Blackbird Fly

D1193750

Lise McClendon

THALIA PRESS

Smithville Public Library
507 Main Street
Smithville, Texas 78957
512-237-3282 ext 6

Blackbird Fly. Copyright © 2009 by Lise McClendon.

All rights reserved. Printed in the United States of America. No part
of this book may be reproduced or used in any manner whatsoever
without written consent of the publisher, except for brief quotations
embodied in critical reviews and attributed to this work. This is a
work of fiction. Any resemblance to real individuals, situations, or
settings is coincidental.

First published in the United States by Thalia Press.

Blackbird Fly, by Lise McClendon.
ISBN: 978-0-9819442-7-2

Cataloguing Data

McClendon, Lise.
    Blackbird Fly/ Lise McClendon — 3rd U.S. Edition

    1. Americans in France— Fiction, 2. Women — Fiction, 3.
France — fiction, 4. Female Attorney — Fiction, 5. Title.

ACKNOWLEDGMENTS

Many thanks to the wonderful people who helped me with this book, including my American friends in France, Sharon Tompkins, Tom Jones, Valerie Trevino, Carol Curtis, Robert Cabrerra, and Katalina Cabrerra. A special thanks and *bisous* to Patricia Zirotti who corrected and never laughed at my French, and Laurent Zirotti who helped me plan many trips to his home country and explained the French way effortlessly and elegantly. And to Arjan and Marije Capelle at the Hotel Edward 1er in Monpazier who wined and dined and helped fold those humongous maps. A big thank you to my contacts at the Legal Aid Society in New York City, Alan Gordon and Marie Mombrun. To Robin Taylor who helped me hash things out, and to Sherri Cornett, traveler extraordinaire — when do we leave? To Katy Munger, who thinks big and just gets me. To Kipp who always has my back and lets me daydream. Thanks for all the travel, wine tasting, and brainstorming, honey, you're the best. To Evan, Nick, Abby, Annie, Susie, Natalie, Barbara, Dean, and my darling mother, Betty.

I appreciate all of you so much. *Merci beaucoup.*

Read the next Bennett Sisters novel
The Girl in the Empty Dress
May 2014

Also by Lise McClendon

The Bluejay Shaman
Painted Truth
Nordic Nights
Blue Wolf
One O'clock Jump
Sweet and Lowdown
All Your Pretty Dreams

Written as Rory Tate
Jump Cut
PLAN X

Dedicated to my father. Miss you, pops.

John Haddaway McClendon
1921 - 2004

BOOK ONE
THE DEATH

He who binds to himself a joy,
Does the winged life destroy;
But he who kisses the joy as it flies
Lives in eternity's sunrise.

William Blake

1

ON THE DAY HAROLD STRACHIE DIED New York City struggled to slough off the lingering chill of winter and he struggled with his spare tire. Twenty pounds had crept up on him, without his consent. He gulped down the usual double-double espresso to get the juices flowing. The early morning was dark and echoing, his only company garbage trucks and young people jogging, their feet slapping the sidewalk, oblivious to middle age.

Getting fit was a bitch. Walking from the train or subway was the extent of his exercise up until now. The extra pounds made Harry feel old at 54, someone who had lost control of his own fate. He refused to let his champagne belly keep him down. He would be muscular, strong, a master of his universe. Confidence was everything.

He'd spent the night in the City as he often did when his deals were soft. For several hours before the markets opened he would work while the office was quiet, researching trends and companies, so he was ready to pounce. But he didn't feel too cat-like climbing the seven flights of stairs to his office, his new daily workout. He stopped on each landing to catch his breath.

In the empty lobby, he fumbled for the light switch and swayed on his feet, woozy. Cold sweat ran into his collar. He blinked, hung up his coat, and sat down. If he'd had a picture of his family on his desk, which he didn't, he would have picked it up. His boy — so smart and tough and, yes, awkward at 15, but he'd grow out of that and be better for it. And his darling girl who looked so much like him with dark curls and mournful eyes. He wished he'd stolen into her bedroom this morning and ruffled her sweet hair.

A horrible squeeze of his chest made him grab his shirt. He gasped, waiting. As the tightness eased, he saw his daughter again, ten years from now, in makeup and mini-skirts and all her innocence lost, and he felt the pain again, harder.

Black spots floated before his eyes. He sat back in his chair, trying to relax. Christ, this wasn't good. He shouldn't have had that espresso. If this was heartburn he'd be buying antacids.

The squeezing lessened. He'd get an appointment with his doctor for later in the week. He could already see the smirk on the doctor's face when he told him to stop being such a nervous nelly. A moment of calm. The office quiet was soothing. He took a light breath and blew it out.

Harry clicked on his computer. As the reports streamed in he clicked through prices, checking analysis. The sweat on his forehead began to dry. Just another day, he thought. Then, the last, the worst — the pain seized him again, and the black spots grew and merged into one.

2

WHEN SOMETHING SHATTERS, when whatever you're attached to ends, definitely, the moment rises up like it's been hanging there for years, a lead balloon waiting to drop with a heavy thud into your life. All that living leading to this exact moment in time. Where has fate been hiding? Doesn't matter. Here it is. Here it is, by God.

Merle stared at the phone, heavy, institutional beige. She'd arrived at the Legal Aid offices in Harlem a few minutes before. She was still wearing her boots. She hadn't touched her coffee.

He was dead. Harry. Husband. Deceased.

She felt the air move around her, solemnly, gently, as if she was a pile of ash a strong breath might blow away. Outside her office voices filtered in, the chatting of colleagues, the insistent tone of an angry client evicted from her apartment. The sounds grounded her, the endless litany of troubles to be untangled, emotions to be soothed, hands to be held. Just the name Legal Aid — aid was so basic, so important in this hard world — made her warm.

Here she was necessary. Here she did good in the world.

Her little world, so ordered and sane. Her nest, every twig in place. The selfless lawyer, fighting for the homeless and disenfranchised. The charity work on her days off, boring or annoying at times but always fulfilling in the end. Tomorrow there was another luncheon, a benefit for African orphans organized by her sister. Francie was so excited about the celebrities, a baseball player, a talk show host, that she had lined up.

No luncheon now. Merle knew she should make a list of what tomorrow would look like but the murmur of the office captivated her, the buzzing like a hive, as if she'd never really listened before, never felt the ordinary blessing of her colleagues and their routine.

"Merle?" One of the law fellows stood in front of her with a quizzical look on her face.

The receiver was still in Merle's hand, making a noise. Laura took the phone and replaced it on the cradle. Merle swallowed, frowned, and stood up.

"I have to go."

"Oh," Laura said, fluttering the way young people did. *When had she started thinking of new graduates that way?* "Your appointments? Mrs. Elliot is waiting, then — " She stopped, seeing Merle's face. "Sorry. I don't need to tell you that."

"I'm sure you can handle them," Merle said, putting her coat back on. It was still damp with morning rain. "I have an emergency. I must go."

"Oh," Laura said again. "Can I help?"

Not unless you can bring a man back from the dead.

OF HER FOUR SISTERS, the one she wanted at the hospital was Annie. It was sad, really, that Stasia was her second choice because she was so strong and capable. A magazine editor these days — not the lawyer she'd trained to be but no one blamed her for that — and damn good at it. An organizer, a do-everything gal. She and Merle lived close together in Connecticut but they were so different. Merle and Annie, her oldest sister, shared an intangible something. In this emergency Merle never thought of Francie or Elise; they were younger and if she had to say so, a bit shallow, despite going to Whitman Law like their older sisters. Someday they would lean on Merle, the middle child. They would need her like she needed Annie. But Annie lived too far, in western Pennsylvania. You had to be practical.

Stasia came, promptly, and held Merle until she didn't want to be held. Dried her tears, called everyone. She made the lists that stubbornly jumbled up in Merle's head. She was so efficient.

In the end Stasia arranged the funeral, wrote the obituary, talked to everyone for Merle. Arranged flowers, watered flowers, threw away flowers. Arranged meals, heated up meals, threw away meals. And so, when it was time, two weeks later, for the visit to Harry's lawyers to hear his will, there was no question which sister went with Merle.

DEEP RUGS, OLD OAK, leather-bound tales of mishaps and bad decisions and the appalling nature of life: The Law Office. With eyes closed Merle caught the smell of the time crumbling, the fruitlessness of human endeavor, of — mortality. Well, it was on her mind.

In the law you could change lives, you could make a difference. You learned the rules then you bent them. But justice was a slippery devil. Hard to quantify, impossible to hang on to. She concentrated on the endless rows of dusty books, not justice, searching the shelves for the earliest court records. New York District Court, 1878. Harry's lawyers, and his father's before him, were a very old, very white-shoe firm, not unlike Byrne & Loveless, firm of her misguided youth.

Harry. She couldn't stop thinking about him, now that he was gone. Trying to remember little things, it was hard. She hadn't really noticed him recently, besides his dry-cleaning and a cocktail party or two. She stared at his suits in his closet, lined up the oxfords he would never wear. He wasn't in the best of shape, never had been, with that paunch and double chin. He hadn't told her but apparently he had a plan to get healthy by exercising, or at least climbing stairs.

Genius, that Harry.

She gripped the arms of the chair, trying hard to picture him the first time they met — the day she made partner at Byrne & Loveless, at the bar after the party after the celebration. She tried to remember the feeling of being valued, loved, feted. All she could remember was barfing in the women's room. And Harry taking her home.

When he told the story he was the gallant knight, swinging the limp princess over his shoulder. She may have knocked into him coming out of the restroom. Yes, that was it. Almost fell down and he saved her from cracking her head.

Out of the blue, the question boomed inside her head: *What-what.* What? What?! It was back, like a disease never quite cured. She hadn't heard it for weeks, that little voice that plagued her.

These last weeks everybody knew what was what: Harry's dead, that's what. *Shut up.* She looked out the window and silenced it.

Stasia sighed and looked at her watch. The lawyers were keeping them waiting. At the funeral Stasia had surprised everyone by sobbing, loudly. Strange, since she never cared that much for Harry. She thought he didn't love Merle enough, and told her so one famous Christmas in front of a roaring fire before she knew about the baby on the way. Maybe that's why she cried at the funeral.

Merle's cell phone vibrated in her slacks pocket. Tristan's school calling. She went into the hallway. Trouble. The Headmaster (unbelievably they still called him that) would put the boy on the bus, if she agreed. She sighed, closed the phone. Back in the office she shook her head at Stasia: *not now.*

Harry's ancient lawyer, who he'd called The Geezer, was shouting in the hallway. The door opened and he shuffled in with a younger man who introduced himself as Troy Lester, a partner. The old man, eighty-five minimum, Landon McGuinness the Third wore neatly-pressed gray flannel almost as ancient as he was.

His thick glasses perched on a beak no doubt less prominent when his cheeks had flesh. The younger partner, Lester, was close to their age but bald on top like the geezer. He was obviously the old man's right-hand everything.

McGuinness peered at them, his eyes magnified behind his glasses. "Which one of you is Mrs. Strachie?"

"That's me, sir. Merle Bennett. Strachie," she added, though she didn't use Harry's name. "And this is my sister, Stasia Bennett."

McGuinness cleared his throat noisily and began in a sonorous voice to outline her future. Stasia was taking notes, thank god. *The house is mine.* Paid off thanks to mortgage insurance. Harry only rented his apartment in the city so nothing there but some junky furniture. Life insurance. *Good.* How could she not know about life insurance? Do you get that in one lump sum? Do you pay income tax on it? She would ask when he finished.

Silence. The geezer sat back in his chair and folded his hands.

"But —?" Had she blacked out and missed a section? Harry was an investment manager. He set up a trust fund for Tristan, he had stock funds, pension plans, all sorts of retirement plans.

She couldn't speak.

Stasia could. "That's it? Where's the pension fund? And the trust fund for the boy?" Landon McGuinness III blinked at her, mouth agape. Stasia leaned in and shouted: "Where is the boy's trust fund?!"

Troy Lester, standing at the old man's shoulder, squirmed then tried to hide it with a smile. "The good news is that Mr. Strachie set this up so it won't have to go through probate. You'll have the proceeds of the insurance within thirty days and the deeds will be changed quickly. The joint accounts stay the same, of course — "

Merle sat forward. "But he told me he set one up for Tristan years ago. A trust account."

"Not at this law firm," McGuinness said, smacking his lips.

"Could it be with someone else?" Stasia asked. "At a bank?"

"Harry did all his legal work here. His father too. "

Troy Lester cleared his throat. "The addendum," he muttered.

McGuinness blinked. "Oh, yes. A special addendum." He shuffled papers on his desk and batted off Lester's help.

He found the paperwork and held it at arm's length. "I bequeath to my wife, Merle, because of her love of old houses, the property in Malcouziac, France, a house and real estate surrounding."

The sisters sat in stunned silence. Stasia looked at her. "Do you know about this?" Merle felt float-y, disconnected from the room. Her ears buzzed. Who were these people? *I'm watching an old Perry Mason re-run. Harry will be alive at home when I get there. We'll squabble about dinner. We'll listen to each other snore.*

She pinched her arm. Nothing changed.

The old man was saying in his clear and not-very-aged voice, "Harry inherited this house from his parents when they died. You knew his mother was French?" Merle nodded, unable to speak. A house in France?

"It's in the Dordogne," Lester added brightly. "Southwest France. A small town. Very picturesque, I hear."

"A villa? Could it be worth something?" Stasia asked.

"No acreage, I understand. No vineyard. Sorry."

"Is there a photo or map or something?"

Troy Lester looked at the old man. "We'll see what we can find. Maybe Harry kept something in his own files. You could check."

He called in the secretary and asked for the file on Harry's father, Weston Strachie. They waited in awkward silence. Merle worked over her cuticles. She didn't feel like she would float away anymore, now that she had both ankles wrapped around a chair leg. *Be practical. He's dead. This is what happens when people die.* She was nothing if not practical. Life would go on. Sometimes you just had to remind yourself. Merle felt the hard rock in her chest press against her ribs, making it hard to breathe.

The secretary returned and handed a slim brown file to Lester. He leafed through the papers before handing it to Merle. "I don't think we'll need this anymore. There's some old paperwork, work Mr. McGuinness did for the elder Mr. Strachie years ago, as well as the obituary. Your husband's parents died together, in a car accident in —" He glanced again inside — "1954."

Harry was four. That was all Merle knew about his parents. He never talked about them, probably didn't even remember them. She glanced at the faded newspaper clipping, then at the letters behind them: a description of the property in French, and correspondence about Harry's father's wine and spirits importing business.

She thanked the lawyers. She felt a powerful need to get on with things, to make lists, to organize. To silence the *what-what?!* in her head. At the café down the block she sat with her hands wrapped around a coffee cup. Her mind began to put things in columns. But Stasia looked furious, her color up. "I knew it. I knew it. Where is his pension fund?"

"He liked to play the markets."

"You think he lost it all? No way. He had something stashed away, he must have. Away from the hawk-like eyes of Landon McGuinness the Turd." They smiled. "You need to go to his office. Maybe that's where Tristan's fund is."

Merle knew nothing about that part of Harry's life. She'd never wanted to. It reminded her of corporate law, the open greed, the phoniness, the back-stabbing partners. But obviously a little more attention to the financial aspects of their lives would have been, well, practical. Maybe she wasn't as practical as she thought.

"Is Blackwood paid for?" Stasia asked.

Tristan's prep school. "The first half." He would be arriving on the bus in an hour. "He got in a fight at school. They're sending him home."

"Poor kid. Maybe he just needs some time with you." Stasia patted her hand. "Public school isn't that bad. And there's Country Day. It's college I'm worried about. The good schools are ruinous."

One of Stasia's obsessions, getting her children into A-list schools, the Ivies and near-Ivies, and paying for it.

"Stace, did you know something was going to be funny with the will?"

She sighed. "He was rich when you married him. Those are the ones to watch."

Harry had it all when they met, downtown loft, swank corner office, Fortune 500 clients, summer lease in the Hamptons. But that was 20 years ago, the boom years when he'd been doing investment banking. A familiar guilt crept through her: all the money she spent on the Connecticut house, the pool, landscaping, windows, kitchen, carpet — anything to make the house warm and welcoming. All a waste, a failure. And now he mocked her in his will: 'Because of her love of old houses.' Had he thought she'd done all that remodeling because she loved crumbling foundations and roof rot?

Stasia took her hands. "You don't deserve this. *He* didn't. He was good man, an excellent father. You didn't do anything but love him, Merle."

She felt her chest cave in. The words hit her hard: *Love him.* Love. What was it? The realization came in a flash. She hadn't loved Harry, not at the end. It was hard to admit. Her reflection in the window as he must have seen her last — haggard, gray, pale. Did he know? Did he care? She couldn't remember when it stopped, it had been dying for so long. *I didn't love him.* The realization filled her with something not quite like sorrow: a feeling of shame, of neglect.

And yet. Now you are free.

Merle shook her head to cancel the words. This was no time for happy thoughts. She'd just buried her husband. Whether he loved her, whether she loved him — it no longer mattered. He was gone. She could get a new job if necessary. She had marketable skills. She had the house, and the life insurance. Tristan would go to college on that. Her life before he died, the busy-ness, the calendar full of appointments, the new drapes, charity auctions, even jogging, all now seemed like filler in a hollow life. *Her* life, one she didn't even recognize.

Stasia put on a smile. "So what about this house in France?"

A house in France: it only sounded romantic. "Thanks for coming, Stace."

TRISTAN'S BAGS LAY IN A HEAP in the hallway. A television blared upstairs. Merle turned on lights in the dark house, following the sound to his room. The door was open, which might be construed as a good sign. Still, she knocked before stepping inside.

His room still had its semblance of order from his months at school except for the giant television he had dragged up from the family room. Harry had forbidden TV in his room so this was no doubt a message. It perched unsteadily on a tiny side table from the living room. Cords criss-crossed the moss green carpet. Last summer he had picked out a new bed and desk, along with the beanbag chair in bright yellow faux suede where he sprawled now. He didn't look as cheerful as the egg-yolk chair, not with the black eye.

"I hope the other guy looks worse," Merle shouted, perching on his desk chair while a scantily-clad blond gyrated on the screen.

Music thumped through the furniture.

A pale but strong boy whose face had hardened into a man's in the last year, his complexion was never bright. Thin, dark whiskers sprouted at the point of his chin; his Gallic nose was so like Harry's. His brown hair was hanging in his eyes — he'd lied about a haircut in March and no one cared when he returned for the funeral. At fifteen he was six feet tall, four inches taller than his father and five inches taller than Merle, a strapping lad as his grandfather said. His legs stretched over the beanbag in rumpled khakis and on his size-12 feet, old-school Adidas. His right eye was purple and swollen shut.

"Do you want to talk about it?" He shot her a one-eyed glare. "Let's eat first then. Pizza?"

She made the call from the kitchen then turned on more lights. The house lived in perpetual shadow, surrounded by enormous oak trees and blue spruces, and protected by deep, overhanging eaves. Square and solid with dark wood trim, it sat back on a respectable suburban street that screamed 'lawn freaks.' Sixteen years ago, when she was pregnant, it reached out to her, speaking the language of security, family, and roots with its pre-war homeyness. But when winter came it was dark and depressing with thick trees and small windows. She painted the rooms bright colors but it didn't help. She hated it before a year was out but she never told Harry. He had been against Connecticut. He loved the city, the restaurants, the theaters, the music. The suburbs were sleepy, boring, bourgeois. But he sold the loft for her, downsized to a walk-up apartment he laughingly called a *pied-a-terre*. A few years ago he'd sold it and rented a small studio near his office for nights he worked late.

How could she tell him this dreary house had been a mistake? It was impossible. She bought high wattage light bulbs.

She stepped onto the flagstone patio. April usually filled her with hope, the promise of sunlight and warmth. Another winter gone. The white dogwoods lit up corners of the yard, the cherry tree on the edge of the patio dropped pink petals. The petals were brown now, rotting in puddles. A chill rose up from low end of the yard, bringing with it the heady sweetness of hyacinths. In April she could forget about the mistakes she'd made, the problems, the silence, the darkness. Except for this year. Tristan had gone back to school three days after the funeral, yes, probably too soon but what he wanted. How could she stop him?

She took a deep breath of moist evening air. If she could focus on her financial needs, hers and Tristan's, she could see her way out of this mess. Grief — or guilt? — is a horrible thing. She couldn't define her emotions any more. Her mother said grief was a 'me feeling,' feeling sorry for yourself. Harry is at peace now, Bernadette said, not hurting or sad or missing you. *Helpful, Mom.*

Harry had taken a chance, something he felt he was good at, and married her four months after the night in the bar. They just clicked, that's what everyone said—they just clicked. What did that mean anyway? Click on/click off? It didn't matter. She kept saying it to herself: *It doesn't matter.*

So now she would gather all the information she could, then make a plan. Grief — or fear — lodged in her chest like a rock, making it hard to breathe. Information, planning, numbers would lift the rock, and her life. She would attack this problem like a case at work, as if she was homeless, living on the street. She would find shelter and security. She would sort it out, get things back on track. She was a big believer in the power of her will. Plus she was practical, like all of the Bennett girls. Even Elise, just finishing law school after a series of resort-area jobs in Aspen and the Virgin Islands that their mother called "perfectly understandable play time," was practical. Law was something that fed on that, nuts and bolts, rules and regs, law and order. No sad romantic notions, just the facts. Well, she had no romantic notions, sad or otherwise, not any more.

The pizza came, thick with cheese and pepperoni, smelling of cardboard box. She took it up to Tristan's room, with paper plates, napkins, Pepsi. He set the box in his lap, let her take a piece.

The peculiar loneliness of the only child sometimes broke her heart. If Tristan had a sibling to share his grief, he would be better off. If she had another child to focus on, he would be better off. But because she couldn't have any more children — Tristan himself had been a surprise to her doctors — here they were, a twosome locked in battle, fighting their way out of this blackness together.

"Did you put anything on your eye?"

"Bag of gel."

"Who was the culprit?" He squinted with his good eye. "The guy who socked you."

"Just an asshole. One of millions at Blackwood."

"Right. It was in the paper. They're calling it a public health crisis."

He grunted and stuffed another piece in his mouth, washing it down with soda.

"So they tell me two weeks, is that right?"

"There's a letter in my backpack. They want me to see some quack. But I'm not doing it." A frightened, belligerent look crossed his face.

"Did this asshole get suspended?"

"I guess." He looked at her. "It was Lancaster."

"Billy?" Tristan's best friend. Or had been. "Billy hit you?"

"I hit him first."

"Ah. Good thinking. Catch 'em unawares."

"Ha ha. You aren't Dad."

Merle felt her stomach drop. That was Harry's line. *Catch 'em unawares*, along with other moronic pointers on fighting that he bragged were from his years on the streets. A family joke. None of them believed that Harry had been a bare-knuckle street fighter. Not with being short, pudgy, and better suited to *foie gras* and martinis.

"Sorry," Tristan said. "I mean, I know you're not."

He must have seen her picking at her cuticles, the delightful new habit that made her hands look like a battle zone. A twist of his lips indicated a teenage smile. He laid a hand on the top of her head. A big, warm, greasy hand.

"It's okay you're not Dad. Really. I wouldn't have it any other way."

THE WIDOW. She read about them in the newspapers, heard about them at parties: wives of fallen soldiers, firefighters, policemen, executed criminals. Men whose lives had meaning, whose deaths were heroic or justified. But Harry was no hero. Just a middle-aged man trying to fleece the world.

The concept of 'widow' was semi-romantic, at least in novels. The curse of adolescent reading, dozens of gothic romances she chewed through in her teens where the heroine mucks around in a creepy old mansion, looking for treasure and true love. Annie or Stasia read them then handed them down. They all saw themselves as that brave girl, searching for love. How young they were.

And now she was the widow. Not the heroine. The widow was usually a crazy old bat. Merle remembered one of the first gothics she read, 'A String of Pearls.' The widow was scary for having lived alone for years pining after her dead husband, but generous to the naïve but plucky slip of a heroine. The wild-haired crone gave the girl a string of pearls that helped her survive the storm that battered the mansion and turn the smelly stable boy into a perfumed prince, or some such drivel.

Merle lay on her bed staring at the ceiling, wishing someone had magic pearls for her. Instead of being the slip of a girl she was the scary old widow with crow's feet and bunions. How had it happened? Just yesterday she was sixteen, with dreams. And now, no Harry — but was that so bad? That little voice returned: *Now you're free.* She hadn't loved him. Why was that so hard to accept?

If she was honest with herself — and why bother with the truth when it causes wrinkles, constipation, and other joys of adulthood? — she'd stopped loving him a long time ago. Maybe the week after he'd saved her from a concussion on the restroom floor. Or maybe when he forgot their first anniversary and worked late. This was no gothic romance. There was no magic moment when the spark went out. Maybe it was just a shallow flame after all, not the raging fire they imagined drew them to the altar.

What had she loved in him, all those years ago? She scrunched up her eyes and tried to think back. He was generous, he'd given her flowers unexpectedly, diamonds from time to time, this house she hated. For a man driven by money he wasn't stingy, not at all. Except perhaps with his time. The only time they went out together was for business. That had been his way for years. And she had never complained.

She got up and stared at herself in the bedroom mirror. Her dark hair was streaked with gray, and stringy. The mascara she'd put on for the meeting with the lawyers had smudged. Her lips were thin and cracked. She closed her eyes and tried to take a deep breath. The rock was lodged there, but somehow a tiny bit smaller. For an instant she saw a glimpse of herself when all this was over: attractive, smiling, lovable. And younger: *how was that going to happen? Wake up, Merle.*

The doorbell rang. She rubbed her cheeks, and marched to the door, eager to pounce on another cheesy casserole or gooey dessert. Betsy stood on the porch in her clogs and barn jacket. Faithful friend and cheerer-upper, Betsy had been stopping by each evening, when she knew things grew too quiet. They had been friends since their kids were in preschool, and still jogged together once in awhile. As Merle made them both herbal tea, Betsy's eyes turned toward the thumping ceiling.

"He got in a fight at school. I probably sent him back too soon." Merle set down her cup. "I heard the will today." She summarized the inheritance, such as it was.

Betsy's eyes widened. "Wait — no trust fund for Tris?"

"I guess he never got around to it."

The word hung in the air: *Bastard.* "But what about you? Will you stay at Legal Aid?"

"For the time being. I've been trying to think. Do you know anybody else whose husband died young like Harry?"

"Well. You remember Margo Willoughby. She was about forty-five when Gus died." Betsy bit off her next sentence as they both remembered Margo had flipped out, treated herself to a bad face-lift then married a guy who owned a strip club in New Jersey.

Merle drained her tea cup and smiled. "Time to perfect that cannoli recipe?"

SHE TOOK THE FILE Troy Lester gave her to bed. The obituary for Harry's parents was something he'd never shared. Despite his material generosity he hadn't really been the sharing type, always buzzing off to his meetings and reading endless financial newspapers. He'd rarely sat down in the kitchen to chat like she'd just done with Betsy. Had he ever seen this clipping?

New York Herald Tribune. March 2, 1954.

Weston Montgomery Strachie and his French bride, Marie-Emilie, died tragically on a rainy night as they returned to their home on Long Island from a romantic outing in Atlantic City. Their auto skidded off the road on a curve and struck a large oak tree that has claimed the lives of more than a few drivers over the years. Husband and wife were pronounced dead at the scene. They leave behind their four-year-old son, Harold.

Weston, 37, was a devoted husband and father. He met his bride in France after his Army service during World War II. His business as a wine and spirits importer brought him frequently to the country. They married in 1947, and their son was born several years later. They moved back to the United States in 1952, settling in Levittown.

Marie-Emilie, 26, who preferred to be called Emilie, will be remembered as a sunny, lively girl, a devoted wife and mother. She will be sorely missed by all who knew her.

Weston is survived by his loving sister, Amanda Wilson and her husband, Sylvester, who have opened their hearts and home to little Harold, and by his mother, Louise Strachie, of Buffalo. Marie-Emilie is survived by many relations in France.

There was another, smaller announcement in the *Times*. The only new information was Marie-Emilie's maiden name, Chevalier. She reread the *Herald Tribune* obit; it had the touch of Aunt Amanda, last seen in a dinner plate hat at Harry's funeral. After Sylvester died she traveled the world with friends from her days as a dress buyer at Macy's.

"Marie-Emilie Chevalier," Merle whispered aloud. Was she really sunny and lively, or was that just Amanda's drama? Merle closed her eyes. She'd missed having a mother-in-law, all these years. Amanda had played the part but not exactly, not being the maternal type. Merle tried to imagine Harry as a little child, round and smiling, playing in the fields of lavender — the way she imagined the French countryside, bucolic and fragrant.

The bass and drums of music videos thumped through the ceiling, bringing her back to the present. She put the obituary aside. Like so much in the past, it didn't matter. Not any more.

3

1949

"COMPLAINING WILL NOT KEEP YOU ALIVE."

She backs through the gate with the chicken held by its legs as it flaps and squawks. Pausing inside the garden she looks up at the window. Cigarette smoke curls out, which means Weston is working at his typewriter. No tapping sounds so he isn't actually typing. She wonders if that is good or bad. He believes, like the chicken, that complaining will change his fate. He truly thinks that sour thoughts, and words, about his writing not selling will magically make it sell, when it made sense to accept defeat.

Marie-Emilie sets down the vegetables and the bread on a spot of shade behind the outhouse. She has been lucky at the market, the first real piece of good luck they'd had in weeks. There had been potatoes and leeks, and some asparagus for the first time. The chicken is scrawny but will provide a week's worth of soup. The bread was cheap because it is last week's, hard and dry but she has a method to make it right again. Normally the farmers are hard on her at market, raising their prices out of spite. They are suspicious of strangers, from the war, she imagines, but why they take it out on her, a real Frenchwoman, is beyond her. The villagers' coldness hurts her. She would move back to her own village in a moment, but there is no house to live in there.

The chicken scratches her leg with its beak, causing her to cry out. Weston comes to the window, frowns, and disappears. Jaw clenched she grabs the neck of the bird and gives it a violent twist. With the axe she dispatches its head. Basket between her legs she plucks its feathers, then cleans it. Inside she lays a fire, filling the kettle with water and hooking it onto the iron arm. Weston hollers down from upstairs.

"What the blazes are you doing now? It's so hot my fingernails are sweating and you build a fucking fire."

He appears on the stairs, cigarette hanging from his mouth, in his undershirt. She dislikes seeing him this way, half-dressed in suspenders and wrinkled trousers. Sometimes he goes out on the streets, walking in the evening, like this. Is it any wonder no one likes them?

"Fresh chicken," she says. "For soup."

"It's too fucking hot for soup," he growls. "Where'd you get the money?"

"Barter," she says, smiling. "No money."

"What did you barter then, *cherie*?" His eyes are hateful and black. Money is his biggest worry since things went bad in Nice. They had come with such hopes, with money in their pockets. All gone now. Between the wine business and the writing, they haven't seen any money for a month. But he finds wine to drink. His fingers are stained with it.

"Old clothes," she says, smoothing her cotton skirt. He would never know if she had sold clothes or not. He hates all her clothes.

He takes a long drag on his cigarette. "What clothes?"

"Some old ones I do not wear." In Nice he bought her the satin dress, fancy shoes, the lovely soft jacket. She sold them months ago.

He looks her over with his hard eyes, not lingering, as she hoped he wouldn't, on the faded blue scarf she wears on her head. Planning this day she wore the scarf for a week, hiding her long, black hair until this morning when she sold it for sixteen francs to a woman from Bordeaux who makes wigs for whores.

He frowns at the kettle, now bubbling. "I'm going out." In the garden he washes himself in the American way, she supposes, of splashing a few handfuls of water on one's neck, and slams the gate behind him.

Sitting on the stool in front of the hot fire, she thinks she will write to her aunt. Ask her why she gave up this house, if there is some curse on it. Maybe there is a way to find happiness here that she is too blind to see. With the curse lifted, Weston will be happy and they will have a baby.

She chops leeks and tears flow from her eyes. As she throws

the vegetables into the kettle she prays once more for a child. Then they will both be so happy they will love each other forever.

4

IT WAS LATE MORNING by the time they arrived in the financial district. Fifteen days since Harry died, a Wednesday. Merle was missing a staff meeting at ten-thirty, a lunch meeting in Queens, and six afternoon appointments with clients, one of whom was an old black man named Elmer she'd been helping for years.

She sighed and tried not to think about Elmer and his problems. She was a walking appointment book, her mind fixated on the calendar the way others memorized football scores and bird lists. It was a curse to be so obsessed with days, hours, appointments. Calendar Girl, Harry used to call her, teasing her as he asked on what day of the week the Fourth of July fell three years from now, as if she were a parlor game. And she knew, she always knew.

Tristan sulked in the train. Merle forced herself to look at the scenery and feel joy — or something, *anything* — whenever she saw a redbud or crabapple in bloom.

Why was she so obsessed with time? Now the future looked fuzzy, and it scared her. She had no idea what was going to happen, and felt herself clinging to her old life, unwilling to let it go even though the reality was that it was gone already. And shame, that was a big one. Her failure to love her husband hovered at the edges of everything. She was deficient. That was obvious. She hadn't admitted it to her sisters yet but she would. She couldn't keep something so big, so emotional, from Annie especially.

She watched Tristan, his black eye and sad face full of boredom and pain. She loved her son deeply, but that was organic, wasn't it? She reached out for his hand on the train. He allowed the touch for exactly ten seconds. She didn't have to consult her watch.

Don't think: of pain or regret, love or hate, past or future. Just be in the world. She breathed out, slowly. *Relax, this is your life.* Why is that so hard? Her mind spun, torturing her. The past was a minefield. The future refused to show itself, as murky as the puddles in the streets.

HANFORD WELSH WAS ON THE ILL-FATED seventh floor of the building, not far from the Stock Exchange. They took the elevator.

"Whoa, buddy," said one of the traders in the lobby, Mike, or Ike, or Mickey. "I hope the other guy looks worse."

Tristan put up his fists. "You want some?! Come on!" The trader laughed and edged away.

Dragging the boy into Harry's corner office Merle shut the door. "This is hard enough without you acting like a child." He stalked to the corner windows. Everyone had stared at him on the train. She could kick that trader except she'd said the same dumb thing.

Harry's secretary poked her head in. "Hi, Merle. Do you need anything?"

Merle tried to smile. People were scared enough around the Widow. "Thanks, June. A box maybe?"

She returned with two paper boxes with lids. June was a tiny, young thing, just Harry's type, with wispy light brown hair and big gray eyes. "I'm working for Mr. Marshall now. He said to help you, if you need me."

"I want to look at Harry's computer files before I leave. I need his password."

June frowned. "I'll check."

Merle looked over Harry's desk, the death site. There was no sign of his last breath, of the ambulance workers who pushed him to the carpet and pounded on his chest, shocked him with paddles, gave him mouth-to-mouth. Everything was tidy, as if he'd be back tomorrow. There was his nameplate, which she dropped in the box. On a spindle a stack of pink "While You Were Out" messages sat skewered.

"You want all these pens and stuff?" Tristan was staring at the open pencil drawer.

"Why not." He grabbed two handfuls. "Do you see any passwords?" The boy pushed the mess of papers around and said no. "Keep an eye peeled."

The message slips were old, from people who must have

given up weeks ago. Should she call them? She owed Harry a little dignity. She dropped them into the box. His gray overcoat still hung behind the door. She folded it and set it in the second box.

There was a solid wall of file cabinets across one wall. Last night when she couldn't sleep she'd spent a couple hours poking aimlessly around in Harry's den. She didn't have passwords at home either. What was she looking for? His life, in a thousand manila folders. It was depressing.

She was fingering files when Steve Hanford burst in and enveloped her in designer cologne. If there was a fine grooming class at business school, Harry's manager had aced it. Steve oozed success, from his tassled Italian loafers to his dyed brown coif that swirled elaborately over his forehead.

"How are you? You look great, Merle. But you shouldn't have to do this. I'm so sorry. It can't be fun."

Tristan was making a face behind Steve's back. Merle said, "Life goes on."

"That's what they say." He put an arm around her shoulders, easing her away from the file cabinets. "What can we do to make things easier?"

"There's a steep learning curve here. I let Harry do all the financial stuff — " Steve winced dramatically. She felt a jolt: *What-what?!* "What — is it?"

"Dee Dee was just saying that. She wanted me to explain everything to her. And it's taken me years to get things balanced — Oh, listen to me. Please, go on."

"I need to see Harry's personal accounts. I have to know everything that went on here with our money."

He flinched again and stepped back, hands deep in fine gabardine. "Of course, Merle. That's your privilege. Let's — can you follow me out here?"

In the hallway he stopped, lowering his voice. "Merle, did Harry tell you about his trading account? What he did?"

"I assume he traded stocks."

Steve rubbed his forehead. "Right before — you know — he

ran some options, you know, futures? Trying to predict if prices of stocks and commodities will go up or down. He was selling short because he thought prices were going to fall. He would have cashed them the next day, probably, because prices did go down a little. But he didn't, because, well." *Because he was face down on his desk.* "Nobody looked at them until the end of the week. By then it was too late. The options were called."

Merle felt bile rise in her throat. Called options meant you had lost your bet. You had gambled and lost. And you had to pay up.

"His clients' money?"

Steve shook his head.

She felt her breath catch. "How much?"

"He never did anything halfway, you know that. He loved rolling the dice. "

"How much did he lose, Steve?"

"Six-hundred." She squinted at him. "Thousand. And change."

AFTER A MICROWAVED CASSEROLE that night Merle spread the day's booty across the kitchen counter to commence a stare-down. Almost immediately her parents called. They were "in the neighborhood." They lived about an hour away and had only returned from Florida a few days before Harry died.

Although moved by their concern, what she really needed was some quiet time. After Steve Hanford's little revelation that her husband had lost over half a million dollars and she could be sued for even more lost dollars from his chancy option trading, she had gone to the bank. When she tried to clean out the joint account, she found out Harry had taken almost thirty-thousand dollars out of their checking account the day before he died. While she was fuming about that she emptied out the contents of his safe deposit box into a McDonald's sack still warm with grease from Tristan's lunch.

Then, after the bank, back to the lawyers.

"Anything I can do to help," the younger partner boomed. They must love him in court. Troy Lester was the Brooks Brothers version of Steve Hanford, but bald and smelling of spearmint chewing gum.

"At Harry's office," she said slowly, trying to breathe. "He was trading options when he died, and they were called. He lost whatever he was trading, our money, and a lot more. I won't be liable for that, will I?"

"Normally, no."

She stared at him, willing him to speak. "Normally?"

"The house is safe, since he put the mortgage insurance in your name. And the French property is too complicated to touch. That leaves the life insurance policy — " He paused, frowning, as if life insurance was nauseating.

"Do you mean — can they garnish that?"

"I think we can avoid that. But there's a problem Mr. McGuinness wasn't aware of."

The other shoe hovered, preparing to drop. She felt it deep in her guts, the looseness, the hollow sense of doom. *You thought that was bad, eh? Well, let me tell ya.*

She swallowed hard and looked him in the eye. "Tell me."

"Creditors would have to sue the estate, which if the debts were large enough — and from what you're telling me maybe they are — they definitely would. Even I would sue."

"And litigation isn't your bag. What are you saying?"

He grimaced. "Lawsuits are potential problems, if there are creditors. But the immediate problem is that he borrowed against the life insurance."

She stared at Troy's oversized forehead. She had already decided how much she would set aside from the insurance for Tristan's prep school, then college, and the funeral expenses. But this was what Harry had used to play the options market. This was how much he cared about the security of his family. Damn him. It was gone, all of it. Harry had borrowed against it and lost it all.

She may have swatted Troy Lester with her purse. Lawyers! Who could trust them?

In the kitchen Merle stared again at the meager list of sums on her notepad. Her parents would want to help if they thought she was in trouble. She swept up the checks and statements into her address book and put them on the shelf over the kitchen desk. The last thing she wanted was their pity. They had their own problems, everybody did. One thing she'd learned already since Harry's death — there was only so much sympathy in the world, then people turned back to their own woes. And who could blame them? The world was a hard, unfair place. She would lie and tell her parents Harry left them secure and well-off.

They stood under her father's big golf umbrella then shook themselves in the front hall. Her mother was still an elegant woman, not as straight and tall as she used to be but always finely coiffed, her gray hair pinned up in a twist. Tonight she wore a simple black dress and pearls. They were at the age when funerals were unfortunately common. Maybe they'd come from one. Merle glanced down at her sweatpants and Harry's old Penn t-shirt. Making an effort was, well, such an effort.

"Someone here?" her father said, fixing his blue eyes on her as if she was hiding a boyfriend upstairs. Jack Bennett never lost that protective feeling toward his five daughters. He looked tired though, the bags under his eyes tinged with blue. He was dressed in a dark suit from his attorney days, a blue shirt with no tie. He missed the law, he told her at Christmas, missed the action, hated being old and put out to pasture. She would tell him about old McGuinness the Turd one day, whose retirement plan was to keel over at the water fountain.

"Tristan's home. He was having trouble studying. Maybe he went back too soon."

Bernie — her mother Bernadette — insisted on going upstairs, exclaiming over his black eye, and swearing to keep it secret from Grandpa Jack. She loved having secrets with her grandchildren and could be trusted for six or seven minutes. In the hallway outside Tristan's room, she took Merle's hand.

"Everything is all right then," she said in her firm schoolmarm tone. "You're strong and young. It seems hard now but you'll be all right, both of you. Tristan's had some trouble but he should go back next week. "

"He's supposed to see a counselor."

"Oh, rubbish. I knew a thousand boys like Tristan." Bernie taught junior high school algebra for twenty-five years but always sent the bad boys home to their parents. "Good boys who are picked on by bullies. It's been going on for centuries. You just have to put on a face and go back."

Bernie's advice for most everything was to 'put on a face.' If they didn't think you cared they couldn't hurt you, and the piddling little concern, whatever it was, went away. It worked wonders in the courtroom and the schoolroom. But in your family it let you hurt in silence and fester in privacy. Merle was an excellent pupil; she'd been putting on a face to Harry — and maybe to herself — for years.

"And what about you?" her mother said. "You're thinner, not that it doesn't look good on you. But you have dark circles under your eyes like when you were in law school."

"Sleeping's not so good."

"Do you have pills? Dr. Farouk gives everyone pills."

They left a half hour later, after two cups of milky coffee and a full rundown on their Florida neighbors who had cooked a giant octopus on a charcoal grill and made such a stink they got cited for a public nuisance. Her parents came from the pull-yourself-up-by-your-bootstraps era, when everything bad could be pushed down and hidden, when to get by you pretended you didn't care. You carried on, until carrying on — and not caring — became your life, robotic shell of existence that it was.

Merle poured herself a large glass of red wine and set Dr. Farouk's pills next it, spreading out the financials again. They meant well, her parents. They tried to distract her with coffee and octopus. She'd just have to figure out how to help herself. Maybe that actually was the old bootstrap approach. Maybe it would work if she applied herself. On a new sheet of paper she made lists: Connecticut. France. IRA statement, bank statement, Legal Aid salary. Potential lawsuits. Lists would keep her sane. Well, as sane as she ever was.

She drank wine, poured more. The financials didn't change.

They didn't grow zeros. The lists grew longer but not in the plus column. There was no money for college. No money for prep school. Her salary would barely pay the utilities and train fares. Property taxes were out of the question. The sleeping pills stared at her until she dumped them in the toilet. The swirling black capsules stayed in her mind as she poured more wine. *Don't need no stinkin' pills.* She felt stronger then, like she might find an answer to the rest of her life, somewhere, somehow.

Tristan bounded down the stairs, waving his English book. He read her a poem by Dylan Thomas; he was trying to write a short paper on it. He stood in the middle of the kitchen, one eye swollen shut, and read it theatrically, arms waving, one toe pointed just so. He was so adorable, hair uncombed and shirttail out, she had trouble focusing on the words, let alone their meanings. When he finished he reread certain passages.

"'A weather in the flesh and bone/ Is damp and dry.' What do you think that means? How can something be both damp and dry?"

"Well," she began. She had struggled in English, at least the interpretation of metaphor that was the heart of poetry. She was too literal. "Um. Let's see. Flesh and bone. So the flesh is damp and the other is, like, bone dry?"

"Yeah, but." He frowned at her. She apparently wasn't helpful. "What about this line: 'the quick and dead move like two ghosts before the eye.'"

She knew this! "Quick means alive, so dead and alive."

He squinted at her and slammed the book. "Dylan Thomas liked to think about death. Mr. James thinks he was obsessed."

Merle bit her lip. Was this Tristan's way of telling her she was thinking about death too much, that she was obsessed? If anything she thought too little about Harry. She didn't miss him, not really. Was this Tris's point? Did he know she didn't love Harry? She glanced up at her son. He was getting out the popcorn popper and looking for oil. Life went on. It was just poetry. Strange, pretty words that she couldn't figure out, just like when she was in school.

She put on a smile. "Oh, those poets."

Tristan made a huge bowlful of white kernels. Before he took it upstairs she enlisted him in breaking-and-entering on Harry's home computer, a job that had more appeal than Dylan Thomas. Then the Widow, numbed with wine and poetry and parental advice on culinary octopi, slept in her sweatpants, disturbed only once, "in the darkest hours when the mansion lay still in the icy moonlight and the silent hand of the future held all in its clammy fist," [*String of Pearls*] by a victorious squeal from the young prince down the hall.

5

THE TELEPHONE RANG ON HARRY'S DESK, buried under towering piles of files that Merle had pulled from cabinets. She'd decided to go back to work on Monday, even though Tristan had another week at home. The calendar in her head was on overload, screaming in the night about the things she had left undone, responsibilities untended, duties ignored. The calendar didn't care about dead husbands or traumatized youths. It demanded her presence.

Anyway she had to get out of the gloom and back to what she loved. So with only the weekend ahead, she'd plowed through her dead husband's computer files, printing out obscure stuff, rifling his cabinets for investments he didn't tell her about (no luck there), and generally making a mess in the room that was always off-limits while he was alive. Betsy had come by in the afternoon to help sort through the debris of a lifetime, drink tea, and once again cheer her up.

A dusty account book she couldn't understand fell to the floor as she answered the phone. There was a lag, and the echoing sound of faraway. "Harold Strachie, if you please." A British accent.

"He's not — in. May I ask who's calling?"

"The name is Rogers. Atlantic Investments. Mr. Strachie is a client. I've been trying to reach him at his office for several weeks."

Merle remembered the name from the pink call slips. One of many unreturned calls. "Well, there's a reason for that. Harold is — dead." It was odd to say. It stabbed like a nail in the heart.

"Sorry?"

"Passed away." People liked that better. "No longer with us. He had a heart attack three weeks ago. "

"I see. Oh dear. And you are?"

"His wife. Widow."

"Yes, well, my condolences." He cleared his throat. "Mrs. Strachie, your husband had promised a sizable investment in Bordeaux futures, some fifty-thousand pounds. We were to receive a wire on the 15th."

"Bordeaux futures?"

"Yes, for this year's wine. We simply cannot wait any longer."

"That's impossible, Mr. Rogers." Did she owe him an explanation? "There is very little cash in the estate."

"How odd. He was a wealthy man, was he not?"

"Well. I hope you can sell the futures elsewhere."

There was a pause, and Rogers's voice smoothed out. "I'm sorry for your loss. I'm shocked that Mr. Strachie, as a man of financial brilliance, did so little to protect you — and your children? You have children?"

"We — I have one child. Thank you. It was all pretty shocking."

"He left you a house, I hope, your home there in — is it New York?"

"Close by. And another property. Which is nice, but it doesn't pay the bills."

Rogers sighed. "Poor man, so young. He had a brilliant nose and an instinct for investment. He bought futures from me for several years. This year's were special to both of us, it being such a fine year for French wine. Do you know France, Mrs. Strachie?"

"Not really. No."

"Did he never take you there?"

"I have to go."

ROGERS SET DOWN the phone and called his assistant in. "Strachie's dead. Get Marseille on the line."

Who to trust, and how much, was a constant juggle but one he enjoyed. He didn't think of it as a problem, just a sort of masked ball. A bit of theater, actors playing their parts. He almost liked it better before the curtain went up, and definitely a lot more when it fell. It had taken so long to set up, to find the right sort of sap who would play along. He had been worried that Strachie had caught on and was stonewalling him. But he'd only died, that's all.

Rogers's eyes went to his father's photograph, framed in a battered wood trim. The old man was young then, wearing a poncy suit and full of himself. His niece, pretty and delicate, sat on the grass at his feet. The black-and-white photo didn't show his father's determination to live large in his world. But the brittle slip of paper tucked in the corner of the frame did. His last dinner at his club, on account and never paid so Hugh had kept it as a reminder of how to live, as if death were around every corner. Might as well have oysters and champagne because tomorrow you might die.

Like Strachie. Dead at what — fifty? Not much more. And now Hugh would never get his father's full revenge. It was disappointing. His father would have been proud of him sticking it to the Strachie's after all these years. Prouder than he'd ever been while alive. But the game would still be played, and won. And it would still be sweet.

MERLE LEANED BACK in the leather chair, feeling the sway it had cradled Harry's back. French wine, of all the asinine ideas. He probably bought all sorts of crack-pot investments, if the state of his file cabinets was any clue. Swamp in Florida, Internet porn, penny stocks: nothing was too mundane or ridiculous.

She pulled open the heavy drapes that covered the window overlooking the pool. Harry never swam, never had time for such a frivolous activity. He worked all summer, preferring air conditioning to cool water. Soon Stasia's kids would come over every day to swim. Tristan loved his cousins. He was spending the night over there.

The words of the man on the phone: *Did he never take you there?* Of course not. They hadn't had a vacation together in years, not since the three of them went to Disney World when Tristan was seven. She took Tristan on trips, once to the Grand Canyon with Stasia and Rick, another time to Vermont. Why hadn't she insisted Harry come? She couldn't even remember trying to convince him. There was no point. He was a workaholic.

He never talked about going to France, or mentioned this house where his parents had lived. She'd found nothing in his files about it, nothing about France at all. It was the one place he'd made no investments. It was clear: he didn't care. Probably why he foisted it on her in death.

Suddenly she had to see what that part of France looked like. Logging onto the internet from his computer she did a search for the little town, *la petite ville*, Malcouziac.

6

THE FIRST TIME SHE SEES the village she's riding in a dusty *autobus*, holding Weston's hand. The dry wind blows back Marie-Emilie's hair and settles a fine dust on their clothes. She wears her last good pair of stockings, and the new shoes he bought her, delicate Italian leather with small heels, so soft they feel like slippers. He wears a linen suit and has taken the jacket off and folded it over the seat. The weather is warm, much warmer than Nice where the breeze off the Med cools the city, and in the evening the pine-scented air drifts down from the hills.

There are pine trees here, and hills, yet the Dordogne seems like a foreign land. Weston's business dealings in Nice had gone well for almost a year and they had been able to save a little. He spent too much on clothes for her, she scolded him even as she adored the things he gave her. He wanted to get away, he said, to see another part of France, do some writing. But she had also heard a man talking loudly to him, grabbing his lapels. They left the next day.

The rolling hills, dotted with sheep and goats, are brown already. Along the creek bottoms the trees are lush, a tangle of green. Pretty country, but hard, very hard during the war. Her uncle had been gone for years during the fighting, her aunt told her, and she didn't know if he was alive or dead. The women had persevered alone, even as the Nazis came through, vanishing those they considered traitors or conspirators or Resistance. Aunt Josephine likes to say she helped in the Resistance, but Marie-Emilie thinks it unlikely, an old woman, almost thirty then. What could she have done? Besides the Nazis would have shot her.

No, Aunt Josephine is just a sweet woman who moved away after the war and left the house she inherited from her mother vacant. She thought she might come back someday. She lives on some rich man's estate now, helping with the animals and working in a produce market, selling fruit. Times are hard, she can't afford the taxes any more. So she gave Marie-Emilie the house with the stipulation that she keep the garden alive, water the lime tree and the wisteria, and keep the birds out of the attic.

The village is quiet in mid-afternoon as the *autobus* stops near the *place*. The walls of the city are tall, sloping down to the green sward and bushes in the ditches. She hadn't realized it is an old bastide town, walled to keep out the nasty English. At the top of a hill, surrounded by thick stone, she feels safe, as the ancient French must have felt. The plaza in the middle of town is ringed by arched market stalls where Marie-Emilie will soon be browsing, basket over her arm, smiling at the farmers as she, only nineteen but so, so happily married, picks discriminatingly through their produce.

Marie-Emilie helps Weston open the shutters and let out the stifling air inside the house. It is quite large, five rooms, bigger than any apartment in Nice she's ever seen. The back garden takes her breath away: walled with a pretty arched gate, bursting with flowers she has yet to learn the names of, anchored by a sturdy stone *pissoir* and a large cistern to catch water. Big enough for outdoor meals all year, for intimate candle-lit parties, for tomatoes. She stands in the middle of it, turning slowly round and round, mouth agape in wonder, until Wes calls to her to help with the mattress.

Here, she thinks, beating a rug in the garden, here we will be happy. Here we will make babies and fill the house with love. Here, she thinks, looking at her handsome American husband, we will be a family.

7

ANNIE BENNETT, ANTITHESIS OF REGIMENTED TIME, arrived too early and without an appointment. Merle was doing laundry and avoiding her face in the mirror. Sunday morning, the most depressing hours of the week. She opened the front door, stunned for a moment by sunshine and lilacs. She had forgotten about their power. The oldest Bennett sister — and the shortest — stood under the oak tree, pulling a string of colored fabric squares along low branches.

"Are we having a yard sale?"

"Great idea. Get loose of excess. Free the mind and body of clutter."

In a pink leather motorcycle jacket Annie wore her wiry hair in a tangle of gray and brown tamed by combs and clips. She consulted for environmental groups and governments, about landfills and recycling and generally keeping the land and water and air as clean as humanly possible. Merle's hero, the activist lawyer fighting the corrupt corporations to save the planet. She took Merle's hand, dragging her to the curb to admire the handiwork. "Tibetan prayer flags."

"Ah, so you're a Recycling Buddhist."

"Hey, good karma is where you find it. They bring you happiness." She explained the colors of earth, water, sun, sky: white, blue, green, yellow, red. The neighbor across the street peered suspiciously out of her tidy saltbox colonial. Merle gave her a wave. She'd either be calling the neighborhood association or dropping by for a great deal on a good used car.

Inside Annie settled herself at the kitchen table. Their faces had similarities, the same nose with a bump on the end, same widow's peak, now too apt. Annie's eyes were hazel, lighter than Merle's, and sparkled as she told her sister about the convention in Manhattan for mayors of all stripes. "Where are you staying?" Merle asked.

"At the Rabid Capitalist Repressive Inn. Unless I get a better offer."

"Ah, well, there are ground rules—no jumping on the beds or playing 'Eleanor Rigby.'" They had strict ideas about Beatles songs, from a childhood full of them.

"What about 'When I'm Sixty-Four'?"

Merle snorted. "Absolutely not."

"'Dear Prudence?'"

"Oh, all right."

Annie disappeared in her environmentally-friendly car to find the nearest organic market. Rick, Stasia's husband, dropped off Tristan. In the kitchen Merle made him a tuna sandwich. "I made an appointment with this Dr. Murray. Betsy says he's a very nice guy."

His eyes flew open — at least one did. "I'm not going. You can't make me."

"No, but the school can. You can't go back until you talk to Dr. Murray. It doesn't have to be all touchy-feely."

"Right. We're going to talk about the Yankees."

"It doesn't matter what you talk about. He knows what's going on. He'll be nice. The sooner you go, the less behind you'll get."

Tristan had inherited her compulsive time gene so he agreed. Anything but getting behind in studies. She just hoped he didn't develop the full-fledged calendar in his head.

That night Annie cooked mushroom-filled crepes, two colors of asparagus, and strawberry sundaes for dessert. She made Tristan laugh and help with the dishes while Merle forgot about the future, and the past, for an hour. Afterwards, curled up on the sofa in the cold living room, Merle told her sister about the will and the life insurance, about her chat with Harry's lawyer.

Annie cocked her head. "Hold on. Troy Lester? Yalie with fat sideburns?"

"He's bald now. You know him?"

"We spent one ill-fated year together. Met at a mixer. Remember those?" She shuddered. "He wore full Yale regalia, right down to his regimental socks."

"What a turn-on. He was your boyfriend?" *Gad.*

She laughed. "We wrote to each other. We pretended

faithfulness. Then he met some chick from Smith or Vassar and that was that."

"You must have been crushed."

"Devastated. Now. You and Tris. No starvation in the immediate future?"

"There are debts, *his* debts, and I won't pay them. I can't pay them." She sighed.

"You'll figure something out, Merle. You always do."

Merle looked at her sister across the room. She wrapped a wool shawl around her shoulders. It was a struggle to bring the words into the air, but she made herself do it. "What if I told you he was — you know, dead to me. For a long time." She was whispering.

Annie crossed her arms. "Are you saying that?"

Merle frowned. "I should have told you. I just — I hardly noticed."

"You didn't *notice*?"

Merle cringed, shrinking into the shawl. It sounded, it *was*, so lame. There were so many ways to fail in life, but she hadn't had that much experience with failure until now. She'd always been buoyed by her family, her sisters, her choices. She'd never let herself fail. But now — she stared into her wine glass, horrified at the mess she'd made.

"I haven't told anyone. But I —" She gulped a breath. "I didn't love him. There's some — something wrong with me."

Her sister moved to the sofa and put her arm around her. Merle felt the tears rise in her throat. "Now listen, Merdle. There's nothing wrong with you. It's just the shock of all this. You've got some of the most productive years of your life ahead of you. You could get married again — god forbid. Or get an incredible new job doing something you love." Annie got her a tissue and Merle wiped her eyes. "You have to open yourself to possibility."

"Possibility? Now that worries me."

"Because you can't schedule it into your Day-Timer?" Annie smiled. "It's the stuff that's not on the calendar that's most interesting."

It seemed too late to change her internal workings. She was 49. Life inside the brain was fixed. Even if she wanted to change, which she wasn't really sure she did, how did you do that? How did you change who, and what, you were? She would just have to live with her calendar.

"I should have paid more attention. To him, or at the very least, to myself, to my lack of feelings for him. I've already forgotten what he smelled like. I can't remember the last meal we ate together."

"You had a good life together. You have a wonderful son. No regrets now."

"Yes. I guess. I mean, I know. But — was I sleepwalking all those years? Why didn't I wake up one day and say, this isn't how I want to live my life? I mean, I'm fairly smart, aren't I? Why didn't I notice?"

"Let's see. Skipped two grades, graduated from law school at twenty-one — "

Merle smiled. "In the top quarter, as Mother always says."

Annie grinned. " — In the top fucking quarter, partner by thirty. Wife, mother, housing rights crusader. You are an embarrassing overachiever."

Their usual shtick. They buoyed each other. When one was down, the other sister lifted her up. No small matter, and she never forgot that, even if she didn't believe the shtick anymore. Annie's opinion mattered, it always would. She cared, that was the important thing. Now more than ever.

"But why did I let him handle all the money?"

"You were too busy saving the poor from slum-lords? It's not a crime. Millions of women do it." Annie cocked her head. "You know what you've got, don't you?"

"A financial nightmare? Acid reflux? An AARP subscription?"

"Come on, Merle. Repeat after me. Case of courage — "

The Bennett girls' code, first a joke from the summer they took golf lessons, an experiment that didn't stick, then a solidarity hand-smack between sisters. When all else failed, they had each other.

Even when they didn't get along, even when they didn't talk for months, if disaster struck there was a shoulder to cry on. When they had a fight with a husband or got divorced or somebody died or got expelled or lost a job, or any other crap that life threw your way from time to time, the sisters had each other. Sometimes Merle forgot, but it was only a matter of time before one of her sisters reminded her.

"Come on now. We're together. Case of courage," Annie repeated. Merle held out her fist. Annie whacked it, then they reversed.

"Bucket of balls," they crowed.

WHEN SHE TRIED to sleep that night, Merle had too many thoughts. She reminisced about Dr. Farouk's pills, swirling in the toilet. She got up and went back to Harry's office. Dumping all the files into a corner, she cleared the desk. Behind the chair was the McDonald's bag full of stuff from the safe deposit box. She'd been putting off looking at it, afraid there might be some grim secret about Harry, something that would make her feel even worse about her loveless marriage.

Documents, photographs, passports. The usual stuff. She relaxed, pawing through it. Harry's passport had expired three years before. He never traveled, why bother. A stack of folded papers, the deed to the house, the marriage license. Also, a large, yellow, brittle envelope. She looked at the documents and set them aside.

Inside the manila envelope were old photographs and more papers. She'd never seen these photos. Harry's parents, Marie-Emilie, small and fair, Weston, dark-haired, squinting into the sun. Harry looked so much like his father: thick, wavy hair, sturdy chin, barrel chest. Only names on the back: 'Wes and Emilie.' The house in the background had brick walls, hollyhocks, mullioned windows. Could this be Long Island? No, she'd seen that house, it was clapboard. This must be the house in France. It looked peaceful and sunny, a cottage from long ago when things were simple.

In the photograph Weston wore a wide-collared shirt, Emilie a flowered dress, her hair in a quaint sausage roll above her forehead. Gone for so long: fifty years. It would have amazing to have known them. Maybe she would have understood Harry more, loved him more. Things couldn't really have been simple then. Not right after the war.

A photo of Harry at three or four, sitting on a tricycle in front of a ranch house. Probably after they moved back here. Maybe the last one his mother took of him. Dark curls, fat cheeks, the vacant toddler stare. Then, a school portrait from the late fifties, Harry in a school uniform, a serious expression, eyes glassy, his hair slicked down. He looked, well, not very happy.

In crackling old envelopes she pulled out two death certificates, for Weston and Marie-Emilie. So they were actually gone, there wouldn't be any surprise visits. What a silly thought.

Merle opened a sheet of paper. The blank, engraved letterhead with Weston Strachie's address in Levittown had a large, rusty skeleton key taped to it with stiff old cellophane tape. Now this was mysterious. Maybe Weston had a sense of humor beyond the grave. No writing, nothing to identify the lock the key would open. A trunk in the attic? A grandfather clock? The house in France? The thought kept coming to her, that house, what it might be like. She would never see it. Why was she imagining what color the shutters were, whether there were flowers like in a Monet painting? She'd been to France once, a college trip in the summer, and never forgot the sunshine.

The amazing light. As opposed to this dark, depressing house. She put her chin in her palm and sighed. Oh well. With the new revelations about Harry's financial genius she had to be even more practical than usual. Her sister Francie had found somebody who did international property law. Merle had an appointment with him to start the process for selling it.

Also in the big envelope was a battered gray menu from a restaurant with three curled, dry wine labels hooked to it with a rusty paperclip. Souvenirs of their life in France, she supposed. The menu was in English while the labels were from French wineries.

Two packets of envelopes remained. The first were yellowed,

thin envelopes with faded, spidery script, surrounded by brown string. The tiny stamps were peeling, and French. They were addressed to Marie-Emilie at the house in Levittown. Pulling out the letter from one torn envelope, she tried to read the script, faint as it was. The blue ink was barely legible. The postmark was December 1954. The other two envelopes were similar, postmarked 1955, all of them after Marie-Emilie and Weston were dead. She held one up to the lamplight. French, it seemed. She could make out a few words but her French was mediocre at best. She would get it translated, one of these days.

The last small packet of papers was wrapped in a rubber band which broke as she slipped it off. The deed to the apartment on Twelfth Street: she stared at it for a minute before she realized what it was. Harry said he'd sold the apartment five years before, so this was just an old copy — or was it? He moved on, to that crappy little studio near the Exchange for when he stayed in the city. She remembered him being vague about the price of the Twelfth Street apartment, and who he'd sold it to. Or maybe her memory was just vague. She stared at the deed a long time.

He told her he sold it, she was sure of that. Five or six years ago. But where had the money gone? Down his options rabbit hole with all the rest, no doubt.

8

MONDAY MORNING. The Legal Aid Society offices at 128th & Madison. The list of appointments ran through her mind. She felt a jump in her step. It was good to be back.

Noisy, chaotic, piles of papers everywhere, the smell of unwashed clothes and hope: a little bit of heaven. Merle was immediately swallowed up in correspondence, filings, briefs, arguments, disputes, and rulings. By the time she looked up staffers were back from lunch. She kept working, making one pile to take home, another to give the new fellow starting next month, another for cases that needed attention this week.

Most of the critical cases had been taken over, rather too ably, by Laura Crandall, the current law fellow. She'd taken to tenant rights like she was born to it. Her hard work made it possible for Merle to take two and a half weeks off without feeling single mothers, disabled veterans, and the illiterate would be living on the streets. Laura reminded Merle of herself, twenty-five years ago, energetic, idealistic, full of crusading fervor — not to mention attractive, articulate, smart, and her whole life ahead of her.

"I've set up a workshop with the Tenants Council, on improving communication with your landlord," Laura said, checking things off on a pad. "The new fellow starts Monday so she can help with that. Also I've started interborough lunches with Brooklyn, Lower Manhattan, Queens, and the Bronx. Once a month, brown bag thing, no big deal but we kick around ideas. The first one is Friday."

Filing away those details in her head, Merle scanned email correspondence, trying to get rid of a backlog the size of the Britney Spears Fan Club. "Who is the new fellow?" she asked.

"Oh, she's fantastic, from Harvard Law. She's been clerking in Brooklyn and before that for the Second Circuit. Her name is Nina Cortez."

"Latina? Good." Merle frowned over Laura's shoulder at the

receptionist, standing in the doorway.

"Someone to see you. She said it was personal. Should I send her back?"

Laura got up. "I'll come back later."

Merle turned off her monitor. Probably a courtesy call from someone she'd helped over the years. Mabel Siddons, maybe, who had been evicted and sued for back rent because she couldn't read the notices for renewing her Section 8 certificate — or anything else. Or, Tanya, living on the street with her baby until they found her an apartment and government assistance. Every so often someone would come by and tell her they had found a job, graduated from trade school — or needed money.

The visitor stepped into the open doorway, glancing at the nameplate. Merle didn't recognize her. She was thirty-ish, with blond hair to her shoulders. She wore a black suit with a blue blouse and heels, and could have passed for a thousand other professional women in the city.

In other words, not a client. Merle stood. "Can I help you?"

The woman smiled slightly, her eyes darting around the office, but didn't speak.

Merle said, "Sorry. Do I — have we —?"

The woman clutched a black briefcase on a long strap over her shoulder. "My name is Courtney Duncan. I am — was — a friend of Harry's."

"Oh. Sit down."

"I just wanted to say how sorry I am. That he — " Her face flushed. "I couldn't make it to the funeral." She half-turned to the door. "My — my condolences to your family." And she was gone.

Merle stared at the spot she had vacated, blinking.

Laura returned. "Who was that?"

"A friend of Harry's. Or so she says."

TRISTAN HAD HIS COUNSELOR APPOINTMENT Monday afternoon but didn't go back to school. He pecked away on a paper for his history class and the Dylan Thomas essay, and watched a lot of television. Annie went home on Tuesday. Merle worked long, satisfying days to clear the backlog of cases and slept soundly, from exhaustion, every night. She looked at the old photos once, and the obituary, then put everything into the manila envelope. On Thursday afternoon she took the subway to Brooklyn to meet the property lawyer Francie had recommended.

Hoffmann Suisse International's brownstone sat mid-block among residences in various phases of renovation and decay. As she pushed through into their reception area the smell of bread baking made her smile.

The receptionist's desk sat empty so she lowered herself into a hard, modern chair padded in purple velvet. She picked up a copy of the *International Herald Tribune* as a stylish woman with a European up-do returned and ushered her into the lawyer's office.

Ramon Sauvageau stood, smoothed his tie, and shook her hand. He wore a gray suit with a white shirt setting off his tan and black hair slicked back in an outdated Wall Street look. His accent was soft, indefinable. On the corner of his desk sat a small vase with three perfect pink roses. The receptionist returned with coffee and a plate of warm pastries. Merle chose a square cookie. The buttery crumbs melted in her mouth.

"Now. The inheritance," he said, looking at her under his thick eyebrows. "Under French law all children of the deceased, as well as the spouse, inherit equal shares of property, no matter what the will says. Am I correct that you have just one child, a son?"

"Yes."

"So you and your son will each inherit half of the house and land. Then there is the issue of inheritance tax. It is probable that because the house was held for so long by your late husband that the tax will be lowered substantially. We will work with the French government on that on your behalf."

"But there will still be inheritance tax?"

"It is the way."

"Has someone been to the village?"

"My contact in Toulouse." He moved his coffee aside. "This

village, Malcouziac, is small, with some services, a small grocery and tabac, that sort of thing. Medieval with some of the old walls."

"How small?"

"Three hundred. More in the summer when people go to their vacation homes. Not an unpopular area for summer people."

"Good. I've decided to sell it."

"Very good. We can help you with all the details. I should warn you, it may not be quick."

"I heard these small cottages were sought after. Lots of British in the Dordogne, right?"

"But yours has had no one in it for many years —"

"Fifty."

He frowned. "If you will indulge me, I'll read you what Monsieur Rancard reports." He put on wire-rimmed glasses. "'House sits on the street, approximately twenty feet of frontage. Wooden shutters, paint gone but solid, on all windows and door on the front. House is constructed of local yellow stone in fair condition. A seven-foot wall of stone surrounds the building, including a large rear yard. An alley provides access. Some signs of water damage and mortar in need of repair on both house and wall. Tile roof needs work, tiles missing, birds flying in and out. Possible interior damage from the hole.'"

"He couldn't get in?"

"One moment. He continues: 'Location at edge of village, adjacent to destroyed fortress wall, is desirable except for wall debris along the street, with excellent southern exposure and windows which face the many vineyards and hills.'"

"That shouldn't be difficult to sell."

He held up a finger. "'Shutters on the street padlocked from inside, on first and second floors. Attempt to open door shutter with bolt cutter brought gendarme and neighbors. A Madame Suchet across the street informed me that someone lives in the house. The local gendarme confirmed this. Said occupant has paid the 'taux occupier' — this is the tax a renter must pay to the state each year — they paid 'the taux occupier' dutifully and on time for ten years.'"

"Someone's been in the house for ten years?"

"But not legally, madame. "

"A squatter."

"Who has made all believe that the house belongs to her, even to lawfully paying her tax."

"The house isn't recorded in her name, is it?"

"It appears, no. She has no legal claim to the property."

"Did Harry pay taxes on the property?"

Sauvageau handed her the sheet with tax figures for the last twenty years. "When he was 21 and came into his trust he paid the back taxes. He kept up the payments. That will strengthen your claim. With a house unoccupied for so long, it is not unusual to have a squatter."

Homeless, and French. The squatter was probably like one of her clients in Harlem, destitute, toothless, and clueless. Of course there was a squatter. But one could always hope for an unscrupulous opportunist with bad intentions. Much easier to toss into the street.

"Monsieur Rancard will find out who the woman is. We pay the tax. We record the property for sale with the real estate company."

"Can we sell it if the ownership is in question?"

"Technically we wait until we have access to the property. But Monsieur Rancard knows many people."

"How much is the tax?"

"About two thousand euros."

More money out the door. "We don't know anything about the squatter then?"

"The gendarme indicated that she was a known person in the village. The people in the village are likely to take a elderly Frenchwoman's case over yours, you being a stranger to them and so far away."

9

THE RETURN LETTER from her aunt is several weeks old by the time Marie-Emilie receives it. The postman must have refused to give it to Weston. By the time she is answering the door again he appears with it.

Her bruises have faded; her face is no longer swollen. Her arm only hurts when she raises it over her head. Several nights after she made her soup he had thrown her drunkenly onto the bed and her head scarf had come loose, revealing her chopped, ugly hair. He was always rough in bed but she supposed all Americans were. She had only one boyfriend in France when she worked in the pharmacy, sweeping floors and washing windows. He was the son of the druggist, a brute himself. Weston is no different, except when he drinks.

He had beaten her then made love. It seemed wrong to her. It is wrong. But she wanted a child so she received him on whatever terms he offered. But she has not been able to go out of the house for two weeks.

According to her aunt's letter, there is no curse on the house. Marie-Emilie had hoped for a simple cure to her unhappiness, something she could say or do that would break the spell. The letter is long and reassuring, except for one part:

> 'There was much love in that house, *cherie*. The pain of war too. So many souls lost. I kept their pictures on the wall, clipped from newspapers, to remember them. How I tried to keep house for your dear uncle so that when he returned he would find flowers blooming in the yard, the grapes ready to pick, the shutters painted and secure. But I was only one, I could not do it. You cannot do it alone either. You must insist that your husband help you with the house. He is young, he can fix the roof, plant a rose bush, build a fire. Make him be a man. You are not a slave to him.'

Tante is wrong. Marie-Emilie sits next to the garden wall in a slice of shade. She is so tired. Weston goes out every night and rarely comes to bed before she gets up. He sleeps during the day and goes out again. He no longer even makes a pretense of trying to write. She suspects he sold his typewriter. Her only reprieve from his disapproval is now, these last days, when he has gone on the train to Paris for business.

She is so hungry. There is no food, no money. If by some chance she carries a child now he would surely die from hunger.

She washes herself under the cistern, the warm water rinsing away her tears. She is fortunate that she no longer owns a mirror to see her butchered hair. Dressing again she finds one of Wes's handkerchiefs to cover her head and goes to the market.

One of the old widows gives her two eggs; another woman grudgingly offers her some cream. It won't go far but she is grateful. The men will have nothing to do with her, call her 'gypsy blood.' The priest won't even speak to her. On her walk home she wonders what she's done to offend them all. And thanks the Lord for kind old ladies with good hearts.

Weston arrives home that evening in a singing mood. He swings into the house, takes her into his arms, and gives her a green scarf and nylon stockings from Paris. He had made a deal with someone abroad. They fronted him money for a big delivery of wine, many cases, he says. She is happy but afraid he's already spent the money and the businessmen will be angry. He laughs when she tells him that, saying he's already paid for the wine, and has plenty left over. "Although you'll never know where, my pretty," he laughs again, tweaking her still-sore chin.

Just as quickly, he is gone again. American husbands didn't have to say where they were going, she thinks bitterly. He hasn't touched her since the beating, much too long for him to be without. She imagines the perfumed whores he's been with in Paris, the trinkets he bought them, the wine they drank, the beef they ate, until she curls up in her bed and cries.

10

FRIDAY CAME, LIKE EVERY WEEK. Merle walked into the Legal Aid building, five stories of reassuring brick, utilitarian and unfussy, and ran through the day in her head as always. She'd come in early, hoping to actually take a lunch break today. Then, at ten o'clock her boss, the head of the Harlem Neighborhood Office, called her into his office. She was on her second cup of coffee.

Jeff O'Donald, once a campus radical at Columbia, was now balding and plump with an unruly beard and wire rim glasses. On his window sill white orchids bloomed.

"How are you, Merle? Things okay at home?"

"Sure. The bed's a little cold, Jeff. You looking for some action?"

He cringed. "Sorry. I said that wrong. Are you coping all right?"

She was sounding more and more like the scary widow. Ready to bite off the head of anyone who dared to be nice. She tried to smile. "Thanks for asking."

He let her sip her coffee then leaned forward. "I've got something on my mind." He was an intense guy, and this was his intense way of preparing you for his pronouncements. "This Skadden fellow, Cortez. Crackerjack, according to her rec's. Her proposal is a new intake system that could really shake things up for us. We're very excited."

"I'm excited too."

"Super. I'd like you to train her to take over your job."

Merle set down her cup and stared at him. He squirmed and explained. "She'll be full-time, you're still part-time. She's fully funded by this fellowship. Then we use you in Development. Get us more fellows, and all that."

"You want to send me to Development. After all these years. Just what I need right now in my life, Jeff. Because I don't have enough changes."

"It's called a promotion, Merle. They can really use help liaising with the big firms in Development. You know those corporate boys from your Byrne & Loveless days, right? Lillian thinks the world of you."

She knew 'those boys' all too well, and never wanted to break bread with them again. She and her coffee steamed for a full thirty seconds. Lillian Wachowski, who Merle had met once or twice at social events, was rumored to be a bitch-on-wheels.

Jeff blurted, "Can I set up a meeting with Lillian this afternoon? And of course it'll take at least a week to train Cortez."

A week to learn what she'd been doing for almost fifteen years. She felt old, useless, unwanted. And tired. She hadn't gotten a full night's sleep in weeks. She didn't have it in her to fight. What would she say? She couldn't leave because she had the next two months blocked out in her mind? That she needed to work to stay sane, to conquer the calendar in her head? To deal with financial ruin and the fact that the only man she ever loved turned out to be somebody she didn't love at all? Plus he was dead?

She looked at Jeff, twisting his beard. *Calm yourself.* He had his own issues, no doubt. He must have gotten the word to trim the budget, to transfer out the high-salary veterans, to get more cheap fellows, to serve more law to the poor for less. Or else.

She sighed. "Sure, Jeff, give the old gal a call."

MERLE SAT ON A BENCH in Central Park and stared at the yellow tulips instead of attending the interborough brown bag lunch. She should have gone, but Laura would be fine, better no doubt, without her. Tristan had settled down, doing his homework without nagging, and talking about going back to school in a hopeful, even eager voice.

She dreaded this new job. She didn't want to schmooze corporate lawyers, ask them for pro bono time and fellowship dollars. She hated asking for favors. She disliked most of the lawyers she'd worked with, at least the partners and old-timers she'd be begging for dollars. Most had a rich sense of entitlement, and a nose for where the

SMITHVILLE PUBLIC LIBRARY

money was buried. From a personal standpoint she'd have to get new clothes and the thought of shopping made her feet ache. She'd have to start getting manicures and dyeing her hair and wearing makeup. She smiled at a dog who sniffed her. He eyed her suspiciously and moved on. Even stray dogs rejected her.

Who would she be if she changed everything about herself, put on a fancy new face to the world?

A Lawyer, of course. Someone in touch with her emotions but able to totally compartmentalize, to understand the motivations and emotions that are part of being a human yet stand apart from them, use them, use others' emotions to get what you want. Analytical, suspicious, duplicitous, ruthless. The perfect lawyer: your worst nightmare.

Merle sighed. That wasn't who she was, not any more. She graduated from high school early so she could be a lawyer sooner. Maybe it was just a goal she could see, a clear choice, a set future. It was on her list, Annie would say, something to be checked off, a goal met. Her father was proud, she knew that. Maybe she'd done it for him. Annie, four years older than Merle, graduated law school just a year ahead of her. Merle and Stasia ended up in the same class. Annie, so brilliant, and Stasia, so everything. How could eager, precocious, gung-ho little Merdle be as wonderful as they were? By being a lawyer too, of course.

The lawyer, the attorney, the counselor. The choices we make. She sighed again and pulled at her bangs.

What-what?! Damn. The bugger was back, asking too many questions. It had been silent, she realized now, for weeks. Then, in the the geezer's office, listening to Harry's will, it flared up like hemorrhoids or a bad enchilada.

The voice was familiar, her old friend after all these years. How had it begun? Maybe a line in a movie, maybe overheard from the noisy reception area at work: What? What?!

She had said it just once out loud, in the car after a tedious dinner party at the home of a partner of Harry's. The partner's wife had irritated her with nonsense theories about the cause of homelessness (laziness, a taste for narcotics, bad choices, prostitution: take your pick) and the rest of the women had abandoned her to the hyena. The men were no help, sequestered with whiskey and cigars, conspiratorial and secretive, as if letting anyone overhear their strategies would derail their rocket ride to riches. On top of it all she had a headache, a doozy, and the red wine hadn't helped. So when Harry had asked as they drove home in that mock-meek way he had, what was the matter, she had exploded. "What! What?!"

He had reflexively braked, as if she'd seen a deer or a raccoon in the headlights. She turned to him, almost screaming. "What do you want from me? What? What?!"

He lapsed into silence. His typical reaction to female hysterics, with which he had little experience. She was usually calm, rational, practical, sitting back at these awful business dinners, reflecting on her virtue, her dutiful nature, her patience at putting up with idiots.

After that the *What? What?!* came back — silently, in her head — when confronted with ridiculous questions or inane people. That happened just a few times, but enough to stick. It began to haunt her thoughts, as if questioning what she was doing, what she wanted, what the hell was going on with her life. She tried not to wonder what it was really asking. Mostly it was just there: the *what-what*, like a tic she sometimes managed to ignore, but mostly tolerated.

Maybe it had been her subconscious trying to get her to realize she didn't love Harry and what the hell was she still doing married to him. It was a theory. Then why had it returned after Harry was dead? What did her subconscious want now? She'd had her chance to ask Dr. Murray, the tweedy, soft-spoken counselor who had examined Tristan on Monday. He would have listened, even if he'd looked askance at her. But she couldn't bring herself to mention it. Like a scary relation never visited, the *what-what* was best left in the dark, unexamined and un-poked.

She stood up and stretched her arms at the pink tulips. She wouldn't go back to the office today. No, she had a life of uncertainty to get on with, a meeting with her new people. Her old people could start learning how to cope by themselves.

THE APARTMENT BUILDING in Greenwich Village was nothing to get excited about — dark red brick, five floors with the fire escape hanging on the front. Harry had paid a pretty price for his *pied-a-terre* despite its ugliness, although Merle still couldn't remember how much. Or how much it'd sold for. His New York real estate adventures had been out of her league. When they moved to Connecticut he bought this second-floor unit lacking anything special besides its location a block or two from the Gotham Bar and Grill, one of his favorite restaurants.

She'd had lunch at the Gotham, a wild indulgence considering the state of her finances, sitting at their elegant bar. Lovely over-priced food and bright, almost sunny interiors bursting with huge flower arrangements. The bartender had been kind and a little flirty. She felt raw in the face of handsome, too-friendly men, something she'd had no trouble with in the past. She had smiled at him, drunk a glass of wine, then a strong cup of coffee. Still she had fifteen minutes before she was to meet her new boss.

So she'd wandered over to the old Twelfth Street building. She had just enough time to get the name of the current owner of Harry's old apartment. With luck she'd also satisfy her curiosity that Harry had indeed sold it five years before, and if the stars aligned, for how much. Last night in Harry's home office she'd come up with zero about the apartment. Wouldn't he have had to claim capital gains the year he sold it? Maybe he lied on his tax return. He'd lied about the trust fund and spent the life insurance on his crazy schemes. At this point everything was on the table.

Pushing into the cramped lobby she eyed the mailboxes. On Harry's old box was simply the number — 202. Merle pressed the doorbell and was surprised when the buzzer to the door opened without a word. Maybe this would be easy.

The door to the apartment was freshly painted in spring green. A young woman opened the door the width of the chain and peered out. Hanging on her leg was a small girl, dark-haired and barefoot.

"I'm looking for the owner of the apartment," Merle said, smiling. "Would that be you?"

The woman, with long black hair and heavy eye makeup, brushed crumbs off her fingers onto her tight jeans. She looked to be in her early twenties, chewing gum as she looked over Merle. She undid the chain and opened the door. "I'm the nanny. She's not here."

"Oh, well, she bought this apartment from — someone I know. I have some papers for her." Merle patted her purse where nothing more official than her Metro card was stashed. The room beyond them looked cozy and warm, strewn with toys. The television trilled with the sounds of Sesame Street.

"She'll be back in a hour. If we're lucky. Can I take them for her?"

"Uh, it's one of those legal things." Merle looked down at the little girl, dressed in pink sweatpants and a t-shirt with spangles, and wondered why she'd lied. She hadn't planned on lying. She looked over the girl's head, focusing on the living room. There was Harry's brown chair that she'd made him replace in his office at home. And the red velvet footstool, with gold fringe, from the family room. The little blue rug from Tristan's room. And the painting, that small one of sailboats she'd never liked.

Merle swallowed, her throat tight. Maybe Harry sold the woman some things with the place. But it was only last year when she'd gotten rid of the footstool, and Tristan's rug.

"What's your name, sweetie?" she asked the girl.

The child hid behind the nanny's leg. The woman patted her head. "This is Sophie. She's having a bad day."

Merle felt her heart clattering. She took a deep breath then squatted down to the child's level. "Hi, Sophie. My name is Merle. Can you shake hands?"

Sophie peeked out from behind the nanny's leg, then slapped Merle's hand. "How old are you, Sophie?" She held up four fingers.

"Do you go to preschool?"

The nanny said in bored voice, "Normally."

"Sophie is a pretty name," Merle said. "Do you have more names?"

The girl stepped forward, holding onto her nanny's jeans. "Sophie Lou — " She took a breath. "Sophie Louisa Duncan."

"Nice to meet you." Merle stood up. "I'll stop back later. Thanks." She headed for the stairs. A woman was making her way up, struggling with grocery sacks. A blonde, in a dark suit with a black briefcase. Merle blinked. She held the handrail and felt the cogs click into place.

"Courtney? Courtney Duncan?"

The woman looked up the stairs. Her mouth dropped open as the grocery bags slipped from her hands, spilling oranges, milk, bagels.

THE WEATHER HAD TURNED MILD AND HUMID. Merle rushed blindly down the sidewalk, late now to her meeting with Lillian Wachowski. Her mind raced and her blood pressure was probably through the roof.

With a pointed glance at her watch Lillian ushered her into the office. Spare as law offices go, it was sumptuous compared to the windowless cave in Harlem. An exposed brick wall gave it a downtown look, and the fern. Lillian was a small woman with fine features, wearing a turquoise silk suit with a white shell, her gray-blond hair cut severe and short. Her intense blue eyes and dagger-like wit scared the crap out of everyone. Merle found herself trembling.

She sat without being asked, crossed her legs, and leaned back. Techniques to calm herself and show outward assurance, long-ingrained lawyer tricks. Never let 'em see you sweat. Lillian spoke about the weather and Merle admired her view of the river.

Something — black curls, pink sweatpants? — was preventing her from concentrating on Lillian. The conversation with the lawyer in France, Monsieur Rancard, last night, rattled in her brain too. She couldn't focus. Her life was no longer predictable.

Everything had been tossed into the air.

Rancard was making some progress with the squatter. It was cheaper to have him wrangle with the mayor and the old woman even at 200 Euros per hour. A nun was helping the squatter now, making matters worse. Maybe Merle and Tristan could go see the house, just once, if it didn't cost too much. The property lawyer said it would help the situation if she was there, help press her case for ownership. But now, there was a new job to contend with.

Courtney Duncan. Sophie. Their existence slammed against the defenses of her mind. Harry's lover, Harry's daughter. Courtney's tears, her sobbing explanation, her pleas for understanding. Her pitiful voice echoed in Merle's ears, making it hard to hear Lillian and her small talk.

Merle pushed the voices aside. No matter what sort of messes Harry left behind, she had to support herself and her son. Lillian represented the stable, secure future, for which Merle had just enough concentration to play the game. Stability, security: that was all she could ask for now. Now that she'd screwed up her own life.

The older woman crossed her legs. "How is it going with you and your son — since your husband's death?"

Had she been talking to Jeff about her? Everyone was always hoping they could stop pussyfooting around you. That you will bounce back, smile, carry on. So they can forget that people die. Even you, Lillian, so in charge of your life, will give up the ghost, buy the ranch, sleep the big sleep. *Even me.*

"We're, well — we're coping."

Lillian's eyes blazed. "You look tired."

"That's a frequent observation." Merle straightened, pulling herself together. "Look, Ms. Wachowski, this isn't an assignment I asked for. I was told you wanted me here, that you could use me, and that's very flattering. But I'd rather be on the front lines. I don't mean to be rude. I am grateful," she added.

Lillian's face hardened — further — and she walked around her desk. "Would you like to go back to Harlem? Or the Bronx maybe?"

Merle may have flinched. "Ah. Is that an option?"

Lillian squinted. "I'll be blunt. You need a lot of energy to do fundraising. And a very positive, balls-to-the-wall mentality. You're our cheerleader, our frontline. You can't have bad days in development. You can't *rather be* somewhere else."

A shiver made her twitch. Was there a job in the Bronx? She couldn't go back to Harlem now, no matter what Lillian said. Jeff had cast her off without a backward glance. Did she want to go to the Bronx, start over in another office? Or was this some kind of test?

Merle sat taller. She wasn't going to get fired because of bags under her eyes. "I'm sorry, Lillian. May I call you Lillian?" The older woman gave a curt nod. "The job sounded good to me when Jeff described it. It still does. I didn't mean to give the impression that I wanted to go back."

"Yes, well. It's a struggle raising money. It's never easy. It's like getting blood from a stone. You have to pound, pound, pound, until finally somebody cracks."

She tried to look bright and eager. "I love the sound of cracking."

Lillian looked her over with sharp eyes. "So you're taking a couple weeks off? Rest and recover from all your changes?"

"I — I could. Sure."

Lillian flipped through her desk calendar. "Most of the big firms have mass holidays in July and August. Partners come and go like lemmings. Not to mention this building's air conditioning is ancient and the caterers are all busy with weddings. So, what do you say — September one?"

THE AFTERNOON SUN blinded her on the sidewalk. Merle's arms ached, her head hurt, her stomach had clenched into a ball. All this new information was too much: rejection by Jeff, Harry's daughter and mistress, scary Lillian, the summer off with no income, and the obvious glee her new boss took in employing her. She felt like a punching bag. Could she take a few more body blows please?

She stumbled down the steps of the Legal Aid Society, straightened her shoulders, and headed west into the sun. The

Hudson River lay ahead, wide and gray all the way to Jersey but sparkling in the light. Where was that river going? Where did any river go? She'd never thought about going anywhere. She stayed and persevered, that was who she was. She took the safe path. Kept the calendar full. No sudden moves. It had always seemed the sensible way to live. She wasn't interested in glamour or excitement, just doing the right thing.

An Irish bar had its glass-paned red door propped open next to a blackboard listing today's specials: corned beef, cheese omelet, steak and fries. The smell of fried food, ever comforting, beckoned her in. Doyle's Public House was dark and cool, the wood floors dusty. Besides grease, it smelled of brewer's yeast, cigarettes, Lysol. The bartender brought silverware and a cloth napkin and a dry white wine.

Courtney Duncan. It all made sense now, these last years. The woman had been honest at least. Courtney and Harry worked together at the brokerage, before Harry joined Steve Hanford. She was just out of NYU. She had loved him, that was clear, something Merle hadn't managed to do for a long time. Maybe Harry should have left her for Courtney. Merle tried to decide which was worse, a divorce or a dead husband. Dead was definitely worse. Or what about this? A dead father-of-your-toddler.

She took a deep breath and a gulp of wine then called Stasia and left a message with her secretary. Grinding her teeth, she dialed McGuinness and Lester, Esq., and held while Troy Lester was rounded up. She ordered another wine before the secretary informed her he was out of the office.

"Give me his cell number." She wouldn't. "Then give him my number. Tell him it's an emergency."

All very well about Courtney then. Just the shock of discovery, being blindsided. She should have guessed something like this — years ago. But what about Sophie? How was she going to tell Tristan that his father had another family, that he had a half-sister? That Harry hadn't been all the father Tristan had wanted him to be, because he was father to another?

Suddenly tears leaked out of her eyes — oh God why now — then as the bartender brought the wine, sobs erupted, blubbering noises. Probably not the first heard in an Irish bar but the bartender looked appropriately shaken. He returned with a stack of napkins.

Merle dabbed her cheeks. Very thoughtful. Love that bartender. "Is that your phone, miss?"

Of course it was. "Merle? Troy Lester." Traffic noise, heavy breathing.

"Mr. Lester. When were you going to tell me about Courtney Duncan?"

He stammered and spit. His discomfort made her happy. It was good to have someone repulsive like Troy Lester to be angry at. She couldn't be mad at Harry any more. He was gone, and philanderer that he was, cheat and betray as he did, she deserved it. She had let him go, from her heart, a long time ago.

Reluctantly, Lester spilled the beans. Harry had left Courtney and Sophie the apartment, and the slender remains of his pension fund, also plundered. A second, secret will. Merle threw the phone down on the table.

Stasia arrived fifteen minutes later and, with the help of the bartender, forced coffee down her throat. They were out on the street, walking to the subway, before Merle could tell her.

"He never sold the apartment," Merle said, stopping for a light.

"What apartment?"

"Twelfth Street. He gave it to his blond thing, and their daughter."

"You're drunk." Stasia glared at her. "Are you serious?"

"The lawyers did it in secret. The bastards. He has a four-year-old daughter. Her name is Sophie. She's *four*, Stace."

Stasia turned instantly crimson, a specialty of hers. "Filthy, lowdown son of a bitch —" She stamped her foot on the pavement.

Merle felt calm now that her sister was mad. "Do you think it was because I couldn't —" She felt hollow, the way she felt after the hysterectomy. Not her old self, never would be again. Something gone and gone forever. "Did you know? Do Mother and Daddy know?"

"Nobody knows. If he was good at one thing, it was keeping secrets." Stasia took her arm and led her toward the subway stairs. "Move, now. We'll talk about it later."

A picture of Harry came into her head, an outing to somewhere, when Tristan was three or four — Sophie's age. Mystic Seaport, that was it. Tristan high up on Harry's shoulders, pointing at the big sailing ships, their tall masts, a clump of daddy's hair in his little fist. Harry holding his feet, smiling. They were a family that weekend, a strong yearning in her satisfied for at least one weekend. They jumped on the motel beds, sang songs in the car.

Had she loved him then, or just the idea of a family? Was her heart a stone? He had left her, years ago.

Merle stopped. "I don't blame him. Or her. He deserved love — everyone does — and she loved him. I didn't. I didn't love him. Not for a long time. I — " She shrugged. "I just didn't."

They were next to a flower stand overflowing with color and petals. Buckets of tulips vied for attention. Which one is the prettiest, the red, the yellow, the pink, the white? Daffodils, pussy willows. Lilacs on woody stems, their smell enticing.

Stasia was talking. Merle could see her lips move. Taxis were honking, an old woman pulled her shopping wheelie down the curb. Merle sucked the air on the sidewalk. Her chest felt like it was in a vise. *Why can't I breathe?*

An open palm crossed Merle's face. The sting felt hot. She didn't blame her sister. What is family for if you can't count on them to set you straight when you need it most, even in the middle of Greenwich Village? Her own sister smacked her hard across the cheek, bringing her back, holding her upright, making her grab onto the scraps of her rag-tag life.

"You didn't love him. It's fine. It doesn't matter."

Merle held onto her shoulder. "Okay. Thanks," she croaked.

Stasia pulled her close and whispered in her ear, "Breathe. And repeat after me: Case of courage. Bucket of balls."

POOR ELISE. She had no idea.

Merle looked over the orderly crowd on folding chairs on the lawn at Whitman and slumped lower in her seat. Her mother gave her a little frown and she straightened again. Must be respectful. A solemn and joyous occasion as the last Bennett girl takes the harness.

Elise clutched her diploma to her chest, flushed, her dark hair pulled back and red lipstick on her baby doll lips. Merle was distracted, sweating in a sleeveless navy shift. She'd had to tell Sauvageau about the new wrinkle, that Harry had another child who would inherit. But only if Courtney found out. And how would she? She didn't seem the suspicious type. On the contrary, she seemed naïve, crushed and pathetic. Another ethical conundrum raised its ugly head. Ah, but to a lawyer, that was nothing. Just a thought to be compartmentalized.

The speeches were mercifully short, the May heat rising from the damp earth to surround the well-wishers in the steamy scents of spring. Finally they rose and gathered around the graduate on the lawn. After an interminable, clammy hugging session they decamped for a cool restaurant.

The Bennett clan was tricked out in understated prep-wear. Her father had gone with the red bowtie, always a winner. Bernie wore a navy blue suit with a collarless white blouse that dated from the sixties, somehow surviving a thousand washings.

Her father had insisted on Merle sitting next to him. Jack Bennett had given her shoulder a pinch of affection and sat silently through the toasts. His hearing wasn't great so he liked to just smile at these big gatherings. The salad came and he dug in.

On her other side Francie wore a low-cut flowered dress that showed off cleavage and tan. Francie was the knock-out sister, with auburn highlights and turned up nose, a smattering of freckles across her cheeks and bright blue eyes. Merle had invited Betsy, who knew all the sisters and got along especially well with Elise, but her daughter Lynnie had a soccer game. Just as well, Merle thought. No point in the friends suffering.

At the kids' end of the table, Tristan wore his black blazer and a half-pressed blue oxford cloth shirt with a wonky collar, both last seen at his father's funeral. Francie had picked him up at school — she lived near Blackwood. She worked in Greenwich but couldn't afford to live there. Her clients had a different set of problems than Merle's, lawsuits between neighbors over dogs and parking, bankruptcy, prenups. Francie waffled between loving it and hating it on a weekly basis.

There were sixteen of them around the table, the sisters, one spouse, Stasia's three kids plus Tristan, a couple boyfriends (Francie's was chiseled and very young), Aunt Gloria, Bernie's sister, a cousin or three. Stasia and Annie talked across the table, heads together. They couldn't look more different: Stace in red polka dots and bangles, Annie in something tie-dyed and a big, furry scarf around her neck. Merle wished she were over there instead of by her father and Francie. She wanted to hear their gossip, laugh a little.

Stasia and Rick's oldest, Willow, had brought her boyfriend down from college. Willow lived up to her name: tall and slender with gold waterfall hair. Her boyfriend was scruffy, with dirty brown hair and a black t-shirt, but hung on Willow's every word. Would the children be happy, Merle suddenly worried, examining their expressions. Tristan frowned at her then elbowed Oliver and laughed.

Stasia caught her eye and winked. Annie, who was told the sordid story of Harry's other life just last night, gave her a 'buck-up' smile. After the salad and a polite inquiry into Merle's state of mind, Francie, not as yet clued into the latest revelations, launched into a lament about her job, social life, and lawyering.

"I can see the appeal of Legal Aid, I really can. At least you get to do some good."

"There's that," Merle said, chewing lettuce.

"If I have one more sixty-year-old chief executive marrying his twenty-something bimbo and wanting to keep all his cash from her, I'm going to kill myself. Why does he even bother? I mean, marriage isn't all that great. I should know." Francie had tried it once, briefly. The airline pilot she married was hardly ever home. Her boyfriend gave her a lascivious smile. He was home free.

"I'm taking the summer off," Merle said. It had a nice ring to it.

Francie smiled. "Sure. What would you do, Merle, paint your toenails every day? No, wait, you're going to a Buddhist retreat. Yeah, that's it. Ommmm." She laughed and her boyfriend, Willie or Dick or somebody, laughed along.

"I'm done in Harlem. I got packed off to Development. They don't need me until fall, or until I get my attitude adjusted."

"They said that? Come on." She squeezed Merle's hand, suddenly serious. "You're really taking summer off? Are you all right?" Despite her stunning beauty and a bright, easy charm unknown to the other sisters, Francie could be a loving sister. Merle squeezed back, thinking she should call her more often. Tell her about the nasty family secrets. One of these days.

Merle raised her glass. "To attitude adjustment — it's not just alcohol anymore."

Francie giggled. "I'll go drinking with you any time!"

Someone called: "To Elise!"

As they clinked crystal Merle stood up. "Excuse me, Elise, for using your graduation day for this." Elise smiled, dipping her head in gratitude. She was a little tipsy, draining her glass as if another toast in her honor was in the offing. She turned for a refill to her boyfriend, a pudgy classmate who wouldn't last, they all could tell.

"As you know in his will Harry left me — and Tristan — a house in France. His family home. Sort of a surprise but what the heck, right? Who are we to look a gift-horse in the mouth? Let's just hope it's not a Trojan gift-horse. Anyway, at the end of the term we will be traveling to the small village of Malcouziac, somewhere in France, to throw out the freeloaders and see if we can sell it."

After a shocked pause Annie said loudly, "Hey. You mean, no work? A vacation? An honest-to-God summer holiday?"

Her father turned to her frowning: "You're going where?"

"To France," Bernie shouted in his ear.

A holiday. Mystic Seaport popped into her head. That was a holiday. Those days, whatever they were, were over. Long over, if they only knew.

Put a face on it, Merdle. Vacation sounded a whole lot better than the drudgery, legal wrangling, and endless spending ahead. Harry would have liked that. He goes his own way and she gets stuck with his dirty work.

Oh, yeah, let's see that smiling face.

She raised her glass. "To vacations. What a concept."

BOOK TWO
FRANCE

11

AFTER ALL THESE WEEKS, from a wet April morning to a hot June day, not so long in time but emotionally an obstacle course of peaks and valleys, she was here. Across the sea, over the deep blue ocean. Exactly ten weeks and three days, nine Sundays, a Memorial Day. Over the miles and the hours, after packing and arranging and explaining, here she was, in France where Harry was born. Where he lived. Where not a trace of him remained.

They stared at the house. Monsieur Rancard — 'Arnaud' after four hours together in his perfumed Benz — rolled down the window, letting in hot, dry air. The lawyer, although handsome in that suave Mediterranean way, was business-like, even blunt. No passes, no intimate taps on the knee. She had sweated through her safari shirt and stuck to the seat. They talked nonstop and she was exhausted. Yet, a flutter of anticipation rose in her as they turned the last corner, pulled up to the curb.

No cottage, the house rose two stories of washed-yellow stone with a tile roof at various angles. Four windows, one extra-wide, faced the street. Only a narrow cement sidewalk with a granite curb separated the living quarters from the cobblestones. The shutters were devoid of paint, a weathered gray, an upstairs one hanging on one hinge. A high wall circled the place, starting at both front corners. The only house on the block with side yards, it was slightly grander than most yet looked abandoned.

The house sat adjacent to the crumbling city wall, six feet high here, eight there. Across most of the street it was lower, knee-high, as if a Nazi Panzer tank had crashed through. Beyond the broken wall the slope fell away into rows of staked vines. Across the swale stone-and-tile houses nestled close to the earth, thick forests darkened the hilltops, more grapes undulated with the curves of the hillsides, marching relentlessly toward wine.

They got out of the car and stretched. Merle had seen a lot of country with Arnaud between Toulouse and Malcouziac, villages along streams and on hilltops, bigger towns with gas stations, supermarkets, and modern buildings, but this land of vineyards and buttery stone was as pretty as it got. Maybe she was already biased toward the village, proprietary in a way. Maybe she was just tired.

"It's big," she said, taking off her sunglasses to look at the house. The day was sunny and warm in a way a Connecticut summer so rarely was. Heat reflected off the stone house opposite hers, a tidy, plain house with geraniums in pots. Next door to her house the shutters and door were freshly painted in a glossy royal burgundy. Upstairs music and a lace curtain blew out the open window while at the Strachie's all was closed and silent.

"So you see, all these shutters are locked," Arnaud said. He rattled the door shutter, its curved top matching the rock framework. "I can see the padlock there, through the crack."

As Merle peered through the half-inch space between the shutters the shouting began inside. Through the inner glass she caught a glimpse of movement, a shadow. She looked at Arnaud and raised an eyebrow.

"That is the lady," he said, sighing. He yelled back at her in French.

"What is she saying?"

"Babble. This is her house. Leave her alone." He took Merle's arm and led her back toward the middle of the village. "Perhaps best not to provoke her too much," he said, though he obviously had. "She has the ear of the village now, some of the old people especially. They had no good to say of her when I first came but now? Suddenly, pfft! She is the poor old lady, the martyr."

SHE HEARD THEM AGAIN, outside the shutters. Devils, trying to enter her sanctuary. Evil ones.

Sister Evangeline said God would smite them, but He was

taking His sweet time. Justine called out with her own curse. Satisfied they had gone, she turned from the dark room back into the sunshine of the garden. Eden, she sometimes called it, it was so lovely. She lived out here in the summer. With the hammock stretched into the corner, the only reason she had to go into the house was to store her meager ration of food and to curse the Devils.

The batteries on the radio seemed to be going out. The music sounded faint. She must ask Sister Evangeline for more batteries. Carefully she picked at the plastic cover on the back of the pink box radio, trying to ease it off with a fingernail. She knew how things worked, she'd been around. This radio had been with her for years, a reliable friend.

The sun beat down on her head. Her grip turned moist with sweat. Her finger slipped, slipped again, and suddenly the radio lay in pieces at the bottom of the wall. No sound came from it — no music — no Piaf — nothing. She stared at the pieces. It was the Devils' fault.

Evangeline came through the back gate, locking it quickly behind her. Justine became aware of the tears on her face from Evangeline's shocked look.

"*Qu'est-ce que tu fait?*"

Justine let the sun dry her cheeks. "Batteries," she mumbled.

Evangeline frowned at the broken radio. "It'll need a whole lot more than that." She took Justine's hand. "Did you have trouble with it? Don't worry, dear. Sister will get you another. Sister takes care of her flock."

The woman's hand on Justine's bony shoulder was warm and sticky. Justine didn't like to be touched. She frowned at the old nun. Sister E was to be tolerated. She was kind, she brought food, and a pretty rose-colored blouse just yesterday. And she kept the Devils away, those who would take Eden away from Justine.

Still, she couldn't help but step back, away from Sister's humid grasp. What did the old nun really want, her mind shouted. Why had she showed up here? Who had told her to come, that Justine needed help? Did she hear it directly from above?

"I've brought you something," Sister E said, smiling, holding a paper bag. Her hair made her look like a man, Justine thought, a friar really, with the short, bowl shape. And so gray, very sad. Nuns disliked their hair — why was that? Hair was meant to be adored by all, even God loved hair or he wouldn't have put so much on the angels. Justine patted her own locks, once famous for blocks and blocks, all the way to the Gironde. She felt pity for Sister's plainness, her ugly shoes and baggy trousers.

"What?" Justine said.

Sister reached into the bag and pulled out a small bottle of pills from the pharmacy. "Some pills to help you sleep. See? One before bedtime," the nun said.

"I sleep fine," Justine said. She eyed the small bottle warily. The Sister was trying to poison her now?

Sister E looked at her, making her squirm. Justine felt like she was under a microscope. "The American is in town. I know how that upsets you," the nun said. "Just take one at bedtime."

Justine hesitated then took it.

Sister E smiled. "I'll clean up the radio. Okay?"

"They were here."

"Who, dear?"

"The American. I saw her and her trained dog of Hell."

"Did you speak to them?"

"I called on St. Joseph to curse them for their greed."

Sister Evangeline paused, a piece of broken pink plastic in her hands. "We use the church for good, Justine. It is up to God to judge, not we humans."

"But I prayed to St. Joseph to find me a home and he brought me here. So he must curse them." Justine sat down on the low terrace beside the hydrangea bush. "He must."

Sister Evangeline laid her hand on Justine's shoulder again. "You must have faith."

Justine looked at the bottle of pills in her hand. She wanted to have faith, really she did. But everyone wanted something from her, that was too obvious. Even Sister E. She wanted her to sleep.

Why? So she could ransack Eden, steal her belongings? Was she in league with the dogs of Hell?

While Sister E was bent over the pink plastic chards, Justine poured the pills into the watering can. She smiled sweetly at the old nun.

So plain. Such a plain woman. Poor old thing.

ARNAUD STOOD AN INCH TALLER than Merle, with longish dark hair. His olive green summer suit and starched white shirt, immaculate yet casual, set off his deep tan. His Mercedes sedan was equally well-groomed; he had carefully wiped out the leather passenger seat for her. He was well-versed in the twists and tangles of French estate law, and had given her a tutorial on the drive from Toulouse.

Outside the café under an umbrella they drank iced coffee while he smoked and made phone calls. They had an appointment with the mayor in an hour. The stone plaza was large and square, empty except for café tables. Curved arcades ringed three sides for covered market stalls in medieval days and perhaps today. A few tourists rested on benches in midday shade. The village was sleepy, almost deserted at this hour. As they drove up from the south she could see it perched on the side of the hill, surrounded by vineyards, looking like Cinderella's ruined castle with its crenellated towers and sloping defensive walls.

Merle looked over the notes she'd made in the car. French law was confusing and yet precise. Interesting too, as it reflected a completely different set of values than American law. She'd always thought of the French libertine ways, the keeping of mistresses, the lack of matrimonial rites, as a little too loose and leaning toward men's rights over women's. But now she wasn't sure. Marriage or not, the law was clear. Maybe that was why the ceremonial was deemed unnecessary. Keeping property in the family was valued — one couldn't cut one's children out of a will here — it was also excruciatingly complicated. And therefore, expensive. Lawyers like Arnaud did not lack for work.

He would only be here today. She couldn't expect him to stay and hold her hand. He had found her a small hotel that was stuffy and cramped but would do for the week she planned to stay. Tristan, Stasia, and Oliver would be enjoying their first day in Paris. They'd gone to the airport together but Merle flew alone to Toulouse. By Saturday she hoped to have her business wrapped up and join them. She had debated about bringing Tristan here, showing him his grandparents' home, giving him a little history. But Paris beckoned. The countryside had no chance.

Arnaud set his phone on the table. "Pardon, madame. Business never stops. You should feel lucky you are not that woman I am speaking with. Her husband had two mistresses over the years, and three other children besides their own. Now that he is dead she must share the family villa with five children." He held up all fingers of his manicured hand. "And the kids don't even know each other. Can you imagine the troubles?"

"Will she buy out the children?"

"Possibly. She will try. But as you know, money in hand is not the same as stone walls."

"Yes, well, there is one more child, as Ramon must have told you."

He nodded and had the grace not to comment. Merle had tossed the subject around in her mind. She had to tell Courtney, for Sophie's sake. It would be dishonest not to. She would tell her when they sold the house for lots of money. Courtney, who had called once and been given ten minutes to complain, had enough on her plate. She didn't need these headaches now.

"American law is much different," Merle said. "You can leave whatever you want to anyone you want. Even leave your house to your cat."

He laughed and stubbed out his Gauloise. "A cat would be easier to deal with than Justine LaBelle."

The *hotel de ville*, city hall, was an unpretentious, tidy stone building, recently scrubbed, with geraniums blooming on the windowsills. The French flag flew over the door.

As Monsieur Rancard introduced them and the clerk went to fetch the mayor, he took Merle aside. "I will speak for you. "

"But I can speak for myself. I'm prepared," Merle protested. She had taken several years of French. Awhile back.

"In French?" Now he raised an eyebrow. He said something fast and complicated in his native tongue.

"All right," she said. "But you must tell me exactly what he says."

The mayor came through the swinging gate. He was a tall, thin man, with thick gray hair and an imperial manner. His eyebrows were large and wiry, his clothes timeless and elegant. His slender hand was cool to the touch and he did not smile at her. He invited them back into his office, holding the gate for them both. His office was large and sunny with flowering plants on the sills and maps everywhere.

The mayor's name was Michel Redier. He and Arnaud talked in clipped tones to each other, with Arnaud gesturing to Merle passionately. The lawyer's voice rose as he got shakes of the head from the mayor. Suddenly Arnaud stood and leaned against the desk to get closer to the stony-faced mayor. Merle was impressed but wondered if this was for her benefit alone. The mayor didn't seem to care. He sat back and crossed his arms.

After ten minutes of this, Arnaud returned to his chair and was silent. Was this a cue for her to speak? The mayor leaned forward and spoke in low tones.

Arnaud listened silently, his eyes narrowed. When the mayor finished Arnaud jumped to his feet, shouted, and stomped out of the office. Merle looked at M. Redier who finally was beginning to smile. She shook his hand and said goodbye.

Outside, Arnaud paced back and forth on the sidewalk, flinging his arms around, talking to himself. Merle waited in a spot of shade by a rose bush that grew out of an impossibly small square of earth by a downspout. Eventually Arnaud ran out of steam and looked at her. "*Pauvre con*! If he thinks that is common behavior — " He threw his hands up, disgusted.

"What did he say?"

"Stupid peasant. He thinks you should pay him to evict your squatter!"

Merle thought about that. "How much?"

Arnaud's face was red. He stuck his neck out. "You will not pay him! It is your house, legally. And that means he is your mayor. The gendarme is your gendarme. What have you been paying taxes for all these years?"

"My husband, you mean."

"You, your husband — it is *your* money already paying their salaries. It is bribery, plain and simple. And there are principles at stake. You will not pay him one centime, Madame. Not one franc!" He held up one finger.

"Not one Euro?" she said, smiling.

He waved his hands again. "If he thinks I am so low, so ineffective as to have to bribe village mayors, he does not know who I am — *Vous ne savez pas qui je sais, monsieur!*"

People looked at him curiously, waving and mumbling to himself, this well-dressed man so obviously from out of town. But they looked at her the same way, with bright-eyed curiosity and whispering. It was a small village; they had probably all heard about the dispute over the house. She smiled at a few old women who looked stunned and scurried away. Across the street she saw a man staring openly at them. As Arnaud calmed down, the man, an elderly fellow in a blue jumpsuit and black beret, came toward them.

"*Monsieur Rancard, bonjour encore!*"

The attorney looked up, still frowning. He gave the old man a nod. "*Père* Albert." The old man looked at Merle expectantly. "Oh, yes, this is one of your neighbors. Father Albert from across the alley."

The old man had a round face and a double chin, with black eyes and a near-constant smile. He asked her to call him Albert as he was no longer a priest. She smiled at his jowly, pleasant face. After all she had heard about French formality these two men didn't fit that mold.

"How did it go with the mayor?" he said in heavily-accented

English.

"Not well, I take it," Merle said. "You speak English."

"He is a buffoon, this mayor," Arnaud grumbled. He shot Merle a look as if to say, don't repeat that. "Are elections due soon?" He laughed nervously.

"I'm afraid he was reelected in the autumn," Albert said. "And you know the gendarme too? His nephew?"

Arnaud burst into another string of expletives. "Conspiracy of dunces! Idiots!" He suddenly looked at his watch and said in a normal voice, "I must go, Madame. I have business in Cahors very soon. You will excuse me?"

"I'll speak to you tomorrow?"

"*Mais oui.* I will call your hotel in the morning." He hurried off toward his car. Merle suddenly felt the weight of the trip, all the plans and airplanes and time zones, crash in on her. Without Arnaud the likelihood of getting anything accomplished here seemed hopeless. Maybe even with Arnaud.

The old man was still at her side. "A coffee, madame?" he said, indicating tables outside a tobacco store, *le tabac.* A ten-hour nap was what she really wanted but a chat with the old priest might glean some information. Besides, it couldn't hurt to have friends here, especially English-speaking ones. She sat in a small wooden chair while he went inside to order. He bounced back across the terrace and sat at the round table graced with a dirty ashtray.

"You have a long trip, madame," he said, seeing her stifle a yawn.

"Yes, sorry. A very long day."

A young woman brought out two small espressos on saucers with lumps of sugar on the side. She took a long look at Merle then went inside.

"Does everyone know who I am?" Merle asked.

The priest shrugged. "It is a small town."

"And they're all related, like the mayor and policeman?"

"Oh, no," he laughed. "But they all talk. There is not much else to do."

"Have you lived here long?"

"As a child, yes, then I went away to school, to the church. I only moved back two years ago, when I retired. I live behind your house," he added.

"And what do you see going on over at my house?"

He leaned in, over his coffee. "I only see a little from my upper window. The old woman with the orange hair, she lives on the grounds, inside and in the garden."

"Who is she, this Justine LaBelle?"

"Ah, you know her name. She was living there when I arrived. I see in the village sometimes. Not often."

"She's not friendly?"

He shook his head. "I do not believe she has friends in the village."

"Arnaud told me that she was being protected by a nun, and some of the older people in town."

"The nun, yes. She arrives last week. Calls herself Sister Evangeline but she does not dress like a member of an order."

"What does she want?"

"To help Madame LaBelle. Who plainly needs help, poor woman."

"Is she unbalanced?"

Albert sighed. "She is old, and clearly had a difficult life."

"What did she do?"

Another shrug. "I think she has no family. So I am glad that the nun has come to help her because Madame LaBelle seems to accept her. She has given her the key to the gate so she can come and go. She comes bringing the food and the clothing."

"Maybe the sister will take her back to the convent."

"*Peut-être.* Maybe."

"Do you think this Sister Evangeline will talk to me?"

"Perhaps. If you can catch her."

"Would you help me set up a meeting with her? I would be so grateful, *Père* Albert."

"Just Albert, please." He drained his cup. "I will try, madame.

I will try."

A group of young men burst out of the tabac in soccer shirts and baggy pants. They smoked cigarettes; one had a beer bottle. They stopped laughing and stared at Albert and Merle. Albert looked away, ignoring them. A cocky, short-haired one called, "*Vous êtes le* Merle?"

The other boys began to crow like roosters and flap their arms like wings. They danced raucously around the table then nearly collapsed in laughter before Albert stood and shouted at them. "*Allez! Allez!*"

They ran down the side street laughing. Albert shook his head. "Pardon, madame. Boys."

"I'm staying at the Hotel Quimet. Please call if you have any news about the house or Sister Evangeline."

12

Cher Marie-Emilie,

What you are telling me in your last letter is — if
true — a grievous sin. You must be sure, absolutely
positive, before you say anything to anyone in the
village. Think of the family — of both families.
Your own reputation, at the very least.

Have you spoken to your husband about this?
Please do not be so timid as to hide from him, hide
your knowledge, your feelings. This is too
important. He must be ashamed. Accept his
forgiveness. That is your duty as a wife.

How I wish I could come to you. Your dear mother,
may she rest in peace, would have wanted it so. But
things are not easy here either. Jacques and I must
be present for the birth of the lambs belonging to
the Grand-Duc as well as preparing the fields for
spring crops. You are surprised I call M. LeGrand
such? His family was stripped of their title centuries
ago but to himself he remains the Grand-Duc. He
keeps us in many ways.

So, you see, we all have our troubles. We all struggle
to live after the horrible war. Be glad you are
married and settled. It will get better. Already I see
signs.

Be brave, my darling niece—
    Josephine.

SHE FOLDS THE LETTER and tucks it into her bodice. Be brave, yes,
she needs those words. Wiping her tears she ties the scarf around her
head and picks up the basket. She will walk to the next town, maybe
find something growing along the creek. Anything to leave this
village.

13

ARNAUD RANCARD CALLED before Merle had gotten out of bed the next morning. She woke up at three a.m. then coaxed herself back to sleep on the lumpy mattress.

"I cannot come to the village today, or even tomorrow, it appears. Too much driving, and now that you are there you should be able to have some success with the locals."

"Like who, for instance?"

"The gendarme, for one. It appears Pére Albert is correct. He is the nephew of the mayor. But he is sworn to uphold the law and the law says that the house is yours. Show him your papers, the registry. And take Albert with you, for the translating. *Á bientôt, madame.*"

After a breakfast in the outside terrace with the other guests — croissants, yogurt, orange juice, and coffee — Merle put on her running shoes and a pair of loose pants. She soon found the light sweater too warm and tied it around her waist as she walked through the streets of the village. Exercise, she told herself, and god knew she needed it both mentally and physically. She tried not to think much. That is what walking did for her. She stared at the houses and cobblestones, their jeweled shutters and tidy stoops, the rich golden stone of their walls traced with centuries of war, children, heartache, joy, death, and rain showers. The stones had a thousand stories. She headed through a massive arched gate into the countryside, down a hill to a creek overgrown with wild shrubs. Past a farm, some cows, more vineyards.

When she returned to Hotel Quimet, a staid, yellow-trimmed building a bit out of character with the medieval village with its greasy brass fixtures and excess bric-a-brac, a message from Albert waited at the front desk. He had written out his address and told her to come by in the morning if she wanted to try to talk to Sister

Evangeline today. He had seen her early, going to the grocery. "Often," he wrote, "she is gone for most of the afternoon."

Not that he is spying on his neighbors, Merle mused as she stuffed her wallet, a bottle of water, and the manila envelope with papers, documents, and photos from the deposit box into her backpack. The plaza was a little busier here this morning with a few farmers selling eggs and jars of preserves even though it wasn't market day. That, she'd discovered, was Thursday. By then she would have this house secured — or not. She would not be bullied into doing something insensitive to the strange and elderly, orange-haired Justine LaBelle.

ALBERT'S HOUSE was like many others in the village, an ancient stone village house among a block of similar townhouses. His front door was wider and a little more ornate than most, with his green shutters pushed open. Over his door an iron scroll held up a fan of clear plastic as an awning. He came to the door, smiling, in what she would find his usual cheerful mood.

Inside the rooms were small and tidy as befitting a priest, full of books and little pretense, the old paint faded and gray. Before she sat down she told him about Arnaud's early phone call. Albert promised to talk to the gendarme with her then insisted she sit in the garden for a moment first for coffee and something called *quatre quart*, a pound cake.

He said he had rarely seen Justine LaBelle, but with her orange hair and odd dress she was easy to spot. They sat in the morning sun in his small back garden, dominated by a large plum tree and a tomato patch.

"Odd dress?"

He grimaced. "I should not say."

"She dresses differently than other women? How?"

"Well, like a younger woman."

Scantily, she guessed. Was she hawking her wares on the streets of Malcouziac? That might make her unpopular. "What do you do here, then, Albert? For fun."

"I have my plums," he said, bright eyes looking for the developing fruit. "I will make the *eau de vie* from them. And the fencing."

"Like the musketeers?"

He laughed. "Nothing so fancy. No feather in the big hat! I teach some local boys, a few girls but mostly boys. At one time I was the fencing, how do you say — teacher?"

"Coach?"

"Yes, fencing coach at a boys' school in the Savoie. It is good skill, very ancient. It teaches quickness in mind and body, to be light on your feet."

Merle felt the weight of her legs. Ah, to be light of foot. The bed at her hotel was calling. But this third cup of coffee was keeping her going. She only had four days to get this thing done. She thought about what Annie would say: why not have a real vacation? She wanted to be in Paris with Tristan and Stasia. Not mucking around here with weird old women. She sighed.

"We should go see if we can catch the gendarme," she said, wiping her mouth with the tiny embroidered napkin.

"But what about Sister Evangeline?"

"First, the gendarme."

THE VILLAGE OF MALCOUZIAC, with its thick defensive walls and narrow streets, was like a miniature New York, an island barely connected to the outside world where walking was the preferred mode of transportation. There was nowhere to park a car. Either you had a garage or you parked outside the city walls. She liked that. Everything you needed was a seven-minute walk away.

At one of the arched gates into the city a small bus was loading a line of tourists. Albert explained. "They go to the shrine. Many tourists, and pilgrims, come for miles."

"Where is it?"

Albert turned back in the direction they'd come. He pointed to a rocky cliff across the narrow valley to the east. "There, on top of the rocks. See the chapel?"

The domed rooftop stuck out from the forest surrounding it. "How do they get up there?"

"The road goes in that direction." He pointed north. "Then back again, like a snake. But you can walk up the steps. You can see just the top of them."

A flight of steps was carved directly into the stone face of the cliff. Bushes and the tops of trees obscured their lower reaches at least a hundred feet below.

"They look dangerous. And tiring," she said.

"Oh, yes. Take the bus," he laughed.

"What is the shrine called? I'll look it up in my guidebook."

"The Shrine of Lucrezia. Not a saint but revered by the faithful. A beautiful little chapel there." He stopped in front of the building where the mayor officiated. "Here we are. Around the back."

The office of the gendarme was small and gray, a post-war addition to the traditional stone *hotel de ville* in front. Utilitarian would be the kind term. She had hopes that meant the gendarme would be a logical, literal man who would see the justice of her claim.

A gray counter ran across the room, with two desks behind it. At one desk sat a woman, plump-faced with dyed blond hair. She stood as they entered but stayed behind her desk.

"*Bonjour,* Madame Cluzet," Albert said, pulling off his beret politely. He spoke rapidly. She replied in clipped tones.

"The gendarme is away, having his coffee," Albert explained.

"Let's go see him there then," Merle proposed. Albert held up a hand as the clerk spoke again. "She will call him to return. That is her job."

They sat on the hard chairs beside the counter. Albert was quiet, and with the woman obviously listening at her desk, Merle sat silently too. The clock ticked. Forty-five minutes later, the gendarme, who from his expression had forgotten about them completely, stepped in the door.

Hatless, he wore the dark blue uniform well with his broad chest. He was younger than she expected, around thirty, tall with thick light brown hair parted carefully on one side, olive skin, and an air of authority that she'd seen on policeman before. Before they were introduced she disliked him. Be nice, she told herself as she shook his hand.

His name was Jean-Pierre Redier, but Albert called him *Monsieur le Gendarme*. Redier stepped around the counter and leaned on his elbows, waiting for their pitch. Albert translated.

"These papers show I have full claim to the property. Here is the original registry from 1949, and the transfer upon death of his parents. Here is the new transfer registry, the certificate of inheritance tax paid. . .." She pointed out each document that proved her claim. "The woman living in the house has no right to live there. However, I wish to be fair. I do not want to make anyone homeless. So I would like to speak to you, or whoever is the social welfare authority here, about finding a residence for Madame LaBelle."

The gendarme listened then shot a look at Madame Cluzet, his lip curled in a half-sneer.

"You will buy a house for Madame LaBelle, he asks," Albert said.

"No. *Non*," she said to Redier. "I want to help find her a place to live. There must be some place for the elderly who have no homes."

"Not here, he says."

"How about in a larger city, Bergerac or Toulouse or Bordeaux?"

"You would send her away to Toulouse, he says." Albert frowned at her. "There is the general perception that Toulouse — and Bordeaux — are, um, full of the vices."

"Tell him I just want her to have a safe old age somewhere. Besides my house."

"This is where she comes from, he says."

What the hell did that have to do with anything? She could see why French lawyers got angry. Everything went in circles. "What about my house?"

"He says, there is another claim on the property, from Madame LaBelle. You can sue her, then the courts will decide who is right."

"I don't want to sue her. I want *Monsieur le Gendarme* to do his duty. Protect my property rights."

"He says you are not a citizen of the Republic so you have no rights here."

In dizzying circles, the gendarme wore her down with his glib, nonsensical answers to every parry she made. He could have been a lawyer, she thought, for all his dissembling. He never broke a sweat. Supreme confidence could be very aggravating, especially from someone in uniform. She felt like taking Harry's old advice and throttling him while he wasn't expecting it.

She gathered up her papers, stuffed them into the envelope and backpack, and stepped away from the counter before she lost her temper.

"*Merci beaucoup*, Monsieur Redier. We will meet again." He gave her a little bow as they turned away. "Isn't there someone else here, like a welfare officer, who can help Madame LaBelle?" Merle asked outside, walking so fast through the square that Albert had to jump a little to keep up. "Is there a state office here?"

"Just the *hotel de ville*. Everything goes through the mayor."

"How convenient."

"You will come to see Sister Evangeline now?" Albert asked, taking her arm at the corner to halt her. "*Pardon, Madame*." He was out of breath and red in the face.

"I'm sorry, Albert. Are you all right?" He was struggling with his breath but nodding. "I'll get you some water."

At the grocery she bought him a bottle of water and made him sit in the shade while they both cooled off. "Are you all right?" she asked him again.

"Yes. Thank you for the water."

"Thank you for the translating. What a jerk that policeman is."

Albert smiled weakly. "But he is the gendarme. You must respect that."

"I know. I was just angry with the way he never gave me a

straight answer. Or the answer I wanted to hear."

"I do not think he will help you."

Stymied by authority, abandoned by her lawyer: she had to get into that house, make nice with the squatter, and figure out a suitable housing arrangement for her. She'd hoped to get the house cleaned out, at least, and workmen hired to repair the roof, to secure it from the elements. Her lists so dutifully made before she came lay unused.

Her only hope was Sister Evangeline.

"It is her custom to leave between noon and one in the afternoon," Albert said as he stepped up the tall ladder into the arms of his plum tree. They sat in his garden again, this time with his gate to the alley propped open with a large rock. Opposite was the gate to the Strachie house where, with luck, they would intercept Sister Evangeline.

Merle had gone back to the hotel after the meeting with the gendarme, to take a quick shower and gather some lunch items for the vigil. On the dusty iron table she'd laid out grapes of two colors, red and green, cheese of two kinds: known and unknown, and a sliced baguette. One thing she could get used to, the food of France.

"I will just check from up here," Albert called from the plum tree.

"Be careful," Merle said, watching him disappear into the leaves. She steadied the ladder. "What do you see?"

"Plums," he whispered back. "Wait, someone left the back door. I think the Sister. Wearing a hat, it's hard to tell. I wouldn't know Madame LaBelle without her orange hair."

Her hair must be an amazing color for everyone to keep commenting on it. "Anything now?"

"Can't tell."

With a creak the gate to the Strachie garden opened and quickly closed again behind a short woman wearing gray cotton pants, hiking boots, and small-brimmed sun hat. She had a walking stick and a small backpack as if she was ready for a hike. Gray hair, not orange. Merle jumped up. "*Madame! Soeur* Evangeline!"

The woman paused, looking over her shoulder. *"Oui?"*

Albert was halfway down the ladder. She asked the sister to wait. But she had taken a few more steps toward the street. *"Pére Albert, il est ici!"* As she hoped the invocation of Father Albert's name made her stop.

He appeared with a leaf in his hair, smiling. "Ah, *Soeur* Evangeline." He spoke to her quickly, asking for a moment to chat in his garden. He pleaded, it was very important. Five minutes was all she had, she declared.

Despite the gray hair she was a fit woman, energetic with those well-used hiking boots. Her face was round under the hat, with a sunburned nose and large teeth. She wore no makeup and her hair was cut like a young boy's, all one length mid-ear. Her chambray shirt was clean but frayed, and the same could be said for her hands and nails.

Albert sat opposite Evangeline in the shade and offered her food which she declined. He spoke to her with a slight irritation for that. She replied with the same tone.

"She says Madame LaBelle has no intention of moving out of the house. That it is legally her home from an inheritance."

"An inheritance? Who gave it to her?"

More words flew. "She says a relative years ago, Marie-Emilie Chevalier, who was her mother. *C'est vrai, Madame?*" he asked the nun again.

Sister Evangeline shot a look at Merle and mumbled more French.

"Not her true birth mother, she admits. At first the sister thought it was a blood relation. But Madame LaBelle says she was her spiritual mother, her godmother as you say."

"Does she have proof of any of this?"

"A letter from Madame Chevalier that proves their strong feeling, their close relationship."

Letters. "Her name was Strachie. Marie-Emilie was married to my husband's father. Can we see this letter?"

The sister disappeared back into her garden and returned,

giving Albert strict instructions before she would hand over the letter.

"She says she has the original in a safe place." With that the sister turned on her heel, swinging her walking stick.

"Just a second, Albert." Merle trotted to the street and looked in the direction the nun had gone. She was a block away, walking purposefully, swinging her stick and taking un-elderly strides. At the far corner she turned right and went through the city gate into the countryside. Merle returned to the garden where Albert was reading the letter.

"What does it say?" she asked, looking over his shoulder.

"It appears to be a letter to the convent — I shall read it? 'There is so much I wish to say to her, so much I wish I could say. Someday I will return and make my feelings known. But for now let her know she will always have a home with me, wherever I am. She will never be without someone looking over her, someone who cares. I have not abandoned her. I never will.' It's signed: Marie-Emilie Chevalier."

"Can I see it?" He handed her the Xeroxed page. There was no mention of Justine LaBelle. It was meaningless, legally. "Where did this come from?"

"I assumed from Justine, but now reading it, I wonder. It doesn't mention her and is addressed to the prioress. The Mother Superior."

"Why would Marie-Emilie use her maiden name? She was married before she came to the village," Merle said. "I have some other letters, ones my husband kept. To Marie-Emilie from someone. They're in French. Do you think you could take a look at them?"

"If you wish."

She pulled the small packet from the manila envelope in her backpack. "They're hard to read, they're so faded." He took them, peering closely at the old, brittle envelopes. "Take your time. I think I'll knock on her garden door."

They stood in the alley. Merle was determined to speak for herself this time, woman to woman. She rapped on the solid wood with peeling blue paint. "Madame LaBelle?"

No answer. She put her ear to the gate. "*Je m'appelle Merle Bennett. Je suis Americaine.*" In French she continued: "I want to help you find a new home."

"*Allez! Fiche le camp!*"

"*S'il vous plait, madame.* Can we talk?"

The first rock sailed over the wall and hit Albert's wall with a thud. They turned, startled, watched it roll down the alley. The second caused them to duck then dropped onto the mossy alley floor.

Albert called out, "*Madame! Arretez!*"

Merle backed away from the gate. This wasn't going well, she was thinking, as the third stone hit her square on the forehead. She staggered, stunned.

"Oooh la la, you bleed, Madame!" Albert cried as two more rocks arced over the wall, one barely missing him. He yelled again at Madame LaBelle to stop then insisted they take cover behind his wall. He made Merle come into the house for examination, where, it was true, she was bleeding a little. The goose egg would be a fascinating addition to her forehead.

She held ice in a dishcloth to her forehead. Things were going badly. Maybe she should just wait for the lawyer to get back. She closed her eyes and was back at her desk at Legal Aid, filling out a Section 8 form for an illiterate client. It seemed so safe, so orderly, so *normal*. She opened her eyes. This was the new normal: strange country, strange people, strange laws. For a moment she wished herself back in the dark, rainy suburbs, changing light bulbs.

Ice water tricked down her nose. On Albert's dark wood table was an open bottle of wine, a bouquet of pink wildflowers in a cracked crystal vase, a small dish of black olives. The sun shone through his lace curtain at the front of the house, landing on a purple orchid. On the breeze, the smell of lavender.

The odor of France went into her brain. Was she crazy? Did it take a hard knock to the skull to make her wake up? Did she want to be back in the shadows of Connecticut, or in a windowless cubicle in Manhattan? Here she had sunshine, fresh fruit, warmth.

This is France, stupid. Here, now.

When Albert stepped into the room with his first aid kit she stood up. "I'll go lie down at my hotel."

"I have medicines, no?" Albert's face creased with concern. "Perhaps we should tell the gendarme that she is dangerous?"

"He doesn't care, Albert."

"They like to know, these gendarmes," he said. "Leave it to me."

14

STEFAN WHISPERS, "Leave it to me."

How has it come to this — hiding, whispering, touching, like some common peasant who doesn't know the meaning of time, of commitment, of consequence. Marie-Emilie doesn't know, doesn't want to know. He brings her food, for her mind and her body, that is all she knows.

Maybe she is careless now that Weston has gone. Maybe she doesn't care what her husband feels or thinks, what any of them thinks. The village turned its back on her and it isn't in her to fight any more. Yes, she is careless. She knows it is wrong, this thing, whatever it is, with Stefan. But there it is and she can't fight it. He is her friend, her only friend. When she so needs a friend.

"Leave it to me and all will be well." He kisses her hand, like a gentleman, looking into her eyes. That is as far as she lets him go; she is no whore. She has felt his lips on hers, just once. She closes the door and watches him run with his long legs and floppy blond hair, around the corner. A Dutchman by birth, he moved here as a boy. Who would think, a Dutchman?

On the table are the books. This is how it began, at church, over a discussion of a book. She had not read the one he mentioned although she was quick to tell him she could read, that she had passed all her tests. He didn't make her feel stupid; he listened. This book is just a story, nothing particular, about a young man in the first war who meets a woman, fights and kills, then comes back to her. She knows the type, she had read them. Fantasies of what war meant, as if every man came back to love again, as if nothing had changed. As if hearts didn't need to be mended, as if men were not shattered and children starved, as if the land hadn't gone to rot.

That Stefan had liked the story was what mattered. That he had given her the book mattered.

Weston has been gone for months. She hasn't heard from

him. She is glad. Things have been very bad in town. No one will sell her even an egg at market, not a potato. She rides a farmer's cart to outlying villages where no one knows her and spends what little money she earns helping at harvest and at planting. The farmers use her then, they have no choice. Men with strong backs are scarce, women too. She was the youngest woman bent over the grapevines last fall, the youngest to plant seeds in rows this spring.

For the first weeks he was gone she worried, keeping the house the way he liked it, making sure she looked decent. He might come home unexpectedly, just waltz in the way he'd done. But when he doesn't write or return, something changes in her. She feels loose from him, as if a terrible burden has been lifted. As if he had died in the war and she was a widow who was destitute but could go on without worry now. She crossed herself and begged forgiveness for her evil thoughts.

But he is dead to her. Now she could see he used her, for this house, his carnal ways, whatever he wanted. He no longer cares for her, if ever he had. From the moment Stefan walked her home from church and she told him her name was Marie-Emilie Chevalier, she was free. Her mother's name, the good knight, the avenger of sins.

Now to right the wrongs. She has no illusions about changing the villagers' minds. They will always hate her for Weston. Doors will always slam. Children will be sent indoors to avoid contamination. It doesn't matter. She has a plan and Stefan, who has a bicycle and a job at the *boulangerie*, will help her.

She walks out into the garden and feels the sun heal her spirit. She will not live like this forever, hungry and alone. Things will change. With all her power she will erase his wrongs from this earth. Then she will be a free woman.

15

AS SHE UNLOCKED THE HOTEL ROOM Merle smelled the air change of someone strange, their sweat. Every dresser drawer was pulled and dumped, the closet thrown, suitcase upended. She stood in the doorway, stunned, grateful she'd taken her wallet, passport, documents with her. There was very little else she cared about. The mattress had been searched, lying at an angle on the frame. She backed out of the room and went to find the manager.

"A thief, madame? *Zut alors.*" Guy Framboise was young, a tall man who spoke several languages. Together they walked up the stairs to the second floor rear guest room. "Oh, madame!" The manager apologized, mortified. He insisted she return with him while he called the police.

As he sat her down in the empty dining room, he noticed the bump on her forehead. "Did he hurt you?"

Her hand flew to her head. "No. *Un petit accident.* Could I get some ice for it?"

In a moment the chef brought out a glass of red wine and a bowl of ice, pausing to listen to the commotion in the lobby as the gendarme arrived. Monsieur Framboise cleared his throat as he approached. Merle pulled the ice off her face.

"Monsieur le Gendarme would like you to accompany us back to the room so you can identify any things that may be missing."

Jean-Pierre Redier, the gendarme, seemed a lot friendlier to the hotel manager than he had this morning, although his manner was still a mixture of arrogance, laziness, and too much wine with lunch. The manager translated, so she didn't have to actually speak to the policeman.

"He would like you to carefully enter the room," the manager said, "and see what is missing."

As she stepped inside, moving around a mound of underpants in their perpetually frayed state, she vowed to buy French lingerie for the next viewing. All the undies were unfortunately accounted for, as well as the stretched-out bras.

"He asks if you left your passport in the room," Framboise called from the hall.

"No, I had everything with me. In here." She patted her backpack. She pointed to a pile of clothes. "Can I fold these?"

She picked up her slacks and t-shirts, folding them onto the top of the dresser. She looked around, poked her head inside the lavatory. "My watch is missing. I left it in the bathroom." Not like her to forget her watch but she'd had that quick shower. "And a pair of gold earrings worth about fifty dollars American."

"How much is the watch?" Framboise asked.

Harry had given it to her years ago. *Time has run out, King Harold.* A birthday, or something. Had they even celebrated her birthday together last year? No, she'd gone into the city and had dinner with her sisters.

"Maybe five-hundred dollars. It had a few little diamonds on it."

The room seemed even smaller with the mess. The thief had ignored a pair of earrings worth more and amazingly had left a packet of traveler's checks she'd stuck in the desk drawer. The manager sighed dramatically.

Redier shrugged. The thief had been careless, that was all. Or maybe disturbed before finishing. He turned his dark gaze on her. "*Qu'est-ce que c'est?*" What is that, he asked, pointing to his own forehead.

"*Rien,*" she said. Nothing. He asked her something else and she waited for the manager's translation.

"He asks if that is from Madame LaBelle's garden."

Albert wasted no time calling him about crazy Justine. "*Oui. Un pierre à la tête.*" A stone to the head. She mimed an overhand toss.

"He says, are you going to press charges against her."

"No. *Non. C'est* okay."

Redier looked at her for a long, silent minute. He was just creepy, she decided, giving him an equal stare. He left with the manager to question the housekeeping staff. Merle straightened the mattress back on the bed and lay down. The smell of the room's violation made her uneasy, and her head hurt from the rock. She got up to find her aspirin, scattered on the cracked tile of the bathroom floor. She picked up two, blew them off, and washed them down with water.

Just a quick nap.

At five in the morning the birdsong woke her. She'd slept through dinner and somewhere around midnight managed to get under the covers. Behind the hotel the sun hadn't yet risen over the chateau on the hill. She put on running shorts and shoes, pulled back her hair. In the bathroom she examined the bump over her eye: purple but not too terrible, she dabbed a little makeup on it and went downstairs. In the kitchen the chef slumped sleepily over a cup of coffee. Now that they were friends he waved her on to help herself. She drank a glass of orange juice then walked outside.

The cobblestone streets were silent. A rooster crowed somewhere on the edge of town. Yesterday had been a disaster. Maybe she had been too aggressive with Justine. And not enough with the gendarme. *Step back, make some new calculations.* Turning right she decided to make a pass by the house in case someone was up early. Albert said Evangeline often went out first thing in the morning, possibly to church.

A block away from Rue de Poitiers Merle saw them. Orange hair, short skirt, and baggy pants, hiking boots. Evangeline and Justine walked arm-in-arm out the alley onto the street. Merle jumped into a doorway. Where to hide? She crouched into a ball behind a large flowerpot, tucking her head down. Their shoes squeaked against the cobbles as they passed, quickly, silently.

When they were well past Merle peeked out. Hiding behind a flower pot, really. Why hadn't she just spoken to them? If she could just talk to Justine, get her to understand she meant no harm. But she needed a new strategy, something to break down the defenses, get them to listen. Hopefully the old woman wasn't armed with rocks today.

They turned at the city gate as Evangeline had done yesterday, so they weren't going to church. The medieval cathedral was in the other direction, in the middle of the village. At the corner Merle peered around the stone wall of a house.

The bus to the shrine, squat and blue, stood idling in the parking lot, loading passengers. As Merle hugged herself in the morning chill, tourists materialized on the streets, each holding a sprig of green leaves. Was it some sort of ritual? She'd forgotten to read up on the site. The old women smiled politely as they passed. Old men ogled her bare legs. Groups of middle-aged women huddled together, talking, laughing quietly, all clutching the branches as they passed under the gate and boarded the bus.

She'd lost sight of the two women. Had they gotten on the bus? She waited until the bus started moving, turning laboriously in the parking lot. As it pulled out onto the deserted road Merle walked to the gate. Justine and Evangeline were nowhere to be seen.

The sun popped up over the eastern hillside, sending a beam of light directly on the Shrine of Lucrezia on the cliff above. It was beautiful in this light. No wonder the faithful wanted to see it at dawn. The steps in the rock were also illuminated.

"It's a sign," she muttered, jogging down the path toward the creek at the bottom of the cliff.

Tall grass, a cloud of gnats, and a riffle of fog made the going tough until she came into a small grove of trees. Under them she could see the path, worn in the leaves and pine needles, leading to the cliff and the stairs. She paused at the bottom of the limestone wall and looked up. The treads were worn, slick with dew. No railing — and quite a lot of steps.

The things I do for you, Harry Strachie.

No, make that Tristan Strachie. She was doing it for the future, Tristan's future, not for anyone's memory.

It was a whole new world. The past was done.

When Merle reached the top of the stairs, out of breath, legs screaming, the bus was already parked in the gravel lot behind the building. She let herself look down finally, now that she was safe. The view was dizzying. The village looked toy-like from here, the morning sun glancing off its honey walls.

The Shrine of Lucrezia was a classical building with block walls and a carved portico and columns. It was small and windowless like a crypt. People were lined up outside waiting their turn to enter. Merle watched from behind a pine tree. A car pulled into the lot, then another. More faithful emerged, clutching sprigs, milling with the others. The crowd grew outside the Shrine, quiet and reverential. Mostly women, the crowd increased when another bus arrived, this one full of nuns in long brown habits, complete with blinding white wimples.

Tearing a small branch from a tree to simulate their devotional sprigs she walked around the buses to emerge from the parking lot. As one person left the shrine another was admitted. Merle skirted the edge of the crowd, looking for Justine.

There she was, her orange hair glowing, third in line to enter the shrine. She was tall in platform shoes. There were three other orange-haired women, all short. In front of her was Sister Evangeline. A woman in a red crocheted hat opened the door to the shrine and walked to her right, away from the crowd. To intercept Justine Merle would have to be on the other side of the crowd.

Back around the bus she bumped into a middle-aged man with a bad toupee climbing down its steps. "Pardon," he said with a British accent. Merle picked up the sprig she'd dropped and went around the other end of the bus. Evangeline was leaving the shrine in her uniform of gray pants and hiking shirt.

Justine disappeared into the shrine only to burst out again almost immediately. Jerking slightly she held the door for the next woman, then stepped away and stopped, her head down. Merle moved closer.

"Justine? Madame LaBelle?" She asked softly if they could talk.

The old woman's head jerked up. Her eyes were unfocused. She seemed older today, more fragile. Up close Merle could see the lines of age on her face, the heavy eye makeup that gave her a clownlike appearance, especially with the orange hair that stuck out in all directions.

Merle tried to catch her eye. She smiled, trying to look friendly, and told her that she was the American, that she meant no harm. That she wanted to help. Justine's eyes grew wide.

"*Vous!*" You!

Her shrieks attracted the attention of the crowd. Merle put her hands up and backed away. Another blunder. The woman was not sane. Sister Evangeline trotted to Justine's side and joined in the harangue. Several of the nuns walked over and tried to ask Merle — well, something, but she could only shrug and say, "*Je ne parle pas Francais.*" She thought she spoke French, but not like this, thank you very much. "*Pardon, pardon, je suis desole,*" she apologized as she backed away.

Evangeline put her arm around Justine's narrow shoulders. The old woman wore what looked like a dress from the '50s, yellow and tight against her bony chest and short enough to expose her sagging knees, bare of stockings. Albert's version of odd dress. A habited nun approached Justine, stroking her narrow shoulder as she began to cry. Poor, crazy old woman. How could she expect anyone to help her evict the woman?

AT LUNCH IN THE HOTEL dining room, Merle sipped a glass of white wine between courses and read about the Shrine. Lucrezia was an Italian nun in the Renaissance era. She suffered at the hands of local authorities who believed she practiced witchcraft. She was banished to France where her following grew. She established a convent and set up her own order of nuns.

The pamphlet described the inside of the shrine as "damp." Today, June 19, was the day she was buried, a traditional time for the faithful to honor her.

Monsieur Rancard had been out of the office when she called earlier, but would return her call later from the road. He was in Cahors again, his secretary said. The waiter brought her main course, chicken with a light sauce. As she looked up to thank him she saw the gendarme in the lobby. He was starting to get on her nerves: always present, never helpful.

The food was heavenly, sweet and tender. She finished her main course and sipped her wine. Then, in front of her table stood the manager and the gendarme. "*Madame, pardon,*" Framboise stammered. He tipped his head toward the door. "If you please come?"

Redier had his usual insolent look on. She wiped her mouth and followed them into the manager's small office.

"Have you found my watch?" she asked.

Framboise blinked nervously, listening to the gendarme. "There has been an accident. Madame LaBelle," he whispered. The gendarme growled some more. "She fell from the Shrine, down the cliff. She is dead."

"What?" Rancard's prediction that she would have to battle Justine's descendants for the house was looking prescient. Merle frowned. "I'm sorry."

"He wants to know your whereabouts early today. This morning."

"Well, I saw her. I got up early. Jet lag." Framboise translated. "I went out to go for a walk about six and saw Sister Evangeline and Justine get on the bus to the Shrine, so I walked up the steps. I wanted to talk to Madame LaBelle about the house."

"The house?" Framboise asked.

"The one that is legally mine," Merle said. "The gendarme knows which one." Perhaps she shouldn't be quite so forceful, she thought, watching the gendarme's face. Getting the drift, finally. She could almost hear his thoughts: Greedy American tries to steal house from the poor, lonely Frenchwoman, by hook or by crook. "I tried to speak to Madame LaBelle yesterday. As you know. I thought with the crowd there I would have a better chance. I wanted to tell her I meant her no harm, that I would try to help her."

"And did you speak to her?"

"Very briefly."

The gendarme waved her to stand. Framboise said, "You

must go with him and make a statement."

  She examined the cold, black eyes of the gendarme. The embodiment of authority. He, who smelled like cigarettes and garlic. Albert's words: *Must show respect.* She stood up. "With pleasure."

THE SMALL GRAY INTERVIEW ROOM in the small gray gendarmerie still had a photograph of Charles de Gaulle on the wall. There was a tiny window at chin-height that dropped a square of sunshine on the wooden table. The gendarme and a new man, someone she understood was from out of town, sat firing questions at her. So far she'd managed to say, "*Je ne parle pas francais,*" at least a dozen times.

  "I want a translator, um — *pour parler les mots entré anglais et francais.*" How did two tribes ever communicate?

  The out-of-town officer, introduced as Capitan Montrose, barked at Redier. They both left the room, locking her in, cigarette-free when she really wanted one. She had brought one pack of Slims with her and vowed to stop when they were gone. So far she'd only smoked one, out the window of the hotel after returning from the shrine.

  Cigarettes. The telltale sign of nerves. It was only a statement. She had spoken to the deceased. She was accustomed to working with cops in Harlem, they didn't intimidate her. So what were these nerves?

  Having your attorney present during questioning was possibly not a right in France, but she wanted one. It was the language barrier. Capitan Montrose returned and sat down, his notepad on his knee. He was one of those indeterminate-age Europeans, somewhere between thirty and fifty, a bit jowly, hair still dark but a few strands of gray over his temples. His head was flat on the sides, his mouth small. Thick eyebrows looked crayoned onto his face. His skin was office-work pale and he wore a rumpled gray suit with an ill-fitting shirt.

  Expressionless, he offered her a cigarette. Brown Gauloise, strong and bitter: after one puff she put it out. Redier returned, ushering in an older woman with a patrician air and blond hair she fashioned after Catherine Deneuve. The Capitan offered his chair.

"My name is Jacqueline Armansett. I am the head teacher at the school. These men — the inspector — have asked for my services in translating your statement."

Merle smiled at her, hoping for some sisterly bond but feeling only a chill.

"The inspector asks for you to take him through all of your meetings with Madame LaBelle."

"Today?"

"All."

Merle began with the death of Harry and the inheritance of the house. She told of hearing about the squatter and her own work helping the homeless find shelter. Of coming to France and trying to speak to Madame LaBelle with her lawyer, and through the garden gate. She pointed out the bruise on her forehead.

"He says, do you have a witness to the rock-throwing?"

"Albert Tailliard. He lives across the alley."

Merle repeated what had happened that morning, taking care not to gloss over witnesses, people who saw her come and go. She mentioned the man getting off the bus. The nuns in their robes, Sister Evangeline.

"Have you spoken to Sister Evangeline?" Merle asked them.

"Who is this please?"

"According to Albert she showed up last week to help Madame LaBelle with the legal battle over the house."

"Legal battle?"

"Madame LaBelle thinks — thought — that she owned the house. My documents show that my late husband owned it, for fifty years. I inherited it when he died."

"How did your husband die, Madame Bennett?"

"A heart attack." They stared at her through the smoke. "Oh, come on." Merle rolled her eyes. Now she was a serial killer? "I had nothing to do with my husband's death, nor with the death of Madame LaBelle. I walked down the road from the Shrine. Several people saw me as they drove up."

"Can you give us names or descriptions?"

"A white van. I didn't see the driver, I was too busy jumping behind a tree to avoid being killed. A green — one of those little cars. A woman was driving." That should narrow things down. "I had a croissant and a coffee at the patisserie about eight o'clock. I bought a paper at the tabac, the *International Herald Tribune*. The agriculture strike is on the front page. I went back to my room and straightened it up. Monsieur le Gendarme can confirm that it was broken into yesterday and several things were stolen."

The gendarme spoke to the captain. "What are they saying?" Merle asked the teacher.

"He says you reported a burglary." The teacher listened to the captain. "What does your watch look like?"

"A gold link band, small with a pearl face with four tiny diamond chips. A Tag Heuer, old, scratched."

The captain spoke to Redier who left the room. In a moment he was back with a small plastic bag with black writing on it. Inside was her watch.

Merle pushed the plastic down around the face of the watch; the scratch on the crystal, just as it'd been for years. "Where did you find it?"

The teacher blinked. "On the arm of the dead woman."

ARNAUD RANCARD ROARED INTO TOWN in late afternoon, just as Jacqueline Armansett tired of the translation game and said she had her own work to do. Merle had told and retold the details of her meetings with Madame LaBelle to the point she had nothing left to say. Capitan Montrose seemed to be satisfied, although the connection between her watch and the arm of Justine LaBelle was troubling. Redier seemed to think this constituted a smoking gun. His reasoning was classic: Since the American wanted the house she had to eliminate the squatter. Americans take what they want by force. Americans bribe people with expensive watches. Montrose, clearly the brains and her new best friend, shook his head at each of his proclamations.

Arnaud had called the hotel for Merle and received the news she had been arrested, true enough to get him to race his Benz over the roads to Malcouziac. Merle heard him shouting at Redier outside the interview room. The calmer voice of Montrose intruded and finally Arnaud was allowed to see her.

He kissed her on both cheeks. His color was high, and he spit out his words. "What the hell is going on in this little *ville*? They are crazy, all of them! I wouldn't be surprised if the mayor was behind all this, that idiot!"

Merle felt confused, and a little frightened by what was going on, but she didn't need to get as riled up as Rancard. *Stay calm.* "What are they going to do with me? Have they told you?"

"It is all a terrible mistake. I will call the Embassy for you. There is an American consul in Nice."

"What can they do?" Nice was far away.

"Make sure your rights are not violated by these peasants." He gestured wildly then sighed. "I will help you too, Madame. Whatever I can do, although of course I am not a criminal lawyer. Capitan Montrose, he is from Bergerac, from the courts. He will take over the investigation. In France we do not let the crazy gendarmes do investigation. They are too close to the population."

"He seems reasonable," she said.

"The Capitan will do you well." He stood up suddenly. "I must talk to him."

"Am I being charged with something?"

"Not yet. Do you have with you all the documents about the house?"

"In my backpack. They have it out there."

She thought of Tristan in Paris again. His father dead and his mother in the Bastille. Merle hadn't spoken to any of them since she left the U.S. Now she would have to call. She didn't want Stasia to come, to get excited about all this. They didn't need an international incident.

She put her head down on the table and felt the sun from the tiny window on her neck as if saying: *See— France can be gentle and lovely.*

No need to go back to the 'burbs. No need to go home at all.

16

Merle sat on the tumbledown wall looking out over the vineyards. A bird flew to one of the stakes, perched there, singing. It made her forget about her headache for a moment. High on the tops of the hills, where the old forest still grew tall, wind tugged at the treetops. The sky was so blue it made her eyes hurt.

Harry never wanted to go to France. He lived for work. He would have missed out on great opportunities to make money, his most compelling desire. That single-mindedness defined him. She saw now, in a flash, that he could never have cared as much for her as he did about his money. Maybe he loved Courtney. Maybe he was incapable of that sort of love.

He did love Tristan. They had him in common. She would see her son tomorrow, either here or in Paris. Arnaud had been arguing her case relentlessly for the last twenty-four hours. For an estate lawyer he did like to argue. She smiled, thinking of him waving his arms in front of the stony-faced inspector. They would smoke Gauloises and decide her fate.

They had kept her overnight at the tiny gendarmerie, giving her a cot with fresh sheets and a cold dinner of chicken and salad and a glass of wine. She hadn't slept well. The wine took the edge off her tension but she woke again at midnight, smelling their cigarettes outside the room. They talked on and on. The French have a great capacity for debate.

Early this morning she was served coffee and a croissant. An hour later, the inspector released her. Arnaud Rancard was not there. The inspector told her slowly: do not leave the village. *Absolutement*, he said gravely. Then handed her a note.

'Meet me at the house at 11:00. A.R.'

Now, on the wall, Merle checked her watch but it wasn't there. She had left the hotel at ten, after a shower and change of clothes. Who had ransacked her room? How had her watch gotten on the arm of Justine LaBelle?

Strange that they didn't even know who Sister Evangeline was. She must have been at the Shrine when it happened. Maybe she was even the guilty party, although Merle didn't think so. A nun? Well, was she really a nun? Either way she didn't come off as an evil person. Could someone have merely frightened Justine by the edge of the cliff, causing her to lose her balance?

Merle checked her backpack again. Everything she owned of importance was in there, except her passport. They had confiscated it. She had tried to call the American Embassy this morning about it, but hadn't gotten through. She'd catalogued the contents of her backpack in a notebook. The documents about the house were there, the photographs, the mementos from the deposit box. They had rifled through it all then put it back except for the passport.

The stones of the wall were uncomfortable. She stood up and stared at the house. So silent, closed, absent. Was Sister Evangeline inside? What life had gone on there? She closed her eyes and imagined all the shutters painted — Sky blue? Grass green? Apple red? — and open to the breeze. The glass washed, the air changed. It would be a revival, a resurrection. Would anyone ever do it?

She hadn't called Stasia yet. One more day and she might have some answers. Let it ride, Harry would say. Commit yourself, then let it ride. All you have to do is hang on.

Could it be the ride of my life, thanks to you, Harry Strachie?

He was dead, gone, buried. But he remained a force, a consciousness, a way to look at life. Not her way, but she had learned from him. To trust her instincts, to not be so rigid, to play the occasional hunch. She couldn't deny the years they'd had. As much as she wanted to erase them from memory.

What would he say now — what the hell do you want that old wreck of a house for? She sighed. He didn't care about houses, but he thought she did. Was he wrong?

The tires of the Benz squealed on the cobblestones as it turned the corner and came to a stop in front of the house. Arnaud wore the same clothes as yesterday, except for a clean shirt. He looked tired but immaculate, as always.

He kissed her on both cheeks. "How did they treat you? Okay?"

"I'm fine. How did you get them to release me?"

The old woman from across the street (Arnaud said her name was Madame Suchet) appeared on her stoop with her broom. She wore a scarf and high heels, watching and listening as she took tiny strokes with her broom.

"Through logic, of course," Arnaud said as he opened his trunk. "Why would you, an American, come over here and murder an old woman? You are a lawyer yourself, one who helps poor people find housing in the United States. An officer of the court, a good citizen, an exceptional citizen. Not a greedy person but one who works for the state just like he does. Several times you spoke about wanting to find housing for Madame LaBelle. That is not someone who has villainy in their heart."

He pulled a pair of long-handled bolt cutters out of his trunk. "And now, the house is yours."

"Wait," Merle said as he walked to the door and wedged the tool through the crack in the shutters. "Have you discussed this with the inspector?"

"Oh, yes. It makes the most sense of any alternative. He wants you to stay in the village, yes? Then return the house to you. And so — " He positioned the cutters around the padlock and with a grunt pulled them together. A second try, with a grimace on his close-shaven face, and a clunk as the lock fell to the doorstep. Madame Suchet dropped her broom and disappeared into her house, presumably to call the gendarme. "*Voila!*"

"Did the inspector look at the papers?"

"Oh, yes, he looks over them all, and agrees that the house belongs to you. You pay the taxes all these years. That is evidence. The taxes are accepted because the state recognizes you — your husband — as the owner of the house. The inspector speaks to the mayor who has nothing to say. There is no argument, unless you are an insane gendarme who has your head up your arse."

He set down the bolt cutters and pulled on the door shutters. The rusty hinges creaked. The left one refused to move. The open one revealed the front door with its multi-paned window and pretty, carved wood with faint traces of blue paint.

"And now, madame?" Arnaud said. "Your French home."

Merle stared at the door. "You have a key?"

"You did not bring it?"

She unzipped her backpack and found the big skeleton key loosely taped to the letterhead.

"This is not for the door, madame." He handed it back. "One moment." He went back to his trunk, throwing in the bolt cutters and returning with a small tool kit. "We will change the locks anyway." He stuck a small screwdriver into the lock, twisted it around, and gave the door his shoulder. On the third push Merle could see it was about to go and offered her own shoulder. They tumbled into the dark, moldy room.

Arnaud paused to brush his shirt clean as he looked around the room. Merle stood blinking, letting her eyes adjust. The front room was large, with a head-high mantel over a blackened fireplace complete with iron tools and a large pot. The air was dank and foul. A large table with thick legs, scarred with knife wounds, dominated the room.

The lawyer ran a fingertip across the windowsill on the side wall. "Not much of a housekeeper, was she?"

Merle took small breaths through her mouth. "Have the police been here?"

"Yesterday. There was so little, the inspector said, he wasn't sure she even lived here."

"So it's all right to move in? It seems — disrespectful."

"He took her things, what little there was. Some clothes, some food."

"What about Sister Evangeline?"

"She was renting a room over the bistro. But now she has gone, I hear. Her self-proclaimed duty was to help Madame LaBelle. When the woman died, her responsibilities ended. So she told the owner of the bistro."

Arnaud disappeared into another room. Merle walked to the side of the large room, near a side window. There were stains on the wooden ceiling as if water had come through the roof. Spider webs and dust everywhere. The smell of mouse droppings and mildew. A staircase rose from the far corner into the dark. She looked up the stairs and saw a door at the top was closed.

"*Mon Dieu, quel boue.*"

Arnaud stood in the back room holding his nose, staring at burlap sacks of grain piled in the corner. Corners of them had been gnawed by rodents, with corn and wheat spilling onto the floor. The smell of rot hung thickly. The floor in this room was different, stone versus the dark-stained wood of the front. Arnaud opened the back door, letting in fresh air.

She stepped back into the parlor. On either side of the room sat a moth-eaten armchair and a tall, battered cabinet nearly six feet wide. Dozens of jars of ancient preserves in shades of gray, covered with dust, on the open shelves. She kicked the chair. Squeaks of vermin confirmed her fears.

"Merle! Come quick!"

Arnaud stood outside the back door in a flower garden bursting with blossoms. Lavender grew in a fragrant hedge, its purple spikes held over the gray leaves. Delphiniums, daisies, hollyhocks grew six feet high, blue, pink, white. On one wall red climbing roses, next to a framed grapevine with tiny grapes hanging in clusters. Arnaud pointed to the house. A pear tree had been trained onto a metal frame, flat against the stone house. Miniature green pears hung from the branches.

"And more, look," Arnaud said. On the other sidewall, lavender wisteria had been trained to grow along the top. By the back gate, clematis bloomed white and purple in intertwining vines, covering the arch. A small stone building with a mossy tile roof was covered with a red clematis and pots of geraniums stood on either side of its door.

The garden was bursting with flowers. Under an acacia tree in a corner was a hammock. There was a graveled seating area, with two iron chairs and a small table. On the table was a potted yellow marigold.

"Wow," Merle said. "Wow."

"This jardin — it is like the Luxembourg Gardens!" Arnaud said, spinning to see it all. "These grapes will give you wine. Your own French wine, madame. Not much, maybe one glass, but your very own."

Merle looked around, seeing the old woman's work. "But — it's her garden. Justine's."

"She was only the gardener."

Some of the rose bushes were ancient, and the trunk of the grapevine was as big as her arm. He was putting on his jacket. "I'm sorry, madame. I must drive to Cahors again. The widow with too many children awaits me."

"You'll be back?"

"My work is done here. Ah, the name of the criminal lawyer." He pulled a slip of paper from his inside pocket. "Antoine Lalouche, in Bordeaux. Excellent man. Give him a call." He passed her the paper with his phone number on it. "It has been my pleasure, madame."

"I can't thank you enough. You — you saved me, not to mention my — my house."

He gave her a little bow. "That is what I wanted to hear — my house. Congratulations. A lovely one it is."

Then he covered his nose from the stench as he walked through the house. She felt her heart sink. Would the Inspector make a case against her? Is that why Arnaud had given her the name of a criminal lawyer?

From her doorway, Madame Suchet watched, arms across her ample chest, a frown on her face. After Rancard drove away Merle swallowed hard and walked across the street toward her. As she approached the old woman stepped inside and shut her door with a definitive thud.

"And a *bonjour* to you too," Merle muttered, turning back to the house. Inside the front room she attempted to open some windows, hitting the sashes with the heel of her hand. Two complied, revealing generations of moths. She unlocked the shutters, sweeping the moths outside. She sneezed, and sneezed again.

A utilitarian space, both sitting and dining, basic, utilitarian. For a moment she thought she dreamed it, the sunlight streaming through the dust motes, the footprints across the dusty floor, the rough beams of the ceiling strung with spider webs. On the mantel was a small vase, white china painted with a delicate but unremarkable blue design. It was a cheap thing, yet it had somehow survived.

Nothing but dead flies inside. Maybe it was Harry's mother's, a relic from her French life. Marie-Emilie had dumped the last flower out with the water, onto the ground, then set it on the mantel to say goodbye.

She wandered through the ground floor, eyeing the piles of grain sacks with disgust. It was soon apparent to her there was no electricity in the house. Not an outlet or a light fixture. The only water was rainwater caught in a metal cistern sitting on hefty posts ten feet off the ground. Gutters off the roof funneled the water down to it and with a pull on a chain it flowed into a large washtub on the ground.

The stone house in the backyard was a latrine, an outhouse complete with rough stone stool topped with a porcelain ring. A rank odor and a multitude of dead insects as well as their buzzing descendants filled the small, dirt-floored space. A small, filthy window at eye level provided light. Merle hurried out into the garden, gulping air.

Summoning her courage, she mounted the stairs. The door at the top was stuck. She pulled on it until the doorknob fell off in her hand. Behind the door she could hear cooing and the occasional flutter of wings. A regular covey of pigeons, it sounded like. Back downstairs she pulled out her notebook and began making a list.

TO DO — *Les choses à faire*
    Install new locks.
    Drag furniture outside and wash.
    Drag grain sacks outside.
    Patch glass in windows as necessary.
    Wash walls and ceilings.
    Sweep & wash floors.
    Clean chimney/fireplaces.
    Fix shutters, paint.
    Find roofer.
    Arrange electrical hookup.
    Ditto water service.
    Find electrician.
    Find plumber.
    Take trash, chair (upstairs junk?) to — dump?
    Paint walls.
    Replace floorboards.
    Wash windows.
    Buy beds/furniture.
    Plan bathroom.
    Call Stasia in Paris.

JEAN-PIERRE REDIER WATCHED HER leave the hardware store with a slip of paper in her hand. The American looked in both directions, gave the policeman a look as if to thumb her nose at the French state, then walked south. He flicked his cigarette into the gutter and followed her.

At the corner she consulted her paper then entered a building he knew to be Andre Saintson's, the locksmith. Andre was an old man who kept a messy shop but he was the only man in town to change a lock. Jean-Pierre waited, smoking another cigarette in the doorway to the bistro where he sometimes drank after work. This block of Malcouziac had defied all efforts by foreigners to modernize it. Three townhouses were vacant. One had been broken into and vandalized repeatedly over the years, at least since his own youth. It was a party venue for the delinquents in town. Sometimes he had to walk one home after a night of drinking, but who could blame them? There was nothing to do in this little town.

This foreigner, this American, had created a problem however. She was not to be tolerated, according to his uncle. So Jean-Pierre had the boring job of following the silly woman around and finding something else to hold her on because apparently murder wasn't enough. French law was adaptable. A person, especially a foreigner, could be held without charges for weeks if necessary. And according to some plan his uncle had yet to inform him of, it was necessary to get the American out of the way.

The problem was the inspector. Capitan Montrose was of the old school, a methodical and rational man who wasn't likely to look kindly on any sort of covert action like throwing the woman in jail for littering. The jails, he had already proclaimed, were too full as it was, that was why he let her out, sure that she would obey his order to stay in the village. Let justice take its course, he said in his arrogant city way. Banned from Paris, Jean-Pierre thought, or else why would the inspector be assigned to the death of a *putain*, a whore? There was talk that the murder had made the newspaper in Bergerac, although Jean-Pierre doubted it. No one cared about an ugly old whore, least of all city people.

The old man emerged with the American, his tool box under his arm. Andre's face had more lines than a French road map, from his previous profession as a grape-grower. His family had once owned the big mansion, the chateau on the hill, now a winery run by a multinational insurance company. No one liked the company, least of all the local grape growers who had last year accused them of importing cheap grapes from South America and calling it French wine. Nothing proven, but resentment ran high. Last week Jean-Pierre had run across a group of farmers plotting something in the parking lot of the village. They had smiled and slapped his back as if they were just having a friendly chat, but he knew otherwise.

On Rue de Poitiers, Andre bent over the front door as the woman talked in what Jean-Pierre knew to be the worst French ever to come from the mouth of a human. He stood at the corner, saying good day to an old woman. She looked down the street and in a second had him all figured out. It was impossible to fool the old ladies in this town. His mother had known them all, and now they all knew him.

Suddenly there was the old priest, walking up to him with that stupid smile. Jean-Pierre tried to nod and turn away but the old man caught him.

"Have you found the killer yet, Monsieur le Gendarme?" Albert asked. He was the only person in town who didn't call him by his first name and for that Jean-Pierre gave him grudging respect. He had no use for priests normally.

"Of course, *Pére*. But she had a Toulouse lawyer and she is out. You see? She is in the house as she wanted. She got rid of the old woman and it is hers."

Albert's smile fell as he looked down the street. "Madame Bennett? Oh, you make a joke. She is no more a killer than you or I."

Jean-Pierre shrugged. Better to have lost a possible murderer to a bad system of justice, than to not have found the killer at all. "She wants the house, she seeks out Madame LaBelle at the shrine, she pushes her over the cliff." He dusted off his hands: *finis*!

Albert frowned at Jean-Pierre. "*Que tu est fou*," the old man muttered under his breath as he turned and walked toward the woman and Andre.

So now he would have to watch the old priest too. For an old man he had too much interest in things that did not concern him. Even his uncle the mayor had mentioned the meddlesome nature of Pére Albert who had come to the gendarmerie to plead a case for Madame Bennett. The captain had listened to him. They had some school tie. For Jean-Pierre who had not gone to university at all this was loathsome.

So he would keep his eye on Albert too. He had nothing

better to do, or so his uncle would say. He was only one man, one simple gendarme for the entire village. But his uncle promised a cut of whatever he had planned, so Jean-Pierre would keep both eyes open.

17

MERLE HANDED THE OLD MAN the big skeleton key. "Does this fit?"

The locksmith examined it, hobbled out to the back gate and tried the key in the keyhole. It was too big.

"*Desolé, madame*," he mumbled. Their communication was limited. Merle was tired and her French wouldn't come. She resorted to hand gestures. It had taken him quite awhile to get the idea that she wanted her locks changed. He'd done the front and back door and now he wanted to know about the garden gate.

"Please. *Oui*," she said. But he held out his hand again, as if he wanted the skeleton key, and mumbled something. She had no idea about the key to the gate. Except that Sister Evangeline had one. She'd seen the nun lock up the gate from Albert's garden.

Andre fumbled around in his bag and tried a few things to open it. He couldn't do it today, he possibly said, as he waddled back out through the house. With her new key she locked the door. Another trip to the hardware store netted a new padlock for the door shutters, this time accessible from the outside. She locked up and waved at Madame Suchet on her stoop.

Back at her hotel Merle put through another call to the U.S. Embassy. This time she got a live person and requested help with her legal situation. She was given a name and number of a functionary at the Nice consulate, but when she called there the phone rang unanswered. Next she called Stasia's hotel in Paris. Tristan answered the phone.

"Mom! Why haven't you called?" He sounded worried, very unlike a fifteen-year-old.

"Sorry. Are you having fun?"

"Yeah. But I've seen enough churches for awhile though. And rose gardens."

"A person can never see too many rose gardens," Merle said. "Listen, I have things to do here. The house is sort of a mess. Would you like to come down?"

"I thought you were coming here."

"I could use your help. The house is awesome, Tris. Much bigger than I thought. It just needs some TLC."

"Is it a mansion?"

"Not that big. But it's got a beautiful garden. A huge fireplace. I could use your strong back, kiddo. We could work together. Just till time for camp. I miss you, honey."

He probably missed her too, she thought after hearing tales of Oliver buying beer and being grounded by his mother for a day. Stasia had waltzed them through six museums and eight cathedrals, Napoleon's tomb, the Louvre twice, and a *bateau mouche* — her schedule was like the Bataan Death March.

Stasia got on the line and the sisters worked out the details. Stasia wanted reasons, which were faked. Tristan would take the train to Bergerac tomorrow.

THE INSPECTOR SHOOK HIS HEAD so slowly she wasn't sure if he was nodding off or saying no. Merle had tried to explain that she needed to pick up her son tomorrow in Bergerac and bring him here. She had perhaps said she needed to see him instead of get him. Conjugating verbs was a pain in the ass.

Finally she was sure he said no. Stay in the village. That is the bargain.

Albert might know if there was bus service from Bergerac or how much a taxi might cost. The gendarme followed her from the police station, his insolent face and boot steps everywhere she went. The old priest came to the door in his fencing jacket and tight white knee-pants. He had been practicing with a student in the alley because the school was closed today.

"You look very —" she wanted to say 'jaunty' but said, "— professional."

He waved his hand. "A glass of wine?"

Merle sat in the garden while he poured her the dark, oaky wine, a black Cahors. She hadn't eaten anything since the croissant at the jail. In a moment he was back with some of the cheese she'd left him a few days before, still wrapped in its paper.

"You are so kind, Albert. I don't know how to thank you." He didn't answer, just smiled. "What did you think of the house?" She'd taken him inside while Andre worked on the locks.

"The garden is so lovely."

"You don't have a key to the garden gate, do you? Andre couldn't get it open."

"Sorry, no. You should get Evangeline's."

"She's gone, according to the inspector." Merle set down her wine glass. "Is there a bus here from Bergerac?"

"Once or twice a week. I am not sure of the schedule."

The wine made her melancholy. How did she, an upstanding citizen, a moral person, become a murder suspect? "I can't leave the village. The inspector's orders. And my son is coming down from Paris tomorrow."

"I will pick him up. Think no more about it."

"You have a car?"

It appeared he owned one of those curious beasts, an ancient Citroën, the Deux Chevaux. His was blue, and a bit rusty. In the morning she saw him off in it, with its roof rolled back, the bug-eyed headlamps wobbling, the bicycle tires bouncing. It barely made thirty miles an hour as it puttered away from the city parking lot. She'd given him a small list of things to buy for her: fly paper, scrub brushes, disinfectant.

At the hotel she asked the manager if she could rent two rollaways with linens. A few minutes later, and several euros, a bell-boy helped her roll them over to rue de Poitiers. They walked back together, rattling over the cobblestones, around corners, up curbs, ignoring the gendarme. Back at the hotel she paid her bill. With her suitcase rolling behind her, she bought towels and soap, mousetraps and buckets at the grocery. At the hardware store she asked for the name of an electrician, and called him from the *tabac*. Giving his wife a garbled message, she crossed her fingers, dragged her suitcase along the stones, and unlocked the doors to her house in France.

SHE HEARD THE LITTLE CITROËN before she saw it pull up outside. Tristan looked good, tanned, rested. He explored the house, curled his lip at the mouse corpses his mother had dumped into the water tank and christened the outhouse.

"How was the trip?" She handed Albert money for gas and supplies.

"A beautiful day. This garden, madame. So lovely." He looked around, smiling, then turned back to her with a tap to his beret. "Tristan and I talked about him fencing with my boys."

"Really?" She laughed as her son fell out of the outhouse, gulping air just as she had. "That would be terrific, Albert. But first we have some serious work to do."

"Jeez, there's a lot of crap." Tristan stared at the pile growing by the locked garden gate. Merle had dragged out the grain sacks, and the ruined armchair.

"You haven't seen nothing yet." Merle turned him back toward the house. They climbed the stairs and confronted the stuck, knob-less door.

"Now what?" Tristan asked. "You want some of this, Albert?"

"I have to put my car — "

A crash. Tristan had broken the door's hinges, flattening the old panels to the floor. Merle caught the back of his pants to keep him from falling on his face. Squawking and flapping of wings made her squawk too, as pigeons came at them, flying madly in circles. Tristan broke free and waved his arms, shouting at the birds as they beat their wings to lift that fat bellies off the crown of an armoire, windowsills, and a large hole in the ceiling. Two got by Merle and flew down the stairs.

"Shoo them out, Albert!" Merle stepped over the door and pried open the front window and flung open the shutters. "Out!"

In a few dirty minutes the room was cleared. Coughing, Merle stared up at the hole in the ceiling. Blue sky shone through a hole in the tile roof. A pile of sodden plaster had dried on the floor beneath. A window that faced the garden had two panes gone and a shutter. Tristan stood covered in feathers and white powder, hands on his hips. "Wow, this is so great. Very exotic." He picked a feather off his tongue. "Ack."

"Look at this." Merle pushed open a door to a side bedroom. A carved wood bedstead and moldy mattress sat in the middle of the room. The pigeons had partied in here too, along with a mouse colony of legendary proportions. But with a new mattress, a lot of scrubbing, a luscious color on the walls? She shivered. Maybe Harry was right about her. Harry — when would she stop thinking about him?

"Awesome." Tristan frowned. "Looks like a park in New York."

"Having a house in France is a filthy business," she said, leading him back downstairs to find tools and plastic to cover the holes. If only he knew how dirty it could get. She tried to put the legal problems out of her mind. Enjoy these moments. Not the past or the future. Right now. It could be over tomorrow, or next week. This time would end — but for once in her life she intended to live right here in the moment.

18

MARIE-EMILIE WALKS UP the road, her feet aching from the long day. No rides for her, not this day. Some Malcouziac farmers had slowed, saw who she was, and snapped the reins again. So she walks on.

She can see the village ahead, up the hill. Sitting on a log to rest she examines the soles of her shoes. The hole is growing bigger on the left one, almost through. The right wore through yesterday. Still she has no regrets. She has made it to the convent and delivered her message. The sisters had been understanding and given her meals. Without that food, and the loaf of bread and cheese they pressed on her for her journey, she would never have come back.

Perhaps she shouldn't, she thinks, staring at the dark cloud passing over the city walls. But Stephan is waiting for her. He promised they would leave as soon as he arranges everything. So she gets back on her feet and walks on.

Spring is almost over and with it the rains. Soon the summer heat will return. Why is she still in this village where everyone hates her? Soon, soon, she whispers to herself. She turns the corner to her house. Someone has splashed red paint on her shutters. She touches it, still damp. Unlocking the door she takes her bucket to the garden and fills it. In minutes she has scrubbed the shutters, leaving only a shadow of stain not unlike the stain this village has imprinted on her heart. She looks down the street in the evening dusk, an eerie purple bruise of a sky. Not a soul watches, not a soul cares.

Exhausted she falls into her bed. She wants to stay awake for Stephan, in case he hears she is back. Should she go to his rooms above the bakery? She is too tired. Tomorrow is soon enough. She's walked nearly thirty miles today.

When the knocking begins she barely hears it from upstairs. She is deep in a dream. She pulls herself up and walks down the stairs. As she reaches the floor below she wakes up and feels a flicker of happiness. It will be Stephan. He can't wait to see her. She runs her hands through her tangled hair and pulls her dressing gown together as she unlocks the shutters.

19

FERNAND, A BANDY-LEGGED, LEATHERY-FACED old coot who smoked a crusty pipe, got to work on her plumbing needs with his homely son, Luc. They searched gamely for underground water lines. After days of searching she felt lucky to find a willing plumber at all. There was hope that a drain in the stone-floored kitchen actually led to the sewer. Merle left them to explore, and Tristan to scrubbing upstairs, to beg *Monsieur le Maire* to expedite her utilities. The candles and flashlights, not to mention eating all meals out, were getting old.

A waste of time with the mayor at city hall. The same with tracking down the locksmith for the garden gate. His shutters were closed, his door locked. She so wanted the pile of vermin-infested debris in her garden to disappear. The only way to do that was to open the locked gate. Could she take it off its hinges? Break it down? She hated to ruin it. She stepped into the bistro across the street to ask if they'd seen old Andre. The waiter shrugged at her Idiot French and turned his back.

On the street this morning no sign of Jean-Pierre. She ducked into the alley behind Andre's shop. Maybe the old man was hiding from her. Possibly the mayor and the gendarme had warned him about helping her. She walked up the mossy cobblestones, looking into open windows. These houses were in bad shape, in need of even more help than hers. She stopped to peer inside a vandalized house. A tree was growing in a pile of debris, right through the roof. Beer bottles and trash were everywhere. Graffiti covered the walls. Suddenly she was pushed from behind, into the doorway.

"Quiet," the woman hissed, her fingers tight on Merle's wrist. She was shorter than Merle with a blue knit cap pulled low on her head and brown curls poking out below. She wore large sunglasses.

"You speak English." Merle had been mugged twice in Harlem. Strong as she was, the woman wasn't a threat unless she had a weapon. She was slight, and weapon-less. "Let go of my arm."

"Don't talk." The woman took off her sunglasses and Merle saw the bruise on her cheek, just below her eye, angry and purple. Her accent was French, but British.

"I don't have any money. Look." She pulled out her pants pocket with her free hand.

"Here." The woman opened her fist to show a large key. "Take care of her memory — her garden. Whatever it is, they will kill for it. Be careful." She pressed the key into Merle's hand, wrapped her fingers around it, then ran out the door.

"Who? Wait!" Merle jumped back into the alley. The woman ran hard to the street. Tightening her hand around the key Merle ran down the alley to the street.

Was that — yes, it must be. Sister Evangeline. Who had the key to the gate. The knit cap and brown hair were a disguise — or a new disguise. The baggy pants, the small nose: it had to be her. Merle slipped on the mossy stones, ran in the direction she'd gone but the street was empty.

TRISTAN LEANED THE EXTENSION LADDER against the house, estimated the distance to the roof and raised the top section. He climbed slowly up to the edge of the sloped tile roof slick with moss. His mother was tearing around the village, mad to get the utilities hooked up and handymen hired. He might fix the roof. Or just take a look.

He squinted into the sun, getting a long view of the vineyards that wrapped and twisted around the hills that surrounded the village. Tall trees swayed in the wind on top of a hill next to a large house which he guessed qualified as a chateau. A creek ran down the opposite hill, bisecting the vineyards laid out in careful rows that matched the topography like a tight glove. The hole in the roof was almost two feet across. Major. He climbed back down and went to check on the plumber.

Fernand stood scratching his head in the back room of the first floor where his mother wanted both a bathroom and a kitchen, even though it wasn't even half the size of their kitchen at home. She also wanted to make the stone outhouse into a real laundry room. But first Fernand needed to get water into the house. He shook head sadly at Tristan.

"No water?"

"*Non, rien.*"

Fernand went on in French but Tristan couldn't follow it. He pointed down the drain in the floor. "Where does this go? To the sewer line?"

Fernand held up a finger. "Ah! *Oui!*" He motioned Tristan to follow him into the living room where the big cupboard had been pulled back from the wall. He leaned down, stuck two fingers in knots and pulled up the floorboards.

"A trap door! Cool."

Fernand jabbered away then began to close the door again when Tristan held his arm. Grabbing a flashlight out of the tool pile Tristan shone it down the opening. He made walking motions with his fingers. Fernand looked alarmed. "Wait here. *Attendez-moi ici.*"

Tristan stepped onto the wooden stairs, tapping each one with his toe for rotten planks before shifting his weight onto it. Lower and lower he went, until only his head was above the floor. He waved at Fernand and disappeared.

MERLE PUSHED THROUGH the front door of the house, noting again the weak hinges and need for grease. Tomorrow she would paint it. Yesterday she'd scraped and sanded the door and found the wood in decent shape, its curved top too pretty to replace.

"Mom!"

Tristan and Fernand turned toward her. Her son was covered with dirt, cobwebs on his eyebrows. "There's a cellar. It's full of old junk." Tristan shone his flashlight down the hole in the floor. "Fernand says that hole in the back room hooks up with the sewer."

Merle looked at the plumber. He shook his head. "*Pas d'eau.* No water. *Mais* — How you say, sewage? I put zee water down the hole and voila! It disappear!"

"But you have to dig?"

"Ah, *oui, madame.*" He said the water line connected from the alley. "Tomorrow, we dig."

"And today," Merle said, marching outside, skirting the debris, "we open the gate." With a sort of magic, the key slipped into the lock. She wiggled it and pushed down the handle. It swung open.

She held the key tightly against her chest. The encounter with Sister Evangeline, if that's who she was, seemed like a dream. Why had she given Merle the key? Did she kill Justine LaBelle? It didn't sound like it but who knew. She would have a chat with the inspector.

But first, a trip to the dump. "Fernand? Do you know a man with a truck?"

The next morning digging began in earnest. Merle primed the front door as Tristan helped Fernand and Luc in the yard. The blessed event of taking all the mattresses, upholstery, preserves, and rotten trash to the dump had taken place late the previous evening. The yard looked three times bigger without it.

In late morning they took a break. Merle motioned Fernand to the outhouse while Luc and Tristan draped themselves over chairs, exhausted. The plumber called the small building *'le pissoir'* with a sneer. He measured it and discussed — mostly with himself — the legal, physical, and environmental problems of closing up a centuries-old crapper.

Merle put her hands on her hips. You had to take a firm line with workmen, she knew that from previous renovations. "I want a laundry room. This is perfect."

He took off his little hat and rubbed his nearly-bald head. "We have no water."

"Keep digging and we will. We must, Fernand." She stuck her head through the outhouse door, a true act of courage. "Is this wide enough for a washer and dryer?" She stepped inside, stretched her arms and could touch both walls. Clothes dryers were not common in rural France with all its sunshine. Especially in medieval latrines.

Fernand got out his tape measure again and measured the inside dimensions. He wrote in a little notebook, tapping the pencil lead to his tongue like a character from a '40s movie. Frowning, he measured again. "Bizarre. Forty-seven centimeters wider on the outside." He held his hands eighteen inches apart.

"Maybe it's the thickness of the walls."

They were only four inches thick. The latrine appeared to match the stone on the back of the house, a more recent addition, down to the stone sills on the windows.

Fernand walked around the latrine, tapping the walls with his metal tape measure. "*Voila!*" He said one side wall, left as you entered, was thicker. There was a false wall on the inside. They could make the laundry wider by taking down the interior wall.

"*Très bien,*" she said. His face dropped. He didn't do stonework, he said sadly.

LOW CLOUDS CLUNG TO THE HILLTOPS above the vineyards when the man from the water department showed up, to everyone's surprise, with his shovel. Merle suspected the mayor's hand in this; he wanted her finished with her house and out of town — or behind bars — as soon as possible. Was this an anti-American thing, she wondered, or did he hate all foreigners? She watched as the work began in earnest. With the plumber and his son and Tristan there were four strong backs. They took turns with shovel and pickaxe on the rocky earth and had made it through the gate and six feet into the garden when the rain began to fall. Merle moved the metal tub from the garden to the second floor to catch rain that fell through the hole, and then used it with a dose of bleach to give the armoire another scrubbing.

By mid-afternoon the rain was steady. Fernand and his crew took refuge somewhere and would probably not be back. Merle gave Tristan the sledgehammer she'd bought at the hardware store and put him to work inside the pissoir.

"Just prop the door open," she said. "If you hit the rocks

enough to loosen the mortar you can pull them out. And try not to hurt yourself."

Tristan flexed his muscles and gave the wall a whack, dislodging dust mostly. He grimaced. "This should be fun."

Merle watched him swat the wall again with the enthusiasm of Mighty Mouse. They had been getting along well, with minimal carping. He even seemed to enjoy the hard work. She knew the feeling. Hard work kept the mind occupied, relieved the stress of grieving. She backed away, feeling the rain run down her neck. It was welcome rain, warm and nurturing, and felt good on her face. Then she remembered the roof, frowning at the hole and the pigeon perched in it.

"Madame Bennett?" She turned to see Albert standing under an umbrella in the arch of the gate.

"Hello, Albert. Any word on that roofer?"

"I will call him again. Can you come for some tea? I have looked at those letters you gave me."

After a check on Tristan she followed the old priest through his garden. Settled into a corner of his kitchen, she used the tea towel he offered to dry her face and hands. She'd hardly had time to say more than 'can I use your telephone' to Albert for the several days. "The rain is nice, isn't it?"

He put the kettle on his stove. "Very necessary for the grapes. I am going out to a vineyard tomorrow, would you care to come? You get wine, very cheap."

"I'm so busy, Albert. But thank you." His face dropped, worry replacing his usual smile. Could he be lonely? She had seen the gendarme pass by Albert's house, eyes dark. Maybe he had no friends here anymore. She hadn't heard him mention any relatives. "Sure, I'd love to go." The smile returned as he poured water into the teapot.

She dropped a lump of sugar in her tea. "I saw Sister Evangeline. I think."

"Really? But she left town. "

"They think she did. Do you think her gray hair was a wig? Anyway, she had brown hair and she gave me this." Merle pulled the key to the garden gate from inside her shirt where she'd strung it on a chain. "The key to the gate. But what she said was strange. She said 'they' would kill for it."

"They?"

"I assume whoever pushed Justine. But I don't understand why would anyone kill her."

"Do you think she slipped, or perhaps killed herself?"

"My watch was on her arm. There was a deliberate attempt to incriminate me." Merle frowned into her tea. "Maybe that was all it was, but it seems a bit much to kill somebody just to frame me." Albert frowned, thinking. "I don't think Evangline was a nun."

His kitchen had the spare feel of a monastery, cozy and dry while raindrops nattered on the windowpanes. "I had my doubts. I've known a good number of sisters in my lifetime. Shall I read the letters?" He pulled them from a shelf by the table, smoothing the first letter with his gnarled hand. "The writing is faint at times."

'Cher Marie-Emilie. It has been a long time since I have seen you but I think of you every day. Why don't you answer my letters? Here is my address again. 743 Place de la Bastille, Segala. My situation is not good. I work for a family but they have no money. I only have the bread and a little cheese in the evening. Can you help? You said you would help but now I hear nothing. I am alone and sometimes in the night I cry. I cry for all of us.'

"There is more but I can't read it. But it is signed, Dominique."

Merle sat back in the chair. "I saw that. I wonder, who was she?"

"Or he. Could be a man. And this Marie-Emilie?"

"My husband's mother. She lived in the house. Harry — my husband — was born there. But she was dead by the time these letters were sent."

"It appears this Dominique was someone she knew. Have you looked in the old records at the parish?"

If she had time. How many days would she have here before they gave her passport back? The inspector hadn't been by to make sure she was still in town. Even the gendarme had grown bored, making a couple cursory passes of the house each day. "Do you think she would be listed there?"

"Perhaps. If we knew her full name. Her address here is Segala. That is many kilometers away. "

"Please, continue."

"'Cher Marie-Emilie. The days go by so slowly without word from you. How is the boy? I fear when you do not write. Have I offended you? The weather is fine for so close to the new year. The hired man and I will be alone when the family visits to the south. I do not like him. At night sometimes I think of Malcouziac and your kindness and I cry. I hear nothing from Malcouziac. I wonder if you do and what they say about me. I no longer care but my heart remains there and always will. Dominique.'"

"So she must be from here."

"It appears. This is the final one. 'Cher Marie-Emilie. I will not bother you again with my letters. The family has turned us out. There is no money, no food, no roof over our heads. A new owner has come to the *mas* — the farmhouse — and we are all dismissed. If you have a heart send francs to *la poste* in Malcouziac.'"

"A sad story."

"These happened long ago?"

"In the early fifties. Were things bad here then?"

"The war hit this area very hard. It took much time to recover, to get the farms going, to rebuild. There were few men here to work."

Merle finished her tea and shook her head at more. "Albert, do you think the inspector will find out who killed Justine?"

He shrugged. "He is a good man, I think. Honest."

"But — ?"

"He does not know these people and they are not, well, open with him."

"Do you hear any talk about the murder?"

"Very little. They say it is bad for tourist monies."

"I bet they wish I would go home."

Albert blinked. "Oh, no."

"You're too kind, Albert." No, they wished the whole thing — crazy prostitute, greedy American, ugly murder — vanished. Then they — whoever *they* were — could get into the house, according to Evangeline. And do what? Steal pears from the tree? There was nothing there but dry rot and cockroaches. Even the grim, dirt-floored cellar revealed only sodden carpet, spider webs, and moldy kegs.

The telephone rang in the other room. Albert returned, smiling. "Good news. We find a roofer."

20

THE NEXT MORNING, while his mother and Albert went out to a winery, Tristan broke rocks. He stepped inside the outhouse, sweat dripping down his forehead. Luc and Fernand were attacking the ground like wild men, almost to the house with the trench. Swinging the sledgehammer would probably help build up his right arm which had been sore from fencing.

It was strange, fencing, an antique sport, useless but fun. Sometimes you felt a little gay with one hand behind your back — like any minute you'd be pulling on a codpiece and puff pants — but a few swishes of the foil made you forget about it. It was hard work. Albert had given him an old fencing foil. After this chain-gang project his mother had given him he had plans to make a cardboard opponent to hang on the back wall. He was going to call him Billy.

The wall was coming down, rock by miserable rock. A space about a foot high across the top had been liberated. He took a break to put his head under the tank. The rain from yesterday had left the yard steamy. Stripping off his t-shirt he wiped his chest and face. Across the garden the roses were pink and red, perfect buds opening toward the sun. He couldn't remember working in the yard like this, ever. He didn't hate it either. Which was really weird. Maybe he'd be a carpenter or a builder when he grew up. He liked working with his hands. He'd always thought he'd be like his dad, a wheeler-dealer, a Wall Street suit. But maybe not.

He was chewing on some bread when the refrigerator and the electric range arrived. The stove was basic, and the fridge was a quarter size of theirs at home. Now they could have cold drinks, at home. There was a concept. He plugged the refrigerator into the new outlet the electrician had installed and lo, and behold — zilch. No electricity. Not hooked up yet.

He was closing the door after the delivery man when he saw another man on the street, looking up at the house. He held out his hand. "*Bonjour.* You are the man of the house?"

"You speak English."

"Oh, yeah." The guy was kind of cool. He had a crooked smile and long, curly hair. He was taller than his dad, almost as tall as Tristan, but had bigger muscles under his black t-shirt. "I hitchhiked around the U.S. Six months and voila!" He snapped his fingers.

The guy was staring at the front of the house. "Are you here to do something?"

"Sorry. I am Pascal d'Onson. I heard you need a roofer."

"Oh, yeah. We have an attic full of flying crappers." Tristan ran through the garden to Albert's to borrow the ladder. He watched Pascal climb up to the high roof and examine the hole. The roof was too wet so he climbed down again.

"First, the pigeons. We must send them bye-bye. Otherwise, you have a stink like no tomorrow." Pascal said he would be back the next day with a smoke bomb. "You have a very old roof. Perhaps some water damage inside?"

They tramped upstairs, leaving their muddy shoes at the door. Pascal discussed the hole in the ceiling for a long time, staring at the bucket of sudsy water his mother had left and the limp sheet of leaky plastic she had nailed over the hole to keep the birds out of the house. This talking was the French way. No quick decisions. Much talk must take place first, a few cigarettes, maybe a glass of wine or a coffee. Pascal jawed about joists, plaster, tiles, a possible skylight, a possible dormer window.

"A big job, will take time," Pascal said as he left. "But we will get it licked. See you in the morning."

In the garden the heat rose from the damp earth. The man from the water department smoked a cigarette under the acacia tree. He had decided to watch today, it seemed. The plumber and his son were throwing mud like demons. Fernand's wife was complaining about his dirty clothes so they were determined to be done soon. Luc made a scary face describing his mother's wrath. He was a short like his father, but young and strong, and his enthusiastic digging encouraged Tristan to keep swinging the sledgehammer.

An hour later he put down the hammer and sat on the plywood covering the *pissoir*'s hole. His arms burned with fatigue and his back had a cramp. He stepped carefully over the piles of mud and found the flashlight in the kitchen. He had peered over the false wall several times, once when he sent a rock flying over the top, but it was too dark and full of dust to see anything. Curiosity was a good excuse for a break.

"*Terminé*, Tristan?" Fernand said, his muddy hands on his hips. "You are finish?"

"Just want to see what was so secret behind the wall. Maybe a million bucks." He twirled the big flashlight as Luc stepped out of the trench, handing his father the shovel. "Want a look?" Tristan asked.

Luc followed him inside the cramped space. Tristan mimed for him to stand on the plywood toilet top and lean over the now five foot high wall. Luc stepped up and flipped on the flashlight.

"Is it pirate booty? Gold coins?" Tristan crossed his arms and grinned. Luc stood still, pointing the light down into the dust. He stepped slowly down from the wood, solemn as he handed Tristan the flashlight. "*Vous vous regardez,*" he whispered.

"All right. I'll look for myself." Tristan hopped up on the toilet and draped his long arms over the wall. Outside Luc was calling to his father. Fernand and the water department man came to the door.

An odd, musty smell wafted up. Moving the spot of light from one end of the space to the other, Tristan felt a charge of excitement. The space wasn't bare, nor was it just full of dirt, rocks, and mortar dust as he guessed. No money. But there were bones. A lot of bones. He looked up at Luc and his father in the doorway.

"Holy shit." He steadied the yellow beam of the flashlight on the empty eye sockets of a human skull. "We're not in Kansas anymore."

THE OWNERS OF THE LOCAL WINERY were a middle-aged woman and her brother. Tanned, well-muscled, in a flowered dress washed to the point of limpness, Odile Langois had been pretty once but years of labor in the sun had lined her face and bent her back. She was fierce-looking, serious, but gave Merle a courteous shake of the hand. Albert asked for a tasting demonstration for his American friend. "She has only ten minutes," Albert told Merle. "But one glass?"

"*Formidable. Merci.*"

Odile winced at Merle's French then demonstrated how to swirl the wine, to taste, to swish on the tongue, to hold it there. All this had to be told to Albert and translated, but Odile was fast. In ten minutes on the dot, they had swirled, swished, and spit. Albert ordered two jugs of wine, Merle one, and Odile left to find her brother to help them load.

"What was I supposed to be tasting?"

"The delicate flavors of the wine," Albert said, pinching his fingers as if plucking flavors from the air. "Oak, lavender, mint, lemon, blackberry. Did you taste any of them?"

"Is burnt leather a flavor?"

He chuckled. "Highly prized."

"I've never been to a wine tasting. It would be fun to help people educate their tongues."

Albert cocked his head. "You could do it?"

"If I knew anything about wine. Which I don't."

"Odile told me she was looking for someone to give English tours but she can't afford one. There is a school for tour guides. It is *tres cher* to get graduates as not many pass." He looked at her, smiling in his toothy way.

"What?"

"I could put in a word with Odile."

"For what? A tour guide? I'm not a graduate of tour-guide school."

He wiggled his eyebrows. "The French enjoy bending the rules. I will ask her."

"But I'm only here a week or so — "

He slipped out the open door as she began to protest. She didn't know anything about the making of wine. And then there were her personal issues, as in being under village arrest, renovating a dilapidated house, fleeing the country as soon as possible.

The tall silent brother they had seen earlier in the fields picked up three jugs of wine from the storeroom next to the tasting room. He wore khaki field clothes and a straw hat. The backs of his hands were red and leathery. Merle followed him out to the car where he set the jugs on the back seat. He strode off to the stucco building, one of two large warehouse wings. It seemed newer, with a nice clean roof. That reminded her, was the new roofer at the house? One could wish.

The house was a perfect distraction. Thinking about paint, flowers, even a laundry room, kept her mind occupied. It filled her with tasks, duties, and she was a dutiful person if anything. At night reality came crashing back on her and menace floated in her dreams. She didn't dream about Harry much. He seemed to have slipped away from her, and that made her sad. She should have fought for him. Or at least cared. Then there was guilt of getting the house from a murdered woman. All day though, things were good, domestic and containable, under control. With Tristan here there was no one to worry about. The harder she worked during the day, the easier she slept without dreams of Harry or Justine or home.

Albert was waving at her from the line of cypress. Odile stood on the porch of the house with him, chatting in the shade.

"You can lead a tour on Monday?" Albert asked Merle. "She just had a telephone call from the *Maison du Vin*."

Merle smiled at Odile while she whispered to Albert: "What have you gotten me into? "

"It will be fine. Just once. You'll see." Albert turned to Odile and spoke in soothing tones about who-knows-what. They kissed again as they left. Albert took Merle's arm as they stepped onto the gravel parking lot. "You have a date in two days to come back and tour the place with Gerard, the brother."

"Does he speak English?"

Albert opened the car door for her. "Not to worry, we will think of something."

Merle stood on the back step overlooking the garden now ruined by mud, boot prints, cigarette butts, and trenches. A crowd stood huddled around the outhouse: the plumber and the water department man, Fernand's son, the gendarme, and the inspector. And Tristan by the pile of rocks, waving his hands.

"Mom! You won't believe it!" He ran over to her, dragged her by the hand.

Albert trotted behind her. He had come in to talk to Tristan about the fencing tournament. Fernand spoke rapidly to the old priest. Albert turned to her. "There is a discovery, Merle. They called Jean-Pierre."

Tristan was excited. "You won't believe it. We've got a skeleton in the *pissoir*."

"What?" Merle elbowed her way into the outhouse and demanded the flashlight.

"Step up on the toilet, " Tristan called from outside. The gendarme spoke rapidly, in a commanding tone. Too bad she didn't understand a word.

It took a minute for her eyes to adjust. Then, there it was. A human skull, with tufts of hair still attached. The hands, tiny bones collapsed in piles. The ribcage, half-intact. Leg bones, crushed by a rock. She stepped down, bowing her head over the flashlight as she tried to slow her heartbeat.

The inspector's face was implacable as always. He held a stub of brown cigarette in his stained fingers. His eyes, a curious brownish green, watched her. She stepped outside and asked, "What will you do?"

Another investigation file would be opened, but since the inspector was already here his superiors had ordered him to also take this case. He had called for a forensics team to shoot photographs and take the bones to a laboratory for analysis. The gendarme, shunted to one side yet again, left the garden through the back gate. The inspector took Merle to the table, with Albert to translate, and asked her about the house and its history. She told him that the last legal occupants had been her late husband's parents some fifty years before.

The house stood empty for fifty years? Except for the occasional long-term squatter, she said, giving her best Gallic shrug. Madame LaBelle, Albert explained. The inspector asked to look around. He walked away. Albert sat down in the chair he vacated, without his usual smile.

"If I believed in curses I would say this house has one," he said dejectedly.

"Maybe we could use an exorcism," Merle said, trying to cheer him. The skeleton was shocking, yes, but not more so than the recent death of Justine.

Albert sighed. "Too late, I think. When did your husband's parents live here?"

"Nineteen forty-eight to fifty-two, from what I can figure. They were given this house by an aunt, then moved back to the United States when Harry was two. They died in a car accident when he was four."

"Did anyone else live with them?"

"We know very little of their life here. Just the obituary, and those letters." Merle remembered the other things in the safe deposit box. "Wait here."

She returned with the envelope and spread the items out on the tablecloth. "Here is a photograph of them. Not here though, I don't think. See the brick wall?" The old priest picked up the black-and-white photograph and squinted at it, pushing his glasses onto his forehead.

"And look at these." She unclipped the fragile paper labels and spread them in front of the old man. "Do you know these wineries?"

"All famous vintages. Rare too, right after the war. Château Pétrus is very fine, I hear. I myself have never tasted."

"This menu — it looks English. Shepherd's pie, spotted dick." She looked at the front where the tiny bird was imprinted in red on the gray boards. Round Robin Inn, it said faintly. She'd never been able to make it out before, but here in the afternoon sun, it was just readable.

The inspector stepped out the back door. He rounded the outhouse several times, examining the rock work, the mortar, the roof. He went inside again. Tristan said, "What's he looking for, a murder weapon? Pick a rock, Capitan, any rock."

"I have a feeling my laundry room is doomed," Merle said.

"Just when I was starting to love the chain gang," Tristan said, smirking. The skeleton had if anything made him cheerier. "Hey, did I tell you the roofer was here? He went up on the roof with Albert's ladder." He turned to priest. "He's your friend, right?"

"His father was in my parish once, many years ago."

The inspector appeared outside the outhouse and punched a number on his cell phone. A few minutes later Jean-Pierre returned, with a roll of crime-scene tape. The bright orange tape had *'Entré Interdit'* on it: Entrance Forbidden. Together they strung it around the outhouse several times and tied the ends together. The inspector gave Merle and Tristan instructions on not touching the *pissoir*. The forensics team would be here in the morning.

AFTER MIDNIGHT MERLE LAY ON HER ROLLAWAY in the parlor, staring at the spider webs she'd missed on the ceiling. The evening was warm, promising a hot day tomorrow. Tristan had tossed and turned for fifteen minutes but now lay at the other end of the room, snoring. He had a snore very like his father's.

Albert had invited them to dinner. It seemed better to stick together after the day's events. They discussed the skeleton in the *pissoir* so long that there had been nothing more to say. The old man speculated it was the Dominique of the letters. Now, in bed, Merle had a sour taste in her mouth that had nothing to do with the wine from Château Gagillac at dinner. It was Weston Strachie, and his French bride, Marie-Emilie. What were they like? Were they kind and friendly? Were they mean and unhappy? Why had they left? Had they killed someone here? She shivered and pulled up the sheet. She struggled to picture the house with them in it, with Harry as a baby, squalling, toddling, laughing.

Time erased their presence. That was the quixotic thing

about old houses. Maybe the reason Harry mocked her renovation efforts. You put so much of yourself into them, your handiwork, your time, your tastes, as if to make time stand still. And still everything that was you is gone in time, everything you touched, everything you made. Like Weston and Marie-Emilie, who had disappeared into time.

Time. She had been here for eleven days. Or was it ten? The calendar in her head wasn't working. She concentrated, tried to remember what she'd done each day, what day she'd arrived, what day Justine had died — poor thing — how many days the plumber had been here.

Unbelievable! Calendar Girl was no more.

21

IT IS NOT STEPHAN AT THE DOOR. No, the door stands open and a man occupies the parlor space, heaving breaths, a bear panting.

Weston.

Marie-Emilie stands on the stair landing, hoping for invisibility. Too late. He sees her, blinks, and grunts.

"Why are you back?" she asks. Perhaps not the friendliest tone.

"To get what's mine." He stumbles across the room, holding a chair for balance.

"Drunk again. I see your travels haven't changed you."

He glares up at her, takes a step toward her and slaps her hard. "Shut up and get my clothes."

In the corner, hand to her cheek, Marie-Emilie leans against the wall. "Get them yourself."

He wavers for a moment, unsteady on his feet. Then, as if making a decision, he nods. "Open the door in the floor. Light the lantern." He walks heavily out into the garden, leaving the door open to the night.

She wants to run, to find Stephan. But it is late, past midnight and the village is sleeping. She stands at the back door as Weston returns, a wooden wine case in his arms. He struggles toward her. "Open it, you daft woman! The lantern!"

She lights the kerosene lantern and pulls up the trap door as he sets the case of wine on the floor and returns outside. In a moment he is back with another case.

"Hand me that one. Put the lantern here on the step."

She does as she is told. The wine is his business; she wants nothing to do with it, or him. If she doesn't complain, he will not hit her again and he will leave. He is down below, opening the wooden door to the wine cave. Then she is pushing the second case toward his waiting hands.

"Go get another. The truck's in the alley. Hurry, woman."

Despite herself, she helps him. They bring in the wooden cases then stack the bottles carefully on the old racks. It takes almost three hours. She is exhausted. When he tells her again to get his clothes she hasn't the strength to say no. She pulls herself up the stairs, throws his clothes in an old carpet bag.

He emerges from the cellar holding the key to the wine cave. It has always hung on a nail but now he will take it with him. He tucks it into his inside jacket pocket, grabs the carpet bag, and turns toward the alley where the truck is waiting. He stops in the middle of the garden and walks back to her.

"Tell no one about the wine, do you hear? No one. Or I'll beat the livin' shit out of you, woman." His breath is sour and again he is unsteady. She wonders if he will drive on the road wherever he is going, or will end up in a creek.

"I have seen her. The girl, heavy with your child."

He is clear for a moment. Furious, but clear. "What the fuck do you care?"

"You must help her. Send her money."

His chest rocks as if he laughs but no sound comes out. He will not help the girl. He has used her and thrown her away, just as he has Marie-Emilie herself.

"You must care for her, for the baby. You are not so cold, Weston, that you would abandon them in these terrible times." She tries to reach him, to find something inside him that is good and decent. She offers him one last chance to be honorable.

He drops the bag and grabs her shoulders roughly. He opens his mouth as if to agree, or disagree. But he can't. He doesn't care enough for that.

His fingers dig into her back. For a moment she thinks he will kiss her, as in goodbye. As in, we are finished forever. She could take that. She would welcome it. But instead he shakes her, gives her a push that sends her backward. She trips on a rock and sits down hard on the ground.

As he pushes the gate open, she begins to cry.

22

BEFORE THE BIRDS WERE UP, the inspector and his team knocked on the front door. Merle answered, already dressed, and stood between her sleeping son and the forensics crew as they tramped through the house and out the back door. Before she had time to comb her hair the workman from *Electricité de France* arrived to set up her service. Hallelujah.

In the back he climbed up a pole in the alley. He had an excellent view of the *pissoir* where three men dressed in white coveralls, gloves, masks, and paper hats filed in and out. Merle watched from the gravel patio, chin resting on her hand. Fernand and his son arrived with white plastic pipe, ready for the big day. Water and electricity in one day? It was too much. She needed coffee. She went inside to rouse Tristan for his daily trip to get breakfast.

As she shooed him out the door, another man appeared. "It's the roofer." Tristan introduced them then ran off down the cobblestones to the patisserie.

Perhaps the first Frenchman close to her own age she'd met — the village seemed overwhelmingly elderly — who was also taller than a postbox. Probably had bad teeth. She stuck out her hand. "*Bonjour*. Call me Merle. You speak English?"

"Yes. Your son tells me you are —"

Jean-Pierre Redier, the gendarme, knocked loudly on the front door. He spoke rapidly in French to her. Pascal's dark eyes rounded as he translated. "He says he needs to speak to the inspector?"

Merle led the gendarme through to the backyard and closed the door. Pascal leaned against the stair, arms crossed. "This is a busy place."

"You don't know the half of it." She motioned upstairs. "Come on, I'll show you the inside first."

The broken door sat propped against the wall. Plastic covered the broken windowpanes. But the room was showing improvement. The guano quotient was way down. Only a white powdery sheen and a dank odor remained on the armoire and bed.

"Before I work inside, I must fix the hole outside." He walked to the window. "If there is room for my ladder."

"You arrived late," Merle said. In the garden the inspector and gendarme were having a lively discussion, waving hands, smoking cigarettes, as the crew bagged bones. "A little discovery in the *pissoir*."

Pascal smiled — his teeth were just fine — and wagged his finger. "That is not a nice word for a lady, madame. Say *latrine*, or at least *la pissotiere*." He looked again. "What is it they found?"

"A human skeleton, it seems. A bit spooky."

"Ah. Very Edgar Allan Poe." She squinted. "You know. The Cask of Almontillado."

"You've read Poe?"

"My English isn't so bad," he countered. "Now, madame —"

"Call me Merle. It's Pascal, right?" She had laid a hand on his forearm. His muscled tightened and she pulled away. "How long do you think it will take?"

"First, Merle." He smiled as he said her name. Was her name somehow humorous? She remembered the laughter of the boys at the tabac. "First the smoke bomb." He patted his canvas bag. "No more birdies."

Merle drank her coffee, ate her croissant and yogurt, and watched the hive of forensic technicians take photographs, bag evidence, and talk. The EDF man was efficient, now that he'd finally arrived, hooking up the meter at the house and the electricity on the pole. Fernand swore at the crowd. By noon the refrigerator and stove were working. Pascal climbed Albert's ladder, dropped a smoke bomb in the hole in the roof, and sent the pigeons angrily on their way.

Tristan and Albert left in the afternoon to practice fencing. Merle walked to the grocery and stocked up on food, made herself a salad and cheese plate, and ate it on the patio under a cloudy sky. When the forensics crew returned from lunch she took the inspector aside.

"Did you speak to Sister Evangeline about the death of

Justine?" she asked.

He answered something, too fast, and she urged him to speak *"plus tard."* He repeated it slower, that he had spoken to a woman who knew Justine. "Not Sister Evangeline?"

He shook his head, staring in his inscrutable way. The stains on his shirt had increased, and his tie was a mess. The forensics team was finishing up, packing their kits. Merle continued in her blundering French. "She stopped me on the street. Two days after Justine died. She looked different, with brown hair, not gray. I think the gray hair was false." She didn't know the word for 'wig.'

He smoked his cigarette, waiting for more.

"She gave me the key to the gate, there, on the alley. She said 'they' would kill for it."

That got his attention. "They?"

"I don't know who."

"Can I see this key?"

She pulled the chain over her head and handed it to him. The key dangled, large and old. He examined it carefully, turning it over on his palm. Merle knew there was no writing on it, no number or identifying mark. It was just a simple, old-fashioned skeleton key.

"She had a bruise on her cheek, here. As if someone had hit her. She seemed afraid."

The inspector puffed. "We were told she had left town by the owner of the bistro."

"But I saw her."

"Thank you, madame, for the information."

"Is there anything new about Justine LaBelle? Do you know where she was from, who she was?"

"She was from Bordeaux. She was well known there. She had been in police custody." He stared up into Merle's eyes, holding her look. "But she did not deserve her fate."

One of her Harlem clients, Freddie Wilson, came suddenly into her head. She was trying to get off the streets, clearly a working girl with the gaunt look of a junkie, not unlike Justine. They heard she'd overdosed. Merle felt she had ignored the obvious, let down the woman and the entire community. Something might have been done, should have, but sadly, irrevocably, wasn't. It had been years but the guilt, the remorse of doing nothing, remained.

"I agree, Monsieur. She did not."

Perhaps the inspector felt the same way, a little guilty that the state had let down Justine. She felt his eyes on her back as she walked to the house. Pascal was coming down the ladder after putting a temporary cover over the hole to keep the birds from returning. She waited for him at the door, her jaw working angrily at the inspector's implication. *He doesn't know me.* Was he testing her, seeing if she looked guilty?

The roofer stood silently, watching her face. He looked at the inspector watching them both with eyes like slits. Merle gave him a last glare and turned to Pascal.

"I hear a glass of wine is recommended to all workers, if you want them to come back tomorrow." Just looking at him made her feel better, like all of France didn't have the wrong idea about her motives. "*Monsieur le couvreur?*"

He took her elbow, turning her toward the kitchen door. "You promised to call me Pascal."

An older woman opened the door of the church offices, simply dressed in a flowered blouse, but elegant in that French way. Merle had seen her with Albert. Her gray hair was pulled into a chignon, her blue eyes danced over the visitor with the peach paint under her nails.

It was late morning the next day. She'd left Pascal tied to the chimney, high above ground, and the plumbers busy laying pipe. With progress at the house, Merle allowed herself a few hours off. She introduced herself to Mme Beaumount, said she had relatives born in the village and made her request to look at parish records. "*De naissance, mariage, décès, par example.*" Births, marriages, deaths.

Merle stuffed a five-euro bill in the donation box and was led back into the church, down stone steps into a small basement room. Mme Beaumont waved a hand at the shelf of volumes. "*Quelle année?"*

What year indeed. The records went back three hundred years, at least, assembled in a series of large, leatherbound books lined up on a wall of shelves. She pointed to the next to last, printed in gold with '1900-1950.' Mme Beaumont set it on a wooden table. She gave her a pair of thin white cotton gloves and disappeared back up the stairs.

Merle switched on the gooseneck lamp and pulled her notepad and pen from her purse. The room must have been specially sealed because there was no smell of mildew or rot, even with all these old pages in the basement. The gloves were thin and baggy but would keep the old pages clean.

She took a breath. Here were births, confirmations, deaths, banns, and marriages, as well as other curious notations. Families, generations, descendants. She began in the thirties, scanning down the lists written in a black curlicue flourish. Here were Andres and Jeans and Danielles and Jacquelines. But the name she was looking for was Chevalier.

Albert's baptism, 1943. A Laurent Chevalier, baptized in 1919. And his sister Josephine in 1920. Josephine was confirmed in 1931 and apparently her sister, Marie Madeleine, in 1933. Another Chevalier was baptized in 1929, Marcel. His parents were Frederic Chevalier and Angelique Leduc, neither of whom showed up anywhere else.

What about the sender of those letters? The name Dominique was common; she found it on almost every other page as a mother, a child, a man. Without a last name it was impossible.

1948: Marcel Chevalier again, married in the church. He and his wife had a child who was baptized, and died, on the same day in 1949. She wrote his name on a separate page of the notebook: "cousin to M-E?" There was the mayor, Michel Redier, born in 1949.

What relative had given them the house? She didn't know. Were Marie-Emilie and Weston married here? Born here? Confirmed here? It appeared not.

Merle ran her gloved finger carefully down the listings,

ignoring her stomach. Slipping the heavy book back onto the shelves she pulled out the last volume, "1950-2000."

The pages were crisper, less speckled by moisture and time. The same delicate handwriting, flourishes and all, until 1953 when someone new took over, with a less flamboyant hand. It was easier to read, though less pretty.

Where was Harry's birth? That was odd. There were births that year, 1950, several in May, but none named Harold. Had they changed his name? But not a single birth on his birthday, May 30th.

Another Redier, a boy born in 1951, to the same parents as he-who-would-be-mayor. She scanned through the end of the 1950's and half through the '60s and closed the book.

Back at the house she found Albert, Pascal, and Tristan drinking wine in Albert's small yard. They had both garden gates propped open to watch for her. Fernand and Luc had laid all the pipe, connected it to the water line, and began re-filling the trench. They had left already but not without this message, relayed by Tristan. "Tomorrow they're coming early to punch through into the house. Fernand warned us to be out if we don't like noise."

Merle took the small glass of wine Albert handed her and sat at the table. "Where does he propose we go?" She took a sip. "This is good, Albert. What is it?"

"Château Gagillac, of course. Have you forgotten your appointment tomorrow?"

Merle sat back. She didn't forget appointments, and yet. Her calendar mind had fled. She wondered if she'd get it back when she went home. "I don't know, Albert. I know nothing about wine and the brother—"

"Gerard."

"He'll realize it, won't he?"

"He speaks no English. You speak very poor French."

"Truth hurts."

Albert pushed over a tray of sliced baguettes and olive tapenade. "I cannot come tomorrow. The boys have a special practice for the tournament. But Pascal says he can go."

"If you allow me to come down off the roof," Pascal said. "Merle."

He rolled her name on his tongue as if it filled his mouth with something sweet. Tristan was watching her with his chunks of melon paint in his hair and hands.

"You may come down if you use the ladder, Pascal." She turned to Albert. "But you must let me use your bath. Before it becomes an international incident."

"Hey," Tristan said. "It was in the paper. They're calling it a public health crisis."

Merle thought it might be a Thursday. So unlike her. What would Harry say about his Calendar Girl now? He wouldn't even recognize her. The lists, the perpetual calendar in her head: gone. Well, almost gone. It might be Thursday, June 25. If it was, she had been in France almost three weeks.

Albert lent Pascal the Deux Chevaux. The roofer ground the gears but managed to turn the car around, as tricky as a French verb, then drove through the old medieval gates to the city. He'd rolled down the roof and the wind blew through their hair. Merle wished she'd worn the scarf but at least her hair was clean. Albert's tiny bathtub was a lifesaver. She smoothed her skirt over her knees. It was the last clean thing in her suitcase.

"Are you from around here? Originally?"

"From the Languedoc, but I am here one year."

"Do people treat you like you're an outsider?"

"Small villages are like that. They are dying. They have no new jobs, no more land for the sons to take over. So they resent foreigners who have so much money." He watched the road. "They warm up when they get to know you. Everyone knows you."

"I know. I finally had to bribe my neighbor with a tart." Madame Suchet who swept her front steps in high heels and jewelry had still been too wary to invite her in. But it was a first step. And she'd met the next door neighbors too, a young arty couple from Paris, Yves and Suzette who were very chic.

"Did you know Justine LaBelle?" she asked Pascal.

"Um, no."

"Did you see her around town?"

"Once or twice. She was hard to miss. With that hair."

"I've seen other women with orange hair. Did she have friends?" He shrugged again. "What about this so-called nun, Sister Evangeline?"

"Never heard of her."

"Do you know the gendarme?"

"You ask a lot of questions." He glanced at her. "I see him around. Jean-Pierre is a good man."

"You think so? He seems pretty cocky to me." Pascal shrugged, noncommittal. Probably a friend of Jean-Pierre's, they drank together, or played cards in that restaurant where she'd seen him at lunchtime. "The inspector thinks I am somehow involved in Justine's death."

"And were you?"

"No. But here I am living in the house she claimed as her own."

He glanced at her. "They will find the killer."

The small sign for Château Gagillac peeked out of the overgrown bushes in the ditch by the road. He muscled the little car onto the dirt lane. Unruly hedgerows gave way to roses blooming along the rows. The gravel crunched under their shoes as they walked to the stone building. A thought came to her. "What if they ask about a work permit?"

"This is what you say." He shrugged dramatically, palms skyward, his voice high like a girl's. "*Ah, monsieur, peut-être.*" He grinned at her. "Believe me, they will not ask."

And they didn't. An hour later they were back on the road, instructed in the proper sniff, swirl, and spit routine, and marginally familiar with the modern stainless steel tanks of the mixing room, the limestone soil, and the barrels stacked in the *chai* for aging. Odile Langois had been cool and efficient, her brother Gerard moody and brusque.

On the drive back Pascal shook his head in sympathy. All that fancy technology, he said, good for nothing.

"Without '*mis en bouteille au château*' — bottled on site — on the label the wine will go into a cheap bottle at the *super-marche*. Or even," he crossed himself, "a wine in a box."

"God forbid."

"I don't know why he bothers to age it. He will not make serious money from his wine until he can set up bottling." Pascal seemed angry about the whole setup. "All those barrels and a very fine aging *chai* and expensive modern equipment and yet no bottling." He was quiet a moment then said quietly, "I have heard Gerard is active in politics for *vignerons*, grape-growers and small wineries. Be careful of him."

"What do you mean?"

"He is ambitious, that's all."

"Because there's no *grand cru* on his label?" She knew that much, that grand cru and premier grand cru were the grand, old class of Bordeaux wines. "Is this about the strike they keep talking about?"

"What strike?"

"The growers. The newspaper says they're planning some big strike to protest foreign grapes coming into this country for wine."

"It is just politics." He glanced at her knees. "Gerard has no label at all, just juice in a jug. But it is good to improve yourself, be something more than when you were born. Don't you agree?"

"I'm an American. Striving always."

"So Gerard is a closet American?" They laughed. No one could be more French than Langois, so serious about the grape and a little bitter about his ambitions.

"And you? Did you strive to be a roofer?"

"My father was one, my grandfather also. From a rooftop, my grand-papa told me, you can see the world."

"So you were born into it. Me too. My father was a lawyer, and all my sisters are."

"All?"

"Yup. Five sisters, all lawyers."

Pascal put his hand on his heart. "*Zut alors*. I see them coming toward me like Charlie's Angels but in more clothing and briefcases snapping. Ready to — how do you say? — kick my ass."

HE PULLED THE CITROËN into the tiny garage two blocks away from Albert's, a space he rented from an old lady. They walked back toward rue de Poitiers. Back to reality, she thought, feeling the strange lightness of the morning at the winery and laughter with Pascal.

At the corner the gendarme lounged against a wall, smoking. He straightened at the sight of them but held his ground. His uniform was always perfectly pressed. Merle wondered if he lived with his mother, or who was the woman who took such care. Did the vain bastard press it himself?

Pascal nodded to him, as if they were acquaintances. She simply stared at him, turning back as they walked toward the house, to stare over her shoulder. Just to give a good dose of what he gave her. He fumed, clenching his jaw, then crushed his cigarette on the sidewalk.

The front door was unlocked. Pascal told her that was a very bad idea, leaving the door open like that. "You must tell Tristan to always lock the door."

Fernand had made progress. The water heater, sitting out in the bathroom like a fat friend who won't leave, was hooked up and filling the water. The floor was torn up for drains to connect with 'big smelly,' the fragrant drain, and three intakes poked through the back wall for the toilet, kitchen sink, and bathroom sink. Luc was busy outside chipping away a last hole for the shower line.

There was a note from Tristan saying he was practicing until six. The tournament was Saturday and he hoped to compete even though he was a beginner. On the roof Pascal began to pound.

Merle grabbed her notebook and escaped. The gendarme had disappeared from the corner. At the post office she waited her turn at the internet kiosk, slipping her smart card into the slot. She checked her email, wrote cursory notes to her sisters and parents, read one from Annie wanting details, gave them all Albert's phone number and said the house repairs went well. Then she did a search for information about the making of French wine. There was a long, juicy site sponsored by the Bordeaux Wine Office that she printed out.

The line behind her grew longer, techno-savvy seniors and tourists. Ignoring them she entered 'Justine LaBelle + Bordeaux' into the search engine. Nothing but hospitals in Quebec. She went to a French white pages site. This time she got three matches. Scribbling down the numbers she checked her time. One minute left. She entered '*Monastères* + Dordogne' in hopes of finding Sister Evangeline's convent, in case she was a nun. One hit, a Carmelite convent fifty miles away. Then the old woman behind her began to smack her cane on the marble floor.

Back at the house a large truck was unloading at the curb. The beds were here, with bedding, and the dining chairs with rush seats. She ferried the chairs in and grabbed Luc to carry her mattress upstairs. She had decided on a soft yellow the color of sunrise for the bedroom. One day she'd paint it, when she could face that much cheer.

Upstairs she pulled white sheets over the mattress, their clean newness mocking the state of the house. She buried her nose in the fresh linen, savoring its starchy, unspoiled odor. Life could be as simple as virgin white pillowcases. At least for a moment.

23

THE LUSH EVENING SCENTS of moist earth and roses were ruined by the smell of the cigarettes. Last two, and then the pack was done.

It was very late. The surrounding houses were dark. A faint glow on the rooftops from a faraway streetlight, nothing more. Stars were strewn across the sky, millions of them, more than she'd ever seen. As if that milk bucket in the sky had been refilled and spilled using full-fat cream for once.

Merle watered the grapevine and the pear tree and stamped on the loose earth filling the trench. She had tried and failed to sleep. She was so far from home. She had a strong desire to call someone, to speak to her family. The village was beginning to feel very small, especially without a telephone. The distance felt good for awhile. She didn't want her family worried. But now she felt very alone, cut off from the world. How were her parents? Had Elise found a job? Were the cousins swimming in the pool? Did Annie have a new boyfriend? Had anyone asked questions about her character or checked her criminal record?

She and Tristan had a real meal in the garden, made at home, then returned the rollaway cots to the hotel. She'd actually cooked in her new French house. Her new French house — what a phrase! As if it belonged to her, as if she would build a life here. It gave her a moment of wonder, and lightheadedness. But she woke up before midnight, the thought that Weston and Marie-Emilie had slept in that room heavy on her mind. They had conceived Harry there. There was something wrong with that. But what? What could be wrong with a married couple bringing a baby into the world?

The *pissoir* sat dark, still wound up with orange tape, off limits. It had to be a woman, or a child. The skeleton was small. Who had been so hated, so unloved, that they were encased inside a wall and forgotten? It was sad, as sad as the fresher death of Justine LaBelle. She thought of the Bordeaux phone numbers in her notebook. Tomorrow she would get a cell phone. She would get back into the mix, call her sisters. Damn the expense.

Looking at the million stars, picking out constellations, the *what-what* suddenly slammed into her head, loud and insistent as ever. She clamped her hands over her ears. What the hell did it want? What question was it asking? *What? What?!* She didn't want to hear it, didn't want to know what the question was. But it wouldn't leave her alone.

Stop! But it shouted again, the siren cry of the unknown: *What? What?!*

Then she remembered Dr. Murray, the gray-haired, ruddy-complected psychologist. He had peered at her with watery blue eyes full of compassion. It had been hard to look at him, she thought she might start crying. Weeks ago at Tristan's evaluation, what had he said? They had a short, clinical discussion about grieving, about the way different people handle the mourning period. He said you couldn't make rules, set schedules for recovery, for normalcy. That you had to listen to whatever was going on inside you. You had to respect your subconscious, or it would be your demon. Better to listen to your demon, to try to understand it, than ignore it and pay a worse price, he said.

Okay, *listen.* She took her hands off her ears and closed her eyes, tipping her face to the starlight. *I'm listening.* What is the question?

Something to do with life, and the end of it. The finality. Harry's death wasn't the initial trigger, no, it had been coming on for awhile. His presence, his living self, had started it. Or something else, something only she could see or touch or feel. Something deep inside her that required answers, that refused to go stumbling through life, blinders set, doing what she "ought to." The subconscious asked on, even when answers were scarce: What do you want from life? What is it about? What are you doing with your time above ground? What will it take to feel alive?

A fine list of 'what-whats.' Her lists, her sanity-keepers. The calendar with its regiment, its comforting lineup of hours. Was that the real core of the problem, insane list-making, schedule mania, calendar memorization? Or were those coping mechanisms, ways to stave off the scary chaos of the answerless questions: What is life anyway? What is death but an end to the pain of living? What happens after death? Why am I here on earth? Why was I born?

Was there an answer to any of them? No one knows why they're born. You are simply brought forth in love. You arrive, and then everything else is guesswork. You choose a path, or it chooses you. You protest your lot, or accept it willingly. It doesn't matter. It's yours, you own it. And now you have to live with it.

The calendar fixation seemed, now that she'd been away from the office so long, simply a neurotic way to cope with the passage of time. That was what bothered her: Time. *Tick-tock.* The way it slipped away, unnoticed, so that days went by in a flash. Weeks slid by, then months, seasons. Winter blew cold and snowy then before you realized it the grass was green and you'd somehow missed the delicate onset of spring, the opening of buds. Children grew overnight from tiny kissy-face cherubs to strapping, shaving, back-talking sluggers. It wasn't fair, it didn't have to happen.

She felt the rock in her chest again, not so big but still there, pressing against her heart. Life didn't have to happen? Ah, but it did. Time marched on, unbidden by protest and the thin desires of the flesh. It would not stop. It would not slow for adoring mothers or trial attorneys or absent fathers. It would not stretch its languorous minutes for you or anyone. Time was an equal opportunity torturer.

How did everyone else cope? You couldn't control time. You could schedule yourself to death, packing in every second with so-called meaningful work. You could try harder, be smarter, love more. But that was only a torture you did to yourself. It wasn't time's fault you accepted its reins so readily. The only thing was to accept. Accept change. Accept time. Accept death.

The moon poked up over the wall, shining a flash of light on the espaliered pear tree, its fruit now swelling and heavy. The bones that hid in the latrine for so long: who was it? Who had lived, and died here? Who cared for them, who loved and missed them?

Did it matter? Death comes to all of us — *but most of all, to me*. It will claim my flesh, make it weak. She thought of Harry again, as his heart seized, as the light went out of his eyes. What did he think of? Did he know he was dying? Was he afraid? She wanted suddenly to have been there with him, to have held him and comforted him and whispered to him as he went, to tell him she had loved him once even if she'd been so very neglectful for, oh, *years*. She wanted, she realized now, too late, his forgiveness. How would she ever forgive herself without his blessing?

Harry had moved on. He'd adapted to her coldness. He had found warmth in the arms of another woman and the soft hands of their child. She tried to imagine him forgiving her. She tried to hear his voice, those words. She tried to make them manifest on the night air: *I forgive you, Merle. I was happy with my new woman, my adorable girl. Don't feel bad you didn't have it in you to love me.*

But it wasn't right; it wasn't him. Harry didn't care about any of them, before or after his death. Not really. He didn't care enough to forgive her.

It's a mystery, how you'll die. But it wasn't a mystery itself. No, it was very ordinary. The Big D. The Dirt Nap. It would come. And sooner than you expect.

TRISTAN WAS SNORING. The evening had cooled and the turmoil in her head had stilled. Cigarettes and *what-what* done for the night.

As she stepped into the parlor she heard a noise under the floor. She'd put out a dozen mouse traps, baited them with camembert (for world's most pampered mice) but hadn't checked them recently. Grabbing the flashlight she pushed aside the cabinet, pulled up the door in the floor and shone the beam down the wooden stairs. At the bottom step a mouse was caught in a trap, the wire across his back but still alive. She picked up a length of plastic pipe and a plastic bag and started down the steps.

Night or day the cellar was pitch black, no worse than her basement at home except the dirt floor smelled of mold. The mouse was pushing himself in circles on the step, one foreleg functional. No sense prolonging the misery. She whacked him hard over the head. With a flick of the wrist she scooped him, trap and all, into the plastic bag.

Where did she put the other traps? She shone the light into the far corner, behind the tall stack of kegs. Another success, a fat dead mouse. She kicked the old rug rolled in a long sausage. Prime rodent hideout. She'd put a trap at each end of the hole. Another kick then two mice dashed out by her foot, vaulting the trap, causing her to jump backwards and lose her balance. She fell into the kegs, smashing three of them in a loud snapping and crumpling of wood.

Swearing, she got to her feet and brushed herself off. She'd dropped the bag and the flashlight. It shone over her shoulder against the back wall where the kegs were stacked. As she picked up the light she moved closer to the wall. Something was different about this wall.

A light went on upstairs. Tristan bent over the trap door. "Mom?"

"Sorry. Checking mousetraps. I couldn't sleep." She ran her hand over the wall. It was wood, and not a wall at all. "Put some shoes on and bring that manila envelope down here. In the cabinet. Left drawer."

Tristan came down the steps in white socks, tennis shoes, and plaid boxer shorts, his blanket around his shoulders. He held out the envelope. "What'd you find?"

She brushed the spider webs off the wooden planks of the door. A wrought iron lock was set into the surface. There was no handle, just a key hole. "A door." She rummaged in the bottom of the envelope.

"Wait, Mom. Maybe it's another skeleton," Tristan said.

"You think so?" She held up the big key.

He shrugged, frowning at the sealed door. "Could be anything."

She'd seen one skeleton this week; two wouldn't make a huge difference. Besides, there was no skeleton in here, she knew it. What were the odds of finding even one pile of human bones in your homestead?

"Hold the flashlight."

He trained the beam on the keyhole. Jiggling the key, she felt for how it turned, if it turned. Left, right, she pushed it in and out, back and forth. Debris dribbled down the wood, ash or mildew. Then it turned.

Merle looked at Tristan, her face lit up in the beam. She pulled on the key. The door wouldn't budge. "Hit the corners of the door with the flashlight," she ordered, smacking it with the heel of her hand. He banged around with the light until she told him to stop. "Let's try again." She heard the ping of wood separating, then, with a jerk on the key, it opened an inch.

"Stick your fingers in and pull," she said. They each put a foot on the back wall and pried the door six inches wider. "Give me the light."

The door stopped eight inches from the floor, as if to keep floodwaters out. She wedged her knee in the opening and put her face up to it.

"More bones?"

"No." She swung the light back and forth. "Bottles."

Prying open the door farther they squeezed inside the old wine cave. The room was only five feet deep but as wide as the house. The racks were about half full, up to chest height, but lots and lots of bottles. She brushed off a bottle and sucked in a breath.

How long had this wine been here? Since Weston's day anyway. Dust and mold lay thick on the bottles. She pulled out one, rubbing the label. 'Château Pétrus.' That was the label Albert said was very fine. The label was crude and brittle, almost shattering at her touch.

A beautiful, ancient space with a vaulted ceiling and carved racks, this was the traditional place to store one's wine in France, underground, at a constant temperature, in darkness, much like Gerard's fancy oak barrels. Merle counted the bottles quickly. Twelve cases, a hundred-forty-four bottles of wine.

"It must be old," Tristan said, pulling a dusty bottle from the rack and blowing on the label. "1947. Yeah, that's old. Do you think my grandpa hid this here?"

"He stored it here anyway." Why had he never sold it, or taken it with him to the U.S.? Had he died before he had a chance to import it? "Hold up the light to this one."

Inside the bottle the wine looked dark as ink. Some sediment had collected along one side. But the corks looked decent, intact. The lead covering had held. Sixty years though, a long time for neglected bottles. It was probably spoiled.

"Peuw. There's big ol' green mold on these," Tristan said, pointing to one end where water had leaked in from above.

Merle stepped down the rack to examine the end ones. "Let's take one up from here. And one from the other end, and that one." She grabbed one, and let Tristan take two bottles. "Upstairs, don't drag your blanket. Wait." She found the bag of dead mice on the floor, relocked the cave, and followed him up the steps and shut the trap door.

They set the bottles on the oak table. Merle got a roll of paper towels and wiped the bottles clean, dabbing the paper labels gently. The vintages were the same three as the labels in the safe deposit box. Three wine labels to remind him what he had stored here.

Merle sat down. Château Pétrus '46. Château L'Église-Clinet, 1949, a black and white label. Château Cheval-Blanc, 1947, the label faded. She pulled the labels out of the envelope. They matched the bottles exactly.

She opened the old menu and for a moment tried to see if there was some clue hidden among the kidney pies and mutton stews. Murky. Was this what "they" were after? Were these wines rare and exotic? She had no idea. "Tristan. You must not say anything to anybody about the wine downstairs. Even Albert. It's our secret. Okay?"

He was huddled back in his bed. "Okay," he said sleepily.

"Take your socks off, they're filthy."

"You coming to the tournament tomorrow?"

She pulled the blanket up under his chin. He hadn't shaved

in a week and whiskers were sprouting all over his chin, making him look not so much like her child anymore. She bent down and kissed him on the forehead. Hard to believe he'd be going home in a few days, without her. The thought of it made her sick.

"Wouldn't miss it for the world, D'Artagnan."

24

THE BABY. *THE BABY.* THE. BABY.

Marie-Emilie can't get enough of him, the tiny, red creature. So helpless, so beautiful it makes her cry to look at him. She would stare at him all day long, as he slept, as his tiny hands plied the air. But she has to find food.

Stephan has left her a bag of stale bread in the alley behind the bakery. She has not seen Stephan for days, but he does this for the baby. She has searched the hedgerows for fallen fruit. She has begged at the old widow's farm. The woman was unkind at first but when Marie-Emilie got on her knees and cried, she offered three eggs and a quart of goat's milk.

The milk is necessary for the baby; Dominique will not nurse him. She refuses to hold him, turning her head away when Marie-Emilie exclaims about his little curl of hair, his tiny fingernails. She wants nothing to do with her baby. So Marie-Emilie is anxious for his survival. If only she could bare her own breast to feed him, to nurture him. Dominique makes her angry. Then Marie-Emilie holds the baby and the anger melts away.

Sometimes she thinks of Stephan but she is so tired the thoughts don't stay long. He leaves bread sometimes but nothing more. She is devoted to the baby's survival. That is all that matters.

Were there still such women as wet nurses? Marie-Emilie does not know. She has asked at the church and received only a shake of the old priest's head. She fashions a nipple from goat hide, ties it to a bottle. Poor little thing. Poor baby. He suckles the makeshift nursing bottle. He looks in her eyes. There is love there. She sees it.

The priest does baptize the baby. Reluctantly, as long as Dominique doesn't enter the church, he says. The baby is innocent, he must be saved. Both the baby and Marie-Emilie cry when the holy water is touched to his scalp.

The days are busy, finding food for the three of them, hoeing rows for a farmer who needs more help than he has, making Dominique eat broth, changing the baby, feeding the baby who demands so much and yet who is she to deny him? He did not ask for this. He is innocent, a baby.

Marie-Emilie names him Henri-Laurent, a noble name. She does not tell Dominique though, whispering the name to the baby alone. The girl worries her. She grows thin. She lost much blood with the childbirth and is weak. But the days grow warm and one afternoon Marie-Emilie returns from the farm and finds the girl in the garden, sitting in the sunshine with the baby on her lap. She has cradled him in her skirt and swings her legs back and forth as a song comes from her lips. But she doesn't look at him while she hums. She looks away, at the birds flying in the sky, at the pear tree against the house, at the roses opening against the wall.

For a moment, Marie-Emilie is too stunned to move. She stands by the door of the house, watching Dominique and her baby, a horrible feeling inside her. Dominique will leave. She will take Henri-Laurent. She will take the baby away and they will both be gone forever. Her heart contracts at the thought of never holding the baby again.

Dominique's hair is long and blond, and wet, she sees. She has washed at last. Such a pretty girl, small freckles across her nose, sweet lips, a high forehead that gives her a regal look. But young, somehow younger than her fourteen years. Weston had seen that right away, that innocence in her blue eyes, that willingness to follow, to be led astray. As if the world could be nothing but good. Only an innocent would see the world that way after this war. Only an innocent, or perhaps someone not right in the head.

Marie-Emilie takes a step out into the garden. Is Dominique not quite right? She has rejected her own child, refusing to nurture him. Is that a sign of derangement? Would she harm him? A flutter of panic rises in Marie-Emilie.

Dominique sees her, grabbing the arms of the metal chair. "Come then, where have you been?" She looks cross, waving her hand at the baby. "Get him, now. He drives me wild with his crying."

And so the panic falls away. Dominique is still herself, childishly annoyed, selfish, never to be a true mother. Marie-Emilie rushes forward and scoops up the baby from her lap, cuddling him against her shoulder. It is only a small miracle, a mother quiets the son she doesn't want. It won't happen again.

Two days later she is gone. Marie-Emilie rises, carrying the baby down the stairs at daybreak, moving quietly outside to wash him. When she steps back inside a few minutes later she feels the emptiness. Dominique's bag, a ratty thing made of scraps of rug, is gone.

Dominique herself, vanished.

25

THE TOURNAMENT WAS HELD in the small school gymnasium, a multi-purpose space about half the size of a basketball court, with a small grandstand of bleachers at one end. There weren't many spectators, just a few parents. The opposing team had come in on a bus from Bordeaux and looked big and rough compared to the local boys.

Albert was busy when Merle arrived. She edged along the side of the gym, watching the fencing matches already going. A referee stood between two of the boys in white jackets and masks, their baggy pants an odd choice with the sleek protective jackets. The official spoke rapidly to the boys in a cautionary tone. Merle couldn't understand what he was saying. She sat down on the end of the bleachers and searched the far side of the gym for Tristan. He was sitting with a couple other boys on the floor, their masks and foils next to them.

Tomorrow Tristan was scheduled to take the train back to Paris and get on his flight. He started camp at the end of the week. She didn't like to think of him taking the trip alone, but there wasn't much choice. She'd been to see the inspector again to plead with him to let her at least take him to Paris, but again she was refused. She had no passport, she couldn't flee the country. She'd also pleaded with the American consulate in Nice but with legal action pending, a possible murder charge, they weren't encouraging.

She fingered her new cell phone and looked at the people on the bleachers. They didn't look familiar. She had no idea there were so many people this age in town, that is middle-aged. Maybe they ran the shops and restaurants. The phone was sleek and familiar, a Nokia just like her one at home. She'd been pleasantly surprised to find the counter at the back of the stationery store — where she'd also bought a rather bad British novel — to buy phones and start up cell service. The nice young man at the counter explained that with so many farmers and remote homes, cell phones, or mobiles, were gaining in popularity. Don't use it in a restaurant though, he warned her with a smile.

She hoped to see Tristan fence before Annie returned her call. The display of technique, the swooshing and cracking, was fascinating but she had things to do. Would he be done before dinner? Probably not.

She looked up to see Pascal, standing in front of her. A man behind her said something and Pascal ducked down, sliding into the bleachers.

"Aren't you supposed to be up on my roof?" she whispered.

"Albert insisted." He glanced at her. "I will make it up to you."

Merle felt the heat in her face and glanced up at the audience beyond him. Some were staring at them, talking behind their hands. Had her English identified her? Did they all think she was a killer?

"What is it?" Pascal said.

"Nothing." She tried to shake the feeling that everyone had tried and convicted her of murder. "It's good of you. To sit with me."

His dark eyes flicked up the bleachers. "When does Tristan fight?"

"Soon I hope."

They watched two bouts, clapping politely. In one round a small boy fenced a much bigger one who whacked him with a side cut that was apparently illegal. The small boy began to groan and moan and the bout was called.

"Is he one of ours?" Merle whispered, nodding toward the writhing fencer.

Pascal nodded. "On the drama team."

Her phone twittered in the middle of the next bout, causing frowns and comments from all around. "Come on," Pascal said. "I'll walk you out. I have a roof to finish."

She answered the phone on the way to the door, waving to Pascal as he left. It was Annie. It was so good to hear a friendly voice. Outside the gymnasium the late afternoon was warm but not as hot and stuffy as the gymnasium. "You won't believe where I am. At a fencing tournament, watching Tristan."

Merle talked about the house, the colors of paint, the garden. How the woman, the squatter, had moved out. That was the way she was putting it. That her roofer was good looking, all the positive stuff. Annie told her that she had a ticket left over from an old boyfriend's Christmas generosity, a trip to Barbados she declined to join him on.

"It's burning a hole in my money belt. Can I come?"

"I would love it. Just tell — "

Inside the gym Merle heard shouting, a commotion. She turned to the door and heard a name. "Annie? Call me tomorrow, I've got to go."

TRISTAN HAD STEPPED UP TO THE TABLE to register before his mother arrived, her money tight in his fist and his mask under his arm. The small gymnasium was hot and getting hotter. Albert told him several out of town groups were coming, and the boys standing at the far side of the gym looked foreign, all right. They were wiry, mostly tall and dark-haired, with stubble on their chins.

The boy in front of him, one of Albert's students named Francois, finished filling out his paperwork and moved away. Tristan took a step forward and suddenly dropped his mask and foil with a clatter, prompting chuckles. He gathered them up and bent to sign his name on the registration forms.

The man behind the table, a wrinkly old guy who was completely bald, said something in French. "*Pardon?*" Tristan said. He repeated it, just as fast but louder. "*Je ne sais pas,*" Tristan said. He for sure did not know what the old man was saying.

The bald guy turned to a referee standing by the table, and said something about Tristan. The referee looked at him and waved his hand. Bald Guy — his name, Tristan found out later, was actually Guy — took his money and rattled off directions that were incomprehensible. Tristan went to find Albert.

"I couldn't understand what he was saying at the table," he told the old priest.

Albert patted his shoulder. "Don't worry. All you do is start when they say *'Commencez'* and stop when the buzzer goes off."

"Where are those guys from?" He looked toward the bearded crew.

"Bordeaux. They look tougher than they are." Albert lowered his voice. "They are in some kind of summer camp for delinquents, I heard."

Tristan put on his borrowed jacket over his shorts and t-shirt. He slipped on his mask and warmed up with Francois, feeling the muscles in his right arm tense. He was nervous, feeling butterflies in his stomach.

A voice said something over the loudspeaker. Francois, who didn't speak English, stopped fencing and turned to his friends. Tristan saw his mother come in and sit by herself on the bleachers. He watched the first bout, a fencer who was way too quick for the other, with the referee calling off points like an auctioneer. Albert said they were trying to get electronic scoring for the next tournament, that it eliminated lots of arguments, and sure enough, in the next match-up one of the Bordeaux boys erupted after a call, arguing with the ref about where a hit occurred.

His turn finally came. He had drawn a short boy, with reddish hair and freckles who didn't look too tough. Good, there was a chance that he wouldn't totally humiliate himself. He took his position on the line. The referee was the one who had waved him into the tournament, but now he was saying something long and complicated, in French.

Tristan froze, his feet in position to fence but his foil pointed down. Did that mean 'Begin'? The red-haired boy didn't seem to be paying attention. Tristan raised his foil to the 'en garde' position, vertical against the face mask.

"Non, non, non!" The referee was yelling and walking toward him. The boys waiting their turns quieted, watching. Strange words flowed from the ref's mouth. What was he saying? Now two boys jumped into the argument, in his face, talking loudly. They seemed excited and were poking their fingers in his chest. Tristan felt

confused and anxious.

The referee saw Albert walking over and began to point in the old man's face. Tristan felt helpless; the boys from Bordeaux were pissing him off. He pulled off his mask and glared at them.

"Get the fuck out of here! Mind your own business."

The boys looked at each other and burst out laughing. And Tristan did the only thing he could think of to shut them up. He heard his father's advice, dropped his foil, and punched them — one, two — in the face.

THEY DROPPED LIKE TIMBER, crumpling onto the floor. Merle's heart sunk. Thundering shoes of the spectators in the stands running into the fray echoed throughout the gym. A melee ensued, boys fighting, pushing, yelling at each other, parents holding them back and some egging them on, even swinging a few rounds themselves. Bedlam for a few minutes, not long but long enough to get a bunch of adolescents worked up, no matter what their ages. Finally a voice came on the loudspeaker demanding quiet. The fighting stopped as quickly as it started.

She clenched her jaw and stepped up to Tristan. Albert was yelling at the referees who were doing a good job yelling back.

"Catch 'em unawares, did you?" she said to her son. He squinted angrily at her, his face red. He'd taken a hit to the chin. He raised his hand, shaking it. "Did you break your hand?"

His knuckles were swelling. "It was worth it," he grumbled.

The gendarme burst into the gym. The two boys on the floor had picked themselves up, sitting now with friends or family at their sides. One's nose was bleeding. Jean-Pierre was talking rapidly with the referees, who pointed at Tristan. Albert joined the lively discussion, pointing fingers at the two boys. Lots of finger-pointing. Very mature, she thought.

"Come on, buster." She picked up his mask and foil. "You're out of here."

Jean-Pierre, the gendarme, cut them off. He said something to Tristan, about Tristan. Merle turned back. "Albert? Could you come here?"

The old priest shuffled over, his face rosy with heat and anger. "I am so sorry, Merle. If I'd known they had a language requirement I would never have brought the boy. No one has ever said such a thing. I never thought."

All Albert saw, after the referee stopped poking his finger in his face and ranting about fluency tests, was a swarm of boys from the stands and floor. They rose up *en masse* to take sides. The friends of the boys on the floor began to swing at Tristan, and other boys helped Tristan fight them off.

"It's over. Now tell the gendarme that we are going home."

Jean-Pierre yelled again. Albert turned to her. "He says you can't leave until we have a full investigation of what happened."

"Tell him this. These boys were harassing my son. My son put a stop to it. End of story." Merle folded her arms. She had recognized one of the boys now. He wasn't from out of town at all. He had been one of the boys in front of the *tabac* who laughed at her name. "He can find us at home if he needs anything else. He knows where we live." She took Tristan's arm, walked around the gendarme, and out the gymnasium door.

Tristan looked ashamed, appalled, his head bowed. Merle plunged his hand in a bowl of ice to keep down the swelling. The bruise on his chin didn't amount to much but he held ice on it too. She held her tongue. If ever there was a good explanation of consequences of hitting someone, a riot was pretty definitive. He'd never gotten to fence. So much for channeling that aggression. A perfect ending to the rural French idyll.

At six Pascal knocked on the back door, signaling his departure for the day. Merle opened the door. "How did it go, the tournament?"

"Just great."

"Yes?" He looked at her again. "What is wrong?"

"Nothing."

Tristan hollered from the front room: "World class fuck-up

lives here!! Photographs ten cents!!"

Merle closed her eyes. "You better go see for yourself."

Albert showed up a half-hour later with a bottle of wine and a bunch of flowers, like a suitor. He felt terrible, he said over and over. He was so angry with the officials that made rules that they told no one. He stayed for dinner on the condition that he help cook.

Tristan set the old table with a new green tablecloth and the cheap white dishes. The priest had examined him for injuries and exclaimed over the lack thereof. A little stiffness, a little swelling, that was all. Pascal was invited to dinner too. He went home and returned, showered and in American blue jeans, his curls dripping on a chamois shirt, carrying a bottle of Bordeaux, a cru bourgeois but very fine according to him. Only seven euros, he told her with a wink. "You must improve your taste buds."

"What is cru bourgeois then?" she asked, holding the bottle. "The workingman's version of grand cru?"

"If it were only so easy," he said. He ticked them off on his fingers. "There is Premier Grand Cru, *Deuxieme, Troisieme*, and so on. Second, third, fourth, fifth. Then, Cru Grands Exceptionels, Grand Bourgeois, Cru bourgeois, Bordeaux Superieur. And that is just for the Médoc and the Graves. For each classification specific techniques must be used in the making. Only a few are Grand Cru, from the old houses."

Albert beamed at him. "Your father taught you well, Pascal."

"Papa had a keen taste for the grape," Pascal said quietly. "Too keen, some might say."

Tristan's mood improved with the company of men, Merle noticed. He so needed a man in his life again, even if it was someone as part-time as his father had been. She hadn't told him about Courtney and Sophie yet. She hated to burst the shining image of Harry that his son carried in his heart. It seemed cruel, yet it also seemed inevitable. Pascal mimicked a boxing match and made him laugh.

"I have a special wine I want to share with you tonight." Merle had taken the three bottles from the wine cave up to her bedroom, stashing them in her suitcase under the bed. She ran up, pulled out the Château Pétrus, and carried it downstairs. She had to know if it was spoiled. And what better time to see, and to share it, than with friends who know wine.

Pascal looked stunned. He examined the bottle, rubbed the label, showed it to Albert who shrugged. "Where did you find this?"

Tristan opened his mouth and she kicked him under the table. She said, "We don't have to open it. It's probably spoiled. Let's drink yours."

"Not so fast. It looks — well — possible. If it was stored properly, and the cork kept its integrity — " He sniffed the lead and raised his eyebrows. "You never know until you open it."

Tristan handed him the corkscrew.

They held their breaths as Pascal carefully peeled off the lead and tapped the cork with his fingertip. The lip of the bottle was gray with mold.

"Good?" Merle asked. His eyebrows wiggled in anticipation. He positioned the corkscrew and gently pressed down as he turned it. When it was down as far as it would go, he gripped the handle, his elbows in the air, and looked wide-eyed.

"Go on, Pascal. I don't care if it crumbles," Merle said.

He pulled it out slowly, carefully. With a low, mellow pop the cork came out, all in one piece. Pascal beamed as they clapped. "Well done," Albert said. "Smell it."

He unscrewed the cork from the screw. Albert's sniffer was a huge Gallic nose like Harry's. Pascal's was more proportionate and possibly, after that mini-lecture about levels of quality, educated. He sniffed the cork then nodded.

"Seems — okay." He picked up the bottle and put it to his nose. His eyes closed as he breathed in and smiled as he handed it reverentially to Merle. "Pour it."

She poured the wine for the three of them, in small juice glasses. At home she would be bothered by her lack of appropriate stemware, but here it didn't matter. Wine was one of the four food groups. Pascal raised his glass then stopped. "No wine for the mighty warrior?"

Albert cried, "He is a man, isn't he?"

Tristan grinned, manfully. Another glass appeared, and the circle was complete at four. They held their glasses high. "To Tristan who may never fence like a Musketeer but can fight like a man," Pascal said. Merle shot him a warning look that he ignored. He kept his glass high and added, "And American friendliness."

"And French friendliness, wherever you may find it," Merle said.

Pascal held up his free hand. "Wait. You must look the person you toast in the eye as you touch glasses. If you don't it is an insult. Do it again." They laughed, clinked again, then stared pointedly at each other as instructed. "To friends, wherever you find them," he said as he looked into her eyes.

Merle put her nose over the lip of the glass and breathed in slowly. She remembered the proper way to taste, and swirled, sniffed again. The flavors began to change, to move up through the midnight black wine. They each took a small sip the dark, thick liquid from the old bottle as if it might poison them. Merle felt the flavors slide over her tongue: oak, berry, anise, tarragon, limestone, apple, a whiff of lemon. She closed her eyes and refused to swallow, buoyed, caught by the viscous essence. The moment lingered, the fluid thick as motor oil, as complex and layered as an autumn breeze. It sank down her throat reluctantly.

Pascal's breath, close to her ear, whispered, "Ooh lala. You have hit the wine jackpot."

BOOK THREE
WINGING IT

26

SMOOTHING HER SKIRT Merle felt the sun on the back of her neck, a warm breeze drying her skin, the unexpected pleasure of the haircut. It had been a sudden decision, of the moment. Having the same hairstyle for twenty years wasn't a reluctance to face change, now was it? No, it was a terror of it. She felt almost giddy, this dangerous pleasure, this haircut, then felt ridiculous and immediately took it back. What would Annie say? *Don't get your prayer flags in a twist.*

She looked over the crowd milling around the door to the tasting room, a little nervous, counting heads; they were still waiting for two tourists to show. So, new haircut, new job. She took a deep breath, almost afraid of what she might do next.

She touched her bare neck. The haircut was a symbol, of *something*. A new life, a new phase, an imperative that sent her flying madly across the *ville*. Preparations for whatever happened next. She'd be ready, if only because her hair was up-to-date. All her life she never gave her hair a thought until the very last moment, until her mother rolled her eyes, until her sisters dragged her to a salon, until Harry dragged her to a formal party. Then there was no time for changes, for new directions. This was different. This time a change seemed deeply, deeply necessary. She looked at the trees blowing in the wind and nodded to herself: yes, this is vain, shallow, and — and yet. It felt right.

The morning Albert drove Tristan to the train she felt lost, as if she'd never see him again, that he was still that baby tearing away from her breast to live on his own, without her. He stood hunched at the front window, frowning out at the cobblestone street. He was off to camp in four days. She finally had screwed up her courage to tell him that she couldn't fly home with him because of the murder. Who was she, he asked. What happened? She gave him the short version: a woman fell from the cliff, she lived in this house, *their* house, and she didn't want to move. He groaned when Merle made him promise not to tell his aunts, uncles, cousins, or grandparents. A hard secret to keep: your mother under the steely eye of the French police.

She made him a list, of course, all the instructions, the tickets, the directions. He had to find the train, find the right terminal at the airport, go through security alone, go through immigration, find his gate, his seat, fly the wide Atlantic, do customs on the other end. All by himself. She took a deep breath and let it out slowly. He was almost a man. Her little boy. He waved to her from the car, then he was gone.

Tristan the child had been gone for a long time. He had gone where children go, slipped away into manhood as if he'd never fit into her arms, never cried on her shoulder, never run to her with a skinned knee. He was his own person now, not a child but independent, free to make his own choices — or would be very soon. Even though her heart hurt it was everything she wanted for him.

She'd burst into the tiny, upstairs beauty salon on a side street over a florist, holding a magazine photograph of a woman in a short page-boy, bangs, dark-haired, no gray. Audrey Hepburn, without the swan neck. And that was how she walked out. She had been a little breathless the rest of the day. What would the workmen say? Would Albert notice? Would Pascal exclaim about her new look? But the roofer, her roofer, never came, not that day or the next or the next. Albert didn't know where he was.

Now she pressed her lips together. A strange feeling, lipstick and new hair, way too grown-up. She smiled, praying for the lipstick to stay on lips, not teeth. There were a few flecks of paint on her thumb, remnants of the last three days of high-speed decorating. It had seemed important to kick things up a notch, cross items off the list. She painted her bedroom that hopeful sunrise yellow, sweet, innocent color before tainted with the harsh banalities of noonday, counted the wine bottles again (two-hundred-and-one), caught six more mice. She mixed up a batch of cement and rocked up the plumbing trenches across the bathroom. Her back had a sore spot.

And now she was a tour guide, a job which apparently required only the decent mastery of the King's English and the ability to pour lightly. The fact that Odile and Gerard, the owners of the winery, would never know what she told the tourists took some pressure off. Still she wanted to do well, it was her nature.

She straightened her back and rubbed the soreness out. The group included ten or eleven wine lovers, Americans — two couples traveling together — and three groups of Brits. The Americans she could spot for miles, the women with gold jewelry and faces frozen with botox. The Brits were less dressed and smiled more.

Tristan had called her from Stasia's, through Albert, when he got back, tired but happy, and packing for camp. Stasia said they'd been over to the house to get his sleeping bag and backpack and everything was fine. Elise was keeping the pool clean. As if that had been a major worry.

It all seemed so far away. She'd been in France almost a month. The rat-race of the suburbs, of Manhattan, was another world. Here the grass grew tall in the ditches along the road. Two fat ducks flew up from the pond. Roses bloomed in a riot. She had a new haircut, and she was on her own, making her own decisions. Was she the same person she had been in April — full of pain and confusion, kicked out of her job, at sea without her not-so-loyal husband, the woman who dreamed of magic pearls to save her from despair, and wrinkles?

"Good afternoon, ladies and gentlemen." She waited for them to stop talking and pay attention, just like jurors in court. That's the way to think of them. Speak just loud enough that they had to be quiet to hear. Impress and persuade. The only thing they were likely to be persuaded was that wine was cheap and plentiful. She smiled again and felt her teeth go dry.

"My name is Merle and I'll be your guide today for the tour of the cellars and vineyards of Château Gagillac. We'll start our tour in the state-of-the-art fermenting facility built two years ago for over four million euros."

As they filed inside the dim cavernous building one of the Brits, a gray-complected man with amazingly bad hair and small, intense eyes, asked her how the alcohol content in the wine changed from the beginning to end of the fermentation process.

"I'm sorry, this is my first week here," she explained. "I'm still learning. I could ask —"

"Quite all right," he said, smiling. "Anthony Simms." He extended a hand. "Nice to meet you, Merle. You're doing a good job."

"I have a lot to learn."

"If you — " He waved a hand apologetically.

Despite her first impression he seemed dull but nice, with warm brown eyes and an upper crust accent. It was nice to have a conversation with a true English-speaker. A tour guide had to find good qualities in everyone, she told herself. She turned to him and said, "Are you offering lessons?"

The other tourists wandered off, poking their heads into the empty vats and running their hands over the stainless steel.

"I shouldn't presume." He stopped, looking pained. "I'm on a prescribed holiday. My friends made me come."

"Oh." He did look sad. Pathetic really.

"I'm keeping you. Please."

The group filed through the dim, cool space. Merle showed off the huge stainless steel vats, explaining the controlled mix of various grape types, the computerized control room. She was brisk and efficient, and didn't ask if they had questions because, well, factoids were thin on the ground. She felt a little embarrassed not knowing the answer to Mr. Simms's question and vowed to study more about winemaking. She showed them where the grapes were dumped, how they were crushed and separated, where the liquid was strained off.

Leading them outside she pointed out the intricately pruned vines and the grapes hanging under their leaves. She explained about the concept of *terroir*, one of the things she'd read up on and found most interesting about winemaking, the way everything worked together to make wine. She scooped up a handful of reddish soil for the tourists. Earth, sun, rain, clouds, hills — just like Annie's prayer flags, this *terroir* business. Very karmic, grapes. The day was cooler than it had been, with clouds, but still the soil felt warm to the touch, its rocky base holding heat through the evening to release it in the cool night air, keeping the vines toasty and coddled.

She showed them the barn-like chai where the oak barrels aged the wine. They were happy as she filled their glasses in the tasting room. She was exhausted; she hadn't spoken this much or this loudly in months. She had sweated through her blouse and underwear, feeling the slick rubbing of her thighs.

Odile split the cash and thanked her with a nod. The tourists had bought several jugs of wine. The money couldn't have made a big difference to the winery. A hundred euros was nothing for a big operation like this.

Anthony Simms leaned against a small white Peugeot in the parking lot, his arms crossed on his chest, trying to look nonchalant. His brown-going-gray hair was parted too far to one side and his shirt collar was frayed. The tour hadn't improved his looks but he did, after all, have a car. When he saw her he smoothed his shirtfront like an anxious suitor.

"I want to apologize," he began. "For taking time away from your tour. Occupational hazard when you vacation alone. Latching on to attractive women for company."

"That can be dangerous."

"Very." He smiled guiltily. Or maybe he thought sexily. "If you would let me take you to coffee to make it right? Unless your husband would object."

Thinner than she'd first thought, he was not as old either. That hair had to be a rug. So he was bald. Maybe he was ill, on chemo? Was that why he was on a prescribed holiday? She chided herself for being so judgmental.

"He might if he was still alive. He died this spring." Still strange to say, but better. Getting better all the time, as John and Paul would say. She had been playing the Beatles full blast while she painted, singing whenever the mood hit her, which was surprisingly often. So smart of Annie to think of sending the CDs with her. Those old songs made her feel young again.

Anthony winced as if she'd punched him in the guts. "Oh, I'm terribly sorry. I do know how it is. My mother passed away only a month ago. I don't know why it hit me so hard."

"I'm sorry. Was she elderly?"

"Quite. A blessing, I guess. But still." He looked off, biting his lip. A little dramatic, she thought. "Can we commiserate over dinner then? It would be so pleasant to have your company. And I might — I don't know, help in some way?"

Assessing her frame of mind, she thought not. She wasn't in the mood for moping, or sharing death stories with this odd person, this stranger. But the sun had come out. The afternoon was hot and sticky and her feet hurt. "I could use a ride back into town."

Simms brightened, springing into action, opening the door of his little rental car. The air conditioning felt luscious and her feet cooled. He babbled about his vacation, some caves nearby with prehistoric drawings of bison, his brave old mum, his friends who urged him to get away from England after he had spent a week sifting through eighty years of belongings.

"That week almost killed me," he said. "What do you do with your mother's girdles, for godssake?"

Ick. A musty bachelor, devoted to old mumsy and her undergarments. So why was he interested in women? She glanced at him. Harder to tell with Europeans. "Where do you live, Anthony?"

"In London, rather north. Do you know London?"

"Um, no. Turn right here." She pointed at her street.

"Can I make a reservation for dinner then? There's a delightful bistro a block the other side of the plaza."

Someone was sitting on her step. "At the end on the left. You can turn around." He pulled the car into a U-turn at the crumbling wall and stopped. Pascal looked up.

"I'm sorry. I appreciate the ride. But I have a workman here."

He squinted at Pascal, annoyed. "Well, I know where you live. Maybe another time? You're all right then?"

She stepped out. Anthony waited a few beats before driving away, as if he might have to jump out and defend her honor.

But Pascal only stood up and stretched. "*Bonjour*, Merle."

She moved around him to unlock the door's shutters, then the door. France was like Fort Knox, or Brooklyn. She arched an eyebrow at him. He wore clean jeans and another black t-shirt, his usual attire. His nose was sunburned. "Are you here to finish the roof?"

"I got called away to another job — "

"You don't have to explain. No one else does."

The air in the front room rushed out, cool and soothing. She threw her bag on the oak table and kicked off her shoes. She wasn't used to wearing dress shoes, or walking a mile on poor roads. This morning she'd had to jump into the ditch when a truck carrying chickens passed so close his side mirror might have knocked her flat.

"You look different." Pascal was standing at the door, looking out.

She touched the back of her hair, feeling foolish now. She was still the same person, cut or dye or not. She had wondered if he'd notice, and he had. Stop the presses.

"You've missed Tristan. He went to camp, back in the States."

Why hadn't Pascal called Albert to tell her he wouldn't be working? Was that so difficult? She realized she was angry at his neglect of her house — or his rudeness— and tried to take a deep breath and relax. She didn't want to be angry any more, at herself or anyone.

"Will he be back?" He sat down across the table from her.

"In a couple weeks, with my sister."

"One of the Charlie's Angels?"

"The oldest. Annie."

He worked his nails, more solemn than she remembered. She felt the slats of the chair on her damp back. The little clock on the mantle ticked off the minutes. She stared at him, at his dark curls. He didn't look up, just sitting there in silence as if waiting for her to do something, to say something. But what? What did she want from him? She got up and got herself a glass of cold water from the refrigerator.

"Have you heard any more about the murder?" she asked.

"I've been — out of town."

"I was wondering. Do you think Justine Labelle was her real name?"

He frowned as if he'd been thinking about something important and she'd barged into his thoughts. "Why do you say that?"

"I got three numbers for a Justine LaBelle in Bordeaux. At all three she was the same child, now four years old, and no relation to the sixty-something prostitute. So who was the squatter? The Inspector said she was from Bordeaux, but not recently. Did she have a connection here? She thought she knew Harry's mother."

He was listening hard, but tipped his head up. "Harry?"

"My husband. He was born in this house." She looked up at the water-stained ceiling and said, for no reason she could think of later, "He died in the spring." She was saying it today, over and over. *He died. He was dead.* If you said it enough, it sunk in. *In the spring:* as if that was ironic, to die at a time of rebirth.

He caught her eye until she looked away, embarrassed. "I did not know about your husband. I'm sorry for your loss." His eyes flicked down to her shirt sticking to her chest.

The quiet of the house surrounded her, a deep, intimate sound, like the breathing of a child in sleep. Pascal filled the house spaces, just being here made it seem like a real house, not a idiotic remodeling project. He sat, forearms on the table like she would serve him food, like he wanted to stay. The moment was soft, almost languid. She watched him breathe with the house, his chest rising and falling under the black t-shirt. Breathing for the house, keeping it alive.

"Are you back then to work on the roof? From visiting your wife or wherever?"

He smiled. "I have not seen my wife for many years."

Christ. She felt her color rise in her neck. Why had she said that? "I'm sorry, I had no right to —"

"Divorced, we are. She lives in Paris now. And yes, I am back to work on the roof. *Bien sûr.*"

Of course he was. He wasn't there to give her a sponge bath. *Stupid widow.* She picked up her shoes. "I need that roof finished so I can get the big bedroom done. It's the only room that's not been painted."

He stood up and stepped in front of her, blocking her way to the stairs, looking over her shoulder into the kitchen as if admiring the leafy green she'd painted there. "You've been busy."

He stood close enough that she could feel the heat rise off him, smell garlic, sweat, olive oil. Sweat was running down her back again. She wanted to touch his hair, his shoulder, his hip.

"You — um, you know where the ladder is?"

In her bedroom she sunk back onto the bed and looked at the ceiling. The shutters were closed against the sun but she could hear the ladder's rattle as he raised it.

She took five deep breaths, holding them for five beats as Annie had taught her. She used to do this before court or whenever she had to make a presentation. It calmed her. How old was he — thirty-five, forty? Maybe he was only thirty, but she doubted it. He had a few small wrinkles around his eyes, and a face weathered by summer sun.

She tried to picture herself cockeyed and reckless, seducing him. It didn't work, just like Harry's forgiving words didn't work. Seduction: that was someone else, someone younger, someone who understood the world a whole lot better than Merle Bennett did. Someone who lived in the moment and didn't give a shit about the future.

She took off her skirt and blouse, underpants and bra, and changed into shorts and a t-shirt. Outside she ran warm water into the tub from the cistern, squirted in some liquid soap, and washed the clothes. With a quick rinse and a squeeze they were ready for the line.

What would her mother say if she saw her washing clothes in a metal tub and hanging laundry on the line, her panties blowing in the breeze while a Frenchman stared down from the roof? Dear stiff-necked Bernie, who'd passed on most of her straight-laced qualities to her middle daughter.

She'd worn black lace underwear today, purchased in the back of the only clothing store in town. Now the little panties — very small in fact — swung happily, frisky things, on the line. On the roof Pascal was putting the last tiles in place. She went inside and took a shower in the new stall and let the hot water run on her back.

By the time she was dressed she was in possession of her mind again. She was under village-arrest, her passport confiscated. She was just trying to hang on for the ride, as Harry always advised. *Don't get nervous, hold onto the reins and stay the course.* Why she still listened to that chubby, philandering squanderer of fortunes was an issue she couldn't get into right now. She had a house to finish and a life to put back together.

With a salad with goat cheese and bread and olives she ate in front of the cold fireplace, making lists in her mind. She wanted to go back to the parish records for another look. She had missed something there. She wanted to talk to the inspector again, get Justine and Sister Evangeline's real names, track them down wherever they'd been. She wanted to find out if he'd learned anything himself, since he was supposed to be investigating. She wanted to know who the bones belonged to.

She could hear Paul McCartney with his sweet, teenage voice: "Your day breaks, your mind aches."

Every – *bite* – thing – *chew* – will – *swallow* – be – *sip* – all – *bite* – right.

AS THE NIGHTHAWKS CIRCLED HIGH on the thermals, she went outside to take down her clothes. On the back doorstep was a note under a rock. Ignoring it she locked the gate and took the clothes off the line. She folded the underclothes carefully, put the skirt and blouse on hangers, and hung them over the doorframe. Before she read the note she poured herself a glass of wine, Gagillac's red table wine from the gallon jug. She took a long drink of it (the hell with swish and swirl) and compared it — unfavorably — with the magical Pétrus.

> "I have finished the exterior of the roof. Tomorrow I will come with supplies to finish the ceiling upstairs. Pascal d'Onscon."

So formal, his full name, in case she had other Pascals in the wings. What did she expect — sonnets? In weeks, maybe less, the repairs would be complete and she would put the house on the market. If it didn't sell, she would rent it for the winter. She would never come back.

This should have made her sleep soundly, the knowledge that things would be done, her tasks accomplished, her name cleared. But she watched the moon rise in the east, almost full, and shine onto the bed linens. She didn't want the summer to end. She wanted it to go on, full of flowers, wine, olives, and — *possibility*. Yes, possibility, that thing she was so afraid of. Now she hungered for it, she lived for it. She rolled onto her stomach and put the pillow over her head.

Was it possible to hide from your own life, from the prescribed steps, the set-in-stone trajectory? Was it possible to, say, change your name and live in France and be a completely different person, one your parents wouldn't recognize, someone carefree, a nature girl, a *bon vivant*? Was it possible to forget the people you leave behind, those who nurtured and loved you, those who made you who you were? If you wished, wished, wished hard enough, would your fairy godmother, or an ogre-ish old widow, give you a string of magic pearls that would transform you into somebody who could do such a thing? A woman who could decide absolutely and exactly what would make her happy, right there, on the spot, and then actually do those things, without compromise or regret?

She sighed under the pillow. How old do you have to be to stop believing in fairy tales? Because she didn't think she'd actually reached that age.

Good old practical Merle. She would see what was right, what was necessary. She wouldn't flinch from duty, responsibility, a promise made at an altar. She would carry on. She wouldn't — no, she *couldn't* change. She was who she was. Haircuts be damned.

Moonlight was not a string of pearls. She wasn't a princess, or even a *bon vivant*. She was the clear-eyed one, the sensible child, the one who would clear her name, sell the house, and go home.

27

GERARD STOOD A GOOD HALF-MILE OUT, deep into the vines. Rogers found him at last, after tramping over the rocky ground for fifteen minutes. Even in the twilight, the stars popping out, the old boy was out coddling his piss-poor vines, some so old and rotten they should have been pulled years ago. Gerard had a fantastic vision of himself as some sort of maestro of wine-making. As if he knew how to look for noble rot and the precise moment the grapes were ready. Rogers knew more than this French peasant did, and he lived in the Big Smoke.

The only smoke Gerard knew was from his cigarette. It led Rogers down the row in the dusk. The Frenchman looked up at the sound of the crunching of soil under his feet. He stared, the tip of his cigarette glowing. Rogers stopped and caught his breath.

"How's the season going then?" he said to be friendly. They had to trust each other, at least a bit.

"*Pas mal*," Gerard grunted. He wore that stupid smock again like he was auditioning as a mad scientist in a B-movie.

In French Rogers said, "Are you ready then? Have the gasoline?"

Gerard took a draw of his cigarette. "In good time."

"This is a good time. You don't want to be buying it right before. It'll look suspicious."

Gerard shrugged. Rogers bit down on his molars. *Idiot.*

"Just so you have it in time. What's that American woman doing out here?"

Gerard brushed past him, his long legs headed back to the house. Rogers turned, skipping to keep up, stumbling on a wire. He growled as he caught himself, swearing. Gerard didn't turn back. At the house he went inside and shut the door in Hugh's face. And locked it.

Rogers knocked. "Come on, old man. Let's have a little parley. *Ouvrez la porte.*" He didn't dare raise his voice this close to the buildings. He looked around the yard and shrank into the doorframe, knocking again.

Odile answered the door. She didn't like him, never had. If Gerard was the silent, brooding type, he at least could be counted on to carry through with the plan. He had the rebel in him, and that was enough to get him to go along. Odile was not so solid. She suspected Hugh of having motives. Which of course he did have and he wasn't about to share them with a haggard old wreck of a Frenchwoman.

"Mr. Rogers," she said. "Or should I say Mr. Simms. I'm sorry I can't ask you in. I'm in the middle of something."

By the look of her she was in the middle of washing dishes, or plucking a chicken. Her hair had come loose in damp strands around her face. She wore plastic gloves, yellow ones, slipping them off now and slapping them on her thigh like a bullfighter. He took a glance at her steely blue eyes and stepped half a step back.

"Quite all right, Odile. Turn off the porch light, would you?" She snapped it off, leaving them in the shadows. The last light clung to the western sky, a slash of violet. "That's better. Now, what about this American? You can't have her out here snooping around. It's dangerous." She shrugged, the French answer to anything they disliked hearing. "Why do you need tours anyway?"

"For the money of course." Her voice was disembodied in the gloom.

"Then do them yourself."

"It is your people who want to see the wineries, the English."

"It can't be lucrative, Odile. What do you get, ten euros a head?"

"Twenty, plus the wine they buy."

"Twenty? Really. Enough to pay off the mortgage, is it?"

She breathed out noisily. He'd made her mad. He'd been right then, Odile held the purse strings while her crazy brother puttered around with the grapes. But Gerard would do as he was told. If you kept your thumb on him.

"We count on you for that, Mr. Rogers. You were to pay us for our expenses so far and we have seen not a sou. The bottles come tomorrow and who is to pay for them?"

"Don't worry about things like that. Just get rid of the American."

"As soon as you pay us. Where is the money? How do we know you have it for us? We have bills to pay."

"So you've said." He searched the dim light for her eyes. "Get rid of her, Odile."

28

WHEN PASCAL ARRIVED AT EIGHT-THIRTY, Merle was dressed in jeans, shirt, and bandanna covering her hair. She waved him in as she left for the post office, logging onto the internet. A tiny postman named Charles called to her: "*Madame Bennett? Vingt-cinq , Rue de Poitiers?*" He held out an oversized white envelope. It was from the lawyers, McGuinness and Lester, Esq., postmarked a week before.

Back at the terminal she had two emails, one from Tristan at camp. He was fine, he said, and he hadn't hit anybody yet. The weather was cool and damp. He was canoeing most afternoons. She wrote that she missed him, and would bean him herself if he got into another fight. The other email was from Annie, making plans to come to France. She was excited and still hoped to bring Tristan with her if she could get Bernie and Jack to pay for the ticket. Merle wrote back with her credit card number and told her sister not to bother their parents.

At the patisserie she bought herself a croissant and a café au lait, and opened the envelope. Inside was Harry's second, secret will, a legal-size document only three pages long. A note from Troy Lester was attached.

> "Merle: Annie made me do it. Also enclosed are what was left in W.S.'s files. Hope you're doing well over there. T.L."

She pulled the file out of the envelope. It contained only a few papers. The first three were yellowing invoices for wine and armagnac from Weston Strachie's Mediterranean Import-Export Company, carbon copies of the documents in the file she'd gotten at the will reading. All were dated 1953, to two liquor distributors in the U.S. and one in England, all describing cases of wine they had ordered. The last piece was new to her, a letter also from late 1953, from a New York distributor, a name that matched one of the invoices — Empire Warehouses. A demand for a shipment partially paid for but never received. Empire threatened legal action.

Had Weston been sued? Was the wine in the basement the same wine mentioned here? She reread the invoices. No, different vintages. He might have lied to the distributors about what he was importing, but that didn't make much sense.

Merle picked up the will. *'Sound mind,' my ass.* Harry left Courtney Duncan, and her daughter, Sophie, who he acknowledged as his child, the pension fund and the apartment on 12th street. Nothing new. Furniture, gifts, jewelry. Hold on. Harry also left ten cases of Bordeaux to Courtney, bought through a British company. Was this the man who had called? Atlantic Investments, it sounded familiar. He had been rather nice on the telephone, considering a big investor was now both dead and broke. Mr. Rogers, like the sweater-and-sneakers guy.

Ten cases could make a nice nest egg if the bottles aged well, and lasted until Sophie went to college. What was the wine in the basement worth? Pascal had called it a jackpot but she had assumed that meant a jackpot of flavor. Maybe he meant it was worth a fortune. How did you sell a stash of wine like that?

Pascal. She had left him alone in the house. He didn't know about the wine in the basement — did he? The hair stood up on her neck. Was that why he was so quiet last night, he had plans to steal the wine? Maybe he was loading it in a truck right now. She stuffed the papers back in the envelope and jogged back to rue de Poitiers.

As she unlocked the front door Pascal's boots hit the stairs. As she relocked the door he stood at the bottom, covered in plaster dust, his hair and eyebrows white as snow.

"I'll be back in a couple hours. *Après dejeuner.*"

"You're filthy. Would you like to wash? In the garden?" The bottom half of his face the only clean area on him. He must have covered it with a scarf. "You should clean up," she said. "Come on."

Peeling off his shirt he lowered his head while she pulled the chain on the cistern. He ran his hands through his hair, his neck, eyes, ears, then washed his hands. Merle handed him a towel. The sun glistened off his shoulders and chest, not an unwelcome sight. He dried off, shook his shirt and pulled it back on, and went out the back gate.

Merle stood in the sunshine, staring at the white footsteps he'd left in the dirt. If he'd been searching the house while she was gone, he made a good cover of plaster dust. He knew where the trap door was. She ran upstairs to see how much work he'd gotten done, and found a huge pile of debris under the ladder. He'd been up in the attic, cleaning out the birds nests. Twigs, feathers, guano: delightful.

She shut her bedroom door tight and walked back downstairs. She hated to think it but she couldn't take chances. Pulling up the trap door she unlocked the wine cave. The bottles were all there, except for the three she'd taken upstairs. She breathed a sigh of relief and locked it all up again.

Outside she moved around the flowers, watering. Pascal was just a worker, not a thief. That was a relief, and enough. She was moving around the wisteria when she did a double-take. A rose bush she'd never seen before sat in newly-turned earth. It hadn't been there yesterday. Planted next to the white clematis vine, by the wall.

The soil was still mounded and soft around the woody stem. A tag dangled from its base, a label: "Reine de Violette." Queen of Violet. A purplish-red blossom rose toward the sun. Who had planted it — Pascal? She stalked the edges of the garden, looking for new plants. There was a new, tiny clematis, almost invisible, in the northeast corner. A tiny row of marigolds next to the stoop.

She spun around, heart pounding. Someone else had a key to the garden.

THE GENDARME STOOD on his steps, locking the door to the tiny police bureau as she rounded the corner. Lunchtime, time for his card game. He blinked a few times as if trying to place her. This new hair had its devices. "Madame," he said, nodding.

"Bonjour." *Damn, in French.* "Do you know if Madame Labelle had friends or relatives, here in the village?"

He wiped his mouth, narrowing his eyes. His shoes were

suddenly fascinating. "*Non. Pourquoi?*"

She'd been trained to spot liars, and he was one. She told him someone had gotten into her garden. Someone who had a key to the gate. "Did she have any relatives here? Or maybe a close friend."

He brought his dark eyes up to hers and bid her good day. He walked away in slow, steady strides, the swagger of authority as universal as mother's milk. Off to his juicy, card-playing lunch. What had he lied about? Justine had relatives here in town, or friends? Did he know who had the key to her garden gate?

She knocked on the door of the gendarmerie but no one answered. She'd have to suss out the inspector elsewhere. As she walked back through the streets, she looked at the faces that passed. Was one Justine's friend, or a cousin or a sister? They stared back, unsmiling, looking through her as if she was invisible.

PASCAL RETURNED ABOUT ONE-THIRTY from lunch. Upstairs the sound of pounding started. Downstairs she looked over the will and invoices again, spreading them out with the other papers she'd gotten from the lawyers. Weston Strachie had made some distributors angry. He hadn't delivered his wine. Maybe he meant to deliver these cases mentioned, maybe he had paid for the wine in the basement with these men's money. Maybe he'd had problems with customs or something. It didn't make him a thief.

She spread her hand over the will. Not again today, she thought. Reading about Harry's devotion to Courtney and Sophie was too hard. She folded it and put it away.

So, back to work. Next on the list: the rug. She opened the trap door to the basement again. The place gave her the creeps, but since they'd found the wine it had begun to look more pleasant, a disguise of filth and vermin to keep out intruders. The stairs creaked as she stepped slowly under the floor, sweeping the flashlight around the dank, earth floor and the mossy stone walls, eyes peeled for furry rodents.

Most of the junk was gone, old bottles, nests of cotton that were once clothes, ancient preserves and unrecognizable lumps of mold. The wooden kegs she'd fallen into must have once held potatoes or carrots but animals had cleaned them out. She kicked one and saw a huge cockroach skitter away.

The rolled-up carpet, source of whiskered varmints, was large and heavy. Setting down the flashlight, she picked up one end. Under it was a piece of tarp. Oil cloth, it felt like. So maybe it wasn't rotten. She shook it, hoping any mice would run away, but nothing came out. Dragging one end toward the stairs, she groaned under the dead weight. As she backed up the stairs, knees splayed, the length of the rug swung out, knocking over bits of broken kegs like a mermaid's tail.

Heaving it around corners, she pulled it out into the garden into the golden summer light and took a good look at it. The exposed top was covered with mildew. The sides weren't so bad, and the oil cloth had at least partially done its job of protecting it from creeping damp. She kicked it with her foot, unrolling it on the gravel by the table.

An Oriental rug of reds and blues, very faded. Worn too, with places where the backing showed through. She folded it back in half so that the moldy top could be scrubbed, filled the tub with cistern water and got a scrub brush from the house.

The mold was superficial, probably developing since the hole in the roof. With elbow grease and soapy water, it yielded. The hard work was satisfying, the way it had been when they first arrived. She threw the rest of the water on the rug, swished it around, rinsed it with a clean tub then called it good.

The sun had left most of the garden. She had managed to get herself soaking wet. Her pink polo shirt clung to her chest, more than a little transparent, her blue running shorts dripping on her bare feet. Putting the tub and scrub brush away, she considered stripping off her wet clothes right here. The towel would serve as back-up in case Pascal was still around. She unbuttoned a button and stopped. Yves and Suzette had a good view of the garden.

As she stepped into the kitchen she heard footsteps on the stairs. So, Pascal had almost caught her naked in the garden. The thought made her skin crawl, or maybe she was just cold. The house stayed at least ten degrees cooler. She paused at the kitchen door just as a creature, a large hairy mouse, ran up through the trap door and stopped at the bottom of the stairs, staring at her.

The animal sat up on its haunches, the size of a small rat. It didn't look like any rodent she'd seen. It had a long nose and big, round ears but was chubbier, almost Mickey Mouse-ish. His black eyes were large and round, the fur brownish gray. But he was a mouse, a filthy rodent, and he wasn't running away.

Pascal peeked around the doorframe from the lower steps. "I see you have company," he whispered, smiling at the thing.

The creature looked fairly tame, chewing something, unafraid. "What should I do?" she whispered through chattering teeth.

"Say hello." He crouched down on the step. *"Bonjour, petit loir."* The animal turned its black eyes toward him for a minute then jumped backwards like a miniature kangaroo.

Merle backed toward the kitchen door. "Here you go. The big wide outdoors. All yours." She stepped aside. "Tell it to go outside."

He clucked his tongue. The *loir* twitched its long hairy tail. Pascal eased over the stair railing and dropped softly onto the floor. "Close the trap door," she whispered. He tipped the door until it closed with a loud thunk. The animal took off like a shot up the stairs, its skittering claws scratching against the wood.

"No! Not my bedroom!"

"If only I hadn't closed off the ceiling." Pascal's eyes moved over her and she crossed her clammy arms over her chest. "But the window is open. And the chimney. It will escape."

"Will it come back?"

He shrugged. "The loir is a harmless little creature. Nothing to be afraid."

She sat on a dining chair, still shivering. "What did you call it?"

"A loir. You do not have them in the United States? It is

cousin to the English dormouse."

She shook her head, feeling droplets fling off the ends of her hair. If we had them in the U.S. she didn't know about it, and didn't want to know. She really should change out of these wet clothes. Her hands were stiff. Pascal disappeared then returned with a towel he wrapped around her shoulders. "Forgive me. You are the shivers."

"Thanks." She pulled the towel closer. "I think I — I — "

"Wait here. I get you some dry clothes."

"B-but." But he was gone, up the stairs. To look through her drawers. And chase the *loir* out, she hoped.

He came downstairs with underpants, a sweatshirt, and jeans, then went outside into the garden. Stepping into the bathroom, she peeled off her wet things, dried roughly and pulled on the warm clothes. She dried her hair ends and rubbed her face. He had brought her underwear, plain, white cotton ones as if that was who he thought she was: a plain, white woman, slightly worn and a little baggy.

Holding her wet clothes in a ball, she stepped out outside. He was still here. Smoking a cigarette. He crushed it under his boot, picked up the stub and put it in his pocket. "Better?"

She threw her wet clothes over the clothesline. "Have you got another one of those?" He dug the pack of cigarettes out and lit her one. She smoked with jerks, hand to mouth then handed it back to him. "That's enough."

He crushed it under his boot like the other. "You are still cold? I can make *chocolat chaud.*"

Inside Merle climbed the stairs to get some socks and grabbed the blanket off her bed. In the kitchen he stirred milk in the saucepan. She sat on Tristan's bed in the parlor, wrapped in the blanket. When had a man ever cooked for her, she wondered, as he handed her a mug of hot chocolate. "Did you make one for yourself?" He poured himself a cup from the saucepan and leaned against the doorframe.

"You make great cocoa. Thank you." *And you make great conversation, for a brain-dead person.* "How is the work going upstairs?"

"*Pas mal.* I can stay and clean it up but tomorrow there may be more mess."

"As long as I can get, you know, to my bed — my bedroom — my room." Christ. Had her brain frozen? A racking shiver went through her.

He looked at her over the cocoa and then at the liquid in his mug. Merle drank, and finally got warm. He set down his cup on the stove. "I'll see you tomorrow."

"You don't think the little thing, the — ?"

"Loir."

"The loir will be back?"

"He is harmless. You will sleep all right?"

"Oh, sure. I guess."

"Everyone has a loir now and then. It is very French."

So she curled up, extremely French, under her covers, cursing in French to keep away rodents, listening for scratching noises, for claws on wood. Something on the roof woke her at three with its scritch/scritch; by five she called it quits and got up. She felt ridiculous and squeaky, like the silly blond in the old gothics who needed a man to protect her. That was not her.

"Only a fricking mouse," she said loudly to the dust motes on the stairs, hoping to scare *'le petit loir'* if he hid somewhere. The thought of things scampering over her in the night, and their little whiskers and teeth. Pascal hadn't been afraid. But he wasn't sleeping with rodents.

WHEN THE HARDWARE STORE OPENED at eight o'clock she was there to ask about grills for her chimney, to keep out birds and small animals. The clerk showed her different sizes, all rather pricey. She had been expecting a piece of chicken wire but these were ornate affairs, ranging in price from twenty to sixty euros, depending on the strength of the iron bars and the number of curlicues.

What size was her chimney opening, they asked. She didn't know. At home she made an espresso and set Albert's ladder up against the house. The sun was rising over the hills to the east, sending golden rays from behind a bank of deep purple clouds. Halfway up she stopped to admire the sky. On top of the hill to the east, framed by sunrise, the big Château looked like Cinderella's castle, with turrets and flags and shrubs sculpted into animal shapes. The wine-tasting tourists had asked her about it, was it worth the big price tag. She didn't know a thing about it. Over there, still in shadow, was Château Gagillac where trucks were moving in and out around the tasting room. Loading wine? Would they schedule another tour? She did so miss Gerard's scowling face.

Onward, skyward. She passed her bedroom window and kept going. Those shutters needed paint, badly. At the edge of the roof she stopped again. Pascal's work was twelve or so feet to the left but she could see the new tiles, the patched spot. It looked good, blending in with the old tiles and secure from the weather. He hadn't reset the gutter though. It hung, swinging loose.

She set her hand on the tile roof. The clay tiles were slick moss, and steeper than she imagined. Walking across them to the chimney was out of the question. Down she went, looking over her shoulder at the winery again. Now the big barn doors of the ageing room were wide open. A truck was backing into it. Maybe loading barrels to take to the commune.

As she lowered her foot to the next rung the ladder lurched to the left. A jolt of adrenaline snapped her to attention. She had been sightseeing from her perch when she should have been watching what she was doing. She looked down. One leg of the ladder was sinking in the wet dirt below. Her foot slipped but she hung on. Her heart beating in her ears, she waited for more sinking. She was ten feet off the ground and it would be nice to take the rest one rung at a time, thank you very much. Slowly she put a foot down on the next rung. The ladder sunk a little more, tipping west.

Quick or slow, that was the question. She eyed crash sites below, soft mud straight down where she'd washed the rug. Hard rocks of the path or gravel of the patio if she went left with the ladder. The ladder sunk a little more, tilting precariously. On the upper end, where the ladder touched the roof, the left leg was barely in contact with the gutter. Another inch and —

With a two-rung hop Merle pushed off the ladder, falling to her right hip and catching herself with her right arm. Her shin banged against the bottom rung and she cursed loudly. The ladder fell sideways out from under her flying feet, taking down some of the ripening pears as it fell. A loud peel as it clanged against the top of the wall resounded off the stone buildings like a church bell.

Blinking, her ears ringing, she sat up, covered with mud. An inventory of the body found a gash in the shin, rising already into a goose egg. She gingerly rotated her shoulder. It felt all right, despite falling on it. She felt her arm, her wrist. Sore but okay. She tried to stand. Pushing up with her right arm was painful. Not to mention the sore leg. She looked at her wrist again.

"Stupid. Stupid. Stupid," she whispered angrily. This was the problem with being practical. You wanted to do everything yourself to save a few francs and ended up nearly killing yourself. Years ago, in the blush of home-ownership, she'd decided to hose out the gutters, climbing all over the roof, having a good ol' time up in the air until Harry came home and told her she could have broken her neck. She could hear him right now, scolding her from beyond the grave.

"Oh, Harry." She sat on the patio chair, pushing the ladder off it. "I wish I could say this is all your fault."

Pounding at the back gate. "Merle?"

She pulled the key out from the chain around her neck and unlocked the gate. Moving her wrist to twist the key hurt; she switched to her left hand. Albert wore his usual uniform, the blue farmer's coveralls.

"I hear the big boom."

Her wrist was beginning to ache. "I might have broken something."

He insisted she go see the doctor, leading her through the streets to the *Cabinet du Medecin* of Doctor Beynac. Merle played her role as careless child. An x-ray and exam later, she was fitted with a cast made of rolled gauze and some new material simulating the outdated plaster of yore. The doctor was very nice, even nicer because Albert was an old friend. He also checked out the shin gash, dabbed it and bandaged it up.

"Be careful now," Dr. Beynac said, wagging his plump finger. "You should not be doing these things. Is your husband not able to do these?"

"I am a widow, *docteur*." A stupid, careless widow.

"That old ladder," Albert muttered on the walk home. "I will get a new one. That one is bad, very old, very bad."

Merle stood in front of her house, holding her cast across her waist with her good hand. This could be awkward, not having a right hand. The fingers could wiggle but they couldn't reach her thumb. "The ground was soft. It went — " She mimed the sinking ladder with her good arm. "Then I jumped off."

"*Mon Dieu*. I am feeling terrible. And the worst of it is, I must use that ladder to pick my plums this week."

She led him through the house into the garden where the ladder sat where she'd left it, leaning on the wall. "I hope it still works."

Albert grumbled, angry with the ladder as he carried it over his head and then out the gate. What was she going to do about the chimney grate? Pascal stepped out the kitchen door.

"I began upstairs," he said. "The door was unlocked. That is not a good idea, I told you, leaving doors unlocked, even in the daytime —" He stared at her cast. "What happened?"

"The ladder," she said. "It toppled."

"What were you doing on the ladder?" His dark eyes looked angry. "That is not for you to do."

"So said the doctor. I was looking at the chimney. I want a grate over it. I think the loir came down that way." She sighed. "I kept thinking about his little whiskers."

She lay back on Tristan's bed after Pascal went upstairs to work. No work for Merle today. Next door, in Yves and Suzette's bedroom, the lace curtain blew out on the breeze. She opened her own window to feel the air and heard Yves's voice, murmuring, and

Suzette's high-pitched laughter in response. Were they making love? A hand appeared and their window snapped shut.

Upstairs the hammering began. It sounded like the clatter of her heart.

29

THE ROOM IS DARK and Virginia is tired. She's been struggling with the baby for at a good half-hour and he won't settle down. She'd found milk for it, then changed the diaper so she knew he was a boy. He wore rags, nothing more than strips of fabric wrapped around his strong young body.

Outside the noise has been muffled and gone out. That was so brief she thought maybe she dreamed it. But Weston came inside and told her the woman had run away. Without her baby, Virginia asked. It seemed unnatural. She had no business here, she was a squatter, a whore.

The baby tires of squirming and wailing, nestling into her shoulder. He is quite big, not walking yet so she thinks maybe a year old. She doesn't know much of babies but this one is not a newborn. He is heavy and uses his hands well, grabbing her hair, her earrings.

Virginia looked into her purse earlier and found a few francs. Weston was busy in the back as she slipped out and bought milk and a loaf of bread. The baby quieted as she walked across the square.

But that was hours ago. Now he has awakened again, though it appears another sip of milk has calmed his fears. He looks at her with wide, startled eyes, as if she means him harm. Then his body loses the tension and he melts into her shoulder, rubbing his face on her dress.

Soon his breathing slows and he is sleeping. The quiet of room is deep. She rubs his little stiff back and he wiggles, sucking his thumb. Outside Weston is working. She knows better than to ask what he's doing. She adores him but she knows the limit of his patience.

She strokes the baby's cheek. Someone loved him, he is fat and adorable with black swirls of hair and big serious eyes that make love to her.

Weston is washing outside. She has never known him to be so industrious. He has sweated through his shirt, made his trousers filthy. She laughs at him, but he is in a black mood, angry about something. Probably having to work. He goes upstairs and comes down with a suitcase. He changes his shirt, brushes off his pants. He is ready to go.

Virginia bundles up the baby, finding a blanket, some diapers, the bottle of milk. Weston barks at her, what the hell? She insists, the baby must come. They can't just leave him. No, he yells. Yes, she says again. He will be ours now. She holds him tight against her, perhaps too tight. He whimpers.

We'll take him to the convent, Weston says. She holds him tighter. No, she says. We will call him Harold. My father's name. He is ours now.

30

IN THE MORNING the sun promised a hot day. Her wrist had ached all night and she scratched her forehead with the cast in her sleep. She was struggling with the espresso maker when Pascal arrived.

He brought cans of paint and bags of dry plaster along with plastic bags and a broom. She watched him mount the stairs with only a nod her direction. Could it be he was almost done? She'd gotten nothing done yesterday, the ache was so bad in her arm. Today work called out to her as if punishment for her stupidity.

Odile Langois called on the new cell phone. She'd gotten the number from Albert. Could she tour a group tomorrow? Oh, why not. She wouldn't be painting. Merle wrote down the time with her left hand and hoped she could read it tomorrow.

The espresso wasn't happening. She walked down to the square to buy a *café au lait* from a small bar where men stood even at nine in the morning and had a glass of wine or some *eau de vie* in their morning coffee. Merle hadn't tried that unique concoction — a pear or plum liqueur, heavily alcoholic, that oldsters like Albert made at home. It looked like the white lightning of her youth.

She nursed her *café au lait* at a table on the sidewalk and made some phone calls. At least she could push buttons with the fingers on her bad arm. Arnaud Rancard was on vacation now. She called one of her colleagues at Legal Aid and tried to have a short conversation about getting a name of a homeless agency official in Bordeaux before she realized it was after midnight in New York and apologized. She dug out the phone number of the criminal lawyer in Bordeaux, and called. She explained to the secretary, at least she tried to explain, that she couldn't come for an appointment, she had to stay in the village. Could Monsieur Lalouche call her on this number?

As she turned to signal for her check, she saw the old locksmith, Andre Saintson, at the bar. He leaned forward, barely upright, raising a cup to his lips. She gathered herself, bad arm and purse, and went inside.

"*Bonjour, Monsieur. Comment allez-vous?*" He frowned at her from under bushy eyebrows. "Merle Bennett," she reminded him, and they shook hands. He did not comment on her cast, just shook the ends of her fingers.

"How is your house?" he asked.

"I tried to find you to open the garden gate. But I got it open. Someone gave me the key." He nodded warily. "Remember the garden?"

The bartender, a round man with a three-day beard and black hair, wiped the bar and listened. She turned to him. "My garden is like the Tuilleries. Justine Labelle took great care of it."

The man flinched. She said, "Did you know Justine?"

"*Non,*" he answered quickly, eyes darting at the other man at the bar.

"Did you know Justine Labelle?" she asked the stranger, a farmer by his looks. He threw down some coins and stalked out. She turned back to Andre. "*Et vous?*"

He sneered, nodding. "*Une putain,* a whore."

"Where did she live before she came to my house?"

He lit a cigarette, taking his time. "I don't know where."

"Bordeaux," offered the bartender. "So says Jean-Pierre."

"Why did she come here? Did she just like this town?" Neither man commented. "Or for business?" The bartender leered and muttered something.

"*Qui sais?*" Andre mumbled. Who knows.

What had happened to him after he changed her locks? Had he been threatened by the gendarme? Or had he just decided to hang out in bars all day, avoiding her? She didn't think she'd get an answer.

"It must have been disgraceful, having a *putain* here." The bartender squelched a smirk. "Are there others? My husband's parents would not have liked her living in their house. You, monsieur," she said to the bartender. "Do you know anyone of the Chevalier family?" He said no. "The family gave the house to my husband's mother. She was a Chevalier. Someone must know them."

The bartender spoke rapidly to Andre who told her, "They

all left town years ago, when he was a kid. Some kind of *scandale.* "

"About what?"

Andre and the bartender talked so fast she hardly caught a word. Andre, who spoke slowly, said, "His mother was very upset. She was a friend of one of them and she never saw them again."

"Does his mother still live here?"

"She died last winter."

"Can you think of anyone who might remember the scandal?"

Andre smoked. The bartender had no ideas up his wine-stained sleeves.

"This town is full of old people. You must know someone who likes to wag his tongue."

"Not many in this town." Andre drained his cup. "How about your neighbor?"

"Madame Suchet? She's not old enough to remember, is she?"

The bartender was glaring at the old man. "Perhaps not. You're right. Too young."

MERLE HELD THE SMALL PLUM TART from the patisserie against her cast as she knocked on Madame Suchet's door. The pear tart had broken the ice, she was hoping plums would continue the thaw.

Madame opened the door, smoothing down the front of her blouse. A full-breasted woman, she often left her blouse unbuttoned to her décolletage, probably because the buttons refused to hold. Today she burst from a white blouse with tiny blue flowers embroidered on the collar. Her skirt was pleated in green. Her hair was simple, bangs across her forehead and a platinum dye on her chin-length bob.

"*Bonjour, madame,*" she said. She presented the tart and smiled, and with hesitation, Mme. Suchet invited her inside. She was just having her morning coffee. She sliced the tart and served it on china plates. They tasted it in her small living room, a salon that had a formal air with doilies, old black-and-white framed photographs, and a bit of dust.

Madame asked how the house was coming. "*Bien, bien, merci,*" Merle smiled. A little accident with the ladder yesterday. She grimaced and held up her cast. *You have a lovely home.* Have you lived here long, she asked.

"All my life," Madame said, smiling. "Except for the years I was married and lived in Paris."

"Then perhaps you knew the owners of my house?"

"My parents knew them, the people who lived there during the war."

"The Chevalier's?"

"That was not the name." Madame frowned, looking out the window at Merle's house. "Sebastien? He was Italian. Sabatini, that was it."

"And his wife, she was Italian?"

"No, she was from nearby. Perhaps here in the village. "

"Was she the aunt of Marie-Emilie Chevalier?"

Her finger flew to her chin as if this had not occurred to her. But yes, she said, that is how the house passed to Marie-Emilie and her husband. During the war the Sabatini's left, abandoning the place. Things were very bad here then. The resistance fighters were everywhere, working against the Vichy government. That often brought retaliations, accusations of spying or hiding Jews or black-marketeering. People learned to keep to themselves, to lay low. Monsieur Sabatini had fought for the French and was gone for much of the war.

It didn't take much to get Madame Suchet remembering the past. Mme Sabatini had asked the young Madame Suchet, she was only a girl then, to help in the garden, to pick fruit or hang laundry or help pluck chickens. Things children did in every house. The woman softened into the chair, cuddling her cup in both hands. Her face had lost that hostile air as she remembered the old days. Merle felt the wall fall away between them. They were just two women, alone, and not so very different.

"Where was your father during the war?"

"He had gone into the army early, drafted because he did not have a farm to maintain. He was a mason here but in the army he learned explosives. But after the surrender he was taken prisoner. He came home after the war a broken man."

Madame went to the mantel and took down a faded photograph of a young man in uniform, so proud, so young. He was twenty-seven at the war's start.

"Did the Sabatini's have children?"

"No. They were young too, younger than my parents."

"Do you know what happened to them?"

"For the first few years of the war she took in laundry, bartering for food. But as things got worse and he didn't come home, she grew thin and sick. Finally she went to live with relatives somewhere. She came back for a little while after the war, but things were very bad here. No jobs, the farms abandoned, no animals or men to work the fields."

The woman was talking slow enough that Merle could understand almost everything. Maybe her French was getting better. "But your parents kept their house."

"And so did the Sabatini's. But eating was another matter. Unless you had land, with animals to slaughter, chickens for eggs, a goat, room to grow vegetables, you didn't have food. My mother and her older brother went to work for a dairy, and that kept us alive."

"Did you know Marie-Emilie?"

"*Non.* After the war I went north to find work, and met my husband."

Interesting but a dead end. She tried to think of anything else but there was only the squatter left to discuss. "Did you know Justine Labelle?"

Mme. Suchet grew very still, pursing her lips. "*Non.*"

"You saw her. Living there." She didn't answer. "I heard that there was a scandal attached to the house, from years ago."

Madame cocked her head. "*Je ne sais pas.*" She didn't know.

She suddenly had to go run errands. The visit had been a good one, and they now had had a real conversation. She learned the name of the previous owner, before Weston and Marie. Maybe she and Mme Suchet would talk again.

In the garden the rug felt dry and looked clean enough. She rolled it badly with one hand and tried to pick it up. With a grunt she dropped it again. This busted-wing business was a pain in the ass.

Pascal leaned out of the second floor window into the sunshine. "Can I help?"

He came down and heaved the rolled rug over his shoulder. Staggering he lurched into the house and deposited it in the front room. "Here I hope?"

They rolled it out and Merle swept it awkwardly with a clean broom. Straightening it so that it defined a sitting area around Tristan's bed they stood back and admired its frayed splendor. Shabby, faded and worn, the rug was far from elegant but the bed with its open springs was not exactly the height of interior design either.

"Lovely," Pascal said. "*Merveilleux*."

She laughed and took a swing at him with the broom. He said, "Ow. You want both of us to be cripples?"

"I am not a cripple!" She would be happy with Pascal as a friend, someone to share a laugh. "Only half a cripple."

"You should rest. Wait for your arm to heal." He rubbed his hair, causing plaster dust to fly. "I can help you. If you can't find anyone else."

"Are you offering your services?"

"At your pleasure, madame."

Despite her fresh pledge of friendship she felt the heat rise in her, warming her neck and face. Why did he keep grinning at her and offering her pleasure? He looked quite serious now, as if he didn't have a sexy grin at all.

"Let's see what you've been doing upstairs."

The loft was a picture of demolition with very little construction apparent. A three-foot high pile of plaster, lath, pigeon feathers, sticks, string, and mud from nests, and unrecognizable crap sat in the middle of the room. The stepladder stood under the hole in the ceiling. The rafters were visible, and above them a piece of plywood sealed off the attic space.

"All this was up there?"

"I left some for the next hole." Pascal handed her a bandanna and pulled his over his mouth and nose. "You hold the bags, I fill."

Eight trash bags later the loft floor was mostly clean. Pascal carried the bags down the stairs and set them on the curb. He had arranged for a man with a truck to take them to the dump. Merle tried to sweep with one arm and did a poor job of it. She held the dustpan instead and they filled one last bag.

"What now?" Merle pulled the scarf off her face, admiring the semi-clean space. It would have to be mopped again, later.

"Now I put up new lath —" He pointed to strips of wood piled in the corner. "And do the plaster." He frowned at the now large hole.

"You've done plaster before?"

"Oh, yes," he said confidently then hung his head. "Once."

"Did you do it well?"

"*Formidable, bien sûr.*" He smirked then looked out from under his eyebrows. "Do you want to see if I can find someone who really knows how to do plaster? I am not good. In truth, I suck at plaster."

She laughed. "You 'suck?' Where did you learn that word?"

"It is not right, 'I suck?'"

"It's just not something I expected to ever hear a Frenchman say."

"Well, they say it all the time on MTV."

Pascal made a few phone calls. A small job, he explained, one, maybe two days. He could finish it off, sanding and texturing, and paint would be last.

"What other jobs?"

Merle looked up from the table. "I'm making a list. I'll help you if I can. Until my arm heals, or —" She handed him the piece of paper.

"Or you get tired of me hanging around?"

He had dimples. Dear God. "First, the gutter. You didn't reattach it when you did the roof."

"Back up the killer ladder?"

"Back up the killer ladder."

"But first, lunch? Can I buy you some lunch? It's very late." It was one o'clock. Tragically late.

"I have too much to do. I have my own list." She held it up for him to see how long it was, full of important must-do stuff.

He squinted at it. "Your handwriting sucks."

31

MERLE ATE HER LUNCH in the garden, reading the bad novel and eating cheese. She felt a bit safer knowing someone else was going to do the hard work. She was definitely a danger to herself. And with the treasure in the basement, the wine felt safer too. She stared at her list. Had she learned nothing from France? She pushed it away and turned her face to the sun. It warmed her tired bones, her sore muscles, and her cast, until she moved her chair to the shade, propping her feet on the low wall.

Another heavenly day in the garden. The roses needed deadheading but the climbing pink one on the far wall was busting its guts to please her. Even the new one, the Reine de Violette, had opened a mauve blossom.

She awoke with a start at the sound of the aluminum extension ladder going up. Pascal leaned it against the house, checked the legs for a firm footing, set rocks on either side of them, and climbed. Merle turned back to the book in her lap. Maybe she did need some rest. She tried to stand using her right arm. Ouch. Gathering her dishes and book, she nodded to Pascal on her way into the kitchen.

In the bathroom she took a couple more aspirin then tried to rinse her dishes in the kitchen sink. How in hell was she going to keep this cast dry?

Pascal came to the back door and knocked. He poked his head into the kitchen. "I must find new boulons for the gutter." He held up a bent screw.

"And I need to buy something for dinner. Walk together?"

He had a long stride and she had to step lively to keep up, holding her cast against her stomach. Out on the streets she relaxed, thinking about the menu for dinner instead of crimes past and present. The lavender was blooming in pots around the plaza, scenting the air. In the grocery she bought a small piece of fish with a strange name, some green beans, and a baguette. More than enough for one person.

He was up on the ladder when she returned home. An hour later he appeared again at the door. She offered him a glass of wine. They sat outside on the patio. He sipped his wine, and said, "Something new?"

"Château Cheval-Blanc." She handed him the bottle. "It's good, isn't it?"

He held the glass up to the sunlight. The thick liquid was as dense as milk and tasted a lot better. "*Incroyable.* Where did you get it?"

She wanted to tell him about the cave. But the knowledge, the secret of the wine, was a big responsibility. And who was he? He seemed too well-traveled, too educated to be a roofer. She hated being suspicious, but she had to be careful. She replaced the cork. "I'll pour some more at dinner. If you'll join me."

He put a hand over his heart. "For Château Cheval-Blanc — and your company, madame, I am honored."

She served the fish baked with a cream sauce. Pascal had gone home to wash and change his clothes. His father, he said sipping the wine, would have killed for this one. It was a rare Bordeaux from a small vineyard. Vintages during the war, or right after like this one were very rare because of the devastation of the vineyards from battles and neglect.

As they finished dinner, set outside in the warm evening air, a knock came at the front door. Merle could see the gendarme standing on the step, his hat in his hands. She put her plate in the sink and went to the door.

"I am here to talk to the boy. Your son," Jean-Pierre said, looking around her.

"He's not here." She heard Pascal come into the room.

He reached around her and shook Jean-Pierre's hand. "Come in, have a refreshment." She caught Pascal's eye: what the hell are you doing?

Pascal poured the last of the Cheval-Blanc for the gendarme. At the oak table he sniffed it, sipped, and nodded, licking his lips.

"An old vintage? "

She shrugged. "Was there something you needed from my son?"

"I need to speak to him about the fight. There were complaints we must address."

"He's gone home to America."

"Without his passport?"

"He kept his passport. It's mine you have." She crossed her arms. "Why are you here?"

"The inspector wants to speak to him."

"What about?"

"I just do my duty." He drained his glass and saluted them. Was he drunk? "I will leave you two *amoureux* to your evening."

After the door shut Merle turned to Pascal. "What did he say?" she asked in English.

"Which part, about the passport?" He shrugged, picking up his dishes again from the table then put on espresso.

"What do you think tomorrow? Paint the shutters?"

"I can't ask you to do that, Pascal. You're a roofer."

"I'm not plastering. I must wait for that before I finish upstairs."

"All right. I'll buy paint in the morning." They listened to the night birds circling high in the sky, catching insects. "Has there been talk about Justine Labelle around town?"

"Not since the first few days."

"Do they think I did it? The people?"

"I don't know what they think." He set his cup on the patio table. "I have heard that the Inspector gets pressure from his superiors to make an arrest."

"He's been investigating long enough." She looked up. "You mean me?"

"Are there other suspects?"

The night didn't seem so lovely. "Do you have any theories?"

"I suppose someone who was her customer."

"Here?"

"Or Bordeaux."

"What about Jean-Pierre, our trusty gendarme? Does he know anything about her?"

"I only know him a little."

"Was he drunk tonight?"

"Possibly." Pascal looked serious. "Sometimes he plays cards. A little Jeu de Tarot. At lunch."

"Do you think he would tell you Justine Labelle's real name?"

"Why don't you ask him?"

"I did. He won't tell me."

He looked into his tiny espresso cup, as if reading the coffee grounds for an answer. "You want me to ask?"

THE NEXT MORNING Merle put on her jogging shoes, shoved her good shoes in a bag, and took off walking to the winery. She was early, but wanted to enjoy the morning in the countryside, the ducks on the pond at the bottom of the hill, the wood-cutters taking logs out of the thick forest, the solitary tourists on mopeds putt-putting along the country roads. On some far hill a church bell was ringing. The sky was white, promising heat again.

She took the long way around the city walls, going out the north entrance to the beginning of the path that led to the cliffs. Not so long ago she had climbed those stairs, and a woman had been pushed to her death. Who had done it? Any one of the people on those buses that day. What was the inspector up to? She'd seen him around town, always alone at a table outside the tabac or a café, smoking and ruminating. Pascal said he was getting pressure to arrest her, but he hadn't been back to talk to her for days. This must be what denial feels like. Very nice. Pleasant.

She'd left Pascal with two gallons of sky blue paint. He had started taking down the shutters to paint them in the garden. As she walked her cell phone rang — her mother, calling at some ungodly time of night in Connecticut.

There wasn't much to say. There isn't, when you've been lying for weeks. Your true life can never measure up to the picture you've painted for your relatives. Yes, she was happy Annie and Tristan would be here next week. Yes, the house was coming along. No, she wasn't sure when she'd be home. Yes, everything was fine, just fine, having the time of her life. Vacation like no other. Perfect health.

She'd never lied to her mother. She never needed to. Her life had always been on the up-and-up. But now, as she stepped off the track into the weeds, both literally and figuratively, there was too much to say and too great a distance. Her mother wouldn't understand. Merle would tell them all of it when it was over.

The vines of Château Gagillac trembled in the morning mist. She peeked under the leaves to see the clusters of grapes growing fatter in the summer sun. Something about grapevines was so ancient, so elemental, a link to Romans and Greeks and tribes who cultivated this soil for millennia. Had wine made from grapes planted right here on this hillside once gone down the throat of Caesar? Even the roses scenting the path knew their place in history.

The tour was an hour away. Merle took off her sweater, hung it in the closet in the tasting room, and changed her shoes. In the bathroom she brushed her hair, put on lipstick. She didn't look too bad, except for the cast on her arm. Walking toward the house, she passed the aging room, its big doors closed and locked. What had those trucks been doing the other day, before her fall from the ladder? What was so secret in here?

She looked around. No one nearby. She stepped over to the side door and tried the knob. Locked. Was it lying, the first sin, that made her bold? She walked around the building and found a window unlocked. She reached inside and cranked it wider then peered into the gloom inside. Where was Gerard? She boosted herself onto the sill and slipped inside.

She was behind the rows of oak barrels at the back of the chai. Lying on their sides, two rows high, the top row on heavily supported wooden beams spanned the width of the building. They appeared to be all the same as before, none missing. In front of them was something new. Wooden wine cases, with bottles inside on their sides, two rows deep. So this was what the trucks were doing, loading or unloading these cases. She leaned closer to see the label, picked up a bottle and held it up to the light from the window. 'Château du Saint Clar, Grand Cru Classe, 1992.'

Of course it wasn't Château Gagillac. They didn't bottle their own wine. There would be no Château Gagillac except in big plastic jugs, anytime soon. She looked at another case. 'Château Buzet, Cru Bourgeois, 1988.'

She laid the bottle back in the wooden crate, running her fingers over its mates there, all alike. Similar crates with different wineries stamped on the sides were stacked in neat piles. Voices outside! She crept back to the window. Back over the sash she landed quietly on the grass then peeked around the corner of the chai. No one there, and the voices had gone too. Heart beating fast — what had she been thinking? — she walked slowly toward the house to get her instructions for the day.

The crunching of the stones under her shoes blotted out noises. She raised her left fist to knock on the door. There, again. Angry voices, from inside. She couldn't follow the French, but it sounded like Gerard. Odile answered, equally fast and surprisingly loud, giving Gerard as good as he got. Unfortunately it seemed to set him off further. More yelling, then a bump. Had he hit her — or she him?

Before Merle could turn away from the door Gerard yanked it open, his face flushed with anger. He glared at her and slammed the door shut behind him, shoving past her then tramped up the path to the chai. He disappeared around the building.

Odile opened the door, her face placid and unreadable. Besides a little flush in the neck, you'd never know she'd just had a shouting match. A French thing, Merle supposed, being able to fume and shout then be sweet as pie.

The list of wine-tasters was long, fourteen people. Odile was her usual efficient self, and because of the language barrier, their conversation was over before it started. Odile sent her off as she stared out the window, worry creasing her face.

The tour group arrived in a small white bus, all British. They were a jolly, rosy-cheeked, limp-haired clan, and as they paid their money they joked with her. "How'd you break your arm, dearie? Stayin' clear from Frenchmen, was it?" "If it was you, Jack, it'd be from lifting drinks glasses." "You seem to keep up, Terry. Not that there's a contest." "Lovely having a driver, isn't it?" "A bit too lovely, if you ask me."

Merle took the last man's money, and opened the cash box to look for change. "There you are, sir." She blinked at him. Anthony Simms again, with his bad hair — definitely a toupee — and doggy brown eyes.

He smiled sheepishly. "Hello, Merle. How are you?"

"Another tour?"

He shrugged, opened his mouth to answer. Merle straightened her shoulders as she saw the rest of the group was staring at them silently as if expecting a little entertainment.

"Ready? Let's go to the vinification room and see how the grapes begin their journey into wine."

Tours were shorter now, with the *chai* — where wine was aged — off-limits. She gave a little speech outside the locked doors to describe the oak barrels, explaining the process of selecting new and old barrels and why that was important, the special oak used to build them, the special coopers who did the work. The tourists didn't seem to mind. The morning sun burned off the mist quickly and all felt the contentment of vacation in its rays. One couple kissed at the edge of the vines, much to their friends' amusement.

In the tasting room they admonished each other to taste and spit and not drink too much and to 'bottoms up.' Anthony Simms stood alone, solemnly sipping and swirling his wine. As the tour ended, the Englishmen including Anthony digging in their wallets for sizable and very welcome tips, she ignored him. He walked out of the tasting room with the group. She was glad but not convinced she'd seen the end of him.

Back at the office, Odile didn't answer the knock. The door was unlocked so she'd let herself in, piling half the money at the edge of Odile's desk and scribbling a note.

Outside neither of the Langois was visible, nor the field crew who pruned and watered the vines. The bottles in the chai were a puzzle. Maybe Gerard wholesaled other wines on the side to make money. She changed her shoes in the tasting room, tied her sweater around her waist, and put on her sunglasses. It would be a hot walk back.

Simms waited by his car again, the only one in the gravel lot. He hadn't gotten more attractive with time. In fact, just the opposite.

"Hello, Merle. Very nice tour, as usual."

She stopped, crossing her arms. "Did you learn anything new?"

"You probably wonder why I'm here again. I can see you do. And," he laughed at himself and stepped toward her, "I should explain. I wanted to see you again. But I couldn't get up the nerve to just knock on your door."

"And you, who know where I live."

"And me a grown man, you can say it. It's what you meant. I know. It's silly. I get so — oh, you know. It's crazy. I was hoping I could give you a ride home again? Please. I would like that."

She felt the heat on the top of her head and wished she had a hat. The sweat was already collecting on her back. Yet she really didn't want to ride with him again.

"Oh, come on. I'm not stalking you, is that what you think?"

She squinted at him. "It crossed my mind."

He threw up both hands, palms out. "All right, I confess. I did walk by your house, twice, but I lost my nerve." He looked concerned suddenly. "What did you do to your arm?"

"Fell off a ladder." She sighed. "Look, Anthony. You're a nice man and I would enjoy a cool ride back into town. But as I told you, I recently lost my husband. It probably doesn't look like it but inside I am still mourning. It would be wrong for me to let you spend your money on me when nothing can come of it."

A pretty speech. Being a cranky widow had to be good for something.

His smile frozen, he opened the car door. "A ride then, and nothing more."

She straightened and closed the door. "Have a lovely afternoon."

There was no way she was getting into that car again. He backed up and turned around, glaring at her. The walk home was very hot and her arm ached. A few cars passed going in the other direction. She kept an eye out for Anthony but he didn't show. She didn't have to jump into the ditch — this time.

As she turned onto rue de Poitiers, there he was. The white Peugeot sat in front of her house. The idiot. What did he think he was doing? She walked right up the sidewalk to her door and unlocked the padlock. He was out of his car in a flash.

"Merle, I want to apologize. I just thought we —"

She spun to face him. "No. I can see you are a gentleman. You have to respect that I am saying no."

She fumbled with her key, her hands shaking a little as she shut the door behind her. He sat in his car, looking straight ahead out the windshield, fingers tight on the steering wheel. *Drive away.* He turned to look at the door and she jumped to the side. With a roar the Peugeot, and Anthony Simms, were gone.

For good, she hoped, pulling out some cheese for lunch. In the garden she could see eight shutters propped against the table, freshly painted. She shook out her shoulders, trying to dispel the unpleasantness of Anthony Simms. Had she seen the last of him? She fixed a plate of grapes and cheese and bread, poured two glasses of wine, and took the tray into the garden.

Pascal was under the cistern, washing his face and hands. "After lunch I turn them and paint the other side. Then take the others down." She showed him the food. "I have to go play some cards today."

"Ah, right. Use your charm and guile."

"Charm? *Moi?* "

She drank Pascal's glass of wine as well as her own, then went upstairs to lie down. She gulped a couple aspirin for the ache in her arm. An old person's siesta, for the widowed and the maimed.

She woke up groggy in the afternoon heat. The second-floor bedroom collected it, especially with the shutters off. A ceiling fan over the bed is what she needed. Another job for the electrician.

Pascal was lathering blue paint on the old wood shutters, some of which really should be replaced. Rebuilding a house, making it livable again, could become a mission. This house had become hers as much as it ever was Weston and Marie's. It was Tristan's birthright, his heritage. Maybe she wouldn't have to sell it at all. The wine would be worth a few thousand dollars, maybe more. Maybe enough to keep the house until he went to college.

The rug warmed the room with its faded colors, despite the worn spots. Tristan's little bed made a decent sofa, although she still wanted a gold chenille one, there in front of the fireplace. And an armchair, a big fat one to curl up in and read long novels on wintry days. She couldn't imagine winter in the house, not when the weather was so hot. Would the house be drafty and cold? Did it get cold here, did it snow? She would come for Christmas, someday.

Someday.

ON THE WAY TO THE CHURCH the Bordeaux lawyer called her back. He promised to look into her case, to speak with the inspector and find out what progress was being made. She told him about her confiscated passport and demanded it back. He was polite, if not reassuring. He would call her back again with news, if he had any.

Madame Beaumount didn't seem surprised to see her. Merle stuffed another bank note into the wooden box in the refectory and was led into the basement of the church again. Madame slapped the white gloves against her skirt to clean them and stared at Merle's cast. The gloves were thin, stretching awkwardly over the cast on her right hand. When Madame saw that they would work she left her alone.

She found more names she recognized this time. Redier, Saintson, Taillard. An Yves Estephene Redier was baptized in September, 1923. Another boy, born 1925 to the same parents. She found the marriage of the Sabatini's. How had she missed it before? Josephine Chevalier had married the Italian in 1938. No sign of them after that.

According to the bartender the Chevaliers had moved away after the scandal. If Laurent Chevalier was Marie-Emilie's father, he would be over ninety if he was still alive. Merle kept looking, searching for something she knew had to be here, if she just looked hard enough.

The hours passed quickly in the windowless basement. She went over the same pages, again and again. The routine was like preparing for a trial, looking for precedents, researching back and then back again, farther into history. Finally, when her back hurt and her eyes had begun to burn, there it was. Two names she knew, 'Dominique' and 'Redier.' She had looked at every 'Dominique' in the book. She wasn't sure what she was looking at.

"Dominique Eloise Redier, baptized April 5, 1936."

Her parents were listed as Andre Thomas Redier and Catherine-Juliet (*nee* de Neuvic). Backtracking she found the mother's and father's baptism, in 1918 and 1915. Marriage in 1935, and the father's death in late 1936, just a month after his daughter's birth. Dominique's confirmation in 1946.

Merle scribbled down dates, names, then sat back in the hard chair, stretching her shoulders. Was this the Dominique of the letters? What was her connection with Marie-Emilie?

Merle pulled out "1950-2000." In 1954 Catherine-Juliet remarried, to a man named Carlo Lombardi. Did Dominique marry? She may never have returned to Malcouziac.

Scanning the end of the 1950's and half through the '60s Merle found nothing more. She must have missed something. Back to the beginning, she scanned the '50s where the handwriting was so flowery she had trouble reading it. It looked like the writer had gotten old and feeble. There, at the start, 1950, Dominique again. How had she missed her? A baby boy baptized. She was a mother, at, what? — fourteen. No father listed. No name for the baby, just "*garcon.*" Baptism was June 3.

Writing the information in the notebook she sat back, letting the information sink in. Harry was born in the village. His birthday was May 30, 1950. She felt a chill up her spine.

Could it be? Dominique was his mother? She scoured the births again, focusing hard on every entry for 1950. Only one fit his birth date.

Harry had been adopted? If he had known, he never mentioned it. But he never talked about his parents either. She searched for more on Dominique but found nothing.

But other Redier's— 1971, another *garcon* Redier, Jean-Pierre, born to yet another brother. The gendarme — and the mayor —both related to Dominique. Merle straightened up the room, tore off the gloves, and ran up the stairs.

She watched the cobblestones, walking through the village, the names swimming in her head. Dominique Redier, daughter of Andre and Catherine-Juliet. Mother of Harry Strachie. If it was true, she had given birth at fourteen, then — who was Harry's father?

MADAME SUCHET'S PEA GREEN DOOR opened in a whoosh. Merle handed her a bouquet of red and pink roses in a vase. Madame sat her visitor down, insisting on slices of quatre quart, the ubiquitous pound cake. When she could wait no more, Merle interrupted a treatise on roses.

"*Excusez-moi, madame.* I have a question."

Madame Suchet sat down in a yellow print chair. Merle asked, in French, "Did you know a young girl in the forties named Dominique Redier?"

"*Ici? Dans la ville?*"

"*Oui.*"

Yes, here in the village. Her brown eyes flicked to the window. She arranged her hands, took a deep breath and blew it out. Would she talk, that was what she was asking herself. Should she? Her eyes grazed Merle, then back to the window. A minute passed. Merle ate a bite of pound cake and silently begged for trust, for help.

Then the older woman cleared her throat.

"She was two or three years younger than me. A pretty girl, a blond. I didn't know her well."

Merle felt her breath leaving her. Finally, someone was talking. "She grew up here."

"I haven't seen her since the war, since I left. I never heard of her again."

"Do you know her mother, Catherine-Juliet Lombardi?"

Mme Suchet nodded. "She has been gone some years."

"Died?" Another nod. The older woman was looking at her straight on now, as if waiting for the real question, begging her to ask. "I'm trying to track down Dominique. That little scandal attached to the house? I think I know what it was."

Mme Suchet was silent in her assent. Merle waited, then blundered on, unsure how this next question would sit. "Did she — " It seemed too impolite for the French of Mme Suchet's generation. Was she knocked up, had an illegitimate child, got in the family way? What did you say? Merle searched for the words.

"I think she got herself in trouble." No argument from the old woman. "Was there a place for young girls to go when they were—" She hesitated, searching for a term. "—Becoming a mother?"

Madame looked uncomfortable, then corrected her. "*Avant d'accoucher.*" Before the lying-in. "There was a convent. "

Poking her head out the kitchen door, she wondered if Pascal had found out anything from the gendarme. He was still painting. She went back into the front room and stared at her notes from the parish records. Harry was adopted. It had to be true. He was born here, and there was no record of a birth at that time that could be him except Dominique Redier's son. She got out the letters again. There was the line: 'How is the boy?' That was why she kept in touch. Dominique was Harry's mother.

Merle was pouring herself a second glass of ordinary Gagillac wine when Pascal came to the door. "That for me?" His face was wet, his hair dripping on the stone floor. Pouring another glass, she carried both into the garden. Pascal was staring at the shutters as she handed him his wine.

She walked to the outhouse. "Do you think we'll ever get in there again? Will they open it up?"

"I don't know. And this pile of stones. What will you do with them?"

"Tristan can move them." She sat on a metal chair in the last rays of sun. It felt warm and good. The wine was going to her head.

"Not another fight?" He perched on the low wall.

"Just fifteen year olds on the loose." She leaned over her knees, her forearms on them, and stared at the mud by the patio edge. Harry, adopted. It wouldn't sink in. She felt woozy in the evening heat. At her feet were stones, piles of dirt. The garden was a wreck, hardly the lovely place it had been when they'd arrived. Rocks, leaves, dead flowers, a nasty trench torn through. Their presence was disruptive, there was no denying it.

"I need more wine." She rose unsteadily and headed toward the kitchen door. Pascal took her elbow before she got in the house.

"You need food. You and me, we go eat some dinner."

Her head hurt as it spun. This garden. This nasty little town. She suddenly hated all of it. For so long this adventure, this summer, had been a dream, an idyll, but now she saw it for all it was — the death of an aging prostitute, a rundown house with a dark past, a village full of hateful strangers who decided before she arrived that they wanted nothing to do with her then proceeded to frame her for murder. And Annie! How could she come into all this, expecting lavender and cheese and loveliness? She covered her eyes with one hand.

"My sister's coming and I don't have anywhere for her to sleep. The garden's a mess. There's a hole in my ceiling. I'm suspected of murder. I broke my fricking arm. Why should I — "

The glass slipped out of her hand and Pascal caught it. "Everything will seem more manageable after you eat. We don't allow wine drinking without eating in France."

"Is that so?" His face was dry now, his black curls hanging

over his collar. His neck was caked with grime and small flakes of old blue paint. "You're too dirty to eat in a restaurant."

"You will come with me while I change my clothes."

"No, I won't." He kissed her suddenly. The shock of his warm lips sobered her enough to know she really was tipsy. She pulled away from him and straightened herself.

"Do I — do I get to watch?"

He smiled. "Do you want to watch?"

She took several shallow breaths, so close to him they exchanged oxygen. "Are we still talking about dinner?"

The shower helped clear her head. Everything was manageable. It was just a moment there when things looked bleak. Her list ran through her head the way it always did but fuzzy with the wine effect. Annie needed a bed, didn't she? She wanted the extra bedroom finished. What about Tristan — was camp going well? She hadn't an email since he first got there. Pascal's lips seemed more, well, pressing. She turned to the mirror, rubbing it clear of fog.

"Be logical," she whispered to herself. She rubbed the coarse towel over her body. Thin, with protruding bones, chapped skin, calluses, age spots — plus a damp cast on her wrist — this sack of bones sagged in all the right places. She looked in the mirror. From any angle she looked, well, not that bad, but certainly not young.

She leaned close to the mirror. "But he likes you, old woman."

THE RESTAURANT SHE CHOSE was the one with the truffle omelet she had been dreaming about, Les Saveurs. Everything else was expensive as well, rack of lamb, trout, beef. She leaned over the large menu toward Pascal and whispered, "It's *tres cher*."

He shook his head. "Order whatever you want."

He ordered a small pitcher of house red wine and poured a thimble-full into her glass. Service was quick and friendly, by a young woman who Pascal said was the daughter of the owner. The chef's Cordon Bleu diploma hung proudly on the wall. The restaurant was paneled in dark wood, with a cornucopia of fake fruit and vegetables on the sideboard, unlike expensive French restaurants in New York with their fancy tablecloths and elegant flourishes. In a room off the entry she could see the regulars, laughing and eating at a small table.

"Did you eat lunch here?" she asked, sipping slowly on her wine as they made their way through elegant appetizers of shrimp and asparagus. "With *le flic*?"

"I didn't see him today."

So he wasn't as obsessed with Justine LaBelle and her sad death as she was. Why would he be? That would just be the inspector and herself. Cutting up the shrimp was difficult. It almost squirted off the table. Finally she stabbed it and bit off a piece. Pascal was sipping his wine.

She swirled hers, safer than drinking it. "Do wineries generally buy from other wineries for resale?"

Pascal chewed his bread. "I wouldn't know. Did you see some?"

"In the *chai*. Gerard won't let us take tours through there but I sneaked in."

He shook his head. "Keep out of there. I told you he is —"

"What?" She leaned over her plate toward him and whispered. "Tell me what he's up to. Something — fishy?"

"Stay out of it. No sneaking around." He looked past her to the back of the restaurant. "Isn't that your friend from the tour?"

She glanced over her shoulder just as Anthony Simms looked up. He was sitting alone, stuck in a back corner.

"He's not a friend," she said. "Don't look at him. I don't want him to think I talk about him."

"But you do."

"He's a creep."

"He wants to be your boyfriend?"

She rolled her eyes. Just the word was ridiculous.

Pascal pouted and said mockingly, "He looks so very sad. A plate for one. So terribly lonely."

Merle smiled. "Not my problem." Their appetizers were taken away. Pascal reached into his shirt pocket and brought out a small piece of paper.

"For you," he said, sliding it across the table. On the paper was written two names: 'Justine Labelle — Dominique Redier.'

She stared at the writing. "The same person?" she whispered. She was Harry's mother — ??!. That tired, crazy old whore? Oh, God. What can of worms had she opened?

He sipped wine, enjoying her surprise.

"But — but you said you didn't talk to the gendarme." He hiked his shoulders. "Someone else gave you the name? Who?"

He held up a hand. "I gave them immunity."

"I knew these people knew her." She stared at the paper. "This is the name of —" she lowered her voice "—the mayor." Pascal's eyes flashed. "So, he knew her?"

"Usually you know people with your name in a village this size. There are others as well."

"Jean-Pierre," she whispered. Pascal stared at her, agreeing with his eyes. His lamb with roast potatoes dotted with rosemary arrived. He picked up his knife and fork.

"You must know what this means. Someone, perhaps many people, knew her, knew who she was and what she was."

"She had relatives in this village. Yes." He looked at the people sitting next to them, American tourists deep in conversation about their meal. "Your special omelet gets cold."

It was big enough to feed her for a week. She cut off a piece and hummed with the taste of truffles, woodsy and delicate and unique among mushrooms, dug from the roots of ancient oak trees. The village's mayor and only policeman were in the family of the murder victim. No one talked about the murder. Was that because they knew more about the victim, and perhaps the perpetrator, than they let on?

"How is your dinner, Merle?"

Anthony Simms stood by the table, smiling down at them. "I've had the truffle omelet myself, and also, yours," he nodded to Pascal. "If that's the lamb. Delicious."

Pascal leaned back in his chair. "How was your dinner?"

"Excellent, thanks. The duck tonight." He patted his stomach and looked abashed suddenly. "Nice to see you then. Have a good evening."

He backed away, bumping into the waitress who spilled water from a pitcher onto the floor. He mumbled apologies and ran from the restaurant.

Pascal winced. "Poor guy. What do you call them, a spaz?"

A laugh escaped her, unbidden. "Another naughty word, Pascal." She tried to pull her focus back, to enjoy the rest of her meal. She tried not to think about Dominique/Justine, or the fact that she was Harry's mother. It didn't change who he was, the man he had been. "You didn't learn all your English from MTV."

"I've been to the United States. A couple times."

"Where?"

"New York City, of course. And Washington, the capital."

"There's a lot of territory besides that."

"Where have you been? To Texas and Montana and Chicago?"

"To France, twice," she said, smiling. "But I haven't been to most of the states either."

"I have a confession. I have never been to Normandy or Brittany."

"And so close. Shame on you."

"When you go to heaven you get check marks next to your name for every new place you visit. The more check marks, the bigger your wings."

"A lovely thought. If you believed in heaven."

Pascal reached over and took her hand. "What if — "

"What?"

"Just in case there is a heaven we go on a trip tomorrow. We drive to Provence or Biarritz, or somewhere you've never been."

This was progressing pretty quickly. One drunken kiss and they were off on a trip together. She smiled, a little wary even as she felt — or because of — a rush of desire for him.

"I can't."

"You work too hard. Do you take a day off and enjoy yourself?"

"I'm confined to the village, remember? Besides there's too much to do." Time off made her anxious. She needed progress. It didn't escape her that having true free time made her more nervous than a romp with a fine, young Frenchman. She told her family this was a vacation but it definitely was not. It was work, getting the old place in shape. She needed to check things off her list.

"I have company coming, Tristan and my sister. Tuesday evening."

"This is Friday. That's three, almost four days."

And she knew that. Was her calendar back? It was depressing to think so. "Where would we go? I mean, if the inspector let me go."

"Anywhere. But I see a problem. Between us we have no car."

In her mind she saw the shutters closed, the house empty. Vulnerable. *No.* The wine. She couldn't leave it. Strange how attached she had gotten to her basement treasure. Two or three days with the house unattended? It gave her chills.

"What if —" She put her hand on his now. He turned his palm up and grasped her fingers. "We decide in the morning."

She woke in the night, wrapped in the sheets. He had grunted when her cast rubbed his ribs. Rolling toward him, she propped herself on pillows and stared at his profile against moonlight, the pointed chin, the straight nose, the muscular shoulders. Her body didn't feel old anymore. He made her feel the way Harry had twenty years before, a feeling she'd forgotten, of hunger and contentment.

They had almost run home in the starlight. Whatever had made her cautious in the restaurant had evaporated with the twilight by the time they reached rue de Poitiers. He had kissed her neck as she climbed the stairs, and moved on quickly as they reached the bedroom.

He smelled of garlic, and wine, and sex. She ran her fingers through the thicket of hair on his chest and his eyes opened. She had wanted to touch him, and now she couldn't stop. She felt grateful more than anything. She wasn't the cold-hearted bitch she imagined she was, no — *had been* with Harry. Whatever she'd been, that was in the past, the other Merle who forgot how to feel, how to love. Pascal had found, then revived, something in her that had withered, hardened, and almost died. Always, always she would be grateful to him for that.

He pulled her on top of him, warm and strong. With her face in his capable hands he whispered, "What are you doing, my little blackbird?"

32

THE NIGHT WAS DARK AND FULL OF STARS when Hugh Rogers tapped on the door. The smell of sweet florals scented the air. The house served its purpose, imposing with a blue mansard roof, the sort of grandiosity you would expect from a village mayor. The glow of window light spilling onto the carefully raked gravel path. The wisteria, past its prime, hung limp on the wrought iron fence while the clematis crept over the arched gate. The walk was lined with rows of small flowers in white and orange, militaristic in their precision.

A servant answered, an elderly man in a pinching navy uniform. Rogers gave his name and was admitted to the salon. A squat brass lamp illuminated a circle of light near a threadbare needlepoint chair. He preferred to stand.

Redier entered the room wearing a blue cotton dressing gown over his trousers and undershirt. He looked annoyed. Rogers shook his hand politely. The mayor stuck both hands in the pockets of the thin gown, fists balled. Like his house he was tall and pompous, his gray hair in place and a pair of rimless glasses perched on his nose.

"We need to discuss payment," Redier said. Hugh had expected as much. It always came down to money. "I am taking all the risks. My office, the *gendarmerie*, all will be scrutinized when this is over. You will disappear but I will stay to face the music, as you say."

"You said you could handle the scrutiny."

"Of course. But —" The mayor walked to the cold fireplace and placed a hand on the mantel. An ornate clock whirled behind its glass case. "I have both keys. One to the house, one to the gate. What will you pay for them?"

"She changed the locks, you said."

"The new key, that is the one I have. The locksmith gave it to me in exchange for help with his taxes. There is always a way a mayor can help his populace."

"Bloody patriotic of you. But this concerns me how?"

"You need the keys. You —"

"But there you're laboring under a falsehood. I can get into that house any time I want, without your keys."

The mayor glared at him under bushy white eyebrows, as if the force of his will could move mountains. "You cannot."

"Oh yes. In fact I don't need your help at all."

"We have a deal, Mr. Rogers. On your honor, you will change nothing." The mayor reddened, angry. "You know how we got the gate key? From her, from Justine! One of the men — he was rough, he frightened her but it had to be done. Now we are complicit."

"Ah, the merry band of frog bunglers. Very subtle, tossing her off the cliff. And so now we have the inspector to deal with, complicating matters. If only you people had showed a little finesse."

The mayor stomped over to him and stared down his nose. "Do not lecture me on finesse, Mr. Rogers. The French invented it."

Hugh couldn't suppress a chuckle. "Yes, I see. And tact as well."

"You were to be done a week ago. You must finish and go," the mayor sputtered.

"Right. So the deal is 80/20, take it or leave it. I don't need your filthy key. All I need is for you to keep the inspector out of the way. It's taking a bit longer since you allowed the American to move in. I can't very well barge in, now can I?"

"The inspector thought it was a fine idea. I had no choice."

"Then give the inspector the name of your man who did the deed. That will clear the American and she will go home. Then we wouldn't even need my little diversion, although God knows it'll be a doozy."

The mayor shook his head. "I cannot do that."

"So we see where your loyalties lie. No doubt it's your idiot nephew you're shielding. Well, you've made your choice. Just don't get in my way, old boy." Rogers brushed imaginary lint from the mayor's dressing gown, causing Redier to bat his hand away, horrified. Hugh stuck his finger at the man's chest. "Do your part. Stay out of my way."

33

IN THE MORNING OVER ESPRESSO in the kitchen Pascal turned to Merle. "North, south, east, west. Where shall we go?"

He had told her he would rent a car, a convertible, so they could feel the world go by. But she couldn't. "I have to stay in the village."

"Let me talk to the inspector. He will make an exception if you are with a Frenchman." He put his arms around her. "I can very persuasive."

She wanted to tell him about the wine. She hated that she had lost her trust in people since Harry died. As if his betrayal had soured her belief in goodness. She wanted to think Pascal was good, that he was who he said he was, that he wasn't after that wine he liked so much. She could see goodness in his eyes, in his touch. But she was raw, needy, and that made her wary again.

"What if — we make our own little resort here. Less expensive, and very private."

She kissed him and the regret of the decision balanced with the relief. It was too much responsibility. She couldn't burden him with it.

They set to work transforming the garden. Pascal rallied, finding an umbrella and two fold-up lounge chairs somewhere. A keg from the basement was topped with a piece of wood for a table. She shopped for a special dinner and he shopped for wine and champagne. By noon they had locked the shutters to the house and declared a holiday. He gave her a foot massage. She gave him a one-handed shoulder massage and they filled the big washtub with warm water and bubble bath and soaked their feet and laughed at themselves.

"You have no swimsuit? No problem," he said grinning. So she sunned herself in her black lace underpants and nothing else, after aligning the umbrella to shield the view from Yves and Suzette's upstairs window. He wore a swimsuit the size of a slingshot. She liked it very much.

Several times she felt herself getting up to do "something." This relaxation state, especially in her home environment where the tasks glared at her — FIX ME! — was difficult. Pascal began to massage her palm, which was not only incredibly sensual but made her forget everything practical, all her lists. He made her close her eyes so he could describe where they might be. Biarritz, he said, with miles of white sand and blue ocean, waves breaking against the beach. Fish frying at little shops, the coconut of suntan oil, hairy Spaniards flexing their muscles, buxom Frenchwomen bouncing along and little naked children playing in the surf. The fresh tang of salt and seaweed. The sea wind, raw and wild. Sailboats off the coast, fresh mussels.

"Are we drinking wine?" she asked drowsily.

"White wine. So much we can barely stand up. But we don't need to — we aren't going anywhere. This is where we want to be."

As the sun lowered they made love in the afternoon heat, his hands warm against her body. Making love again, as good as it was, made her feel suddenly sad. For Harry, for all the nights they — or at least she — had spent alone, for the nights she didn't care that he spent in the city, for the relief she'd often felt at his absence. For the time — there it was again, that dirty word — for the time they'd wasted.

After dinner Pascal lay naked beside her on the bed as the sky turned purple. "What was he like, your husband?" He rolled over on his side. "If it is okay to talk about him. Harry?"

"Harry. He was older than me, by five years. Short, in a French way. His mother was French. He lost his parents when he was four. I think it made it hard for him to love. Or maybe I just — " Was it her fault? Was she to blame? She couldn't shake it.

"What?"

"He was a good father, a good enough husband. But something was missing. "

"He had lovers?"

She glanced at him. "At least one. He had a child with her."

"It happens," he said.

"Not so much in the U.S. I didn't find out about it until he was gone. His little girl, the one we never had — I couldn't have any more children — I don't know if it was that or I wasn't — oh, shit." She wiped the tears angrily with the back of her hand. Pascal rubbed her cheek with his thumb and waited for her to speak again. She loved that, just the patience of a man.

She looked away from the ceiling, into his eyes. "You know what? I didn't love him either. Oh, at first, but not for a long time. I made myself believe that I did. All those years. I didn't even realize it until he was gone."

"How did he die?"

"A heart attack, at his desk. He worked a lot."

"So maybe his heart was finished. Maybe he was not lovable."

"But I did love him once — at least I think I did. Then something happened. I stopped. Sometime, somewhere. I don't know why. Maybe I never loved him. Maybe I don't even know what love is."

He licked her neck, slowly, and sucked on her ear lobe. As she held her breath, he whispered into her ear, "Do you want me to show you, cherie?"

THE NEXT MORNING THEY SLEPT LATE, waking only when room overheated from the sun. The make-believe beach didn't seem big enough for conversation. She felt raw and alive in a way she hadn't felt for so long she wondered if she was still practical, rational Merle Bennett. She held Pascal's muscular hand across the gap that separated their chairs. She went topless again, safe in her walled beach. How many summers would it take to go comfortably topless at a real French beach — five? Ten? What would she be doing in ten years?

She shut her eyes, blotting out the future, while Pascal went to a bistro, bringing back goat cheese country salads they ate with more white wine. They did nothing. The word 'NOTHING' careened in her head until she understood. You could do nothing for one day. The world would not slap you down. You did not become a nothing if you did nothing for a day.

Early Tuesday morning Pascal sat in the garden, drinking his coffee, quiet. They were dressed now, back to their old selves. Was he regretting this nothing-weekend, wondering how to extricate himself? Better not to know, to accept this little gift, this sunburn on her stomach, this aliveness, mental and physical, for what it was and nothing more.

Albert came over to introduce his neice. His sister's grand-daughter, Valerie from Paris, was dark-haired and adorable, just fifteen. Tristan arrives tonight, she told them, promising a dinner. Pascal went back to work on the ceiling, nailing up the last of the lath.

Merle walked slowly out to the winery for the afternoon tour. In the tasting room she reapplied lipstick and brushed her hair. Did she look different? A little sunburnt, that's all. When she was young she imagined everyone could tell when she'd had sex, that she smelled different, looked different. But this was France. It was safe to assume everyone made love before breakfast. Even you, Merle Bennett.

The group bought nine jugs of wine, pleasing Odile — if that thin smile could be called pleasure. Merle didn't mind the walk home. A group of workers in a tiny pickup truck passed her, standing in the back, chanting, fists waving. Was there going to be a farm strike? What would that mean to Château Gagillac? She walked on, finally used to French drivers who intentionally passed so close her skirt blew up. She wore scarlet underpants just for them.

The setting sun turned the sky purple, the oaks on the hillside lit through from an inner fire. In front of the house, a little blue car. Annie was here! She saw Tristan's head over the roof and began to run.

34

AFTER WINE FROM CHÂTEAU GAGILLAC, a dinner of pork roast and potatoes with Albert, Valerie, and Pascal, and a tour of the house and garden, the company went home. Annie and Tristan were tired from their travels. In the garden, under the acacia tree, the expected talk of trips around the surrounding countryside came up. Annie was excited to visit old castles, museums, wineries, and babbled about Lascaux Two, the re-creation of the stone-age cave with the incredible animal paintings.

They sat in the garden as dusk fell. Tristan claimed fatigue and went inside to listen to music. "So where have you been?" Annie said, leafing through her guidebook.

"I haven't been anywhere," Merle said. "Tristan didn't tell you?"

"Tell me what?" Annie had braided her hair and wore a peasant blouse with wide, turquoise trousers and Birkenstocks, full vacation mode. "You fell off another ladder?"

Merle told her about the squatter's death and the compromise her lawyer had made to get her the house. "I can't leave the village without the inspector's permission."

"That's bullshit. I'll talk to him tomorrow." Like Pascal Annie had full faith in her skills at persuasion.

"There's another reason I can't go. Come on, I'll show you. We have a secret room," she said, pulling her sister inside and getting Tristan to push the cupboard back. In the basement Merle unlocked the wine cave. Annie's eyes were wide as she descended through the trap door. "Go on, step in," Merle said, pointing the flashlight down at the step, then at the racks of dusty bottles.

"Oh my God," Annie said. "Have these been here for hundreds of years?"

"Just fifty or sixty. But in wine years, that's better than a hundred."

"Really?" She was examining the bottles, holding them up to

the flashlight.

"I searched around on the internet. There are three labels, three different years. The Pétrus could be worth a thousand dollars a bottle, maybe more. The others a little less." The search had actually placed their value much higher but Merle didn't want to count on that. Unlike Harry she preferred to low-ball.

They locked up the cave and pushed the cupboard back into place. Outside, they brushed the spider webs off their clothes. "What are you going to do with it?" Annie asked.

"Sell it, I hope." Merle sat down again on the iron chair. "Someone else knows about the wine. The woman who was living here with Justine LaBelle gave me the key to that gate. She told me 'they' would kill for it."

"Who's 'they'?"

"It could be the mayor for all I know. He hates my guts for some reason." The mayor had been hostile from the beginning. Why didn't he want her in the house — because he knew about the wine? Or was it because Justine LaBelle was a Redier, one of his black-sheep relatives? "Look, it's important that nobody knows about the wine downstairs. I haven't told anyone except Tristan. It's like sitting on buried treasure. It makes me a little crazy."

"Why don't you just get it out of there?"

"How? I haven't even told you about all the stuff that's going on. I'm working at this winery — touring English-speakers around — and there's something funny going on there. There might be a farm strike. And then there's the outhouse." Merle waved her sister over to the latrine. "We were demolishing a wall inside and guess what we found — a skeleton. Somebody had put this woman, dead or alive we don't know — rocked her in behind this stone wall."

"Christ. Have you got any ghosts with chains rattling in the night?"

"Just mice. But I'm on the lookout."

Annie leaned back in her chair and let her head drop back. "I suppose we can't drink that wine. It's too expensive. It'd be like drinking gold."

"We drank two of them. We had to find out if they'd gone bad. We have one more vintage to examine."

Annie's eyes lit up. "You know how to make a girl feel welcome." She looked around the garden, at the crime tape on the *pissoir*, at the roof, and laughed. "I brought twelve books. I thought I could get all caught up on my reading."

Merle lay awake next to her sister, listening to the village go to bed. The sweeping of steps, a rug beaten against a wall, a cat howling, a shutter latched. She made a list in her head for tomorrow. The caulking needed work. The rock pile needed to be moved. Annie might help paint the bathroom ceiling. She'd wanted excruciating detail about how her klutz of a sister had broken her wrist. The stupid thing was hot and dirty and it itched. The grate for the chimney — Pascal, perhaps.

Annie's shoulder was silhouetted against the window. Merle hadn't told her yet about the discoveries in the parish registry. If Merle could have avoided it now, she would. But she owed it to the woman to uncover the truth. Dominique, a blond child playing in Malcouziac's streets, grew up to be a Bordeaux whore named Justine LaBelle.

A sad story but a familiar one. Was it because of her fourteenth year? Who had made her pregnant, debauched her, sent her on a long and winding path ending at the bottom of the cliffs of Lucrezia? Who could be so cruel?

THE NEXT DAY WAS SUNNY AGAIN; it had been weeks since rain had fallen. The stones felt warm to the touch as the sisters passed the houses. Merle opened the door to the gendarmerie where Madame Cluzet pointed them to the inspector's hotel where he had gone for lunch.

The hotel sat on a back street, definitely the economy place. The paint was peeling on the shutters and the carpet in the lobby was worn and dirty. They walked through to a darkened bar where a small group of tables and chairs formed a smoky lounge. The inspector sat in a corner, papers spread over his table, contributing to the fog.

"Capitan Montrose, that's his name," Merle whispered. "We have to speak French with him."

He stood up as they approached through the tables, taking off heavy black-rimmed glasses. He wore a rumpled gray suit and white shirt, more bureaucratic than fashionable. His tie was blue, his fingers tobacco stained. Merle introduced her sister and they shook hands.

"Sit down, please." He waited as they settled into chairs. He discreetly turned his paperwork over.

"We need to speak about the passport, and confining my sister to the village." Annie leaned forward, engaging him with her eyes. "This can't continue. You must return her passport to her or we will have to protest through the U.S. Embassy."

"I am sorry, madame. Your sister is a suspect in a murder investigation."

"And what's happening? Is there progress?" Merle asked. "Have you found Sister Evangeline or any other witnesses to the murder?"

He stared at her silently.

"You haven't found her dead, I hope."

"*Non.*"

"Are you going to charge my sister with a crime?" Annie asked.

"We shall see," he said.

"She has a job in New York City. You can't keep her here indefinitely. She has a family at home."

"I'm retaining a lawyer. Antoine Lalouche in Bordeaux," Merle said. "Do you know him?"

"*Non, madame.*"

"*Monsieur l'Inspecteur,*" Merle began, sitting forward now, "I have some new information about Justine LaBelle. Maybe you already know it." He nodded for her to continue. "She was born here in Malcouziac, and her real name was Dominique Redier. Did you know that? Redier. She gave birth to an infant when she was fourteen years old. My husband was that child. The couple who adopted him owned the house on rue de Poitiers."

"What?" Annie whispered.

Merle stared at the policeman. His stony expression never changed. "That is why, as Justine LaBelle, she returned to live in the house. That was her connection."

He smoked and thought about that. She continued. "Her name was Redier. Both the mayor and the gendarme share that name. Are they perhaps the ones that Sister Evangeline warned me about? The ones who would kill to get into the garden? Was it the bones in the latrine that they wanted to conceal?"

He tented his fingers, concentrating hard on her choppy accent. Could she trust him with the knowledge of the wine? She shivered involuntarily.

Annie said, "Have you identified the remains?"

"Without a missing person report, some idea who she might be, it is very difficult. After the war, records were lax. So many people died or disappeared, or left the country in those years."

"My sister is making progress on this case. Not necessarily more progress than you, *Monsieur l'Inspecteur*." Annie smiled and by God he smiled back. "But please let her work. Let her leave the village for day trips to gather more information. We have been very open with you, Inspector."

"Where would you go?" he asked.

"To a convent," Merle said. He didn't need to know why. Annie shook his hand and turned away but Merle stayed. He asked, "When?"

"Today. Sister Evangeline wasn't a nun. But we will find out today for sure. I think she was hired to get into that house."

"To kill Justine LaBelle?"

"Possibly. But why would she give me the key?"

As serious and solid as he looked, he also appeared adrift, as clueless today as he'd been on day one, the stains on his shirt accumulating. "I do not think you are a murderer, madame, but I cannot afford to take chances. You will not make me sorry."

Outside, Annie waited for her. "What is all this about Harry? He was adopted?"

Merle put her arm through her sister's and pulled her toward the plaza. "Super-genealogy sleuth, here. His birth mother was the woman who was killed. I'm sorry to have to tell you this, Annie. It's embarrassing. But she was a prostitute, that's what everyone says. An ugly old whore from Bordeaux."

"So those people in the car accident on Long Island weren't his parents?"

"Adoptive. I don't even think he knew he was adopted. Guess where we're going now that you got me a day-pass?"

"Lascaux?"

"Equally as thrilling. Right after I give Tristan his duties as guardian-in-chief."

THE HILLS TO THE SOUTH OF MALCOUZIAC rose and fell with each stream and valley, turning at small towns perched on hilltops. The sky was an infallible blue. She drove Annie's rental, a little Peugeot. Annie sat with her knees curled under her, reading her guidebook. A fundamental differences between sisters: Merle had not brought one guidebook with her; she'd had to buy one here. Annie brought three.

"It says here that the Carmelites came to France after the death of St. Teresa. She was that super-nun in the Holy Land who reformed the order. They were wild and she made them all calm down and look inward. Made it contemplative and cloistered."

"I've heard of her," Merle said. "Teresa of Avila."

"Right. That was in the 1500s. The first Carmelite convent was founded in 1604. Now there are almost a hundred in France. No wonder Frenchmen are such horny bastards. Present boyfriends included."

"You have a French boyfriend?"

Annie smirked. "The Carmelites were suppressed during the French Revolution. Oh, this is good. Right before the revolution was King Louis the fifteenth. His daughter Louise became a famous nun. He — *au contraire* — was famous for his godless debauchery. You remember Madame de Pompadour? And Madame du Barry. His lady friends."

"So Louise — his namesake — was the shining example of virtue? Princess and nun?"

"Something like that. This convent we're going to was founded in the twelfth century. That was men — monks. They died out, or something, about the fourteenth century. There were soldiers occupying the place during the revolution and most of the good stuff was stripped out of it."

"So when did the nuns come?"

"After the revolution. They went off to England, most of them, to save their necks — although some of them went to the guillotine to save France — then they came back to France around the 1850s." Annie looked up. "Turn here, left, left. It's only a mile."

A small sign on the lane read: *Monastère du Carmel*. The buildings looked like a well-kept farmhouse, two stories high and large, with numerous stone outbuildings and an ornate iron gate where Merle stopped the car. "Is there a bell or something?"

Annie looked through the windshield. "They might not even talk. You know, vow of silence."

Merle shut off the car. "We've come this far."

A shield with crosses decorated each side of the tall, padlocked gate. "Should we shout?" Annie whispered. A nun stepped out of a building, her long habit, white wimple, and black veil recognizable from the distance. They waited, neither Catholic but sharing a glance of anxiety as the nun approached. This was another world, inside these gates, where virtue and purity ruled.

The nun was young, and surprisingly, wearing sandals. Her scrubbed face was dusted with freckles under the tight wimple. Merle asked her in French if it was possible to research birth records here. That she believed a relative may have spent time here. Not a nun, a lay person.

"Birth records?" The young nun, her hands hidden inside her sleeves, frowned.

"Nineteen-fifty."

"We moved to this location in 1962," she said. "There have been no births here."

"Can we speak to Mother Superior?"

The nun frowned and walked back to the house. The sun was hot, and they had only brought water and fruit and a little bread for lunch. Across the fields they could see women working in the rows, hoeing, harvesting, watering. They wore blue shifts and straw hats. Merle and Annie drank the rest of the water, sitting in the car with the doors open, taking advantage of the shade the vehicle gave them.

A half-hour later two nuns came out of the main house. A tall, older nun unlocked the gate and waved them inside. They passed several buildings then, moving through a large, hand-carved door into a dark interior of a tile-roofed, windowless building. Merle blinked in the dim light. The air was cool, heavy with candle wax and incense. A barn-like space with a soaring roof of rough wooden beams, stone walls, and wooden pews, in the front sat a small altar with a white statue of a woman on it.

The tall sister, a wrinkled, haggard woman, pointed to the back pew. "You may pray." Their light footsteps faded, the door closed. The only light in the chapel was from two small round windows, one at each end in the upper point of the wall, under the roof.

What did a cloistered nun pray for day in and day out — world peace, a calm heart, rain? "I am not going to be a nun," Annie whispered. "Just so you know. And I'll hold you back."

"You could be a Buddhist, wear pink and shave your head."

"Not going to happen. If you become a nun Pascal can't give you hickies anymore."

Merle snorted as the big door opened with a loud crack. They jumped to their feet. The silhouette of a nun, short and wide, her girth accentuated by voluminous garments, blinded them for a second.

The nun with the keys, obviously her consigliore, walked beside her. The round nun was old, they saw as she walked toward them, with triple chins and jowls. Her eyes were bright but her skin had the pallor of failing health. Her name was Madame Françoise. The tall nun helped Madame Françoise into a pew. Merle made her request to the Mother Superior, to look at birth records for information about a relative who may have had a child here.

The tall nun answered first. "We were located in the village until 1962. We have some records from the early years." She looked at Madame Françoise.

"You are American?" the old woman asked.

"Yes, but my husband was born in France. I think he was born in your monastery."

"Where is your husband now?"

"He died. In April." Merle felt her sister's hand on her knee. "But for my son, for his legacy, I want to know who his true parents were. My husband, I believe, was adopted."

Madame Françoise's eyes were not gentle. "The records are very sensitive. These girls came to us for sanctuary when they had nowhere else to turn. We cannot break the trust they showed in us."

"But she's dead — " Merle blurted, then bit her tongue. Madame Françoise and the nun exchanged glances. "All of them are dead now. My husband, his mother, his adopted father and mother. There's no one to ask."

The nun said, "You know who is his mother?"

"I did some digging in the church records. Her name was Dominique Redier," Merle said. "Better known now as Justine Labelle."

Madame Françoise sat very still. The other nun let out a long breath that seemed to echo off the walls of the chapel.

"Do you know her?"

"Dominique came to us many times over the years. Here and in the village." The old woman wet her lips. "She was a troubled girl. We heard about her passing. We prayed for her soul that night as we have many nights before, that she found peace and love in Jesus."

"She was an excellent gardener," Merle heard herself saying. "She must have learned that from you."

"She was excellent in many ways," the tall nun said sharply, "just not in the ways of the world."

"Was she a nun?" Annie asked.

"She could not live a contemplative life."

"Not after what happened to her," Madame Françoise added. "She tried, many times. We prayed together for her salvation, for her acceptance of His will, but there are sins of the world that even God cannot make right. We trust that she made peace with the Lord, as He has forgiven her as he forgives all sinners. We remember her in our prayers."

"But, what happened to her?" Merle asked.

"A man," the nun spat.

"A man brought her to us the first time. She was with child, desperate. So very young," Madame Anne said softly. "He said her family had sent her to live in the street, so ashamed were they."

"A man came with her?" Annie asked. "Do you know his name?"

"He was a stranger to us. A foreigner."

Merle bit her lip and asked, "An American?"

Madame Françoise closed her eyes. "I knew Americans from the war, the ones who came down in parachutes. Yes, he was an American."

"A soldier?"

"In the past, he said. His French was good."

"Do you remember his name?" A long pause. "Was it Weston — Weston Strachie?"

Madame Françoise took her time, searching her memory, as if wanting to be sure she was right. "Perhaps. It has been many years."

Outside the chapel a shuffle of feet began, suddenly, then the chatter of women's voices. The nun's eyes flickered toward the door as if eager to join whatever was going on out there. Merle said, "She had her baby at the convent?"

"No. She was with us for awhile, a month or two, then the woman came to take her home. We didn't see her again for some years."

"The woman?" Annie asked.

"She said she was the American's wife, that it was proper and Christian that Dominique have her baby at the home of the father of her child. That she wanted to take care of the girl, to make amends."

The echoes in the chapel swallowed up the old nun's voice. Had she said the American was the father of her child? Weston *was* Harry's father after all? But that would mean he had —

"This woman," Annie asked. "She was Weston's wife?"

"So she said."

Merle said, "*M-Madame, encore, s'il vous plait.* The American's wife came here, took Dominique away, because he, the American, was the father of her child?"

"Dominique went with her willingly. She had received letters. From the woman, I think." Madame Françoise folded her hands. "I prayed we had made the right decision, that God had sent Dominique to us, and the woman as well. I was a novice then and these decisions were not mine. Dominique was a young girl, so naïve about the ways of the world. She returned to us years later when life was so hard for her."

"It was always hard," the nun said.

"But why? Why would Weston's wife take in the girl that he — you know, debauched?" Annie asked.

"I questioned that," the Mother Superior said. "But she was a very pious woman, kind and gentle. She said this was penance for what her husband had done. To try to make it right. The girl had no one. Her family would not help her. They had disowned her. We prayed that the woman was as full of the light of Jesus Christ as she appeared."

She must have been a saint. Merle tried to picture herself taking in Courtney while she carried Harry's child. As much as she felt sorry for Courtney, it was very unlikely.

"One more question. Did you ever have a Sister Evangeline here?"

The nuns looked at each other. "We don't know that name." Madame Françoise took a rattling breath. "Then Dominique had a boy? She told us of trips back to the village, but not about the child. He was your husband? Was he a good man?"

The sky through the tiny window ached with blue purity, the vast loveliness of ether. Merle thought of Harry, the way he was years ago, when she'd married him. Full of mischief and love. The day Tristan was born, the flowers he'd bought, dozens of roses in every color. It all came back to her now, the good memories. The dark house in the suburbs he'd bought for her, the one he hated. Oh, Harry. She looked out the high window above the altar, where the sky was as bright and new as a robin's egg. *Are you there, Harry?*

"Yes, Madame," she said. "He was a good man."

35

WHEN THEY RETURNED FROM THE CONVENT Tristan announced that Albert had invited them all over for dinner. He had roasted a chicken, and they sat around his table, drank wine, and ate chicken and small potatoes and *haricots verts*. Tristan sat next to Albert's niece, Valerie, who was much more socially advanced than he was. The little vixen flirted and pouted, making everyone laugh and Tristan turn red. Merle sat next to Pascal and tried not to flirt. Annie and Albert got to talk more tonight and were soon swapping stories. Tristan told the story of discovering the skeleton dramatically, with flourishes.

Valerie's eyes glowed with excitement. "But who was *eet*?"

"That is the question, mademoiselle," Annie said. "We'll have to wait to find out."

"Can they tell exactly who it was from the bones?"

Annie explained. "They might, if they had a clue who it was. But as it is, probably not. Just general stuff, like a man or a woman, how old they were when they died. Unless they have dental records. They'll have to check for missing persons."

Pascal said, "During the war — both wars — it was chaos. It could have happened during the war, perhaps. After the last war things were not —"

"Organized. You think fifty years ago then, not a hundred?"

"Hard to say. But no one has lived in the house since, what?"

"Since 1952," Merle said. "That's when Weston and Marie-Emilie went to the States." She looked at her plate, deep in thought. The scandal of Dominique's pregnancy had driven her family from the village. Did the village also drive Weston and his wife away?

Albert told them of seeing a truck full of farmers that afternoon. "I'm afraid there may be a strike."

"The grape-growers?" Annie asked. "What would happen?"

"Nothing much," Pascal said. "At least for the grapes it will be just talk until after the harvest. They aren't doing much now anyway, just worrying about what the prices will be in the fall."

Albert said, "There was a rally last year near here. Some of the growers were very angry. They broke into a large cave and stole bottles of wine in protest."

"Were they caught?" Tristan asked.

"Yes," Albert said. "But they received very light sentences because they were just making a point."

"A mistake," Pascal growled.

Merle squeezed his arm. "You are such a political roofer."

Albert laughed. "Everyone is all opinion in France."

"THIS SOFA IS HORRIBLE."

"As comfortable as I am French. No wonder Albert wanted to get rid of it."

It was nearly midnight. Merle opened the third bottle in the stash in her suitcase, the Château L'Église-Clinet, after dinner at Albert's. They sipped and proclaimed it unspoiled and amazing. The Victorian settee, horsehair stuffed and tattered, found by Albert that morning at the local brocante, was lumpy and unattractive even with the shawl thrown over the holes. They arranged pillows from Tristan's bed under themselves, improving comfort slightly, as he ran in from the back.

"Where're Pascal's binoculars?" He clambered up the stairs. "Where are they, Mom?"

"What makes you think Pascal has binoculars?"

"Because I saw him looking out the window. Up there."

Annie asked, "It's dark out. What do you need binoculars for?"

"There's a huge fire, about a mile outside of town. Valerie and I saw people going out there with hoses and buckets, like an old-time fire brigade."

They followed him upstairs. He was rummaging through the toolbox left in the loft room. Merle pushed open the window and scanned the dark countryside for the glow of flames. "It must be out already," she said.

What was Pascal looking at with binoculars up here? Was he suddenly a birdwatcher? Or had he been using his job as a roofer and handyman to spy on her neighbors? A prickle of suspicion rose up her spine.

Tristan pointed over her shoulder. "There it is, on top of the hill."

The clump of trees on top of the far hill surrounded the large manor house turned into a winery by the conglomerate. As they watched a pine tree exploded in flames. "The house is made of stone. It won't burn, will it?" Annie asked. Another tree went up.

From the garden came Valerie's voice. "Tristan! *Allons-y!* We must go! They need every person to help with the fire!"

THE POPULATION OF the entire village and surrounding estates clogged the tiny lane leading to the hilltop manor. Annie, driving the rental car, observed that it seemed doubtful all these people felt a strong desire to save a multinational corporation from destruction. Cars and trucks, bicycles and farmers and children of all ages, streamed along the lane, parking in ditches to keep the road clear. Somewhere a siren whined, then another. When they'd pulled off the road, Merle opened the back and handed shovels, buckets, and gloves to the Tristan and Valerie. They vanished into the crowd running toward the blaze, into the darkness.

Annie handed her a garden hose. "*Allons-y, ma soeur*. Hit the road."

Merle stood for a moment, watching the chaos and excitement. She had felt uneasy leaving the house, double-checking locks on the windows, doors, and shutters. With the village abandoned, a break-in would be simple. At least Yves and Suzette next door stayed home, *laissez-faire* about someone else's fire, drinking cognac on their front stoop. They agreed to keep an eye out for hooligans.

Annie and Merle joined the stream and were half a mile up when a fire truck arrived, lights, horn, and siren blasting through the vineyards, shooting scarlet on the hillside. The sisters stepped between two cars and covered their ears.

Up on the hilltop flames roared through the dry woods at the hilltop, lighting up the sky. Smoke billowed, dropping ash on the crews, farmers, young men, women, old people. Annie tried to volunteer but the orders were incomprehensible. They saw Tristan, running with buckets of water. The grounds of the chateau were burning, bushes flaring as they incinerated. A gazebo went up in a flash and a whoosh, collapsing as its roof burned. The fire hose shot a stream of water onto the rooftops and the edge of the woods.

Talk raced through the spectators. The old manor house, mansard roof dating it in the late 1800s, was used as a tasting room for the conglomerate's winery housed in large outbuildings — like Château Gagillac but grander. The manager of the winery came back from the edge of the fire, covered with soot, his eyes stinging and red. The women next to Merle called him some unflattering names.

She felt a hand on her arm. Albert stood in his coveralls and beret, staring into the fire and smoke. "Is my niece in there?"

"They're are keeping the kids away from the flames."

He scuttled off to find Valerie. Later she saw him talking to a man at the far side of the singed lawn. As a bush nearby exploded in flames, his face was illuminated — it was Pascal. He was talking, gesturing, then he ran back toward the fire. She wondered again what he was, why he needed binoculars. Did Albert know his true identity? Had Albert "placed" him with her?

After two hours Annie and Merle walked back to the car to wait for Tristan and Valerie. "I'm worried about them, Annie," Merle said, "but I'm also worried about leaving the house. And with one hand I'm not much use out here."

"You mean, the wine?"

Even at two o'clock in the morning the village was lit up, shutters open. Down *rue de Poitiers* women stood outside in their robes and curlers, talking. It was a relief. With all these people about, mischief would be limited. Every other night the village was buttoned up by eleven.

"You'll be all right?" Annie said. "Look around. I'll wait."

The house was just as she left it. Waving to Annie, Merle re-locked the front shutters and door. She turned on all the lights, poured herself the last of the Château L'Église-Clinet, and curled up with her novel on Tristan's bed.

At five Annie drove up with the fire crew. Merle had dozed a little but was up, unlocking the door for them. Tristan and Pascal went into the kitchen to make hot chocolate. Valerie went home with Albert. Pascal was covered in soot, his face half-wiped clean, shirt sleeves rolled up, ash on his shoulders. On his head he wore a dirty red bandanna. He poured them cups of cocoa and they sat around the dining table, stunned with fatigue. Tristan explained his duties, wetting down the lawn, in under three sentences. He drank half his chocolate and put his head on the table.

"Some big corporation owns that winery, right?" Annie asked Pascal. "Do they use imported grapes?"

He raised his eyebrows. "There is a rumor that the fire was set by other grape-growers, *les petits vignobles*, who don't like their practices."

"Like those rabble-rousers Albert saw?"

Merle set down her cup. "Is that what you've been doing up on the ladder and from the second floor window? Spying on the vineyards?"

Pascal's face flattened. Annie looked at her sister. "I'm going to take a shower." She went into the bathroom and shut the door.

Merle couldn't keep the outrage out of her voice. "So all this was just an act? All this — " Kindness? Affection? Biarritz-ing? "You're not really a roofer, are you?"

"Yes. But — no." He looked in his cup.

"You got Justine's real name so easily. You're a cop."

"I wanted to tell you."

"Well, we aren't that close."

He winced. "I am undercover. I can't tell you what I do. Even if I could I wouldn't. It would put you in danger."

"So you are using me *and* protecting me?" She shook her

head. "But what about the rest — about — " She looked down at her son. His eyes were closed. It was all too trite. She wasn't the helpless blond in this story. She was just some fool, the widow on the rebound, an easy tumble for a man with velvety eyes and a cute accent.

He said, "We can talk about it, later when we're not so tired."

"Why should we talk, Pascal? What is it I don't understand?"

He stood up. "When you feel like talking, we will talk. But now, you are angry. And we have been up all night." He looked down at Tristan. "It is not a time for it."

THE HOUSE, AND VILLAGE, lay in silence all morning. The rattle of a truck on the road up the hill woke Merle. She lay on the bed next to Annie, numb. She had finished grieving. But something was undone. Maybe she should just go home and figure out the rest of her life.

She closed her eyes, fell back to sleep, and dreamed about Pascal rubbing the duties out of her palm, as if remaking her lifelines. It was very annoying. She woke up sweating. Today was the day to get the cast removed. Albert had offered to go with her. But Albert was the one who had found Pascal, so he knew Pascal was a cop. He had used their friendship to get Pascal up on her roof.

She went to the doctor's office by herself. So there had been a reason for her mistrust. Her gut was a powerful weapon. But she also believed him good, hadn't she? She refused to believe intimacy meant nothing. But maybe for a man. What kind of man was Pascal?

She tried to put it out of her mind, flipping through ancient copies of Le Figaro and Elle Maison. What she wouldn't give for Better Homes and Gardens right now, or good old Good House-keeping.

A woman came out of the back, holding a bandaged hand and arm. Odile Langois's hair was falling out of its pins, stuck to her forehead and neck. Her sweater was off one shoulder, showing her bra strap. She looked bewildered and tired, her clothes dirty and stained with wine. "Odile?"

She startled. "*Oui?*"

"*Ca va? Votre main?*" Merle pointed to her hand. Odile blinked, turned on her heel, and ran out.

The doctor snipped off the cast with sharp pincher-scissors and rubbed her skin with various potions. The arm looked puckered and damp, almost moldy. The doctor told her to be careful with it for a week or two. No handstands.

"Did you just treat Odile Langois?" He said yes. "Did she get burned in the fire last night?"

"Oo la la, many burns. Docteur Angiers was up all night."

"Was she hurt badly?"

"No, not Madame Langois. A cut. Sixteen *points de suture*, how do you say — stitches. She cut herself on a wine bottle. While packing them for shipment."

Merle flexed her hand as she walked home, dismayed with the wrinkled skin and puny muscles, the tan line from the faux beach. Château Gagillac had no bottles of their own. How had Odile cut her hand? What were they up to?

She and Annie walked to a sidewalk cafe for lunch. They ordered house white with coffee on the side. Their lunches came, huge salads. Annie groaned, "I'll fall asleep before this is done." As they finished Annie leaned close and said, "There's an old woman watching us. Over your left shoulder, on the sidewalk."

"What's she doing?"

"Talking to a shopkeeper, that woman at the grocery store. They are both looking now."

"At us?"

"There's nobody else out here. And they're pointing." The rest of the cafe was deserted. "Okay, look now, she's about to go."

The woman was plump with gray hair pulled back from her lined face, wearing an ordinary black skirt and blue blouse ensemble, low black shoes. "I might have seen her at the market. She's probably just related to the punks who flap their arms and caw like crows whenever they see me." Annie looked incredulous. "Something about me they find ridiculous."

"Did you whoop their puny French asses?"

"I'm trying to set a good example."

THAT NIGHT THE VIOLENCE CONTINUED. Roving bands of farmers tossed empty wine bottles at trucks as they passed on the highway and dropped water-filled bottles from second-story windows in town. Pascal came by just before dark as they were eating dinner, to warn them to stay inside. The rumor was the farmers had set the fire.

Annie pulled him inside and gave him a glass of wine, Château Gagillac from the plastic jug. Tristan jumped up.

"I better go tell Valerie and Albert," he said. "Unless you did already?"

Pascal watched the boy dash out the back. "I think he has, what do you call it, a shine? For the mademoiselle. You have it off," he said, grabbing the jug and pouring Merle a glass. "Your arm."

She stretched out the pale limb. "Gorgeous, isn't it. All skinny and moldy."

He was smiling at her when a crash of breaking glass came from outside. They ran to the windows in time to see a group of teenagers running away from a pile of green glass shards on the neighbor's steps. Pascal said, "Come, let's close the shutters." Outside, they pushed the shutters of the front windows into place. Pascal was last in, closing the door shutters and locking them with a padlock from the inside.

"And how will you get out, Pascal?" Annie said, smiling. "Or maybe you could stay and protect us from roving grape mobs. Just what are they after?"

"A sort of peasant revolt. Probably they are not linked to the fire. They are using the fire, and the news coverage, to stir up things. They get into the paper, get the ear of their representative. When some persons rise up against the government, or corporations, the feelings that they are the little man, the peasant, the oppressed, all boils out."

"Like the revolution?"

"*Exactement.*" As they latched shutters upstairs he said, "A short jump from water in bottles to the Molotov cocktail. Then, whoosh. Another fire."

"Who's behind this?" Merle asked. "Gerard Langois?"

"And others. They want the government to control imports. A little revolt is good for business. The price for grapes is very low because the imports flood the market. Many small vineyards like the Langois's will go out of business." Shouts, footsteps, boots running on cobbles, tinkling of broken glass punctuated the night. "It is a French tradition, I'm afraid, to strike or make a riot to get what you want from the government. The people do not like violence. They will demand an end to it."

"I certainly hope so," Merle said. "Is Tristan back?"

They trooped downstairs into the garden. The gate was ajar. Merle stepped out into the alley, but Pascal took her arm. "Wait. I will get them."

Annie crossed her arms. "Pascal is very protective. Does he work for the government?"

Merle frowned. "I just found out."

Annie put her arms around her. "Oh, honey. It's obvious he's crazy about you."

"That's why he used my — my loyalty, my trust, and my upstairs windows," she said, pressing her face into her sister's shoulder.

"Maybe that was just the way it had to be. He had to find a place to look at the vineyards, and you were the lucky prize in the box of Cracker Jack."

"Like the Junior Birdman ring?"

"That's why those punks are making bird imitations. Everyone can spot a Junior Birdman."

Merle began to laugh, holding onto her sister, hiccupping and laughing. They didn't notice Tristan and Valerie were back.

"Mom? You okay?"

They broke apart, wiping their eyes. "Um, yeah. Fine." Pascal and Albert came through the gate.

"Where's the key?" Pascal asked. Tristan handed it over and he locked the gate.

"I'll take it back." Merle put it back on the chain around her neck. "Did you get your shutters latched, Albert?"

"They called, my sister's daughter, very worried about Valerie, and what can I tell them? I am just an old man. And there are hoodlums running in the streets."

A frightened look made him look old. Annie took his arm. "You can stay here tonight. Safety in numbers." She guided him inside toward the cognac and the music Tristan and Valerie were playing. Pascal stood half facing the gate as if ready to bolt.

Merle crossed her arms. "What do you do in your cop line of work?"

"Anti-fraud," he said quickly. "Wine. Of course."

"Wine fraud? Like what?"

He stuck his hands in his pockets and looked at the purple sky. "Misrepresentation. Labeling fraud. Wine is big business in France."

"Like somebody says it's a '79 when it's really a '99?"

"Or one of the big Burgundy producers uses grapes from Chile in his bottles. A big scandal." He looked at her seriously from under his eyebrows. "I have been watching the Langois vineyard."

"And what do you see?"

"Some things. Trucks."

"Odile Langois was at the clinic today with a cut on her hand from a wine bottle. Broken while shipping, she told the doctor. They must have shipped those bottles on the same night as the big fire. Is that helpful?"

He swallowed. "Merle, I—"

"I understand. It was convenient. My house, my roof, my view. It's all right."

"You hate me."

She walked to him, feeling the air warm. "I don't hate you, Pascal," she whispered.

He softened into her, his big hands around her waist. He kissed her hard then took her face in his hands. "I tried not to like you, to just do the job. I tried, I struggled. But I failed."

"I will have to serve you more Château Pétrus for fooling me."

"More? I like you even better."

He pushed her behind the pissoir, out of the light from the house, up against the wall. She bumped her head on the stone. "Sorry, sorry." He unbuttoned her blouse, kissed her breasts in a rush, ran his hands down her hips then came back to her mouth. He pressed himself against her, wedging her leg between his. They were in that position, her pinned to the wall willingly when the quiet was broken. Screeching of tires, crashing of glass then shouts: "*Arretez!*" Women, screaming.

"*Mon Dieu.*" He rested his forehead on her shoulder. "I have to go."

"Is there fraud on the streets tonight?"

He let his hands take a last ride down her ·body. "Tomorrow, *cherie*."

36

NEXT DOOR YVES WAS SWEEPING up glass from the street when Merle and Annie came outside. It was early, before seven, but they had a long day ahead. Merle had sent Tristan with a note to the Inspector that she was seeing her lawyer today in Bordeaux. Yves stooped to scoop up shards into a dust pan.

"Is everything all right at your house?" Merle asked.

"No damage. But Suzette is frightened. She wants to return to Paris." He dumped the glass in a garbage can.

"Look at the flower pots," Annie said, pointing to geraniums wilting on the cobblestones, pottery smashed.

"*Un policier* from the Police Nationale just came by here, in riot clothes, the vest and helmet and stick, like in Paris." Yves seemed more excited than upset. "I asked him who is doing this. And he says it is farmers, can you believe it? And they caught the one who set the fire. He owns a winery near here with his sister. They were both arrested in the night. They found empty gasoline cans hidden in their chai."

Château Gagillac? Where else were sister and brother in business together? Merle hated to think of Odile in jail. They walked the three blocks to the lot where Annie had parked her rental car. Tristan met them ten minutes later. Broken glass littered the streets but there was very little other damage. It would probably be over when they got back, especially now that the national police had arrived.

Tristan wedged into the backseat with a picnic basket. He curled up and went back to sleep as they climbed the hills and dropped into the valley of the Dordogne River. Merle drove, letting her sister read her guidebooks and look at the vineyards along the river bottoms and the beautiful bridges.

Bordeaux loomed ahead, with all the joys of civilization,

graffiti, traffic, and parking. It took an hour to find the building after buying a map as big as the Peugeot. They split up at the door to the lawyer's building. "Go do some shopping," Merle said. "I'll be back at the car in an hour."

The office was simple, with scratched wood floors and worn furniture. The girl behind the counter looked sixteen and wore thick black eye makeup on her pale face. Merle had to repeat herself to be understood. In a few minutes Monsieur Lalouche came into the reception and shook her hand.

He was short, dark-haired, and younger than she expected, thirty or thirty-five. He dressed well, in a black shirt and tie, gray slacks. "You prefer English?"

"Thank you. Yes." She sat in his office, another worn chair in ancient leather. He sat on the edge of his desk and put on trendy eyeglasses. "Have you talked to the Inspector in charge of the case, Captain Montrose?" she asked.

He hadn't. In fact all the things she had requested he do before her appointment hadn't been done. He was smooth and apologetic; he had a big trial coming up. But she had wasted her time. "Why didn't you call and tell me not to come?"

"Because there is one thing we should discuss." He sat down in his chair. "The new political climate of the area. Because of the recent violence there is more pressure from above to maintain order. Montrose is incompetent. There is little chance he can make a case against you without witnesses. And has he found any?"

"He says not."

"But still the pressure is building. He will have to produce a warrant against someone soon or lose his job."

She squinted. "And that someone will be me?"

A Gallic shrug. "I spoke to someone I know in the courts in Bergerac. One murder of an old *putain* isn't too much to get excited about. But now, with arson and riots, things must stop. The provincial government will not allow disorder. There is too much at stake with the tourist monies."

"What are you saying?"

"I will try to get your passport back, Madame. And when I do, I suggest you leave the country as soon as possible."

THEY RETURNED HOME in late afternoon, hot and tired. At a small bistro, the one opposite the locksmith on the derelict block, they ate an early dinner. Merle felt strange, cramped, having left the village and returned. She wished she'd never seen Lalouche. As they walked home Annie peeked into the abandoned townhouses, talking about renovating this one, remodeling that one, but Merle watched passersby, suspicious of every look. Were they all Redier's? Had they all decided to sacrifice her for the public good? She needed her passport, and she needed it now. But how could she run out on Justine? She was Harry's mother. No one cared about her, not even the police. But maybe it was time. There were no more secrets. She knew who Harry's real parents were, and what his father had done. That was plenty.

In the evening Merle carried the trash to the can in the alley. An old woman stood in the alley nearby, sweeping up shards of glass. She wore a gray skirt and blue blouse, with a red and orange scarf on her head. Pumps even though she was cleaning. She bent down to pick up the dust pan, then met Merle's gaze.

Merle smiled, holding open the lid of her can. Was this the woman pointing at them at the café? "*Beaucoup de verre, oui?*" Lots of glass.

Her earlobes hung with rhinestone clusters below the colorful scarf covering her steely gray hair. She looked brightly past Merle, into the garden.

"*Voulez-vous entrez?*" Would you like to come in? She stood still as a statue for a moment, then stepped into the garden. Immediately she walked to the new bush, the Reine de Violette rose, cupping a mauve blossom in her hand. "*Vous?* You planted it?" Merle asked.

She nodded, her eyes filling as she began to mumble in French. She was upset, rambling. Merle couldn't understand her. "*Lentement, madame,*" she pleaded: slowly. But the woman sat down on the low terrace wall and let the story spill out of her. She sputtered, her face animated, joyful, sad, reminiscing, angry.

Annie stepped out. "Who's this?"

"That woman on the plaza. I can't understand her. I think she's using *patois*. Get Albert."

Merle held the woman's gnarled hand. She kept up her tale like she'd been waiting her whole life to tell the story. What was she saying — the house? Dominique?

Pascal came through the kitchen door. Seconds later Albert arrived through the garden gate with Annie.

Pascal looked like he'd been up all night, hair greasy and clothes sweated through with stains now dried. "I can't understand her." He sat down next to the woman and asked her name. "Josephine Azamar," she whispered then launched again into her story.

Albert whispered to Annie as she talked. Finally Pascal touched the woman's knee, making her stop. "She is the aunt of someone named Marie-Emilie. Madame Azamar owned this house, inherited from her mother, and lived here during the war. Then she went to live with her husband's family. Her husband has died, so she moved back to the village. She says she gave the house to Marie-Emilie when she married the American."

"Weston." Merle turned to the woman. "Madame Sabatini?"

"*C'est moi,*" the woman whispered, eyes wide.

"Lorenzo Sabatini was her first husband," Merle said. "He died in the war or right after."

Josephine said something then jumped up, scurrying out the gate. "She's coming back," Pascal said.

"Did she say anything about Dominique?"

"She says Dominque was the American's ... mistress. He flaunted her, took her places with him. Shocked the village." He looked at each of them, ending on Merle. "She had his child. Did you know?"

Merle nodded.

"He turned the village against her relatives. They had to

move away."

"But the mayor, and the gendarme? They are —"

"It was the Chevalier relatives who moved away. Marie-Emilie's relatives. The Redier family closed ranks, burying the scandal. She says Weston came to her later to borrow money to go to America."

"Did she say anything more about the child?"

"No. How did you find her?"

"She was sweeping in the alley. She had the grocer point me out. I think she's had a key to the gate all these years too. She planted that little rose bush, after Justine was killed. The whole village must have known she was Dominique."

Josephine rushed back through the gate, pausing to catch her breath. She thrust a small black-and-white photograph into Merle's hands. The background was the garden, and the back wall of the house with a climbing rose blooming by their heads. The kitchen window was in the picture. Weston was a handsome man, with wavy dark hair, bushy eyebrows and a mustache like Clark Gable. A brunette woman stood next to him.

"*Qui est la?*" she asked the Josephine. Who is that?

"Marie-Emilie," she answered.

She stared at the photo, the dark hair. Marie-Emilie was blonde. "I'll be right back."

In the front room Merle pulled out the stack of photographs from the cupboard. The old photograph, from the safe deposit box, showed Weston and Marie-Emilie in front of a brick house. A very blonde Marie-Emilie.

In the garden she put the two photographs beside each other. "*Regardez.*" They all squinted at the images.

Josephine said, "*Cette femme n'est pas Marie.*" Marie-Emilie was dark, like a gypsy, with black eyes and nearly black hair and a big bosom, she said. She was taller than Weston. He was very short, like Albert. This woman, this blonde, must be very small, her eyes are light, her nose is wrong. She is yellow-haired and not Marie-Emilie, Josephine said emphatically.

Merle turned the photograph over: 'Wes and Emilie.' She pointed to Josephine's photo. "This is Marie-Emilie Chevalier? Married to Weston Strachie?"

"*Absolutement.*"

So who was the blonde? Merle asked to borrow the photograph. Josephine said she had memories in her heart and some of them weren't very good ones. She shook hands with Pascal and Merle, Albert and Annie, then walked her dignified walk, broom in hand, out the garden gate.

Pascal stared at the photographs. "He must have been very short for Madame to mention it."

"You don't think it's possible she just dyed her hair blond when she got to America?" Merle said.

"It is not the same woman," he said. The sisters stared at the photographs. Annie shook her head. Albert shrugged.

"Where do you suppose the real Marie-Emilie ended up?" Pascal said.

Annie followed his gaze. "In the *pissoir*?"

A man comes to the countryside in France, as Pascal told the story, because his wife has a free house, because he cannot make a living, for a variety of reasons. His wife is not as pretty or young as the young girls who talk to him on the street. So he takes one as his lover, makes her pregnant. And dumps her at the convent, Annie added.

But his dark, gypsy wife wants a child, Merle said. So she fetches the girl at the convent, cares for her, and the girl gives them the child.

"So far only morally repugnant," Pascal said, "But the American decides he likes blondes better, permanently. He finds one, somewhere. He kills his wife, burying her in the backyard, takes the boy and the new blonde off to America, where no one has met Marie-Emilie. They pretend the blonde is the old wife. Marie-Emilie, the gypsy, becomes Emilie, the blonde."

"They didn't believe in divorce back then?" Annie asked, sipping wine as they spun it out. "And who was this blonde?"

"Divorce was complicated then," Pascal said. "France is a

Catholic country. But the bones will tell the real story. For now, I only have my hunches."

He would try to get information about Marie-Emilie into the system. He knew a man in forensics in Paris.

"The blonde was definitely not Dominique — because she was Justine. Right?" Annie shook her head. "Would you like to come for dinner tomorrow, Pascal? At eight. Earlier if there's a riot."

"The national police have arrived. No more riots," he promised.

Merle followed him to the door. "Has Gerard been arrested for the fire?"

"I'll tell you about it at dinner."

"And Odile too?"

He tasted of salt, cigarettes, and coffee. "Later."

BUT PASCAL DIDN'T SHOW for dinner. They were eating custard Annie made in the afternoon, *creme sans caramel*, she called it, when a policeman in camouflage came to the door with a note. His eyes flicked around the room as if searching for arsonists.

"Is it from Pascal?" Tristan asked. "Read it out loud."

Merle took a sip of wine. "*Cher* Merle. I am sorry to miss your fine dinner. There is pressing business regarding Anthony Simms. Gerard Langois — yes he is arrested — named Simms his accomplice in the fraud of the cases of wine you saw at the winery, which were bottles filled with ordinary *vin du table*. Simms's work was in the news recently — selling so-called 20-year whiskey which is, in reality, crapola. His stalking of you brings to mind the wine you said was in your cave. If you were not joking, this could be a dangerous time for it. It would be prudent to move the bottles out of the house. Perhaps Albert has space in his cave. Pascal."

"You have a stalker?" Annie frowned.

"He came to the winery tour twice, and took an unwelcome interest." Merle looked at Tristan. "Did you ever see him, the Englishman with the funny hair?"

He looked up from his second helping of custard. "You

mean Tony?" The sisters exchanged a look. "I told you. He came by the house when you were gone. Didn't I?"

"No. What did he say?"

"He heard we were selling the house. Wanted to take a look around."

"And did you — did he look around?"

"I didn't think it would hurt." Tristan squirmed. "What?! He was just a guy."

Merle tried to calm herself. "Did you show him the wine cave, Tris?"

"You told me not to. So I didn't." He set down his spoon. "He did ask if there was a basement."

"And you told him —?"

"That we had one."

Annie stood up. "I'll go ask Albert."

"No! I don't want to put him danger. The wine is safest right where it is. Someone might see us moving it."

"Someone like Anthony Simms?"

"Exactly. So far only we three know where the wine is. We'll just be on our guards."

"Plus Pascal apparently. Can you tell the gendarme about this stalker? Or the inspector?" Annie asked. Merle bit her lip. That time had passed. "At least tell Pascal."

Tristan jumped up. "I'll go get him."

He came home at midnight, slightly drunk, without having found Pascal. He had found some boys from the fencing club though, and let them buy him a beer or two.

"Great, just great," Merle said, tucking him into bed.

"At least he has friends here," Annie said. "Is he going back to Blackwood?"

His eyes were shut and his mouth open, asleep and snoring. Was anyone going home? She had no fricking clue what happened next. She threw her arm around Annie's neck.

"No plans tonight. I'm going zen on you, sister."

YVES AND SUZETTE CLOSED UP their house and drove away without a word. It was market day but camaraderie was absent. The farmers who sold at market were friends of the grape-growers, brothers, cousins, uncles, wives, sisters, and aunts. Whispers of the arrests were everywhere.

In the garden Annie put a fresh tablecloth on the patio table and they ate lunch al fresco, trying to keep their eyes off the crime scene tape, the strips of barren dirt through the lawn where the water line had gone, and the fading roses dropping their last petals. Merle closed her eyes, holding the wine on her tongue to taste all the flavors of France in the essence of grape.

Tristan went inside with the plates. "Somebody's at the door."

It was a policeman, one Merle had never seen before, young and spruce and serious under his cap. Behind him were Josephine Azamar and Albert. The policeman held a small white box like Chinese take-out.

Albert stepped closer. "These are the ashes of Dominique Redier."

Merle held her breath, staring at the box. She hoped the policeman wasn't going to hand it to her. Albert said, "We thought, Josephine thought, that you might be agreeable to burying the ashes in the garden."

They buried her at the foot of the elegant, espaliered pear tree. After Tristan patted down the soil with the back of the shovel, Albert pulled a cross on a chain from his pocket and recited some Latin. Annie and Merle bowed their heads while the gendarme fingered his cap. They shook hands then Annie saw them out.

Merle stood with Tristan by the tiny grave, thinking about meeting Justine up at the Shrine of Lucrezia. Did she see Harry in that face? Or Tristan — her grandson? Should she tell him? She hadn't even told him about Sophie yet.

"Hey, don't worry, Dominique or Justine or whoever you are," he said quietly. "We'll water your garden. You just rest now."

They went to dinner at Les Saveurs that night, a last splurge before Annie flew home. The meal was exquisite, grilled lamb, truffle omelet again for Merle who couldn't get enough of it, and for the newly adventurous Tristan, who once proclaimed anything but pepperoni pizza 'weird,' a rabbit dish that tasted 'just like chicken.' In the morning Annie drove her rental car to Bergerac to the train station.

Merle and Tristan spent the rest of the day rearranging furniture. She put up a lace curtain in her bedroom. They moved the single bed up the stairs into the finished loft and put wallpaper on the shelves of the old armoire.

She had trouble sleeping that night without Annie. The lawyer's words careened her head. When would they arrest her? Where was her passport? Where was Anthony Simms — had he been arrested? The moonlight shone on her bed again, just like it had months before. Now it seemed like the natural glow of France, just something that was there. No longer soothing, now it seemed cold and calculating like looking for its chance to illuminate the inevitable.

"MOM, WAKE UP. MOM!"

She bolted upright. "What?"

"Something's going on at Albert's. Look."

"What time is it?"

They pushed up the garden window and leaned out into the night. Tristan said it was past three. Lights blazed at Albert's, then, suddenly the house went dark again. Tristan whispered, "I thought I heard glass breaking."

"Get some clothes on."

Hastily dressed they went out the back door, through the gate, and down the alley. Merle had a strange urge to hold Tristan's hand but instead held his sleeve at the elbow. The night was still and lit only by stars. They knocked on Albert's door. The shutters were closed so it was impossible to tell what was going on inside. Tristan pounded on the door shutters and called the old man's name.

No answer. On her cell phone she dialed the emergency

number, 1-8. Where did it go? She tried in broken French, to describe a break-in, an old man alone, Malcouziac. She read his address off his door. The operator, an efficient woman who seemed to understand, said the message would be forwarded to the local police.

Tristan ran back from the corner. "I saw somebody — in the backyard."

"Oh, hell," she muttered, following him to the mouth of the alley. Her heart pounded in her chest. Tristan was at Albert's gate, pounding. "The police should be here soon."

"Damn it, Albert! Open up!" He rattled the wooden gate. "Hey, old man!" To his mother he said, "I was going to go over the wall but it might have that broken glass on top like ours."

"Let's go back to the front and wait for the cops."

On Albert's street, after they knocked on his door again, lights went on across the street, a man's head came out the upstairs window, scolding. "*Taisez-vous! Nous dormons!*"

"*Pardon, monsieur,*" Merle called. "*Peut-être un cambrioleur.*" A burglar, perhaps.

The man disappeared then opened his door with a younger version of himself. The two joined them in the street. The boy looked familiar — was he one of the tabac gang? His name was Henri, his father was Louis.

"*Vous êtes les Americaines,*" Louis said, nodding, as if he knew all about them. "*Les flics,* they are very slow in the night," Louis said in heavily-accent English. Merle was happy for the company, especially after the two boys ran off to check the alley again. In a moment there was a shout from the cross street. She looked at Louis, with his baggy eyes and disheveled hair.

"Come, madame." They jogged to the corner. The street was empty. They walked around the houses to the alley, also deserted. "Where did they go?"

"Let's check his gate again."

Louis was ahead a few steps. He turned. "Is this your *jardin*?"

Merle stared at her open gate. She had locked it, she was

sure. Did Josephine Azamar open it? In the middle of the night? She pushed it wider, looking around the yard. The yellow light from the kitchen windows spilled onto the ground, framing the dark box of the pissoir. "Tristan?"

"Madame!" Louis yelled. "*C'est Père Albert!*"

She spun around. Albert's gate was ajar too. Louis had opened his back door and was bending over a prone figure.

"Albert!" He had a gash in his head. "Get me a cloth." Louis stood over them, fixated at the sight of the priest, unconscious. She pushed him aside, grabbing a cloth at the sink, wetting it, then holding it to the wound. "Can you hear me? Albert! Louis, call the police again!"

The sound of a motorcycle engine announced the gendarme. He roared up the alley and jumped from his bike. Jean-Pierre Redier wore his street clothes, unless leather pants was a night uniform. "Call an ambulance!" Merle yelled. Oh, what was the word? "*Les services d'urgences! Vite!*"

The gendarme took a long moment looking around the kitchen, then pulled out his cell phone and punched in the number. "Breathe, Albert," she whispered. His chest was rising. He was alive.

Louis spoke to Jean-Pierre. They looked out the door to the alley. The gendarme stepped outside. Louis said, "There is someone in your house, madame." Merle stretched on her knees, keeping one hand under Albert's head. Was it Tristan? "The ambulance is here soon. He is okay? Ah, here are the boys. They come from the street."

Merle's stomach dropped. "Tristan! Someone's in the house!"

37

THE GATE HUNG OPEN. Henri peered over Tristan's shoulder into their garden. He heard the panic in his mother's voice. "What?"

"*Quelqu'un, voila! Un homme!*" Henri pointed into their windows, lit up in the dark night. A man's back was silhouetted.

"Mom?"

"I've got Albert. He's okay! The house, Tris!"

"Oh, shit," the boy said. Jean-Pierre was at the gate now, looking into the garden. He pushed the boys aside and strode toward the kitchen door. "It's that son of a bitch." *The one I let in the house.* "Come on," Tristan told Henri. "Around the front!"

They ran hard down the cobblestones. Skidding around the corner, they saw the man come out the front door, kicking out the shutters. "Wait!" Tristan called but he saw them and turned to the wall. Jumping the short section, he disappeared over the side.

The vineyards swallowed him up. The boys watched as he crashed about in the dark. Henri had a foot on the wall, ready to follow, when Tristan saw him slip through a gap in the wall farther down, and disappear into the streets. "This way!"

The streets were dark, shadowy, with alleys and walk-ways and lots of corners to turn down. The village was a maze at night, with look-alike shuttered houses. "Where did he go?" Henri looked familiar, with his flop of black hair and big honking nose. "*Où est-il?*"

"*Je sais pas*," the boy mumbled.

"Hey." Tristan poked a finger at him. Henri took a step back. "You helped those Bordeaux punks at the fencing tournament. You held me down." The boy turned his palms up and looked sideways. "It was you. Okay, you and me. Come on."

Henri took a step backwards.

"So you're chicken without your friends?" Tristan put up his fists. "Come on, asshole. Give me your best shot. You baby. That's right. *Bébé.*"

The boy raised his fists then. "There you go. Let's see what you've got." The sound of footsteps, running on the cobbles. A man dashed across, half a block away. "There he is!" The fists dropped, the fight forgotten.

The chase went down one street and up another, as if the man was lost. It was dark but to Tristan it looked like Tony, the man his mother said was creepy. He ran funny, like he had a bad leg. At an alley he skidded to a stop and turned in.

Henri got there before Tristan, who wasn't used to running on cobblestones. "*Voila!*" Henri pointed down the alley, a dead-end stopping at an iron gate. They had him trapped. They slowed to a walk, advancing on him.

"Get away from me. This is mine," Anthony mumbled, cradling two wine bottles in his arms. "Leave me alone, you filthy delinquents."

"Hey, Tony," Tristan said. "*Bonsoir,* my man. Having a fun evening?"

Surprise then relief flooded his face. "Mr. Strachie. How nice to see you. I thought you were the police. Or a nasty little frog." They each took an arm. "Watch the wine, please! Thanks much but I'll be off now. Hey! Take your hands off me!"

The boys were as big as Simms, and younger and stronger, and had little trouble marching him back to the gendarme. His running commentary turned increasing vile, with slurs against both Americans and French. He struggled to free himself from their grasp but protecting the bottles kept him busy. When they reached the street where Albert's house sat, they saw the lights of the ambulance. In the flashing red his mother and the gendarme and Henri's father were visible.

"*Regardez,*" Henri said. "*Le gendarme et l'Inspecteur.*"

"Keep moving, creep. Mom!" The grownups looked up. The gendarme and the other cop started towards them. "We got him!"

Simms gave a last, grunting effort and twisted out of Tristan's grasp. Henri kept hold of his left arm and they jumped around on the street, barely keeping their footing. Everyone was yelling, trying to catch Simms. Suddenly Henri had one of the bottles of wine in his hand.

"No, no, you little bastard! That is mine. I'll not be cheated again." Anthony grabbed at the bottle, a spastic lunge. Holding the wine over his head Henri laughed at him, taunting. Anthony's eyes were wide with panic. His toupee slipped, revealing a bald scalp. "Now, young man, let's not do anything rash. Give me the bottle, there's a nice boy. *Donnez-moi le bouteille!*" Pascal and the Inspector moved cautiously behind him, closing off the escape routes. "Damn it, you little shit. Give it to me."

Tristan tried to grab him but he jumped aside. Henri moved the bottle higher, turning it to hang on to its neck, like he was going to throw it on the ground. Anthony cried out, "You have no right! My father paid for that wine and it belongs to me." The Englishman sniveled, hugging the other bottle to his chest. "Give it to me, you dirty swine." He took a step toward Henri.

A chorus of 'No!!' rose as the boy smashed the bottle over Anthony's head.

He stood, stunned, red wine dripping down his bald head, his face, like blood. Green glass scattered on his shoulders, then he slumped to the ground.

Someone threw a bucket of cold water over Anthony Simms. He woke up in handcuffs, lying on his side on the street. Everyone on the block was now awake, standing outside in their bedclothes or hanging out windows. Merle held Albert's hand as he lay on the stretcher. He was conscious now, having come to just before the ambulance arrived.

The emergency crew pushed her gently away and rolled Albert inside the vehicle. She winced as they slammed the doors. The sight of his jovial face so unsmiling was wrenching. Pascal put his arm around her shoulders. "He'll be all right. He is tough." He squeezed her arm. "I'm sorry. I haven't been working on my list."

She glanced at him, his half smile. "Yes, where have you been?"

"You are shivers again." Pascal pulled her close. "Go home. I have to arrest the Englishman. You have my number if you can't sleep?"

After thanking Louis and Henri Merle dragged Tristan away from the excitement. She wanted to go check on the wine. The boy chattered excitedly, recounting the chase and the amazing thing about Henri being one of the guys who helped the out-of-towners at the fencing tournament and how he was all right now that he'd smashed a bottle of wine over the burglar's head.

She set Tristan to trying to secure the front door which had been kicked out, both the frame and the door itself were splintered. The door shutters were done for. He propped them up and brought the padlock inside. The gate was in similar shape, broken timbers and lock busted. She tried to lock it and finally gave up.

The trapdoor was open, the cupboard pushed aside. Merle shone the flashlight down the stairs. "How many bottles did he have?"

"Just two."

"There's more on the stairs. Be careful."

A case or more lined the steps. He'd gone straight for the Pétrus. The door to the cave had been hatcheted, the tool lying on the dirt floor. But inside the rest of the wine was safe. "Count at that end," she said, after they had put the bottles on the stairs back into their racks. There were only five bottles missing and they had drunk three themselves.

Upstairs they repositioned the cupboard over the trap door then Tristan went to bed, still excited. Merle added to her list: wine truck and safe storage, flowers for Albert. Then: passport. A policeman came to the front door a half hour later. She pushed aside the broken shutters. He was to stand guard. He had a rather large gun, she noted happily. She put her head down on the table.

THE SOUNDS WOKE HER. She looked for her watch, still a reflex but an empty one. It was dark outside. Through the broken panes of the front door she could see the policeman, walking back and forth like he was a palace guard, probably to stay awake. Had he coughed? What had wakened her?

She curled into the horsehair sofa, feeling the lumps poke her hips. Just jumpy, she thought, turning down the floor lamp to low. She listened again, and lay her head on a pillow.

There! Again, a sound, definitely from the back. She lay still. Should she get the policeman or scare whoever was in her garden off herself? Policeman. For sure. She lay in the semi-dark, listening. Had she locked the back door?

On cue, the glass shattered. She sat up to see a hand coming through the broken pane and unbolting the door.

The hatchet lay against the fireplace where Tristan had left it. Her heart was pounding as she lunged for it, standing in the shadows under the stairs, waiting for — who? She yelled, "Police! Help! Intruder!" Where was he?

She jumped into the light, brandishing the hatchet with both hands. In her kitchen stood Jean-Pierre Redier flanked by a shorter man. Jean-Pierre looked startled then began to laugh. "*Vous êtes en état d'arrestation, madame.*" You are under arrest. He pulled out his handcuffs and slapped them across his black gloved hand.

"Oh, no, you don't. *Monsieur, policier!*"

"He has gone home. He isn't needed, madame." He grinned at her. "Three's a crowd, isn't that the expression?"

"Mom?" Tristan stood on the stairs in sweat pants and t-shirt. "What's going on?"

"Come over here by me, Tristan." She still held the hatchet in both hands, ready to chop off the hands of anyone who came too close. She felt reckless, and sleep-deprived, and generally pissed off. "Get back!" She swung the hatchet in the direction of the gendarme. Black leather pants, my ass.

Her son vaulted the railing and landed on the floor. He slid sideways to her side. "What the heck are you doing, mom?" he whispered. "That's the cop."

"Reach into my pocket," she said softly. "Get my cell phone and call Pascal. Tell him to get here quick. I'm going to turn a little your way. Don't let him see."

"Where is the policeman? What did you do to him?" she said in French to Jean-Pierre. She needed to keep talking until Tris made his call. She could feel his fingers in her pocket. "Did you kill him like you killed Justine LaBelle?"

"*Quoi?*" said the other man, who was bearded and wore a knit cap. "You killed the *putain?*"

"Stop talking nonsense. You killed her, madame. That's why you are under arrest." He took a step toward her. Tristan crouched behind his mother. She could hear the buttons beeping and coughed to cover the sound. "And you broke into my house, Monsieur le Gendarme. How will you explain getting your fingers chopped off, eh?"

The second man's eyes widened. He stuffed his hands in his pockets. Jean-Pierre lowered his head like a bull. He was a big man, young and strong, and she was making him mad. Some things couldn't be helped.

"She was your aunt, wasn't she? You must have been proud. An aunt who ran around in revealing clothes. A famous whore, right here in town. How exciting for you. It must have been hard to explain. So you pushed her off the cliff so you didn't have to see her parading her pathetic old self around town any more. Isn't that right?"

Tristan was whispering. The gendarme looked around her, craning his neck. He lunged forward and she swung the hatchet, catching him on the wrist with the blunt side of the hatchet. "Get back, you dirty flic!"

He grabbed the handle of the hatchet. She refused to let go, skidding across the room with both hands tight on it. "Go out the front, Tristan!" He turned as the gendarme slammed her against the wall under the stair. The boy put his shoulder to the door and ran.

"Don't let him get away," Jean-Pierre told his frozen cohort. He had a boot on her foot, pinching her toes in a crushing motion. Merle howled and tried to chop at him again, but he had both hands on the hatchet and wrenched it out of her hands.

"Go after him, idiot!" The shorter man ran out the front door.

"Quite the tom-cat, eh?" He dropped the hatchet and grabbed her hands. Slapping on the handcuffs he wrapped them around a stair baluster. She struggled to her feet as he let up on the pressure on her toes. "Okay, where is it?" He began to pace around the room.

"Where is what? Your dick? They all say you have trouble finding it."

He laughed and kept pacing. "Wouldn't you like to know? Like a little taste, would you? The door, where is it?"

"Right behind you. Show yourself out."

He had spun when she said 'behind you,' and now grabbed her arm. He smelled of liquor and sweat. His breath reeked of cigarettes. "You are so smart. You arrogant Americans." He brought his knee up to her back. She moaned at the pain.

He pushed the sofa, pulled up the rug, flinging it against the wall. Through the kitchen and bath, he pounded on the stone floor with his boots, then at the kitchen door, he laughed. Quite fond of evil laughter, was he. He had found it. The scratch marks on the floor had clued him in. He pushed the heavy cupboard aside, pulled up the door, and shone a flashlight on the stairs.

Merle tugged on the handcuffs. They cut into her wrists. The banister upright she was chained to — the word came to her: baluster — was halfway up the stairs, at shoulder level. Her hands were going numb. In the cellar she could hear the gendarme moving around, humming over the wine bottles, setting them back on the steps as Anthony had done.

The baluster was two inches across but carved with spiral indentations. She had so enjoyed painting the stairs. But now... She gripped the baluster with both hands. It wiggled when she pulled. If she could break it without alerting him — well, that was unlikely, wasn't it? But what else did she have?

The hatchet lay on the floor, six feet away. She stretched her foot toward it, pulled it with her toe. But how to get it up to her hands? She put her right foot on the fourth stair tread, eased her hands to the top of the baluster, and swung her left leg over the handrail. Her newly-healed wrist screamed with pain. She wiggled her hands into a better position and lifted her right leg over.

On the steps sat Tristan's hiking boots. She slipped her right foot into his boot. It was way too big, almost falling off. She figured she had one chance. Dangling the boot on her foot she tried to tightened the laces but it was too hard. These steel-toe wonders she didn't want to buy him because they were too heavy for camp — well, time to pay up, dogs.

The clink of bottles just below the trap door — he was too close. She waited until he moved away, back in the cave. She counted his steps, two, three, four, five, then drew back her foot and kicked hard. The post bent but held. She aimed again, a little higher, and swung again. This time the baluster shattered. She kicked off the boot and slipped her handcuffs down to the breach. In a leap she was on the floor. She reached the trap door as he looked up the stairs. He shouted obscenities as she flipped the trap door down on his head and jumped on it.

He pushed up, bouncing her. The cupboard was three feet away. His shoulder heaved up under her. He outweighed her by fifty pounds or more. She couldn't hold him down much longer. She dove around the cupboard as he blasted up out the trap door. With a shove, it toppled, crashing, splitting in two with the top section snapping off and landing with all the dishes and glass and shelves on the gendarme's head. She heard him moan and didn't hang around for the crying.

She ran through the garden, out the gate, and into the alley, her socks slipping on the moss. Albert's gate was closed and locked. She ran down the alley. Where the hell did Pascal live? Who could she trust? Running hard, she passed rue de Poitiers and ran all the way to the inspector's back-alley hotel. The windows were dark, door locked.

"Open up!" She rattled the knob, pounding. "Capitan Montrose!"

"Madame?" He stood behind her, materialized in the night air in his sensible gray suit. "*Qu'est-ce que tu fait?*"

"*Allons-y! Vite, vite!*"

She dragged him through the streets. He didn't complain or ask questions. He tripped a few times, but then so did she, in her handcuffs and socks. "*Ma maison, monsieur,*" she said at one corner. "*C'est urgent!*"

Rue de Poitiers was lit up like Albert's street had been hours earlier. Every neighbor was on their stoop or at their window, at least those who hadn't fled to Paris. Madame Suchet stood in a velvet housecoat, arms crossed, chatting. Great entertainment, better than television, these Americans.

Merle dropped her grip on the Inspector's sleeve and burst in the door.

"Mom!" Tristan ran to her and threw his arms around her. Behind him stood Pascal.

"Did you get him?" she asked. "Where is he? I'm okay, honey," she told her son in a rush.

"In the garden. A special spot." Pascal tipped his head to the back yard. She followed him out the door, through the dark to the pissoir. The crime scene tape was torn. He pushed open the door. Handcuffed around the ancient stone stool, his bloody head resting on the porcelain ring, sitting on the dirt in his leather pants, was Jean-Pierre.

"You bastard!" She spun to Pascal. "Get the key for these off him. Is the wine all right? Did you check it? What happened to that other guy? Did he catch you, Tristan? Are you all right? Did he hurt you?"

The policeman watching Jean-Pierre was the one who had been posted outside her house. He looked at her guiltily. "Where the hell was he while I was being forcibly detained? And where were you, Pascal? What took you so long? Were you sleeping? Are all the dishes broken? How many bottles did we lose?"

Pascal took her handcuffed hands and put them over his head, around the back of his neck. He clamped his hand over her mouth as she talked, adrenaline surging through her. "Get the key! Don't fool around, my wrists are killing me! My feet are bruised, my ankle is twisted —"

"I can't hear you, blackbird," he said. "What is that you say? The only way to stop your mouth is another mouth?"

Tristan laughed.

Pascal winked at the boy. "Okay, if I must."

38

THE NEXT TWO DAYS WERE FULL of repair, human and *maison*, and storytelling. Merle recounted her adventure with the thieving gendarme to numerous officials, from Capitan Montrose and again to his superior from Bergerac, then to a high-ranking Policier Nationale officer in a very strange uniform. Most humiliating that one of their own was so bad, caught in the act. She felt a lot better than they did.

Merle, Pascal, and Tristan dropped all their repairs and drove to the hospital in Bergerac to see Albert. They were not allowed in his room so they left flowers and a note for him with the nurses. His sister's daughter, Valerie's mother, was to travel down from Paris to take him home with her for recuperation.

The doors to the house were a total loss — front, back, and shutters. Andre Saintson, the locksmith, conjured up substitutes, probably from the ruins on his street, and planed and sanded until they fit. He put on new locks, with deadbolts. Madame Suchet dragged a pair of door shutters out of her basement that would serve, a flaky red paint on their boards. They didn't have the pretty round top of the broken ones but they would do.

The cheap dishes and glassware were not mourned, having performed their civic duty on the hard head of Jean-Pierre. He in turn broke a Malcouziac rule and ratted out his uncle, the mayor, the original schemer with Anthony Simms. Pascal was very happy even if the Inspector broke out in a sweat, smoked endless Gauloises, and was generally theatrical.

The wine had mostly been saved. Two bottles of Château L'Église-Clinet had broken when the trap door landed on Jean-Pierre. A bottle of Cheval-Blanc had cracked. But the remainder, miraculously, was intact. Pascal arranged for it to be stored at a government facility but Merle felt uneasy and made him take her with him. It was inside a prison yard in Toulouse. Better than any other alternative, she thought, re-reading the detailed receipt for the 99th time.

THE NEXT MORNING Tristan was clumping down the patched up stairs in the famous hiking boots as she walked in the house. She handed him a pastry.

"Pascal was here. He wants you to meet him. There's a note. He said I was too sleepy to remember." He pointed out the slip of paper on the table. They bit into their *pains au chocolat*. "Mom? Are you going to marry Pascal?"

She choked. "What?"

"He likes you. And you like him, don't you?"

Her boy, almost a man, wore his youth fresh on his early-morning face. His hair stood out in all directions and he gave her that half-smile, just like Harry's. "We live on different continents. But we'll come back here, don't you think?"

"Not if we sell it." He flopped in a chair and inhaled another pastry.

"Would you like to keep the house, come back here in the summers?"

"Would Valerie come back too?"

"Maybe." She read the note: 'Meet me for lunch at Cafe Eloise, one o'clock.'

"I might, like, get a summer job or something."

She ruffled his hair. "Keep your options open. Like Dad always said."

PASCAL LEANED AGAINST THE BUILDING, smoking, as they rounded the corner. He stamped out his cigarette, kissing them on both cheeks, then led them into the bistro with an old checkerboard tile floor and red tablecloths. For some reason she'd never found this restaurant. But she'd be back. If they needed money for college she would sell the house then.

After lunch Tristan left to buy ice cream on the square. Merle and Pascal had peach sorbet and coffee. He reached into his pocket and slid her passport across the table.

She set down her spoon and stared at it, fingering the inside, her old picture with her stringy, gray hair. She leaned over and kissed him. "Thank you."

"I am just the messenger. Montrose has charged Anthony Simms in the murder of Justine LaBelle."

She frowned. "Did he confess?"

"I don't think so. But the intent was there. The wine was a powerful motive." He sipped his coffee. "What?"

"It's just — remember when I was babbling that night? I know you do. When I was facing off Jean-Pierre I blurted out, did you kill your aunt the whore. I don't know why I said it, but it makes perfect sense. She embarrassed them. They'd been shunnng her fifty years. Plus they wanted her out of the house so they could get to the wine."

"Perhaps. Maybe they did it together. We know Simms was at the shrine that morning."

She would go home, and forget about Anthony Simms. But would she forget Justine LaBelle? Not likely. She probably never knew about the treasure in her cellar. What a life she had.

Pascal leaned forward. "About the wine. It's safe now but we should not tempt fate. You know how to call the auction houses?" She nodded. "Did you hear Simms say something about 'my father's wine'?"

She frowned. "Do you think he actually owned the wine? There were invoices in an old file left by Harry's father. One of them was from a British company, in London."

"An invoice for these wines, these vintages?"

"No. Other wines."

"Then I doubt it. Hugh Rogers — his real name — he has a pretty good rap sheet in England. His father tells a tale, he says, of being swindled."

"Out of this wine, *my* wine?"

"It's just another of his cons."

"How did he know it was in the house? I didn't tell anyone,

not even you."

He smiled. "But you did let me drink some, *cherie*. It's my belief that he came here knowing that the wine might be here, even though he had this other business, the wine scam. Probably picked this area for his scam because the house was here."

"Wait. What did you say his name is?"

"Hugh Rogers."

"He called the house. Back home. He was trying to get Harry to invest in Bordeaux futures. So he must have known about the connection with Harry's father — and the house."

"Did you tell him about Malcouziac?"

"I might have mentioned the house. But I didn't tell him where it was. He must have found out on his own." She fiddled with her spoon. "Do you think he has a legal claim to the wine?"

"No." Pascal took her hand. "It is ancient history. An old family story, that is all. He is a swindler, a thief, a killer. I don't believe a word he says."

"You're sure? I don't want to take something that isn't mine."

He looked at her, tipping his head. "The wine is yours, Merle. All yours."

As they walked out into the street she invited him for dinner. "On one condition," he said. "You make your *coq au vin* again. It is just like my grandmother's. And, yes, that's a good thing."

THEY SAT OUTSIDE IN THE GARDEN in the evening, sipping pear *eau de vie* that Pascal had brought. It went straight to her head, making her dizzy even sitting down. Tristan was inside listening to music. The night was quiet, peaceful for once. She listened to the birds in the trees, the frogs in the vineyards. This was the way she imagined her French summer, not full of injury, intrigue, violence. She shut her eyes and tried to forget all that. The music rolled out the open door into the night, American music in a French garden, a perfect match.

She'd thought more about Anthony, or rather Hugh Rogers, and his connection to the wine. If he'd had a decent claim he could have pressed it with her. Instead he chose to steal the wine. That negated any thread of legal claim, she decided.

Pascal held out his hand. "*Vous dansez, mademoiselle?*" The music was Annie's album, old Beatles songs. She swayed in his arms, as he twisted the hair on the nape of her neck. A bittersweet moment made ludicrously romantic by the night sky and his strong, warm hands. Even this — *especially this* — she had never imagined. And why not, her little voice asked, having finally released her from the *what-what?* She felt free, calm. A person who asks *why not?* A new person altogether.

She closed her eyes tightly, memorizing the way he felt, his shoulder under her hand, the smell of his skin, his breath on her ear.

As the song wound down, he took her face in his hands, smoothing her hair. "Blackbird. That is your song."

"Is that what my name means?"

"All your life," he sang in a breathy, French accent. "You were only waiting for this moment to be free."

He pulled her to his chest and sang along with John and Paul — the dark black night, broken wings, blackbird arising — as he stroked her hair. He smelled like fruit and life and sunshine.

Criminy. It was going to be hard to leave.

BOOK FOUR
THE BEGINNING

39

THE SKIES HUNG LOW AND GRAY with flocks of crows squawking in the bare trees. November in London was short, dreary days followed by long, damp nights. A change from her last trip to Europe but Merle wasn't watching the skies. No dawdling this time. Pascal had helped arrange the auction of the "Fine Vintages, Rarely Seen," as the Sotheby's catalogue read. He had called Merle half a dozen times in the last three months. She often missed the calls because she was in meetings or wining and dining the corporates.

She had dreaded starting her new job, but to her surprise she wasn't half bad. She began viewing herself as an anthropologist who studies corporate lawyers, dissects their social structure, mating rituals, and mindsets. They weren't that complicated really. She enjoyed appealing to their generous sides, and most of them were generous if you knew how to press their buttons. Lillian Wachowski called her a magnificent closer and even took her out to dinner one Friday evening to celebrate signing a big firm to a long-term pro bono agreement.

The hotel smelled of fish and chips, full of bus loads of culture hounds. As she checked in, the clerk handed her a large envelope with the auction house imprint. The copies of the contracts she'd signed last month were inside, with more details on the auction. Her father had gone over the fine print and everything seemed in order. She was nervous about the auction. If the prices weren't good, she had decided to refuse the sale. She hoped that didn't happen, but the economy was still shaky.

The auction was in the morning, early, but her internal clock was off and she wandered the streets for awhile, considered a movie in

Leicester Square, watched juggling instead, and window-shopped at rare book stores. A fine mist began to fall as she walked back to the hotel.

"Miss Bennett!" the desk clerk called. He handed her another envelope, letter size with the hotel imprint. Inside was a fax, handwritten. She sat on the edge of the bed.

> *Cher* Merle,
> As you see I am not in London. Things are very busy with the trial approaching. Gerard Langois and Hugh Rogers will be put on trial together for the fraud, a time-saving maneuver which I hope will not blow up in our faces. Rogers now claims Jean-Pierre Redier is responsible for Justine's fall, or alternately that it was an accident. Can you come for the trial, my little blackbird?
> *Pascal*
> PS. Enclosed my translation of the report on the *pissotiere* bones, just completed.

The next sheet, the forensic report on the bones, was short.

> "The bones are female, 20 to 40 years old at time of death, approximately one-hundred-forty-three centimeters in height, brown-black hair, who has not delivered a child. The skull had received a hard blow, fractured: probable cause of death. Bones are contemporary based on clothing fragments and hair samples found within the encasement, possible burial thirty to seventy years past. Without dental records or DNA sampling, identification is incomplete."

She would write to Dr. Beynac, maybe he knew who the dentist was in Malcouziac fifty years ago. But the chances were slim. Weston Strachie had probably wiped out all evidence of Marie-Emilie's existence. The shame of the connection still made her ill. He may be long dead, and good riddance, but he was still the lowest sort of pond scum. She sunk into the worn bedspread. If only Pascal were here, to stroke her hair and tell her it was all over years ago.

THE BIDDING ON THE MALCOUZIAC WINE began at 11 a.m., after a lot of 2000 vintages from Château Latour in Pauillac. Prices for those were good. Merle listened to the talk in the gilded rooms on New Bond Street before the bidding on her wine began, standing with well-dressed men and sophisticated ladies looking at three bottles, the representatives of her lot — Château Pétrus, Château Cheval-Blanc, and Château L'Église-Clinet, their old labels brittle but the glass shiny and bright, cleaned for the day. There was no tasting as they'd done for the new vintages; the bottles were too valuable to open. The Pétrus had the biggest reputation. The wine critic Robert Parker had given it his highest rating, 100 points. You could almost hear him salivating between the words. The L'Église-Clinet was less well-known but might, according to one gentleman, attract those looking for something different.

She settled into the back row, in good line of sight of the auctioneer. With amazing speed the Château Pétrus, 1946, sold for £2200 a bottle. The Cheval-Blanc '47 went for £2100, the L'Église-Clinet, 1949, sold in a split lot, half for £1200 and half for £1450.

Then it was over. Stunned, Merle had to stare at her notes for a moment before the figures sunk in. She punched in the numbers on her calculator, pounds to dollars. On the Pétrus alone, before the consignment fees, over 100,000 pounds sterling. That was more than $152,000 US. On the others, over $240,00. Altogether nearly $400,000. She couldn't believe it. She sent up a silent thank-you to the old bastard, Weston Strachie, then almost fainted from relief.

A ripple, a murmur, then the auction moved on. She drew a deep breath. All that scrabbling, angst, and panic over bottles of wine was finished. Pascal should be here. He had not let her down. He had done what he said he'd do, restoring her faith in men, or at least Frenchmen.

She gathered herself and stood up. She would see Pascal again, sometime. But now there was one more loose end.

THE QUIET VILLAGE IN SOMERSET, a crossroads of two narrow highways, could have served as a set for a Masterpiece Theater program, something from Thomas Hardy perhaps. No thatched cottages, but very nearly. Merle had taken the early train from London after a little solo celebrating — and banking — in London. The village was a couple blocks long in businesses, with old homes mixed in, an inn where she intended to spend the night, a small food shop, a bakery, a garage.

She asked the rental car clerk at the train station for directions to the even smaller village of Hockingdon. A flock of geese honked overhead, pointing her in the direction of the hamlet. Carefully she urged the little car onto the pavement (*stay left/stay left,* her right-handed brain scolded), into the rolling pastures and hills. Hockingdon wasn't far, and she made it there by mid-morning. Fortifying herself with the thermos of tea she'd brought, she parked in front of the Round Robin Inn.

Still there, after all these years, and still open for business. Amazing. Weston's archive of memories, including the menu from the Round Robin, sat on the seat. The fat bird on the sign matched the menu imprint. They hadn't even changed the sign in sixty years. She had found a listing for the inn — complete with plump fowl — in a British touring magazine, but she'd also found six other Round Robin Inns from Leith to Aberystwyth. She hoped she'd guessed correctly. With that sign, she felt sure she had. Closest to London and over a hundred years old, the inn apparently embodied the village, nestled in the center of the single block of buildings.

Pushing through the heavy door, Merle stepped into the lobby. It smelled of grease and wet wool and bread baking. She took a seat in the deserted restaurant. An older woman, plump and red-faced, wearing a dirty apron, arrived at the table with a kettle and teapot.

Outside a motorcycle zoomed by on the street, rounding a school bus and barely missing a small child. Several pedestrians waved their fists in anger. A couple made their way across the street and into the inn.

The man and woman hung up their coats and scarves, chatting as they sat down at the window table. They were both gray-haired but looked youngish, talking in their country accents. Odd to be in a foreign country where you could understand the natives. Merle plucked a scone from the tray.

Tea in a pot was brought for the couple. Merle waited for them to settle in, then stood up. They didn't seem startled at her approach. A good sign, she thought.

"Pardon the intrusion. I was wondering if you might be able to help me," Merle said. "I'm looking for someone in the village who lived here in the fifties, someone who might remember a relative of mine."

They were quick to introduce themselves and find her a chair to join them. "Gavin Towne, and this is my wife, Gloria."

"The fifties?" Gloria said. "Gavin lived here."

"Yes, ma'am. When in particular?"

"Nineteen-fifty, fifty-one."

"I was in school then." He looked over his teacup at her. "Sorry."

Merle told them the memorized fiction, that she wanted to find the woman her father married after leaving her mother. "They divorced after only a couple years, I never saw him again. But I think I might have half-brothers or sisters."

Gloria's eyes twinkled. "Oh, wouldn't that be lovely? Is your father gone now?"

"Sadly, yes. And Mother too." The story of all the related parties being passed and gone had worked at the convent so why not here? But she could feel her mother's fingernails on her neck.

"Isn't there somebody around here who knew everybody?"

Gloria wondered aloud.

They consulted the waitress who suggested the vicar. But Gloria knew he'd only arrived five years before, just as they moved back.

The waitress slapped her cloth over her shoulder. "You should ask Tulliver."

William Tulliver owned the store across the street, and apparently knew everyone. Gloria and Gavin introduced her, telling the shopkeeper of the search for lost relatives. He scratched his head and said, "There's the Westchesters, but I think the old man's gone in the head. Or maybe Lloyd Acres down by Tinsley."

The names flowed out of him. Merle scribbled them down. There seemed to be something wrong with each of them, they were infirm, recently died, or had begun to forget their kin. Then he said, "What about Annabelle Gallagher? She doesn't get out much, but I hear the old girl's still with us."

Gloria had seen the woman several Christmases back — a tough old bird. Liked to talk. Probably knew everyone.

The shopkeeper drew a map to the Gallagher place called Three Oaks, a reference to long-gone trees. The sun came out, scorching the green hills with color as she drove. The old manor house, down a narrow drive, looked neglected, with missing shingles, broken shutters, windblown tree limbs on the shaggy lawn, a tire-less car rusting next to the carriage house. A few decades back the owners of Three Oaks had thrown in the towel.

The knocker was a huge brass lion. A middle-aged woman opened the door — thin, bad dye job, pale skin. "Miss Gallagher?"

"She's in the sunroom," the woman said sullenly, opening the door wider before she remembered to ask, "And who may you be?"

"Merle Bennett. Mr. Tulliver in Hockingdon told me Miss Gallagher was the person to talk to about relatives of mine."

The woman looked her up and down. "Wait here."

Merle looked around at the wide, empty yard, trying to imagine lawn parties and elegant sculpted boxwood and men in top hats. It looked like there hadn't been parties for a long time.

The door opened again. Merle was escorted through the dark house, echoing rooms empty of life and furniture, to a large glass Victorian conservatory with a two limp palms hanging onto life. Under a red tartan blanket sat a shrunken old woman, white-haired and wizened as an apple doll, with bright blue eyes. She wore a pilled green sweater buttoned up to her chin.

Merle introduced herself as a dining chair was dragged in. Jenny dismissed herself to make lunch. Merle pulled the photographs out of her purse. "I'm looking for someone who might remember my father's second wife, in case I might have half-sisters or brothers."

"What's her name?"

"That's the problem. All I know is her first name, Emilie."

"You don't know your father's name?" Merle had a new facial expression, the Montrose deadpan, which she wore now. It was her favorite response to questions she preferred not to answer, something her new job was rife with. The woman squinted at her. "You have a photograph?"

Merle put the photo in her hand, the small, blond Emilie with Weston against a brick cottage. Three Oaks was limestone, not brick, so this was probably the first of a hundred dead-ends. Annabelle Gallagher stared at the photograph, her hand trembling a little.

She handed it back with a sneer. "An awful little man, but she loved him."

Somewhere a clock was ticking. Jenny banged pans in the scullery. Merle blinked. "Excuse me?"

"Never saw the appeal myself," she sniffed.

"You—you know them?"

"I've forgotten his name."

"Weston."

"Ah. 'My Wes,' she called him." Annabelle looked at her sharply. "He wasn't your father. Who are you working for? Are you a collection agent?"

Merle shook her head. "He was my father-in-law. He died a

long time ago."

"Look around. This is all I have left, a few plants and my chair. There's nothing to collect but these old bones, you know."

"Miss Gallagher, I only want information about Weston and Emilie."

"Emilie? Huh." She waved a hand and looked out the greenhouse to the dry yard as if seeing into the past. "He took her away, against all our wishes except her batty mother, and we never heard from her again. End of story. Ran off to France, I suppose — he talked about his business there — or America. I often wondered what became of poor Virginia."

"Virginia?" Merle looked at the photograph. The tiny, yellow-haired woman: not Emilie but Virginia.

"My mother's name. Dear Virginia. Lovely really. An angelic little child, all golden hair and rosy cheeks. My sister doted on her. Until the day she died she fretted about never hearing from her little Ginnie. Tiny, like a child, she was. My sister tried to find her in the States, even hired one of those men, those —"

"Private detectives?"

"Nothing came of it." The old woman stared at her spotted hands. "Is she alive?"

"Sorry, no. She died, a long time ago too."

"In childbirth? I always thought she was too small to have children."

"A car accident. They were together."

The old woman nodded, accepting the facts. "I told my sister it would come to no good. No one ever listened. She's dead then." Annabelle sucked in her lips as she blinked to keep her eyes dry. She tried to say something but covered her mouth with a gnarled hand. Merle waited, the way she did in depositions, for silence to build and emotions to settle. Finally the old woman gasped angrily, "All of them gone. It's so unfair. Two of us left. Me in this wicked old house as good as a jail, and one in a real prison."

"Prison?"

"Very sad the way he's turned out, but after his father's

appalling life —" Annabelle looked sharp again, squinting at her visitor. "You want to hear it? Of course you do. It's made the entire countryside squeal with glee. Me, buried alive in this tomb. Do you know we eat onion soup six days a week?"

Merle bit her lip as the woman rambled on. "It started with my brother. Departed this earth these thirty years. A spoiled, thoughtless man. The heir to this grand estate. He thought he was a fancy chef, or at least could employ one. Bought a lovely old building in London, in the West End. He spent thousands of pounds and lost it all. Terrible business man. And his son is worse. Does something dodgy for a living." She lifted her hands to the glass ceiling. "And that is the legacy of my grandfather, the wise and wonderful Armstrong Aloitius Rogers. Who built this house and had such dreams for all of us."

"Rogers?" Merle blinked, trying to engage this new information. "Your brother's son, your nephew — is he named Hugh Rogers?"

Annabelle narrowed her eyes. "So that *is* why you're here, to squeeze blood from this old stone. Many have tried to recover the money he's swindled them out of. You won't be any better at it. All you'll winkle from this old body is onion soup, I told you."

"No, I — I met him in France. This man, Weston Strachie. Hugh says he swindled his father out of some wine. A long time ago."

A dry laugh came from the old woman's mouth. "Hugh's been barking about that wine for years. Well, don't worry, I want nothing to do with him and his dirty dealings. I'm sure it's some tale Armstrong made up to make himself feel better for throwing away all those pounds. Throw the blame off his own stupidity. Now Hugh appeals to me from his prison cell in Paris. 'Help me, Aunt Annabelle.'" She snorted. "Not likely, laddie."

Merle let her rankle subside. She had more questions.

"Weston came here, did he?"

"Oh, yes. We were all young then. He was a friend of Hugh's father. The restaurant business, always a poor way to earn money, if one must. Let's see. He came several times, I believe. The year

Virginia was here, though, she had just come back from school. It was winter, I recall. He stayed for the season, six or eight months."

"What year was that?"

"Virginia was nineteen, I believe. Sometime after the war. 1950, maybe."

"Why did he stay so long?"

"Armstrong enjoyed having a pal around. Pudge and I were married then but — well. They didn't get along. Wes had energy. He loved to shoot and drink and all. He wooed silly Virginia right from the start. Poor wretched girl. I tried to warn her about men like him but she did love him."

Merle looked at the photo. "Was she wrong, do you think? To run away with him?"

The leafless trees across the back garden made stark designs on the sky. Annabelle's voice was soft. She glanced at Merle then disappeared into her memories.

"Love is never wrong. But where it leads you, that can be the biggest mistake, one you pay for all the rest of your life. I fell in love with Pudge Gallagher against everyone's wishes. He was a buffoon, they said, but I didn't see that. I was blind. I found that out later, to my sorrow. He spent my money and that was that. So were they right about Pudge, about my mistake? The heart doesn't hear that. I couldn't tell Virginia she would be unhappy, that she would, as you say, meet a painful end with him, could I? She would have been unhappy if she'd stayed — although we all liked to think we could have picked out someone better for her than that slimy American. We always like to think we know best for others, don't we." Annabelle sighed. "She was happy, for awhile, do you think?"

"I suppose," Merle said. "Maybe that's —" She stopped. To be happy for awhile seemed like such a small thing.

"All we get. Yes," Annabelle said. "Life is long, I can tell you. It has moments you cherish and those you wish you could forget. You know what the poet said, 'he who kisses the joy as it flies lives in eternity's sunrise.'"

The smell of boiling onions wafted in from the hall. Merle

said goodbye. The Widow and her Gothic Mansion had come to life. The bitterness, the loneliness, the empty rooms and dashed dreams crashed in on her. She shivered, closing the heavy door behind her.

In the car Merle tried to feel the coursing of life through her veins, blood sending oxygen to her brain. *I am alive.* Would she end up bitter and alone like Annabelle Gallagher? *No.* She would not ruminate on her failures, on her faults, on her losses. She *would not.* But she would send Annabelle some money, a ham every Christmas, something to atone for the sins of Weston Strachie. Wait, she had money now. Of course she did. She'd send Annabelle a ham every *week.* She would stop into that butcher shop in Hockingdon.

Yes, and then — she would move on. She sat straighter and said it aloud: "I will move on." Was this the release she'd been looking for? Had she forgiven herself for her blinders and blunders?

The sky was so blue suddenly, the clouds blown off to the west. If this wasn't forgiveness, it was a decent stand-in. It would do. It was reality. She hadn't loved Harry; he hadn't loved her. With any luck she would grow old, he would not. She would hold her grandchildren, he would not. It was a hard bargain but she had no choice. Accept death, she'd told herself. But what about life? Was she ready to accept all it offered, good and bad? To open her arms, her heart to anything and everything?

She opened her bag — that much she could do — to put away the envelope of photographs and memories. There, tucked into a side pocket, was the purple marble little Sophie had given her. They had all met one Saturday in early October, Harry's extended family: Courtney, Sophie, Tristan, and Merle, at a pizza parlor on the Lower Eastside. There were nerves, lots of them, except for Sophie who danced in wearing her red party dress and pink tights. The little girl brought gifts, a marble for Merle and a rabbit's foot for Tristan. It had been so hard to tell Tristan about them. He had cried, pounded his bed with his fists, and cursed his father. Then the next week he sent her an email from school that he wanted to meet Sophie. She was his sister. She was a connection to his father, he wrote, a way to keep him in his life. Tristan was so much wiser than she was, in so many ways.

The marble was smooth, veined with white. She rolled it in her palms. Now that she didn't have to worry about Tristan's future, she was concocting a plan to put aside money for Sophie from the auction proceeds. But first she would invite Courtney and Sophie for Thanksgiving dinner at her dark, shadowy house. It would be awkward, difficult. There would be more nerves and probably tears. But she would be brave. She wasn't afraid of the future now.

She shut her eyes and thought of Pascal. Was that love? Probably not. She went days without thinking about him when she was busy. But she could love again, it was possible. Her heart wasn't cold and dead. There was something left inside her, a yearning for more. Another chance. A richer life. A second half.

Possibility. Was that all that it took to feel alive? Could it be that it wasn't getting the thing you desire itself but the anticipation, the struggle, the dream of it that makes living so amazing? Was it that simple?

The noon sun peeked out again from the clouds, glinting off the car's chrome. The old woman's poem echoed in her head. 'Kisses the joy as it flies'— she got that. Annie would be proud: enjoy the moment. But 'eternity's sunrise'— what the hell did that mean? Hope? A new day? Always living in that moment when the sun comes up, a new day begins and anything is possible — or — or —

Merle touched a finger to her forehead and smiled. The engine roared back to life. She didn't have a clue what the poet meant.

And that was all right.

Get ready for
the sequel to *Blackbird Fly*

winging your way
May 2014

The Bennett Sisters are on a walking tour of France
when they discover an injured dog
Who else is looking for the dog?
Truffles, Intrigue, Wine, and Romance

Come along and find out who is...

The Girl
in
the Empty Dress

Read an excerpt here

Lawyrr Grrl

Where a woman can grrowl about the legal profession

BLOG *Sistrrs in Law*

tagged family matters, vacation, kvetching,
screaming inside, ulcer time
Posted June 13

Grrls, it's confession time. You may have guessed from posts over the past year that I have four sisters and all of us are trained attorneys. Kinda crazy, but there it is. Our father and his father before him were also lawyers. The law is in our blood. We grew up debating, arguing, holding mock trials over dishwashing duties, deposing each other, trying to best one another around the dinner table, running to Daddy's law books if we were stumped.

We sisters are all different and use our legal training in various ways: profit, non-profit, corporate, non-traditional. I'm not going to tell you exactly what we do or where we live. I *will* tell you this: being a non-lawyer in this family was a non-starter. Eventually we all fell into lock step. Some are happy troopers, some not so much. Some enjoy cracking the whip, some like taking a beating. We all have our strengths.

So we're going a trip together! No lounging around five-star hotels or cruise ships for us. No, we're walking through the countryside, reading maps like explorers, getting spider webs in our hair, perspiring like champs, losing our way. Sounds like a bonding experience, huh. I mean, what the hell? We don't wear zip-off pants and hiking boots. We wear power suits and stilettos. We're lawyers: we have manicures for f••kssake!

And yet. Grrl sigh. Not going is also a non-starter. I will report in, or lose my shit, or both.

1

Cresting the hill on the dirt road, Merle Bennett felt the ache of her calf muscles and paused to adjust her backpack. She wasn't breathing that hard, just needed a second to catch her breath. Four days on the trail in the French countryside, plus all that jogging she'd done this spring made her feel strong.

Her oldest sister pulled up next to her, a little red in the face but smiling. Annie was fifty-four, bearing down on Social Security, she joked, but looking fit in cargo shorts, hiking boots, and a tie-dye T-shirt from a CSNY concert. "This is so great, isn't it? Look at that old ruin up there, all Castle Grimly."

Merle followed her gaze. "It belonged to Lord Byron, they say. Very gothic."

Francie arrived puffing, auburn tendrils stuck to her face and freckles blurred by exertion. Sister number four, she was too young to be a reluctant hiker. Forty-three was nothing. Just wait until she turned fifty.

Fifty. It had hit Merle hard. Fifty and alone: the words circled her brain. Even with James. Somehow he didn't change things where it counted, deep in her heart. *Was James not a keeper?* No, no mind games today, not today on the top of a beautiful hill in the Dordogne surrounded by orchards and vineyards and cows with the sun on her shoulders and the scent of lavender and roses on the breeze. This was a good day. Her sisters were here, helping her celebrate being a big, fat fifty.

Focus, Merle. Smile, Merle. This is your life, Merle Bennett.

Stasia was ahead, walking down the hill beside Elise. Number two and number five, the sisters were the same height and walked the same way. Their hips swayed just so, and they swung their arms enthusiastically. Elise had dark brown hair like Merle, but Stasia's was lighter with well-maintained highlights. Merle was the middle sister. The Tent Pole they called her, possibly because of her Olive Oyl figure. The running, the worry, and Harry's death were responsible for that.

"Where the fuck are we?" Francie gasped, pulling out her map.

"Right here, right now, Miss Francine honey," Annie said, smiling like the Dalai Lama.

"That's what you always say."

"And I'm always right," said Annie. "Come on." She linked arms with Merle and Francie. "Let's truck down this hill. We're off to see the —"

"No singing," Francie hissed.

"Tell that to your friend," Merle muttered. She squinted down the hill. Francie's friend Gillian was dressed in safari classic, khaki head to toe with an asymmetrical hat that made her look like Crocodile Dundee. *What was she trying to prove with that get-up?* She hadn't made a good impression on the Bennett sisters. Merle hated to dislike people in general. Everyone had at least one good quality. Lawyers were trained to find the overlooked, that one detail that would set the case back. They just hadn't found that detail, something positive, in Gillian yet. Her presence had upset the sister dynamic, throwing off the finely tuned, five-spoke spin. But it was too late to get rid of her.

Merle sighed, pledging to herself to try harder. She didn't want to *try* to like someone on her vacation. It didn't seem quite fair.

Since they arrived in Paris together, on the plane, on the train, and on the trail, Gillian had remained aloof. She didn't answer when asked a question, didn't listen, didn't offer help or information. She acted like she was doing *them* a favor by going on the trip. Merle had given Gillian a pass for a couple days, but it was the singing that pushed her over.

She had a nice voice, that was true. Besides Annie's folk guitar days, none of the Bennett sisters were musical. They would be walking along, talking and laughing, and Gillian, not participating in the conversation, would nonetheless pick up on some phrase or word and burst into song. Usually Tony Bennett or Frank Sinatra—if someone remarked on the moon, she rang out with all the verses of "Fly Me to the Moon"—which was weird for a woman of 30-something. No one knew how old Gillian was. She seemed older than Elise, who was also celebrating a birthday on this trip, her 40th. Elise, the baby, always seemed young.

But, dear lord, the singing. It drove Merle bat-shit crazy. She was trying hard not to let it show. There were five more days on the trail to go.

Stasia, in a wide-brimmed hat decorated with wildflowers, rolled up pants, and a pink shirt, stopped next to Gillian. Elise pulled off her backpack and laid it on the dirt. A break was in the offing even though they'd only walked for an hour. They'd never make it back to Malcouziac tonight at this rate.

Gillian was staring at something in the ditch, hands on her hips. Merle frowned. There wasn't supposed to be a sixth member of this trip, but Francie hadn't gotten that memo. She'd invited her law firm colleague to go walking through France with them. Francie was the type who always needed a pal at her side, reinforcing her specialness. She was the prettiest sister, auburn hair streaked with sunlight, beautiful skin, the tallest. Pulling in the biggest salary too. But right now she was just one of the hiking Bennett sisters. She'd been cranky from the start.

When they arrived at the bottom of the hill, Gillian was crouched low in the grass, hand extended. Elise turned to them, eyes wide. "It's a dog. Hurt or something. Gillian found it."

They gathered around a filthy liver-and-white dog curled on its side, head up, brown eyes sad. A poodle maybe or a mix, a small one, its curly hair matted. When Gillian reached out a hand to pat its head, the dog thumped its tail.

"Don't touch it," Stasia said. "God knows where it's been."

"Aw, sweetie dog," Gillian cooed, ignoring her. Merle looked at Stasia, who wiggled her eyebrows. This was a new wrinkle, the fuzzy side of Gillian. Stasia had tried to befriend her at the start of the trip, being a pal, calling her Gillie. She'd been corrected.

"He's hurt. He's all bloody on that hip," Elise said, peering down. "I bet he can't walk."

"We'll carry him," Gillian announced. "How far to the next village?"

"Hold on," Merle said. "We can send somebody back for him."

"It's a mile at most." Francie consulted her map. "Loiverre. Not super tiny."

"So they might have a vet." Gillian walked around the back

of the dog. "I'll carry him. Stand back."

"Wait, Gillian. Stop." Stasia held up a hand. "He'll bite you if you pick him up. Then we'll have two injuries."

Gillian handed her backpack to Elise and scooped her arms under the dog while clucking in his ear. The dog whimpered, his injured leg twitching, but laid his head back against his savior. Gillian gave Stasia a look of victory—or possibly *fuck you*—and walked out of the grassy ditch toward the village.

"She won't make it." Stasia marched beside Merle, shaking her head. "So bull-headed. What was Francie thinking? Gillian is ruining everything."

At five-four with an athletic build, toned arms, and muscular legs, Gillian was strong and fast. The rest of them struggled to keep up with her, even with a dog in her arms. Francie skipped ahead to try to help. Elise carried the extra backpack and offered encouragement.

"She must hit the gym more than the lawyers I know," Merle said.

"Don't hold that against her," Annie said.

Stasia laughed. "Oh, I've got a dozen other grievances, counselor."

In fifteen minutes they'd reached Loiverre and gathered in the central square to reconnoiter. Gillian lowered herself to the stone steps by a statue of a soldier and the French flag, cradling the dog in her arms. Annie volunteered to go ask about a veterinarian.

Elise jumped up and they took off together for the post office before Merle could say anything. She'd never found postal employees helpful in France, especially if you didn't speak perfect, colloquial French.

Sandwiches were eaten in silence as they waited. Gillian soothed the dog, talking baby talk. Annie and Elise returned and led them down a side street to the entrance of a medical office. "No vet," Annie explained. "But the doctor treats animals sometimes."

The receptionist in the doctor's office begged to differ. Her eyes widened at the sight of the smelly dog. Merle asked in her re-tooled French if there was someone around here who treated dogs.

"*Ah, oui, madame,*" the young woman said, dashing into a

back room. She returned with an older woman, apparently a nurse. She was tall, silver through her dark hair, and had kind eyes. Merle explained their situation.

"She says she can take him home and treat him," Merle told her sisters. "We can leave him with her. She'll try to find the owner."

"No," Gillian said, still attached to the animal, clutching him tightly. "I want to take him with us."

The sisters looked at each other. "Be reasonable," Francie said. "We're on vacation. What are we going to do with an injured dog?"

The nurse bent down beside Gillian and talked to the animal soothingly in French. The dog seemed very sweet, considering the pain he must be in.

The nurse stood and addressed Merle. "Tell your friend not to worry. She can come back for *le chien* in a couple days if she wants."

The walk that afternoon was hot and dusty. They were mostly on farm roads but veered off onto a trail marked with little pink slashes on fence posts, through woods, and next to a creek. The shade was delicious. The French sun could be brutal in June, baking the hillsides. The roses in the hedgerows grew limp as did the Bennett sisters. Gillian marched off moody and alone, back to her silent self.

The walking was meditative for Merle, calming her overactive mind. Her job in New York helping Legal Aid get Big Law backers kept her spinning in circles. Or maybe that's just the way she rolled, booked to the max, going 110 percent all the time. At any rate, she was back to her mind-set of lists and calendars. Nearly a week in France hadn't cured her of that. She would stay on for a couple extra weeks though so there would be time to unwind. It worked last year in this soft European time, where no one has anything more important to do than buy fresh croissants. She'd looked forward to getting back in the golden light for months. It really was a shame Gillian had to come along with her negativity.

Stop. Calm. Family. Tristan. She said it like a mantra. *Dinner tonight at Albert's. Wine. France. Calm. Wine!* There was a happy thought. Her throat felt parched, even with the last few lukewarm gulps from her water bottle. A cold Sauvignon Blanc would go down nicely.

By late afternoon, they were close to her adopted town. The approach to the walled village of Malcouziac filled her with pride and a kind of longing. Here was her piece of the Earth, a rocky, forlorn shard of charm. Harsh, unknowable, foreign. And yet, she belonged to it. Down a deep valley choked with brambles then up the other side, past high cliffs where the Saint Lucretia shrine guarded them all, around the butte, down another hill and there they were, the golden stone of the *bastide* walls, framed against the sky, curved and delicate, yet sturdy, and satisfyingly permanent. As much as the village had despised her last year, she loved it in all its messy glory. Centuries of fighting, clan against clan, duke against king, outsider against local. The walls of Malcouziac had lasted seven centuries. They would endure long after the petty quarrels of today's inhabitants.

The past year had taught her so much: patience, tolerance, forgiveness. If she could practice those things on herself, she could sure as hell offer it to the unfortunate citizens of Malcouziac. They had a new mayor and gendarme. She'd only been in the village a couple days before the walking tour, but there was a new air of friendliness.

They rounded the cliffs, tall and chalky on their right. An image of Harry sprang into her head, something that didn't happen often anymore. Her husband died last year of a heart attack and set her world on end. He would have enjoyed this though, in his curmudgeonly way. She could see him waddling along in his fancy loafers, tie loose, suit coat draped over a shoulder, moaning about the heat. If he wasn't already dead, the heat would have killed him.

"What are you smiling about?" Annie asked her.

"Nothing." Merle took her sister's arm. "Everything."

"Harry or Pascal?"

Pascal: last summer's curative to her broken spirit. She hadn't told him she was back in France. It would be awkward with James around. It seemed less complicated to just forget about Pascal.

"You know me too well."

Annie squeezed her hand. "Will we have to go back for that damn dog?"

Merle laughed. "Yes, oh wise one. I think we will."

2

The multi-paned door to the house on Rue de Poitiers stood wide open, a gust of wind rattling its dry shutters against the stone. Merle stood on the threshold, heart thumping. Tristan was alone in the house. He'd forgotten to lock the door. Panic shot through her. How close disaster had been last summer.

Laughter in the back garden reassured her. The cache of wine was gone. The bad guys were locked up. She took a breath. Why was she still so jumpy? She and Annie were the last two hikers to arrive. The sisters had felt the need for fresh air. That was all.

The ancient stone house still smelled stale from the winter, its thick walls cool and a little slimy in spots. It needed airing. The blue shutters were old and cracked but freshly painted. The orange tile roof had been repaired and survived the winter intact. *Everything* was intact. No need for worry. In the main room with its huge trestle table and a worn horsehair sofa, she knocked on a window sash and pushed it up. A breeze from the vineyards carried in the scent of fruit and musk.

Stasia called from outside. "Bring the wine, Merdle!"

When Merle arrived after a year away she'd been worried her garden would be a mess, both from neglect and from last year's modernizing. But her neighbor Josephine — who lived here long ago — had delivered on her promise to keep things tidy and growing. She'd watered the grapevine and the espaliered pear tree, trimmed the roses, and swept dead leaves off the gravel patio. Merle was looking forward to thanking her at dinner tonight.

Stepping through the tiny kitchen into the sunshine, Merle felt the same rush of pleasure at the sight of the garden as the first time. An electric charge of wonder: her oasis, her pleasure grounds. Stasia had scoffed when Merle described it, calling her a romantic.

How could a small garden be *all that*? When she saw it Stasia admitted she was wrong. It was a special place. Merle looked around. There, where she and Pascal danced that last night, last summer. There, the old rock *pissoir*, a soon-to-be converted outhouse with a vine climbing over the mossy roof. The wooden water cistern, still used for laundry and gardening, stood guard on its ten-foot legs surrounded by lavender. The roses were all in bloom, the red one busting its guts.

It was all so quaint and harmless and *French*.

Such a contrast, this little paradise surrounded by hard, weathered rock walls. Inside they were softened by wisteria and clematis and grapevines. Outside the world could be hard and cold. But in here, everything was safe and calm.

She delivered the bottle of wine as her sisters took off boots and swilled liquids then went to hug her son.

Tristan and Valerie sat at *Père* Albert's kitchen table, playing cards. Her son had met the girl last summer. She was the reason Merle got Tristan to come back to France with her. Her great-uncle Albert was round and cheerful, a former priest with the sort of beatific air that made you forget not to call him Father. His head injury from last year had set him back a little. He'd lost weight, Merle noted, and was less sure of climbing the ladder to pick his beloved plums for *eau de vie*. But he emerged from the sitting room with a big grin and open arms.

"*Bien venue*, Merle. How was the walking?"

"Lovely. The weather couldn't have been nicer. We stopped for a few *gustations* along the way." The wine tastings only worked at the end of the day of walking, otherwise there was much weary carping. But Merle only smiled. Albert wasn't interested in bickering.

"And your feet? Okay?"

"Not one blister."

"What about Aunt Francie?" Tristan said, his eyes on his cards. "No blisters for Queenie Franceenie?"

"Well, yes. She got a couple." And bug bites, thorn pricks, sunburn, and scraped elbows. Disaster seemed to follow Francie on the trail, at least from her perspective. Each sister's personality blossomed on the trail. That morning Merle had made a mental list of each one's travel mojo.

Annie: Everybody has a good time, right now!

Stasia: Follow the plan or I shoot you.

Merle: I just hope nobody stabs anybody.

Francie: This cheese is so freaking awesome! Ow! Look at me! Pass the wine!

Elise: If you tell me what to do I will pout all day.

And the plus one:

Gillian: My mind is too beautiful to share.

Two days in Malcouziac, resting, then they would hit the road again for three more days in a loop off to the North. The thought of it made Merle queasy. Her sisters were getting along all right, but the togetherness sometimes put a strain on things. If anybody bailed Stasia would be livid.

Merle turned to Albert's niece. "Have you and Tristan had fun, Valerie?" She put her hands on her son's shoulders. Maybe this was all the hug she'd get. Her boy was sixteen now.

"*Oui, madame. Nous* — pardon, I am to speak English." Valerie rolled her eyes. "It sound terrible to me."

"It sounds great." Tristan said. "I love your accent."

Valerie gave him a playful punch. "What accent?"

At fifteen the girl had already perfected the French pout, the ammunition against men for centuries. She turned up her nose, folded her arms, smirked and burst out laughing. She was going to be a handful, if she wasn't already.

"Thanks so much for looking after my boy, Albert," she said.

"Valerie took charge of activities. I only feed the man." Albert wagged his finger. "Not a boy any longer. So tall!"

"And handsome," Valerie chimed in. "With big shoulders." Her violet eyes flashed at Tristan again.

Merle tapped his shoulders. "Come say hello to the aunties, Tris." As he got up, Valerie did too, straightening her chic print blouse that clung to her chest and tugging down her mini-skirt.

"Oh, madame. I will love to practice my English on them!"

"Dinner at nine," Albert called as they trailed through the

back garden to the alley and through Merle's garden gate.

The women dressed for dinner, changing into summer dresses. Merle had been able to rent her neighbors' house as her own was too small for all of them. Yves and Suzette had been very generous. Elise, Francie, and Gillian were staying in Yves and Suzette's house next door. It was much more modern than Merle's, with a full bathroom on the second level and everything very chic. It made Merle's tiny *maison de ville* look medieval.

When the younger three showed up in the garden for wine before heading to Albert's they looked refreshed, shampooed and powdered. Elise, youngest and shortest sister, wore a flowered skirt and crisp white blouse. Francie had on a fitted dress with the kind of low neckline she liked. Gillian had transformed herself with a short lilac dress with black lace insets better suited to New York than rural France. She'd worn it to dinner twice already, with her thick brown hair onto her head. She took a glass of wine and stepped away without speaking, as if fascinated by the ripening pears as she tottered on four-inch heels.

"How much do you think that dress costs?" Stasia whispered in Merle's ear.

"Whose?"

"Gillian's. I saw it at Fashion Week. It's couture, some Italian designer."

"Looks expensive."

"Pucci. That's it."

"Really? I thought he did all those blocky, colored things."

"Look at you, fashionista. That's why this dress stood out. Isn't it divine? I checked it out at Bergdorf's. I lusted after it." They watched Gillian move carefully over the dirt, bending to sniff the roses. The black lace seemed to glow. The dress *was* kind of amazing.

As assistant managing editor at *Gamine*, a trendy women's magazine, Stasia had access to all sorts of insider perks. Last winter she'd arrived at Merle's with an armload of sweaters and let her take her pick. "Wouldn't *Gamine* give you one?"

"Are you kidding? I can't believe she has it. Of all people." Stasia leaned closer. "Way too pricey. Eight-thousand."

Merle sloshed her wine. "Dollars?"

"I have a personal limit for a single item. Kinda way over."

Merle stared at the dress. It fit Gillian like a glove. Those shoes look spendy too. Who would pay eight-thousand dollars for a dress? "She must be making some serious cash," Merle muttered. But Stasia had moved away to talk to Elise. Their youngest sister was already on her second glass of wine. She'd twisted her ankle the first day out, not bad enough to stop walking. No one saw any swelling. But Elise took it as a sign of doom. She used to be such a sunny person before she went to law school.

Wine and *Franglais* flowed freely at dinner, between Valerie, Albert, Tristan, the sisters, Josephine, and Gillian. Josephine wore her ever-present pearls and brought a huge terrine of cassoulet rich with duck sausage. Not a usual summer dish, she explained, but one she'd made so often she could make it with her eyes shut. They were all sated with food and wine when Gillian stood up, clinking her glass with her knife.

"Thanks for dinner. It was good." She nodded gravely at the old people. Merle blinked, fatigue slowing her reflexes. Was Gillian making a speech? "I can't go to that church or whatever it is you've cooked up for tomorrow." She looked at Albert. "We found this little dog, hurt, by the side of the road today. He's in a village with an old lady. I don't trust her. I have to go get him."

She sat down abruptly. Francie recovered first, sitting on her left. "I'll go with you. I don't think I can stomach another church."

"I found him. I want to go by myself."

She glared at Francie who blinked, confused. "I didn't —"

"I'll go, and Valerie can too. I love dogs," Tristan said, carrying dirty plates.

Valerie pouted. "I am to leave tomorrow. Back to Paris."

"Well, I can go. Can I go, Mom?"

Gillian folded her arms. "I don't need anyone to go with me. I just need to use the rental car." She looked up at Tristan, appraising his worthiness or manliness or something. Merle felt a shiver. Gillian squinted against the candlelight. "All right. He can go."

Rapport de Police, Midi-Pyrénées. 18 June.

M. Jean Poutou, resident of St-Paul, Lot, called to report a stolen dog. Poutou, age 82, was confused and upset. Wailing heard in the background. Claims expensive dog used for truffle hunting was released from its pen and taken from grounds. Unsure of date of incident, possibly as long as three days ago. No explanation for why dog was unattended for such a long time. Dog belongs to grandson not currently on premises and has imbedded ID chip (dog, not grandson.) Advised that *les policiers* do not look for lost dogs and to call insurance agent.

Patrick Girard, Commissariat de Police, Toulouse

The Girl in the Empty Dress

Available May 2014
Wherever books are sold

Connect with the author at
http://lisemcclendon.com

Also available from **THALIA PRESS**
these other great novels

by Lise McClendon

The Bluejay Shaman
Painted Truth
Nordic Nights
Blue Wolf
One O'clock Jump
Sweet and Lowdown
All Your Pretty Dreams

◆

As Rory Tate
Jump Cut
PLAN X

◆

Read about all these titles at
thaliapress.com

69620188R00178

Made in the USA
Lexington, KY
03 November 2017